# Fortysomething

NIGEL WILLIAMS

VIKING

VIKING

Published by the Penguin Group
Penguin Books Ltd, 27 Wrights Lane, London w8 5tz, England
Penguin Putnam Inc., 375 Hudson Street, New York, New York 10014, USA
Penguin Books Australia Ltd, Ringwood, Victoria, Australia
Penguin Books Canada Ltd, 10 Alcorn Avenue, Toronto, Ontario, Canada m4v 3b2
Penguin Books (NZ) Ltd, Private Bag 102902, NSMC, Auckland, New Zealand

Penguin Books Ltd, Registered Offices: Harmondsworth, Middlesex, England

First published 1999
10 9 8 7 6 5 4 3 2 1

Set in 12/14.5pt Monotype Fournier
Typeset by Rowland Phototypesetting Ltd,
Bury St Edmunds, Suffolk
Printed in England by Clays Ltd, St Ives plc

A CIP catalogue record for this book is available from the British Library

Hardback isbn 0–670–88647–5
Trade Paperback isbn 0–670–88939–3

For Suzan

'Out of this wood do not desire to go . . .'

*A Midsummer Night's Dream*

# January 12th. 5 p.m.

*Estelle, Ruairghy, Jakob, Edwin and me all at home.*

Feeling depressed. Why is this?

Size of stomach? Loss of hair?

Or is it because I am due to be run over by an articulated lorry on March 15th?

I have been saying for years that I wanted to move on from my role in *General Practice*, but I suppose I always thought that I would have some influence over the timing and manner of my departure. I don't know why I thought this but I did.

My paranoia is made even worse by the fact that I am not quite sure who is behind the decision to end Dr Esmond Pennebaker's life. The new generation of scriptwriters, many of whom seem to be younger than my own children, are trying to pretend that they are only obeying orders. The producer – a bald, shifty-looking Welshman called Karl – has been away at a management training course for about a month. I don't think he was quite so bald before the course. He has spoken to no one since his return. If you try to speak to him he twitches and runs away. I don't know what they did to him. All he would say to Surinder, one of the writers, was, 'It was very intensive.' Surinder said she had heard they spent ten days trying to construct a Wendy house out of old cardboard boxes. Steve Witchett says they were all forced to type eighty words a minute, make phone calls in Italian, etc., wearing only their underwear.

I suspect the idea of offing me may have originated at the very highest level in the BBC. I am almost positive that John Birt was involved. He has got rid of just about everything else at the Beeb, so why not me? It may not have been Birt, of course. It may have been one of his henchmen. But as his henchmen are paid hundreds and thousands of pounds to speak, think and dress like him, it probably doesn't matter whether he himself gave the order. Colin Cross, the spineless new Head of Soaps – Radio Drama Continuing Narrative Strand (Domestic) – *thinks* he may have given it. Like Hitler or Stalin, John Birt's assumed opinions seem to have as much weight as his real ones.

Although I have no evidence, I have become convinced that it is the

Director-General who is trying to have me killed. He probably insisted, too, that my death should not give too many opportunities for bravura acting. Someone at the story conference, the week before last, apparently suggested that I fall out of a window, but this was quickly squashed. I think I could have done something with that. As it is, all I will probably get is one quick gasp of alarm followed by a muffled scream. It may be – although I can't believe they would do this to me – Death by Reported Speech. A way to go that compounds the tragedy of one's death by handing a dramatic opportunity to another actor. There may be a funeral scene. They may even let other actors make speeches. Some of them may even be allowed to cry – something I have never been allowed to do, unless you count the slight tremor at my end of the phone call in which I learned I was being sued by some idiot simply because I had cut off the wrong leg.

Maybe they will let Ronnie 'Very Nice Man' Pilfrey make a speech over the grave. Sick-o!

The one clue I have to the identity of those who are trying to kill me is that the decision originated in a committee called the Core Directorate Policy Unit. No one will tell me who is on this committee – although 'some creative personnel' are part of it. If I can work out who they are, and get close enough to them to lick their boots, I may have a chance of surviving this year.

But do I want to? Haven't I had enough?

It is time I moved on. Twenty years in a BBC radio serial is too long. But the time has, as I was telling Estelle the other day, simply flown by. It seems only minutes ago that Esmond Pennebaker was graduating from medical school. Now, here he is about to kick the bucket. What has he done with his life? Gone into the surgery. Had an affair with his secretary. And now here he is – dead – or well on the way to it.

What have I done with my life, come to that?

In a few months I, too, will be fifty. On the day of our wedding anniversary – June 24th. Estelle does not seem very interested in this fact. I broached the subject, casually, a few weeks ago, hoping that she might suggest a romantic week away. She has not, so far, done so. The nearest she has come to acknowledging this important landmark in my life is to say, last Tuesday, 'I suppose you want a party.' When I said that I didn't want to put anyone to any trouble, she said, 'Don't go on about it. You keep going on about the fact you are fifty. You are not actually fifty yet. You are forty-nine. I am fifty.'

She isn't actually. She is fifty-one. But I did not like to point out this fact. Instead I said, 'I would like to have a few really close friends round me on the actual day.' She looked at me oddly. 'What friends?' she said, in a way that suggested she thought I had none. 'Oh,' I said, 'Nobby. And Good Old Steve . . .' Estelle said that just because you had known someone for thirty years that did not necessarily make them interesting. When I asked whether this applied to me, she said I was becoming very self-pitying. She has become very hard of late. I think this may be something to do with the menopause. I did not, of course, say this.

A party is probably a very bad idea. I can't think of who else I would want to ask apart from Nobby, Good Old Steve and Peter Mailer. What, anyway, is there to celebrate about reaching the age of fifty?


## 9.30 p.m.

Dinner with all the family. This is unusual these days. Estelle made lasagne. She did not, as she once would have done, make the pasta herself. In fact she has shown a worrying lack of interest, recently, in things like hand-crafted tagliatelle. Once, she scoured the shops of south London in search of tamarind and even attempted to smoke her own fish in the garden shed – very nearly asphyxiating herself in the process. But now . . .

When I chewed her dish in a manner I thought just this side of ostentatious and said, two or three times, 'Mmm! Delicious!' she did not react. So I said, 'My, this is tasty!' In case she had not heard I said it again – this time in a foreign accent. She glowered at me from under her fringe and said, 'It's simple anyway.' What does this mean?

Jakob, my middle child, has taken to reading the *Financial Times* during the evening meal. I do not approve of this. When I asked him, point-blank, tonight, whether he would consider devoting more attention to the hors-d'oeuvres, he said, 'I am going back to Oxford tomorrow. And I need to see how Praskein are doing!' When I asked, with just a touch of edge, whether this was the name of a Russian football team, Jakob concealed his face once more behind the paper. At one point he made movements that suggested he might be picking his nose. I suspect the

*3*

boys may be in some kind of conspiracy to annoy me. When I asked his younger brother Edwin to pass the Waitrose Mixed Herb Leaves, he said, 'No FT! No Comment!' During most of the meal Ruaierhgry, their elder brother, had positioned his face, horizontally, above his plate, like a flying saucer about to land. He only raised his features to fork in more supplies. I suspect him of orchestrating this attack.

Jakob back to Oxford! On his own! (Always a secretive child, he has not yet told us how he intends to get there.) It seems only yesterday, although in fact it was last year, that we were running both Jakob and Ruairghy up to my old university in my elderly Volvo. Two sons at Oxford! A fact for which I had to apologize to other competitive parents in the Wimbledon area. Estelle took to saying that they were 'somewhere in the Midlands', which I thought made it sound as if they were in prison. And tomorrow he will leave Ruairghry behind, here with us.

I love my eldest son dearly but I still think we should have given him a name we could both spell.

Estelle offered to run Jakob up tomorrow, but he was most insistent about going on his own. (Why?) It will be strange not to be staggering up the stairs of his college carrying the portable television, the combined CD cassette player and radio, the Compaq Deskpro computer, the Hewlett Packard Laserjet 4 Printer, the portable answering machine, the three electric guitars, the complete works of John Maynard Keynes and the truly staggering number of Megadeth CDs. I had not even heard of them before 1994, let alone been aware that they had a back catalogue about as extensive as Wagner's.

I asked Ruairghy, at dinner tonight, whether he was looking forward to doing some real teaching. He is doing a Diploma in Education at the University of South Wimbledon. His answer surprised me. He said, 'I am not going to be a teacher!' I raised my eyebrows slightly, but did not ask why, in that case, he was spending nine months boning up on the theory and practice of education.

My God, it's not long since the first time I left Ruiarhgy at Oxford! After dumping him in his room with his two mobile phones (in case he lost one, which he did in the first week), his eight T-shirts, two anoraks and three pairs of trainers, I walked back across the quadrangle and sobbed helplessly at the thought that now, at last, 'our boy' was standing on his own two feet.

'Standing on his own two feet' is perhaps, even now, not fully accurate. He asked me the other day where Leeds was. It is possible that we have protected him too much.

Dinner was very pleasant, although Edwin, my youngest, insisted on eating a tin of baked beans out of the can, instead of the lasagne. He said lasagne 'hurt his throat'. Edwin is sixteen but I do not think that is sufficient excuse for his behaviour. As the boys were clearing away the plates — and stacking them, for reasons that are still unclear, on one of the bookshelves — I read out an amusing paragraph from my copy of the *Independent*. 'One of the Jobcentres near Southampton Docks . . .' I began, without, of course, trying to do a funny voice, 'has had to expand due to the enormous amount of seamen flooding in . . .'

Edwin greeted this with a loud cackle. Estelle said, 'What is funny about that?' I explained, patiently, the phonetic similarity between 'seamen' and 'semen'. Estelle said, 'I see that. But I still don't see that it's particularly funny.'

She is a magnificent creature — black hair, huge eyes, big, strong hands. I was struck, tonight, how, in repose, her profile bears a strong resemblance to that of the Emperor Nero.


## 11.30 p.m.

Estelle is asleep. Should I ring Nobby? I don't know why I think talking to Nobby might help me sleep. Hearing about his sex life (which is astonishingly busy for a man of his age) is, of course, nearly always tiring.

Should I call Peter Mailer? I think not. Ever since he was cured of alcoholism he has acquired another compulsion. He stares deeply into your eyes and even the most trivial conversational opener provokes him into orgies of sincere nodding. I ascribe this to group therapy.

Good Old Steve? Good Old Steve will be out. I will go to bed. I have the feeling this year is not going to be an easy one.

# January 14th. 9 p.m.

*Jakob back in Oxford, Edwin upstairs (I think). Ruairghy in pub with Gordon. Estelle in bed. Raining.*

Already missing Jakob. He may be, I now realize, even more secretive than I thought. He has almost certainly been concealing the full extent of his secretiveness. Was he always like this? When he was young he was particularly fond of hide-and-seek – and even when he is in the house he often gives the impression of being on the point of disappearing into thin air, like the Cheshire Cat. But although he does not say much, his remarks often have a gnomic profundity.

He is a tall, thin boy with aquiline features and a shock of black hair. Estelle often refers to him as 'my handsome one' – a remark which I find slightly offensive, but there is no doubt that he has a striking profile and a beautiful speaking voice, as well as an IQ of over 150. Admittedly this was at the age of eight and he may well have dropped a few points since then. But it was tested by no less than three experts, one of whom was German. They all disagreed with each other, and Estelle and I averaged out the results.

Estelle always says his intelligence is something to do with his birth – a process he achieved in the world record time of six and a half minutes from first contraction to first appearance. Apparently (I was in the studio) he emerged, suavely, from the birth canal, finely covered in black hair and giving a small cynical smile – a fact of which Estelle never tires of reminding him, usually, for some reason, at family meal times.

I admire Jakob. I admire his ability to remember long telephone numbers, his taste in shoes, his ability to speak Spanish convincingly, and to understand his degree course (economics, a science that I find not only dismal but incomprehensible).

And yet . . . and yet . . .

When I asked him the other day which way his ambitions were tending he muttered something about 'making some serious money'. I had to tell him that when his mother and I met, in the summer of 1968, money was the last thing on either of our minds. 'No,' he said, 'all you thought about was drugs.' I told him that until the age of thirty-five I thought coke was a variety of smokeless fuel.

Are there women in his life? I asked him last year about this and he said, in even tones, 'It is non-stop sex at Oxford.' When I asked him why he had not yet 'brought a girl home' he said, 'I bring them to the end of the road and hump them there.' I *think* these remarks were intended humorously.

He and Ruairghry are not getting on as well as they usually do. Several times, during the holiday, I overheard them arguing about a girl called Lucy. I am not quite sure what the point at issue was but as far as I could make out (they usually leave most rooms in the house soon after I have entered them) Ruairghry has broken off relations with her. I can't understand why this should bother Jakob. I also heard them arguing about a girl called (I think) Laura. This was a little clearer. It was pretty obvious that they were both keen on her. At one point Jakob used the word 'pork' as a transitive verb.

Anyway, he left this morning. A large black Daimler called for him at a quarter to eight. When I asked him whose it was he said, 'Oliver is driving it at the moment.' I presume Oliver has parents wealthier than me.

Edwin, who will take his G C S E s this summer, has little interest in the academic life. Apart from spray-painting an enormous traffic cone, which he carried home late one night a few months ago and installed in the back garden (announcing it was a 'found object'), his appetite for intellectual stimulus is limited to watching videos of *Trainspotting*. He has, I think, three of them. There is the Director's Cut, the Unabridged Rough Cut of the Director's Cut and, somewhere in the pile, the boring old film that all the rest of us saw. Heinrich, at Blockbuster Video in Raynes Park, actively encourages Edwin's stamp-collector's attitude to the art of film and has promised to look out for amazing rarities like the Director's Cut of a film called *Goblin*, which, from my memory of it, didn't look as if it had a director at all.

I suspect Heinrich of having a more than fatherly interest in Edwin.

Only four of us in the house. In fact, after tomorrow, there will quite often only be one of us, as Estelle has, after twenty-one years of child care, decided to take a job. Should I pack her a lunch? Show how much I support her in this move? If so, what should I pack? A little salad niçoise perhaps? To show her what a superb mother I think she has been?

7

Perhaps not.

The job is something to do with those little things she makes out of old Brie boxes. She has a happy knack of transforming them into useful little trays. I think she will also be making little dough men and selling them to gift shops in the Wimbledon area. I don't think it pays much. But it will get her out of the house. And, as I said to her last night, 'Anything helps, love. Even your little bit will be a help. And it will help you forget the awful empty feeling you get now the children are leaving home and you are going through the Change!' She looked at me thoughtfully, lit a cigarette and said, 'You too will soon be going through the Change, Paul. I will be changing you for Brad Pitt.'

I must remember not to mention the menopause.

## January 16th. 11 a.m.

*Estelle at work. Jakob at Oxford. Ruairghy in bed. Edwin at school. Raining.*

A new job is on the horizon! At the Royal National Theatre! The R N T Or Ram your Nose up Trevor Nunn's Tush (as R. Pilfrey calls it.)

I must admit that the first day without Estelle around the house did feel a little curious. Not that I am the kind of man who can't make his own lunch! I had bought some San Daniele ham, a few olives and a roquette salad which I had hidden in a drawer in my desk to stop Edwin or Ruairghry getting at them. In the day and a half she has been there I have tried not to bother her. I am not even sure I know her number.

But this morning, as I went over my lines for next Tuesday's recording, I kept feeling a bit like that bloke on the Shackleton expedition who was convinced there was someone else in the house. Every time a door banged I raced upstairs to see if it was a burglar. I even went in to look at Ruairghy once or twice but he was lying, in his pyjamas, with his mouth open, making a noise like a steam drill. I have asked him, several times, how his course is going, but all he says is that the University of South Wimbledon 'is not somewhere you want to be around too much'. This seems a shame as we are paying him money to go there.

So when Gustave rang at around ten to tell me there was an exciting offer in the pipeline, I practically threw my hat in the air. If I had been wearing a hat I would almost definitely have thrown it in that direction. There goes the phone! Can this be him?

### 11.23 a.m.

It was Gustave. Apparently there is serious interest in my playing Gumbago in a major production of *Measure for Measure* at the Lyttleton. It is, apparently, quite a good role, but it is so long since I have read *Measure for Measure* that I cannot, for the moment, quite recall what part he plays in the piece.

Gustave, who never reads anything apart from contracts and cheques, said he thought he was 'some kind of duke'. Back to my *Collected Shakespeare*.

### 11.45 a.m.

I cannot find a character called 'Gumbago' in the cast list for *Measure for Measure*. There is not even anyone beginning with G. I have started reading the play, though. It is clearly a work of genius but rather hard to understand. Not many laughs. Perhaps I have spent too long saying things like 'Looks like a fungal infection, Mrs Peet!' or 'I am really worried about this fundholding business . . .' Perhaps he means Claudio. Once upon a time, I must keep telling myself, I was a classical actor. I will call Gustave.

### 12 noon.

This is unbelievable! Gumbago, it appears, is not really a character in the play at all but simply one of the Lords, Officers, Citizens and Attendants. 'Actually,' said Gustave, as if this was going to improve matters, 'they are genuinely keen on having you, even if only as a silent member of a crowd. I think they thought your radio fans might want to spot which one you were!' I said that if he didn't come up with a better idea (and soon) I was going to leave him for someone who would really get hold of my career and push it where it was meant to go. He said to let him know as soon as I knew where that might be.

I should never have given that interview to the *Guardian*, even if the

9

young woman they sent did have enormous breasts. Apparently I did say everything that appeared in the article, but the headline 'GET OFF MY BACK, ESMOND PENNEBAKER' may have given some people the idea that I no longer wanted to play the part.

I will ring Estelle.


12.12 p.m.

Unable to find her work number.

All I know about her workplace is that it is some kind of craft shop, founded by some of the women with whom Estelle worked when all three boys were at Cranborne School, Wimbledon. A period that now seems as far away as the Pleistocene Era. There was Katie 'Cellulite' Wimbourne and Shulah 'They're My Caterers' Arrowsmith and Stella Badyass and an anaesthetist in a sari called (I think) Udpar. There was Angela Lansbury (no relation) and the aptly named Serafina Wiles, and they all got together in each other's houses and made decorated trays, hanging baskets and these little dough men in Cranborne School uniform, which were 'very popular in people's loos'. (Why?)

This was not enough for Serafina Wiles. She has opened a shop in the village and Estelle is going to be Head of Design.

At least it will stop her moaning on about how fat she is. 'Who cares whether you're fat?' I say to her. 'Even if you *are* fat, does it matter? What matters is that you are alive! You can feel the wind in your face! The sun on your upper arms!' She said, 'Do not mention my upper arms. Women over a certain age do not mention their upper arms! They go wobbly!' 'All right then!' I said. 'Feel the sun on your face, then! Isn't that all that matters?'

And, of course, whether John Birt has decided that you should fall under a lorry in the interests of a Better BBC. He is probably working on a pamphlet about it even as I write. 'DO YOU THINK THIS IS VALUE FOR MONEY? LAST YEAR WE BROUGHT YOU 367,000 HOURS OF COMEDY, DRAMA AND TOP-QUALITY LIGHT ENTERTAINMENT AND WE PUSHED ESMOND PENNEBAKER UNDER A LORRY. JOHN BIRT'S NEW BBC WORKING TO MAKE BRITAIN A BETTER PLACE!'

'We will make sure,' said Surinder last week, 'that we replace you with an Asian!' She said this with only a hint of irony. I think that she meant it entirely seriously. When I refer to her as a 'chocco' I make it very clear that I am using the term ironically. Although, fundamentally, we are on the same side and she would only introduce an Asian character into the series (there are already nine of them) if it were absolutely necessary for the story-line, a bit of me thinks she is not really being sensitive to my feelings as a middle-aged white male. After all, I was the man who went on the West London Anti-racism Rally for the Gloucester Road Seventeen!

Estelle is fat. But I do not care about this. She is a lot of other things as well. And I like her fat. I want her to be fat. The fatter she is the more I like it. I am worried that this job will make her thin. I do not like thin women. Anyway if she was thin someone else might pinch her. She's not much but she's the best I'm likely to get.


## January 20th. 1 p.m.

*Jakob at Oxford. Estelle at Work. Ruaireghy in bed. Edwin at school (I think). Raining.*

Just in from the studio. We recorded three episodes of *Practice* this morning. Was it compelling radio, though? I am not sure that we got the sound of the artificial limbs exactly right. I also learnt that it has been decided 'at the highest level' (does this mean John Birt? Or the rather sinister Core Directorate Policy Unit? Or someone else even more import-ant than these two? The Prime Minister perhaps?) that Esmond should commit suicide and not be run over by a lorry. Ruth Lever rather cattily said that this might explain why he had been sounding so miserable for the last three years.

They are all very excited about the fact that it is Mental Health Fortnight in the week I am due to stiff. Perhaps they think my death will give a few practical hints to those thinking of topping themselves.

I liked the idea. If I have to die I might as well do so in style. Esmond has been under an enormous amount of strain and this would be a powerful way of expressing what he feels about his wife and children. And about the way the N H S is being run. I discussed with Surinder the possibility of Esmond having a few failed attempts – 'cries for help' if you like – before he actually succeeds in offing himself. Although cautious at first (apparently 43 per cent of the *General Practice* audience are prone to depression), Surinder got rather involved with this. She suggested I might like to 'start by using barbiturates and work my way up to something dramatic, like a moving train'. I pitched in with a few exciting ideas of my own, including the idea that I might survive, although horribly disfigured, for a few weeks. 'There could be scenes where I reflect on my past life!' I said.

Surinder didn't seem quite so keen on this notion. She said she didn't think I should be allowed to 'ramble on'. Although that is all that I and almost every other character in the series have been doing for the last twenty years. Having dismissed my idea she waltzed off to meet a man, who, she said, was going to let her write an episode of *Casualty*.

Perhaps I will discuss this with Ruairighy. As he is the only other person in the house he seems the logical choice.


## 1.30 p.m.

He is not in bed!

This is really worrying. He never usually gets up before half-past two. Unless he is hiding in the bathroom, waiting for me to go away so that he can nip back under the duvet for the rest of the day. I will call Jakob.


## 1.45 p.m.

Writing this in downstairs front room. Left message on Jakob's mobile. I finally tracked down Ruairghy, who was making an impromptu meal out of all of the nicest things in the fridge. Must remember to hide the Luxury Seafood Goujons from Waitrose. I said, 'I don't know whether I should put my head in the gas oven, take an overdose or open my veins in a warm bath – what do you think?' He went very white and said, 'Daddy, please don't say things like that. I know life is difficult sometimes. I am in a terrible situation with Laura and Lucy, and I get really depressed but I would never do anything like that. Life is good, basically!'

I said I was touched by his concern but explained to him that I was not thinking of topping myself. It took quite a while to convince him that this was the case (he always was a very sensitive child) but he finally grasped that I was referring to Dr Esmond Pennebaker. He seemed to think that the best thing that could happen to Esmond was to be shot in the head 'preferably by an irate N H S fund manager'. I do not think he finds Esmond a sympathetic character. I asked him whether he had any lectures today. He said he had to go and see Gordon 'about going to Chile'. The phone went and I went to answer it but Ruaierghy forbade me to do so, saying that 'it might be Leopold'. I left him chewing a large chunk of smoked salmon.

I do not think his beard suits him.

## 2.15 p.m.

The light on my answerphone is flashing. This must be the call I heard downstairs. Leopold presumably. It might, I suppose, be for me. But it hardly ever is these days.

## 2.30 p.m.

It was Jakob . . . He had got my message. He sounded intensely concerned. I think I may have mistakenly given *him* the impression that I was about to kill myself. He sounded worried about this, which both pleased and touched me. I called his mobile back and found myself talking to a person called Oliver, who said he was 'minding it' for Jakob. I think he sounded genuine enough. I presume he is the one with the Daimler. Mindful of this, I was extremely polite. In fact I had quite a pleasant chat with him. He seems to be president of something called the Whisky Club. At first I thought this might be a theatrical troupe of some kind, but, according to Oliver, it is not that at all. 'It's just a group of students who get together to drink whisky!' he told me. It sounds a jolly enough way to relax after a day in the Bodleian. Though I was a little disturbed to hear that a few of the members had had to be hospitalized after meetings. I told Oliver to let Jakob know that I was not going to commit suicide but that there was a chance that Dr Esmond Pennebaker would be made to swallow barbiturates. Oliver got quite het up about this and asked whether Dr Pennebaker was a prisoner of conscience and, if so, if there was anything he could do about it. I had to explain — slightly piqued I have to say —

that Dr Esmond Pennebaker was the star of *General Practice*. I could tell from the cautious silence at the other end of the phone that Oliver had not even heard of the programme.

What one does about this I do not know. I do not like it when people recognize me and I like it even less when they have never heard of me. And, for a reason I have never quite managed to discover, the people who have heard of me are always people whom I vaguely despise. This is not because they have heard of me. The fact that they have heard of me makes me desperately want to find them interesting. (Quite a lot of them seem to be women over the age of seventy-five.) I once spent three hours talking to a man called Kevin about his goldfish, simply because he had heard of me. But I had to admit, at the end of the day, that the only thing I found interesting about him was the fact that he remembered my Autolycus at the West Yorkshire Playhouse.

Perhaps I should market-test the people who find me attractive. Or, more precisely, issue a simple questionnaire to find out who they are. Because there are not, as yet, enough of them to constitute a defined social group. I could push it through local letter-boxes, as decorators and plumbers have taken to doing. 'HULLO, MY NAME IS PAUL SLIPPERY! HAVE YOU HEARD OF ME? IF YOU NEED ANY ACT-ING DONE I AM IN YOUR AREA AND HAVE BEEN ESTABLISHED FOR NEARLY THIRTY YEARS. I AM A FORTY-NINE-YEAR-OLD ACTOR AND SPECIALIZE IN RESPONSIBLE MIDDLE-CLASS, MIDDLE-AGED MEN. I AM WHITE AND HAVE A CLEAN DRIVING LICENCE.'

I don't think a photo would necessarily be a good idea. That, as Estelle is always reminding me, is why I went into radio. '*I* love you . . .' she sometimes says, with a slight air of being surprised by this news, 'but most people don't like people whose hair sticks up at the back.' The curious thing is that she doesn't like the fact that my hair sticks up at the back. In fact she has spent nearly thirty years trying to get it to stay down.

I tried to probe Oliver on the Lucy/Laura situation. He seemed unwilling to discuss it. All he did say was that 'before it was like so cool and now it isn't cool. Because like Ruairghy can't feel it for Lucy and like Jakob has this thing for Laura and like Laura's Dad is very like psycho-pathic, which is not good, and I would love to help but I'm like . . . hopeless really!'

I do not like the sound of Ruairghiy being in love with a psychopath's daughter. I must probe him on this question.

## 4.30 p.m.

Just picked up Edwin from school. This, I suppose, will be one of my tasks under the new regime. It is, obviously, something I have done before, but now that I am the only person available to do it, it somehow seemed more important. Not, I have to say, to Edwin, who seemed not to appreciate the sacredness of the occasion. He was standing outside the school with a boy called Scagg (this is not, needless to say, his real name) who, whenever he is in the car, never utters more than two or three words. All I know about him is that his father is a committed chiropodist. He even subscribes to glossy magazines about feet, which he reads in his leisure hours. Scagg, too, according to Edwin, is very punctilious about his own feet.

Scagg did actually speak today. He said, to Edwin, 'Can he drop me here?' 'Of course I can, Scagg!' I said, brightly. Edwin gave me a hostile look. It is obviously not the done thing to address Scagg directly. And certainly not by name.

I took a furtive look in through the windows of Craftgirls as we drove past, but did not see Estelle. Presumably she is somewhere out the back stirring up huge vats of dough in order to make even more little men (they are apparently 'going like a storm'). She does not seem to want me to see the inside of the shop. Is she trying to keep her new life separate from me? Is she shagging someone there? As they are all women it will, presumably, be a lesbian relationship. Would she let me join in, I wonder?

# January 23rd. 12 midnight.

*Jakob in Oxford. Ruaighry at Gordon's house. Estelle in bed. Edwin watching Trainspotting.*

Ruairghy announced that he had to go to Gordon's just after he got up today (i.e. at around 3 p.m.). I asked him, with a touch of satire, whether he was planning a trip to Mozambique or possibly the Windward

Islands and he said, rather snappishly, 'I have to be at Gordon's because Laura may be there. We don't know where she is and we're rather worried about her actually.' I asked him who 'we' were and he said, 'She's been wanting me to have a session with Mr Proek for ages!' I was asking myself whether 'Mr Proek' was some appallingly twee nickname this girl had devised for his genital organs when Ruaighiry gave a short, contemptuous laugh. 'Mr Proek,' he said, speaking as if to a simpleton, 'is Laura's father!'

The psychopath!

Hoping to work my way round to a conversation about his diploma, I asked him what he thought of the work of Ivan Ilich. He did not seem to have heard of him.

But I have other things to worry about! Estelle did not come home until ten tonight! Something is up!

I had had a hard day in the studio, trying to deal with Esmond's nervous breakdown. Everyone seems very pleased to have got rid of the lorry. Apparently it is really difficult to get a convincing sound recording of someone being hit by a truck. There was also concern about the Road Haulage Association, who are apparently very concerned to clean up their image. My mid-life crisis is now going to be precipitated by an alcohol problem, followed by an attempt to drown myself, followed by what Surinder describes as 'The Full Monty', i.e. pulling a plastic bag over my head and cutting my throat. The head of our department has said the programme in which I do it must 'carry a health warning at the beginning', and we are 'not to make suicide sound like an attractive option'. He has also suggested a brief statement at the end of the programme, the gist of which seems to be that cutting your throat can be dangerous.

A mid-life crisis! The next few months are going to be a challenge. Surinder has handed me a pamphlet entitled *How to Recognize an Alcoholic* with a picture of a guy who looks exactly like me on the front. Apparently one of the first symptoms is thinking you aren't one. Which is disturbing.

Today I was doing a difficult scene in which Esmond confronts the management consultants who have been brought in to modernize the practice and are attempting to mark his 'decision-making ability' out of ten. He gets three. I go out of the surgery, into the pub and ask for a triple Scotch. I said to the director I thought real whisky would help me get into the role. He told me not to take the piss. He added that he was trying to persuade Surinder to write in Ronnie 'Very Nice Man' Pilfrey, our bumptious junior partner, to speak at my memorial service. When I said the only consolation about being dead would be that I wouldn't be there to hear his speech, Surinder said, 'That's a good line. Ronnie could kick off with it.' Then they both went on about how there should be 'a lot of jokes' at the Service of Thanksgiving for the Life of Esmond Pennebaker. They seemed to think that even the funeral should be a fairly upbeat affair. I was intensely depressed by this.

So I was not altogether overjoyed to have no word from Estelle as to her whereabouts. It was not until eight o'clock that I realized that I was going to have to make supper. I opened a tin of tuna fish, added it to a tin of cannellini beans, and, as I have sometimes seen Estelle do, chopped up a red onion and half a green chilli, which I then stirred in with some lemon and olive oil. By the time I had finished I felt almost calm. When I called to Edwin – who had been playing the chord of G major on his guitar since six o'clock – he said he had 'already eaten'. I said that I wished he would tell me before he ate anything. 'Why,' he said, 'are you afraid I might choke?'

As I paced around the kitchen I heard myself say, 'I have made a nice meal! I have spent half an hour making a nice meal! I wish you would tell me before eating!' In order to stop my voice rising to a pitch usually associated with hysterical old queens, I gave it a lot of stern bass, which seemed to impress Edwin considerably. I held up a forkful of the bean salad to show him how much it had cost me in terms of time. 'I could have been learning my lines!' I said. I swallowed it and chewed it elaborately to show how delicious and nourishing it was. I then cross-questioned him, at great length, as to what he had eaten. In the end he said, 'Some sweetcorn!' 'That isn't a meal!' I screamed, 'You can't just . . . eat some sweetcorn!' He said that that was what he had done. He apologized for having done so. He had been unable to stop himself. He had seen the tin, he said, and he had just 'gone for it'. He went on about the sweetcorn at some length. 'It's so lovely, sweetcorn,' he said; 'it's so chewy and lovely and crisp and crunchy and lovely!' He was quite eloquent about it. In a way, I think he too might have potential as a performer of some kind.

I said that I would remember that. Who cared about cooking? We should probably all spend our evenings crawling into a corner, shovelling a bit of bread down our faces and having what Jakob refers to as 'a really good Jodrell'. I started to become agitated at this point. I think I may have begun to discuss the impending death of Dr Esmond Pennebaker.

Eventually we calmed down. Or rather, I calmed down. Edwin had remained pretty calm throughout this encounter. He said, 'Actually I am quite hungry. It was only a tin of sweetcorn. And that salad looks really nice.' Unfortunately by now I had eaten all of it. He remained calm about *this* which, once again, started to agitate me.

It was at this point that I heard the thump of the front door and realized that Estelle was home. Edwin disappeared with a suddenness that recalled my own departure (as Ariel) in Act Five, Scene One, of Lionel Freebody's 1973 all-male production of *The Tempest*. And then, with some of the drama associated with my entrance (as Gloucester) in Act One, Scene One, of the same director's all-male version of *King Richard the Third*, Estelle Thwaites came down the stairs and into the room. She was carrying three large plastic bags. Out of the top of one of them peered a little dough man. All she said (but she said it before I could open my mouth) was, 'I don't suppose you got any wine.'

I said, very lightly, very calmly, 'There is some red.' This might seem, on the face of it, a harmless thing to say. But, after one has been married for nearly twenty-five years, there is no such thing as a harmless remark. Estelle, as it happens, does not like red wine. She dropped both her bags and said, 'Oh. Well, you'll be all right then.'

This remark was delivered to an invisible arbitrator. One who was, clearly, wise, fair-minded and almost certainly on her side. At this point I foolishly attempted a counter-attack. It was too late. It was not well executed. And it lacked confidence. 'You're late!' I said, as if I was simply commenting on the fact. She gave me a quick, sharp glance from under her fringe, and then, her northern accent becoming a little more pronounced, said, 'I don't see what that's got to do with it.' Then she shook her head like a troubled horse and, lowering her broad shoulders, headed for the door like a woman intending to do it some serious damage. 'No, no, no,' she was saying, 'I'll go! All I've been doing all day is *making little dough men!*'

I simply did not believe she had been making little dough men until ten o'clock. Unless Serafina was running Craftgirls along the lines of a Victorian match factory. She had, quite clearly, been for a drink with someone. 'Making little dough men,' I said, 'is clearly very important. And I am not putting it down for one moment. I am fully behind your involvement with little dough men!' 'Then why,' she said, 'are you sneering about it?' 'I am not sneering about it,' I said, 'all I said was *I am fully behind your involvement with little dough men!*' 'There you go again!' she said. 'Listen to the way you say it! You say it in a sneery way!'

I had spent most of the day trying to say lines like 'I am afraid your haemoglobin levels are giving rise to concern' and 'I asked for the white count, Lola, not the assessment forms!' – and some of these had been subjected to pretty close and unpleasant scrutiny. To be accused of being unconvincing in my own kitchen was too much. In an attempt to calm myself, I went over to the CD player and put on a Beethoven string quartet. As I was doing this, I said, 'You've had a hard day. I've had a hard day. Let's try and discuss this like rational human beings, shall we?'

When I turned round, to my surprise, she had left the room.

I poured myself a glass of Australian Merlot and sat back, trying to enjoy the music. It wasn't as difficult as I had thought when in the middle of the argument with Estelle. When in the middle of an argument with Estelle it is often difficult to conceive that any kind of life has been possible before it started or will be possible after it is over. If it ever *is* over. It is a bit like being eaten by a crocodile. I sat there, marvelling at the way Beethoven manages to conjure up such textual richness out of only four instruments. 'You would have thought,' I said, aloud to the empty room, 'that we were listening to an entire orchestra!' I went over to the CD player and found that I had been listening to Schubert's Fifth Symphony.

I have always prided myself on being musical, and I was seriously shaken by this discovery.

In a mood of real humility I went up the stairs. Estelle was slumped in a chair in the corner watching a video of ER. She glanced up at me, briefly. I sat at the other end of the settee and watched as they performed a rather incompetent tracheotomy. I know enough, now, not to point out the medical inconsistencies in the show. 'You think you *are* a bloody doctor!' Edwin said to me when I, very quietly and gently, pointed out that the recommended dose of carisoprodol was 350 mg a day by mouth. Very quietly and gently I said, 'Look. I realize that I am going through a difficult time and that it isn't easy for me, and I do accept that I am not as easy as I perhaps have been in the past. I am losing focus on a lot of things. I am approaching fifty. It is a watershed . . . I want to make it clear that I take your work at . . .' I paused slightly here, suddenly unsure as to whether Serafina's shop was actually called Craftgirls, '. . . at the shop very seriously and . . .'

I got up, sensing that she was, at last, listening to me. 'All I am saying is,' I said, beating the air with the side of my flattened palm, 'all I am *saying* is that we both have stresses and that you are under a particular deal of strain for a number of reasons, not least because the children are going to be leaving home soon and of course you are going through an enormous number of biological changes in which the whole hormonal pattern of your life is altering in terms of what your system is producing, in terms of ovulation and so on and that will have an effect on you which I am determined to help you deal with!'

I turned, feeling proud of the fact that, in a fairly long speech I had not once mentioned the word 'menopause'. But Estelle had left the room. I went upstairs to the bedroom, prepared to continue the conversation. As far as I could make out she was asleep. At least, the light was off and there was a dark hump on her side of the bed that was snoring loudly. It is still there. I think the snores are genuine. But there have been times, over the last twenty-five years, when both of us have pretended to be things we were not. Perhaps it isn't her at all. Perhaps her friend Rosie, from down the road, is deputizing for her. Perhaps she has nipped over the wall and is in a nightclub in Balham. I am not certain of anything any more. I am sitting at my desk staring out at the rain-flecked street.

Opposite me I can see Porker, lurching around his front room in his towelled dressing-gown. He looks drunk. Upstairs in the bedroom, Mrs Porker is drawing the curtains. Soon Porker will turn off the standard lamp and ascend the stairs. Moments later the bedroom will be plunged into darkness.

What then? Will Mr and Mrs Porker make love? Or will Mrs Porker, like Estelle, be snoring loudly? Next door to them, the Wicketts show no sign of life at all. This is not surprising. They have been married thirty-five years. Wickett is in an even worse position than me. He is no longer even middle-aged. He has, according to his wife, paid off his mortgage. He has actually achieved redundancy – even though his was not gained by gouging out his carotid artery in front of an audience of 750,000 people. I feel, suddenly, a strong bond of love between me and Wickett and Porker – who is now, unsteadily, climbing the stairs. We are looking, unafraid, at what may well be our last twenty years. We are like children lost in a wood, abandoned in our separate houses with women who no longer understand us, who shout and tidy and snore in ways that we have long ago ceased to understand.

And who, if statistics are anything to go by, will almost certainly live longer than we will.

I close this diary tonight with sombre thoughts. Where was Estelle tonight? Why did she not wish to tell me? Was she really simply making little dough men? What does the year hold for me, for her, for Ruaighry and Jakob and Edwin? Who is Lucy? And who is Laura? Why is her father a psychopath? Why is he called Proek? Where *is* Edwin? Did he go to bed at all? Can I be bothered to climb the stairs to his room to find out? Wouldn't I have done so for Ruarghiry? Isn't this enough rhetorical questions for one night?

Yes.

## January 26th. 10 a.m. Sunny.

*Edwin at school. Estelle at work (we hope). Jakob at Oxford. Ruairghy in bed with Gordon.*

I do not think Ruairghy and Gordon are having sex. They simply did not finish discussing their latest plans for a trip (to Malawi) until four in the morning. They finished a bottle of vodka in the process and, when I went down to tell them to shut up, the country of destination had changed to the Independent Republic of Northern Cyprus.

I am writing this in a hurry before I go into work for an urgent meeting called by Colin Cross, Head of Soaps. Is it to discuss my death? Estelle left without speaking to me. This was partly because I was pretending to be asleep, but nevertheless I found it disturbing. She closed the front door in a distinctly hostile manner, perhaps trying to signal that she felt it was not her turn to take Edwin into school.

I must write about our sex life. But maybe not right now. It is a difficult thing to describe tastefully. (Why?) I must get to this meeting. Maybe it will yield some clue as to who wants me dead.

## 12.45 p.m.

I am writing this in the canteen. It is one of the few areas of Broadcasting House that John Birt has not yet attempted to redesign in order to give the impression that it is a privately run concern – go-ahead colours, instead of the comfortable shabbiness associated with an organization funded by public contributions. At the moment it is still referred to as 'the canteen' – very much as it was in 1971, when I first made my bow as Esmond Pennebaker. Soon, Surinder suggests, it will be given the kind of name usually associated with fast-food franchises. 'If they call it Uncle John's Noshery,' she told me, 'people will have the illusion that someone is making a profit.' When I told her that, judging from the amount of meat in the moussaka they almost certainly were, she launched into another hour-long tirade about Producer Choice and the Internal Market, none of which I understood. Apparently it costs three hundred pounds to take out a library book, and seven hundred and fifty pounds every time I go to the lavatory. I told her I thought this was cheap at the price.

Colin Cross, a small weaselly man with a beard, who was made head of department after fourteen people turned the job down, opened the meeting by announcing that there was going to be 'a period of major restructuring'. I assumed he might be referring to the imminent death of Dr Esmond Pennebaker but this was not the case.

Apparently Radio Drama Continuing Narrative Strand (Domestic) is going to be merged with Radio Drama Occasional Documentary Division (Overseas) and there is to be a new head of the new department which will be called Home and Overseas Radio Documentary Drama (Occasional and Continuing). This, as far as I could make out, will be Cross. He will have a new assistant called Sylvia, who was previously the head of Radio Drama Occasional Documentary Division (Overseas.) She is a small fat woman who said that her new position was 'an exciting opportunity' – which is BBC code for saying she was pissed off about not getting Cross's position and was going to resign as soon as she could find another job. 'There are obviously more changes in the pipeline,' said Cross (who used the word 'pipeline' no less than eight times during the course of the morning), 'but obviously I cannot discuss them with you at the moment since I do not know what they are. As soon as they have filtered down from upstairs, however, I will be circulating a memo to everyone setting them out in detail. Assuming of course I am still in place after the changes!'

He laughed lightly as he said this but Surinder tells me he is almost certain to be sent to Scotland, a country from which he has specifically asked to be excused. The fact that he is working on a life of John Birt has not saved him. Cross then went on to tell us that he had brought in someone called Ashley Ramp (a hunchback with a pale face and a corduroy suit) who would be 'coordinating the restructuring'.

This, for reasons I cannot go into here, is ominous news.

What I really wanted to know, of course, was how this affected the (at present brief) future facing Dr Esmond Pennebaker. So after about half an hour of this I looked at Karl our producer, and said, 'Can I know whether the restructuring will affect the plans for my death?' There was general laughter at this remark. 'At the moment,' I went on, 'the people in charge seem to want me to top myself. But if they change – does that mean I might be given a reprieve?' There was more laughter. 'I would settle for a lingering disease!' I added, for which I almost got a round of applause.

Karl pushed back his chair and gave the table in front of him a shrewd, bloke-ish glance. Karl is in his late thirties but acts as if he was older than I am. He has been associated with many successful radio dramas, although all the ones he has actually produced have been flops. Once he had let us know he wasn't going to take any rubbish from the furniture he raised his head and gave the wall behind the people opposite him similarly uncompromising treatment. Finally, after some facial work designed to illustrate the fact that thoughts were supposed to be filtering through to his speech centres, he said, 'Well, Paul – this is a time of change for all of us. All we can say at the moment is that the plan is for you to commit suicide. But that may change. It is a time of change. Some of the people who feel that that is what should happen may no longer be in place after the restructuring.' 'Let's hope so!' I said.

I got another laugh for this remark.

At this point Ashley Ramp himself entered. He was carrying an enormous briefcase. He said, 'I am so sorry, Colin. They were trying to get me to go to Scotland!' Cross seemed to find this amusing. After that Ashley Ramp said the whole department was going to be moved to somewhere called The Building. People started to mutter together, rather in the manner of a Shakespearian crowd turning nasty. Ashley Ramp

*23*

seemed positively to enjoy the sensation his words had caused. I must stop writing now, as Karl and Surinder are coming towards me across the canteen. I wonder, not for the first time, whether they are having an affair. I am always seeing them whisper to each other in corners when they think no one is looking. I also wonder, not for the first time either, why I go around boasting about being a happily married man, instead of joining in the sensational amount of shagging that is clearly going on in Broadcasting House.

I will go and ring Estelle. No I won't. Why should I? She is clearly up to something. As I have only a few months to live – why don't I enjoy them?


### 1.45 p.m.

Still in the canteen. Rang Estelle. I was connected to a crematorium in Raynes Park. I really must get hold of her work number.


### 3 p.m.

Writing this in an outer office. The secretary keeps looking at me as if I was mentally unbalanced. I have noticed that writing things down in a public place tends to make those around you nervous. I intend to do more of it. I am waiting for a chance to talk to Karl about my future. I called Gustave and asked him if there was anything in the pipeline – a word I don't think I have ever used until today. Cross, by the way, used the word 'coalface' five times and the word 'objective' seventeen times. I said to Surinder in the lift that my objective was to take Colin Cross down to the coalface and hit him over his fat head with the pipeline. She laughed. I think I may have a chance with her.

Gustave said there was chance of some commentary work on a programme about fleas. I said I was extremely interested. He said, 'They're looking for a voice that can humanize them. Apparently fleas are not just horrible little things that suck your blood!' 'Not like agents, you mean?' I said, but he didn't appear to hear me.

Here comes Karl, with the furtive air I have often noted in Welshmen.

## 4.45 p.m.

Waiting for Surinder for regular Tuesday meeting in her office. She hasn't, of course, turned up yet. Surinder is the sort of girl who is always late. She also tries to disarm you by laughing about it. I am not sure that I like that.

God knows what she wants to discuss with me. She has probably hit on a new way of ending my life ahead of schedule. Perhaps I am to be burned alive. Or perhaps, unbelievable as this may seem, Karl has had an idea – although he has spent so much of his life taking credit for other people's, I do not think he would recognize one of his own. I can't work Karl out. What is he up to? Is he the one who wants to get rid of me in spite of his protestations to the contrary?

When I went in to see him, he was shifting his (stolen) award statuettes around on his desk. After about two minutes he said, 'I don't want to go to Scotland. Colin doesn't want to go to Scotland. But we may have to go to Scotland.' I remained silent. 'We don't want to go but it's difficult. Peter Skopolos is going to get the planning job and Marie Duveen is very well thought of. She will go to Muswell Hill and sort things out for Lucy Duhuig!' I remained silent. 'I would have liked to go to Wales,' he went on, 'but that is not going to be possible as long as Pike is in place. The man has been promoted above his level of competence.' 'I am sure,' I said, with a look of straight-faced sincerity, 'that that will never happen to you, Karl.' I thought, for a moment, that he was going to cry. Then he gave me a quick, sharp look, as if to check whether he should break into Geordie or, perhaps, try yodelling. 'I may have to go to Radio Aberdeen!' he added. I composed my face into a suitable expression of sympathy.

Then he looked around furtively, as if he suspected someone might be eavesdropping on this conversation. 'It's not me who wants you dead,' he whispered. 'I can't tell you who it is, but it comes from upstairs. Someone very senior has got it in for you.' He tapped the side of his nose. 'If I have to go to Scotland I am afraid you will almost certainly have to die. That's all I can say at the moment.'

Clearly I have to stop Karl being sent to Aberdeen – even though it is probably the best place for him. But who is it up there who doesn't like me? I don't think it can be John Birt. Could it be Colin Cross? Or Ashley Ramp?

25

Ramp and I go back a long way. Of this more later. I had better try and find out what is going on.

Surinder has clearly decided to stand me up. A pity. I was rather looking forward to seeing her. I think I have grown fonder of her than I realized over the time we have worked together. There is something very attractive about the way she —

## 5.45 p.m.

Writing this in the car park.

My diary is written in one of Jakob's old exercise books. And the end of the last entry was just at the bottom of one of the pages. As I was writing it I heard footsteps behind me and, like a kid caught out in school, I put my hand over the last paragraph. Over most of the last paragraph anyway. The only words left visible were . . . 'worked together. There is something very attractive about the way she —' Just as I had realized this and was trying to cover them with my head, I heard Surinder say, 'Who's attractive then, Paul?' She has a light, silvery voice and a laugh that reminds me of a test tube dragged lightly along a glockenspiel.

I closed the book with a snap and said, 'Please do not read my novel without my permission!' Surinder put her head to one side and shook out her long black hair. She has, I found myself thinking, absolutely stupendous teeth. Then, still shaking out her hair she walked across the office floor and sat on the edge of one of the desks. 'I never realized you were a novelist!' she said. 'I'm not!' I said, 'Actually this is . . . er . . . a memo! . . . About . . . er . . . current affairs!' 'There are lots of those in the BBC!' said Surinder, and then gave me a fast, shrewd glance. 'And people write them up in their diaries!'

After a while, I said, 'What was it you wanted to talk to me about?' She seemed to be debating whether to tell me. I was unable to keep my eyes off her legs. She was wearing a short leather skirt — a garment poised delicately between the erotic and the ridiculous — but her legs managed to look as if they had an existence entirely independent of the things covering them. Although she was sitting down there was none of the thigh-puddling observed when Gemma Beesley, the programme secretary, tries unsuccessfully to perch on Karl's desk in her miniskirt.

'Anyway,' she said, 'you are a happily married man!' I looked up

26

guiltily, aware that I had shifted sideways in my seat and craned my head out to the left like someone lining up a tricky putt. The sort of interest I was (involuntarily) expressing was of the kind only really proper in a gynaecologist. I think I may have blushed. 'I am!' I said. Surinder smiled. 'Good,' she said, 'I like happily married men! Let's have a drink one evening some time!'

## 9.30 p.m.

Dinner with Estelle and Edwin. Ruairghry came in halfway through and ate a packet of prawns while circling the table. Consumed with lustful thoughts about Surinder.

## February 2nd. 10.30 a.m.

*Estelle at work. Almost certainly. Jakob 'in Leeds'. Probably. Ruiraghy in bed with Gordon and Leopold. Edwin at school.*

I do not think Ruririghy and Gordon and Leopold are having sex. When I looked in earlier Gordon was asleep on a pile of cushions and Leopold seemed to have curled up underneath Rurighy's desk.

Leopold apparently wants to accompany them to Malawi and they are trying to stop him doing this.

When I rang Jakob's mobile this morning I got Oliver once more, who told me that Jakob had 'gone to Leeds with Laura'. The mysterious Laura again! When I asked him why, Oliver said he thought it was something to do with a cash-flow problem. I was not unduly worried by this. Ever since he sold our used milk bottles to a boy in the class below him at St Luke's Primary School, west Wimbledon, Jakob has had a fairly firm grip on his finances. Oliver also said something about 'white goods'. I hope this is not anything to do with drugs.

I have just got out my mortgage documents. But cannot bear to look at them.

I am staring at Ruairighy's self-portrait, aged six, up on the wall above my desk. It is a curious bulbous-shaped thing with gigantic canine teeth. We showed it to a psychiatrist once who advised us to put it away in a drawer 'in case someone saw it and tried to have him put into care'. Next to it is a photograph of Jakob, aged three, wearing a pair of white lederhosen and a small conical cap of the kind assumed by elves or kibbutzniks. Ruiairghy is standing next to him peering off into the opposite direction. They both have the air of people who have just landed on a strange planet and are anxious to placate the inhabitants.

None of all this is much help with the mortgage, which, as far as I can work out, will not be paid off until the year 2525 (wasn't there a song with that as the title?), by which time I will be just over six hundred years old. Ruairghhy will be well into his half-millennium. Maths was never my strong point.

The BBC Pension Fund, however, stands at over four hundred million pounds. I ought to be able to get my hands on some of that if I play my cards right. Porker, who retired from the National Westminster Bank three years ago at the age of fifty-one, got two thirds of his salary and a gigantic amount in cash. His life has, however, come to an abrupt stop. He spends almost all of every day walking round Wimbledon Common with that whippet of his. I am not sure this is a good arrangement for either of them. He is unloading the dog from the car even as I write this. It hops down on to the tarmac and he snarls at it.

All this mortgage stuff is really avoidance behaviour. What is really worrying me is Estelle.

She is changing. She now almost never says goodbye when she goes out in the mornings. I must admit that there have been times in our marriage when I wished she would stop saying goodbye. There was a period when she would twine herself round me like an octopus if I was planning a trip to the off-licence. But now she marches out to spend as many as *eight whole hours without me* with an air of complete indifference. How can she manage this with such ease?


## 12 noon.

Unable to concentrate on my nervous breakdown. It begins in next week's episode, although it has not yet reached the storming heights of lunacy that Surinder promises me in a month's time. All I have done so far is keep saying things like 'I'll have a large one!' If this is the first sign of a mental breakdown I should have been sectioned years ago. I also start to get obsessed with parking. Which is a hard thing to act. Surinder's stage direction simply says, '*There is something clearly unhealthy about his attitude to parking.*' And the line that follows it is 'Do they clamp in Drasborough Road?' I have tried this several ways. The best seems to be if I emphasize the word 'they', as if Esmond is convinced that the wardens may be from another planet. I tried emphasizing the word 'clamp' but that gave the line a vaguely sexual flavour. When I emphasized both 'clamp' and 'road' it sounded like a quotation from John Betjeman.

Perhaps I could base my performance on Porker. He has been out most of the morning, measuring the distance between every stationary vehicle in Mafeking Road. Sometimes he writes little notes and leaves them under the windscreen wipers. I do not need to examine them to know that they say, 'IS THIS SELFISH PARKING?' I know because I received one from him in the spring of 1993 and that is what it said. I replied by leaving one under his windscreen which simply said, 'Is this?' It created a coolness between us that lasted for nearly a year.

But my mind is not on Esmond Pennebaker. I am going to ring Estelle.


## 12.10 p.m.

Was connected to a Greek restaurant in Ealing. I really must find her number. Is there some psychological reason behind my failure to remember it?


## 12.15 p.m.

Found number on floor under bed. She has gone to lunch! At twelve noon! With someone called Julian! Unless he is one of the little dough men, I think I am going to have to find out more about this!

When I rang, the phone was answered by a woman I used to know. Her name is Stella Badyass. When I knew her, she was a quiet, uncomplaining individual who spent most of her days lugging her son Norman's cello about Wimbledon village, smiling ruefully out from under her fringe, as if it was sheltering her from the rain. Norman wasn't her only son — although, for some reason, no one seems to have seen the boy from her first marriage. She had been married to a high-flying doctor from somewhere in the Third World but he had left her and she had ended up with a rather hopeless surveyor. If there was a criticism to be made of her it was that she walked and talked like a duck, but apart from that she was an extremely inoffensive person.

She has changed.

'Hoo yah!' she said, when I announced myself. It was only as she said this that I realized it was a locution I had heard on Estelle's lips recently. Perhaps it was a form of company song. I could not quite bring myself to say 'Hoo yah!' back so, after a spurious inquiry about her son and his cello, I said, 'Do you happen to know where Estelle might be?' 'I think,' she said, 'she was with Julian!' *Ah hah! Julian! Right! Julian!*

'Hoo kay?' said Stella Badyass. I gave up. 'Hoo kay!' I said. I wondered, as I put down the phone, whether Stella Badyass was going through the menopause. Even if she wasn't before she went to Craftgirls she was almost certain to have caught it by now. Am I becoming obsessed with the menopause? I have noticed recently that I suspect an amazingly wide cross-section of women of going through it.

Julian. She has never mentioned Julian. That is a very bad sign. I think I am going to have to discuss the sexual side of my marriage.

## 4 p.m.

I have just torn a few pages out of this diary. It is not something I want to do again, but reading over what I had written about me and Estelle I decided that it should be destroyed as soon as possible. I did not even dare to confide it to the waste-paper basket. Eventually I tore it into tiny strips and flushed it down the upstairs lavatory.

I think I am suffering from a form of sexual amnesia. I seem unable to remember when I last had sex. I do not know whether this is because it was so long ago. Or whether it is the same order of event as, say, the fact that I keep forgetting the second name of the man who lives at number 43.

This amnesia is probably due to the fact that, on average, we have been doing it about two or three times a week for the last twenty-five years. And in the early phase of our marriage a very great deal more than that. That is a rough total of 1,300 acts of intercourse. It is no wonder they are all blurring into each other. This inability to recall the last sex act I committed is partly due to the fact that I keep remembering occasions that, on reflection, turn out to be at least eighteen years old (the ski-lift, for example). This in turn makes me doubt whether the one I think happened last did actually happen then at all, or is another act transplanted into our current bedroom for some deep and hideous psychological reason to which I do not have access. If, anyway, the last time Estelle and I shagged was as long ago as I seem to think it was, when, if ever, am I going to get it again? At the moment the next available slot for sexual contact seems to me to be on the other side of the Millennium.

She would not see it like this, I know. She thinks that when it comes to sexual gratification, I make no distinction between next Tuesday and the Millennium. And this is absolutely true.

Back to Esmond Pennebaker. I note that my next line is 'Go easy on the tonic, Arabella!' An unusually subtle touch for Surinder.


## 4.45 p.m.

Just been upstairs to tell Ruaierghy that it is time he got up and did some work for his diploma. He and Gordon seem to have sneaked out. Leopold, fully dressed, had crawled under Ruairghy's bed and gone back to sleep. I did not wake him.


## 6 p.m.

I have retrieved Edwin from school.

Today he was with Scagg and Bozz. Bozz is a tall, spectral creature whose hair grows in tufts. His father has retired. Apparently he was allowed to do so on medical grounds, although Bozz says there is nothing wrong with him. Scagg – who is growing more talkative – said, 'Hey, Bozz! My dad told me your dad has bunions!' Bozz seemed pleased and surprised by this news. 'No kid?' he said. 'Like . . . big bunions?' 'Huge!' said Scagg. I said, 'I had a verruca once!' and Scagg looked impressed. I feel he has warmed towards me.

When we got back Edwin went to the garage round the corner and bought three tins of spaghetti hoops, which he ate. I did not try to stop him. He asked me what I had done all day and I said, 'I tried to learn my lines.' I have read somewhere about fathers who had had appalling experiences in the war and were never able to discuss them with their children. I am in the reverse situation. I am aching to communicate not only my experiences but also my inner thoughts and feelings to my sons. Unfortunately I do not have any. He is now upstairs on the phone to Bozz. I stood outside his door to listen. They were discussing a girl. I am almost sure I heard him say, 'It's Lulu, man! It's like love with Lulu!' At this point I lost my balance and fell over on the landing. I heard him coming over to the door and had to scamper off down the stairs.

I have noticed that Edwin prefers to use the telephone to talk to people who he has just left or is just about to see. Although this is probably preferable to his talking to a French or Norwegian version of Bozz, I find it extraordinarily irritating.

Although I did, the other day, find a piece of paper in his room with a suspiciously long sequence of digits written on it. I am almost sure the first few were all noughts. So maybe, as Stella Badyass's son is reported to have done, he has been phoning a sex-chat line in Florida. Apparently they are 'more imaginative'.


## 7 p.m.

Ruairghy phoned in to say that he and Gordon were going to the Chinese Embassy. I did not ask why. He then said he would not be back tonight as he was 'going to try and find Laura and sort out this Jakob business'. I do not like to intrude on my sons' private lives but was unable to stop myself saying, 'What Laura business?' Ruarighry said, 'Can't you see what's happening here? Are you totally blind? Can't you see how it's tearing us all apart?' I said, 'No.' I was just going to ask him why he thought going to the Chinese Embassy would help him with his diploma when he hung up. Concerned, I phoned Jakob on his mobile.

A girl answered. I said, 'Who's that?' And she said, 'Would you like to speak to Jakob?' I said I would. When Jakob came on the line I said, 'Was that Laura?' There was a long pause and Jakob said, 'Very possibly.' I said, 'How was Leeds?' Jakob said, 'Why do you want to know that?' While I was still recovering from this question, he said, 'Leeds is a large industrial town with a great many entrepreneurial possibilities. It was great crack.' I said, 'I am assuming you are not referring to the drug.' Jakob gave a slightly sinister laugh. I did not like to ask him about white goods. He then asked me what the yen/dollar exchange rate was and I had to confess I did not know. It is nice he is taking his degree course seriously. Just before we said goodbye Jakob said, 'Could you not mention to Ruairghy that I'm here with Laura?' I said I would not dream of doing such a thing and asked him whether he was all right. 'It's all a question,' he said, 'of cash flow.'

I presume this is something to do with an essay.

He then put the phone down. Edwin entered my study not long after this and, to my surprise, remained in it, even after he had ascertained I was there. He sat on my sofa as I bent over my script and said, 'How is *General Practice* going?' I must admit that I was instantly suspicious. He never usually asks questions that I might be interested in answering, without an ulterior motive. But on this occasion he did not seem to have one. We discussed my role at some length and he told me that the scene in which I discovered the mouse droppings was 'brilliant'. As he left he said, 'How much does a fridge cost?' I said it depended on the fridge. He seemed to find this a satisfactory answer. In many ways he is the most practical of the three of them. An early interest in the pricing of electrical goods could well lead to a career in retailing.

I asked him if he knew who Lucy and Laura were. He said, 'Are they the ones on Channel Four?'

The creak of the lock and the thump of Estelle's shopping hitting the floor. I suppose I shall have to go downstairs and try not to look as if I am angry with her. It is an impossible task. She will know. I will stay up here.

## 7.30 p.m.

She knew I was angry without my going downstairs. I don't know how she managed this. I quite often don't go downstairs when she comes in. I am quite often learning my lines or on the phone. But somehow or other she could tell, simply by standing in the hall and cocking her ear, that I was angry. Why has she been gifted with extrasensory perception? And why are her exquisitely tuned sensibilities used exclusively to winkle out my baser feelings?

'What's up with you?' was the first thing she said. I said, 'Nothing!' Remember I am a trained actor. I spent three years at RADA. I gave each syllable total conviction.

33

But I knew she wasn't impressed.

She started to climb the stairs. There was something horribly businesslike about the way she did this. But, purposeful as her shoes had sounded on the way up, once she was round the door of my room she did a pretty fair impression of someone coming into someone's room for no reason apart from the fact that the door happened to be open. I bent my eyes over my script and she shouldered her way over to the window.

She stood looking down at the street for some moments, her hands swinging loosely at her sides. There was a brooding quality to her, a sense of contained energy. At any second, I decided, she might hook her long arms up over the pelmet, swing off on to the light-bulb flex and then hand herself out on to the landing by the dado rail. Instead she glared down at me and said, 'You're annoyed because we haven't had sex.' 'I think,' I said, 'that we have had sex. It may have been some time ago. It may have been rather stale and tired but that is only to be expected after twenty-five years of marriage.' She looked at me. Her eyes seemed to suggest a righteous despair that such people as me should be still living in the world. *I feel sorry for you*, said her eyes, *you are so grubby and small and predictable and sad*.

She then gave a small shrug, which, as with many of her gestures, seemed to be for the benefit of someone who wasn't me, and marched to the door. She was out on the landing when I said, 'How was lunch with Julian?'

This brought her back into the room with amazing speed. 'What about Julian?' she said, pronouncing the man's name in a ludicrously affected way. 'How was lunch,' I said, a touch humorously, 'with Julian?' Estelle narrowed her eyes. 'She is allowed out for meals, you know!' she said, 'even though her husband is a *complete pig*!'

I seem to remember reading somewhere, probably in that now forgotten sixties classic *The Divided Self*, by the spectacularly bonkers Ronnie Laing, that referring to yourself in the third person is the first sign that your next most-used garment is likely to be a strait-jacket. I suppose Esmond's crack-up made me unduly sensitive to such nuances.

I laced my fingers together. I had not expected the crisis, when it came, to take quite this form. But it was a relief, in a way, to be dealing with something so obviously serious rather than the usual petty rows about whether we have or have not had a shag recently. 'Why is he a pig?' I said, very gently and quietly. 'Oh,' said Estelle, 'because he shags other women. And he's a transvestite.' 'Is he indeed?' I said, softly. 'Does he wear your clothes, do you think?' She gave me a very odd look. 'He doesn't wear *mine*,' she said, 'he wears Julian's!' I was having a little trouble getting hold of this. I did some more of the finger-lacing and said, 'So Julian likes . . . women's clothes too?' Estelle knitted her brow. 'We shop for them together, for God's sake!' she said.

This was all said in a way that suggested that her involvement with a cross-dresser was the most natural thing in the world. Not wishing to disturb her any more than was necessary I tried to gently steer her in the right direction. A direction that would help her find her way back to herself. 'So Estelle likes Julian because Paul likes dressing up as a woman.' She gave me another very odd look. 'Who's Paul?' she said. 'I'm Paul, for God's sake. I'm Paul Slippery. I like dressing up as a woman. Right?' Estelle's mouth fell open. 'Oh my God!' she said. 'Oh my God!' 'It's what you think, isn't it?' I said. 'It's what you feel. It's what you want me to do at some subconscious level. It's why you've got this thing going with Julian.' Estelle's brow furrowed in puzzlement. 'What do you think I've got going with Julian?' she said. 'Well,' I said, 'you go shopping with . . .' I pronounced the man's name with clarity and disdain, '. . . *Julian* for these women's clothes he likes and you —'

There was a long silence. 'I think,' said Estelle eventually, 'that we are talking at cross purposes here. I am talking about someone called Gillian. Who works at Craftgirls. And who is working with me on the figurine project. Gillian is a woman. A very nice woman. There is no one called Julian at Craftgirls. There are no men at Craftgirls. The only place where there are men is at 52 Mafeking Road and . . .' here her voice rose, suddenly, to a scream, '. . . *I am fed up with them because they all leave the lavatory seat down when peeing and leave shaving hair all round the basin and never clear up after themselves and leave flossing equipment all over the bathroom floor like a nest of snakes and think that saying something in a foreign accent makes it automatically funny!*'

I said that there might be men in Mafeking Road who did these things. But that I was not one of them. She did not seem impressed by this line.

The last thing she said before she left the room was, 'I have had a very tough two hours listening to poor Stella Badyass's troubles. And all you can think about is your willy.' Then she left the room. I am sitting here.

This is all, quite clearly, to do with the fact that the last period she had was on Guy Fawkes's Night.

## 8.30 p.m.

Leopold is still asleep on Ruarighy's floor.

## February 6th. 11.30 a.m. Raining.

*Estelle at work. Ruaiury at the University of South Wimbledon (I think). Jakob God knows where. Edwin at Bozz's house.*

It is a Saturday. Ruairrhy got up at nine and said he had to 'show his face at USW'. Presumably he is doing this on the weekend as there is less danger of his running into any form of organized instruction. Estelle is at a Craftgirls marketing session. Edwin has gone to Bozz's house. From Bozz's house they will go to Scagg's house. From Scagg's house they will go to someone called Lupin's house. There they will meet Lulu, Alice, Dorothy, Francesca and Mary-Anne. Then they will go on to Whizz's house. From there they will go to Lulu's house and there 'probably' they will meet someone called Helen and someone called Snozzer. Then they will all go back to Scagg's house. And from Scagg's house back to Bozz's house. After which the whole thing will start all over again. It seems a desperately sad way to lead your life. But so long as none of the little bastards end up at 52 Mafeking Road, where only last week they decimated the shower curtain, traumatized the fridge and almost certainly walked off with my edition of the complete later choral works of Janacek, I really do not care.

My marriage may have to go. After nearly twenty-five years. It is possible that I have outgrown Estelle. It is possible that these little dough men have tied her to a phase of our life that should have been finished ages ago. But I am not sure that I care. I have to learn to grow. ('Grow what?' I hear Estelle's cynical voice say and I answer, 'Grow me! Grow Paul Slippery! Grow and change and be more myself!') Perhaps I have to learn to *live*! Surinder beckons me towards a more glamorous and feisty lifestyle of the kind enjoyed by the likes of Michael Douglas and President Clinton.

I have been a boringly safe married man for too long. I am going to live and breathe and have sex in strange positions with women half my age.

At least I hope I am. I don't see why I shouldn't. Even if I do have 'a peculiar nose' (Estelle) and 'hair that sticks up like a scarecrow' (Estelle) I am still a man with a bit of poke under his bonnet. I seem to be getting involved with Surinder. In fact I think she is panting for me. I am going to see her this evening. A drink in the Langham Hotel, a place I can remember from the early seventies, when it was known to BBC staff simply as The Langham. Once a gloomy, cavernous building, full of highly trained men in suits writing confidential reports on green paper, it is now an international rendezvous complete with potted plants, country-house sofas, waiters with bow ties and visiting Japanese.

## 7 p.m. Langham Hotel, w1

Scribbling this while Surinder in Ladies.

This is hot stuff.

She arrived at almost the same time as me. She ordered a gin and tonic and I ordered a large whisky. When we were settled in our chairs she swirled the ice round in her glass and said, 'Have you any idea why I wanted to have a drink with you?' 'You ache for my body!' I said. She gave that glockenspiel laugh. 'Of course!' she said, in tones of perfect seriousness. 'All the girls in the office are *wild* about you!'

'I want to talk about Karl!' she said. I felt a sudden stab of disappointment. The last person I wanted to talk about was Karl. 'What about Karl?' I said. 'Oh,' said Surinder, sighing, 'Karl and me. You know . . .' 'What about Karl and you?' I said with a Clinton-style leer. 'Are you an . . . item . . . ?'

'Karl,' said Surinder, 'has Angharad and Bleriod and we need say no more.' I nodded wisely. One of these goons was his wife, although I could not remember which one. It was probably, knowing Karl, Bleriod. Although again, knowing Karl, Bleriod could be his house. Perhaps Bleriod was his daughter. 'Angharad's away a lot,' went on Surinder, 'and Bleriod keeps crapping on the floor.'

Bleriod turns out to be Karl's labrador. Surinder had grown thoughtful. She let her glance range round the others in the bar. In the corner was a man in a suit, studying a calculator. Over by the window was a group of smartly dressed young men drinking beer and referring to each other and to absent comrades by their initials. It all felt pretty illicit and sophisticated. I was about to make a grab for her, when she suddenly sat bolt upright and said she had to powder her nose.

She has been an awful long time in the Ladies. I hope she has not climbed out of the window and made a dash for it. Perhaps she is buying contraceptive devices. It is so long since I have done this kind of thing!

Here she comes. Away with the book!

## 8.30 p.m.

Writing this in car while eating peppermints. Do not want Estelle to suspect I have been drinking. Have also jumped up and down to work up sweat and rubbed face with old sock found on floor of Volvo in order to get rid of Surinder's rather powerful scent. Although our marriage may have to move to an open phase in which we talk honestly about my bonking black women (something that I have not managed to get around to this evening), I do not think the time is yet ripe to even reveal I have had a drink with one.

But Surinder clearly sees me as pretty hot stuff.

'The trouble is,' she said slowly, on her return from the Ladies, 'that Karl thinks he's in love with me. And I can't stand that.' 'Me neither,' I said, 'I hate it.' That set her off laughing again. I found I was doing a little more of the gynaecologist's lurch to the left. Surinder raised her eyes to mine. 'Karl says,' I said, 'that someone up there hates me. But that they may not be there after the restructuring!'

We were now looking directly into each other's eyes. 'It's not Karl who wants to get rid of you! There is no mysterious figure up there who is trying to kill you off!' said Surinder.

This made me think that there is. And that she is lying. But if there is such a person — who is it?

Something about Surinder puzzles me. Is it her clothes — almost like a uniform — incredibly short skirt, black polo-necked sweater, outlandish high heels? Or her conspiratorial air? Tonight, after much staring at people from nearby tables in case they might be spies sent by John Birt, she told me that someone had told her that Karl was 'leading a double life'. 'You mean like a . . . spy . . . or a . . . saboteur or something?' I

38

said. 'Is he being paid by the Iraqis to lower the standard of BBC radio programmes?' She said she thought that that was what the BBC paid him for. She suggested that, as he is the one who has it in for me, we try and get something on him and I said I would keep my ear to the ground.

I hope it is me she wants. I hope that, unlike Mary Hopkinson (Cambourne Girls' School, Wimbledon, 1960–67), she does not simply want to be friends.


## 11 p.m.

Ruarighy has announced he does not wish to be a teacher. He says he is going to go to China 'instead'.


## February 14th. 12 noon. Hail, snow, sleet, rain, etc.

*Jakob in Oxford. Edwin at rehearsals. Ruairghry in bed with Gordon, Leopold, Hannah and Jorgen. Estelle at Craftgirls. Me here.*

At my desk with the latest episode of *General Practice*, which is full of some very powerful stuff indeed. Esmond has just wrongly diagnosed a case of multiple sclerosis. He has done this before – in 1987 – but this one is a real cracker. He screams at the woman when she bursts into tears, and tells her to 'pull herself together'. One of Surinder's boldest pieces of writing. Surinder is confident that she can keep me alive. She writes, in a note enclosed with the episode, 'Once you start to lose your marbles people will identify with you!'

Opposite me Porker is being horrible to his whippet. He has got it out of the car and has lowered his face to its level. Although I cannot hear what he is saying from this distance, I have a pretty good idea since I have seen him go through this routine at close range, from behind a bush on Wimbledon Common. 'Why do you do this?' he said to it, as it cowered away, avoiding his eyes. 'Why do you behave in this disgusting manner? Why don't you listen to anything I say? Why do you just skulk around causing trouble?' And then, 'I hate you. I loathe you. I despise you. I wish you were dead. I am going to sell you,' etc., etc. Theirs is a Strindbergian relationship.

In a minute I am going to go upstairs and scream at Ruairghy. Phone going. Life is so boring I will pick it up.

## 1 p.m.

It was somebody calling himself Proek. Laura's father presumably. Apparently Jakob has been sending his daughter Valentines. He seemed annoyed about this. I suggested his daughter talk to Jakob about it. He said, 'You don't imagine I am going to let her see these things, do you?' I said I imagined that, as they were presumably addressed to her, she already had. He told me he made a habit of opening his daughter's mail, and added that he assumed I did the same. I told him I hadn't got a daughter but that if I had I would not dream of opening a letter addressed to her. He gave a bitter, slightly crazed laugh, and said, 'You would if you knew it contained filth!' I said I thought a little bit of filth was quite a good thing, at which he started screaming at me.

I put the phone down on him. He rang back moments later and told me he was sending the Valentines on to Mafeking Road. I asked whether this was because of my expressed preference for filth or simply that he thought I sounded as if I needed a few Valentines. I said that, as I was about to be (a) fifty and (b) unemployed, I needed as many as I could get. Perhaps his daughter could send me some. He started screaming again. I can't think how he got our number and address. I suppose Jakob gave it to her. Perhaps he goes through her address book as well as her letters.

## 2 p.m.

He has just rung again. This time to talk about Ruarighy. He seems remarkably well-informed about my family. I am beginning to think he may well be a psychopath. Apparently Ruairghry has also sent this girl Laura a Valentine. According to Proek it is the very model of what a Valentine should be. He went on about this for some time. Then he said his wife had knitted Ruairghy a hat. I asked why. This seemed to annoy him. Then he asked me how Ruirghy was getting on with 'Lemmings 3D'. I said I did not think Ruairghy kept any kind of animal. At which Proek said, in heavily satirical tones, 'I can see you and your eldest have a great deal in common!' I said I had not the faintest idea what he was talking about. He then started to go on about Jakob. 'I'm not happy with him being round my daughter!' he said. 'And how do you think Lucy feels about all this?' I said I had not the faintest idea of who Lucy was. Proek said, in, I thought, a highly offensive tone, 'Don't your sons tell you anything?' I was about to say that all four of us talked far into the night when I realized this was demonstrably not the case. Suddenly seized with fury I screamed at him and slammed down the phone.

As I was doing this I heard a suspicious rustle at the door. I rushed to it, yanked it open and Ruairghry fell into my room like a Victorian servant surprised in the act of eavesdropping. For some reason I heard myself say, 'What have you done with the Luxury Seafood Goujons?' (I bought a packet yesterday which has disappeared.) 'I hid them!' bleated Ruairghy, covering his face with his hands. Then he did his hunchback impression. 'Were you talking to Norman?' he said, scampering sideways and brushing the floor with his knuckles. 'Was he asking you about me and Jakob and Laura and Lucy?' Then he scratched himself under the armpits and made chimp noises.

What is going on?

## 2.30 p.m.

Called Jakob to try and find out what was going on. Spoke to Oliver. Oliver said Jakob had had to go to Belgium for a few days. He, or Jakob, seemed to be concerned about the collapse of something called the Rundfundsche Deutschebank. Good to think that the boy is doing some 'hands-on' research. Worryingly, however, Oliver said that Laura had gone with him.

## February 23rd. 11 a.m.

*Estelle at Craftgirls. Me at home. Jakob in Belgium. Raurirghy in bed on his own (as far as I can tell). Edwin also in bed.*

Edwin announced this morning that he was ill. 'I have a pain,' he said, 'in my leg. Or it starts in my leg anyway.' 'What does it do then?' I asked him. 'It goes to my chest,' he said. When I asked him whether it stopped hurting his leg when it went to his chest he said he thought not. 'In fact,' he said, 'it stays on my chest after it's gone to my arm. And it stays in my arm after it moves to my face.'

I said I thought in that case it was probably four different pains, but Edwin insisted it was the same pain. He said he thought it was probably going to move on to other parts of his body. 'It will probably,' he added darkly, 'end up in my arse or something.' He seemed disinclined to go to the doctor with it. 'It's not the sort of thing you'd bother to tell a doctor about,' he said. 'Doctors would be useless at it. It's just a sort of pain.' He has double Latin today. I let him stay in bed, largely because I was supposed to take him in to school and I, too, had a pain that would not go away – perhaps related to the three bottles of Chardonnay I downed last night.

Laura Proek's father has now delivered no less than twelve Valentines to this house. All apart from two are from Jakob. They were enclosed in a sheet of paper on which Proek had written, in capitals, 'YOU SEE WHAT I MEAN.' The remainder, also enclosed in a sheet of paper, which reads, 'A BIT MORE LIKE IT, I FEEL', are from Ruairghy. The first one from Jakob says, 'Let's do it till our faces ache.' All the others are slightly more frank and explicit. I am beginning to have some sympathy with the man Proek. Ruairghy's both simply read, 'Thinking of you with deep affection.' On the second one he asks after her mother and hopes Mr Proek's shingles are better.

I am seriously worried about Ruairghy.


12 noon.

Edwin says that the pain is now 'just outside his head, and sort of circling him'. I think if this goes on we may have to send him to a psychiatrist. He seemed to perk up on being told about the Proek situation and said he might get up 'so that we could go to the pub and discuss it'. I said I thought this was not a good idea and when he asked why I said, 'You have this pain!' He looked at me in a vaguely hurt manner and said that he had forgotten about it until I mentioned it but that now I had mentioned it he had remembered it. In fact, he said, he would now be able to think about little else. 'It's sort of stalking me!' he said, lying back on the bed. I fear I may have started a serious decline.

42

Began to be seriously worried about the whole Laura/Lucy problem (whatever it may be). Does Proek have a point? Do I really know my sons at all? Am I sitting on a powder-keg? Are we in the middle of a situation that will make *General Practice* look undramatic? (Not a hard thing to achieve.) What is my youngest son up to? I would not be surprised if Bozz and Scagg and Lulu and Francesca are not up there with Edwin, doing disgusting things to Snozzer. I am thinking of waking up Edwin and checking to see that there is not a woman concealed under his duvet.

## February 25th. 11.30 p.m. Cold and clear night.

*Everyone in bed and probably having sex apart from me.*

Started to worry, too, about the problems between me and Estelle. I am positive now that it is too long since I have had a shag.

In fact, looking back through the pages of this diary I cannot find a single entry that suggests that Estelle and I have done it. I cannot work out whether this is because I am being tasteful or whether we really have not had a bonk since, and probably well before, January 6th. Surely I would have mentioned it?

I have a vague idea that we have got up to something or other in the early part of this month, but cannot ascribe a precise date to it. If we haven't then I have been without sex for nearly two months and, as I recorded earlier, probably even more than that. This condition of mine is not unlike false-memory syndrome, and if it continues I am going to have to rig up some device in the bedroom that will let me know if and when Estelle and I are shagging. If she finds it, mind you, it will only intensify her long-held contention that I am a perve.

## February 26th. 10 a.m.

*Estelle at Craftgirls. Edwin at school. Jakob in or on his way back from Belgium. Ruairghiry in bed. Me in Reception at Broadcasting House.*

Just about to go into a departmental meeting.

We have been renamed. I now work for the Series and Serial Sound Documentary and Drama Continuing and Occasional Home and Overseas Department. At least I think that is what it is called. Every time I write it out I write it out differently. In fact every time anyone tries to tell anyone else which department they work for, they seem to lose confidence in whether they have got the word order correct and have to go and ask someone else. Karl said the other day, 'The old name was better!' But when someone asked him what it was he was unable to remember that either. Surinder says John Birt is determined to erase the collective memory of all individuals who worked for the BBC before he arrived. She maintains his game plan is to disorientate us so completely that, eventually, we will not remember which building to go to and then we can be sacked for absenteeism.

Oh my God – here comes Ashley Ramp. He is wearing an Armani suit specially tailored to fit his hump. He is rubbing his hands.

I am pretty sure that he is the man who hates me. I am probably one of the few people who remember that Ashley Ramp is the Man Who Didn't Make the Programme about Snails but Pretended He Did. He is also the Man Who Said the Programme about Snails was Too Slow.

He is also the Man Who Tried to Spank Eleanor Gubbins.


11 a.m.

I am writing this in the meeting. I have to do something to keep sane.

Surinder keeps winking at me from across the table. She is incredibly attractive. I have just pretended to drop a pencil on the floor so that I could duck below table level and get a look at her legs. They are sensational.

Colin Cross is 'giving us an update on the restructuring'. He did not even have the courage to use his own jargon but read aloud from a pamphlet called *Managing Interdepartmental Change*. We had all been given copies of this masterpiece, so we were able to follow his performance, prayer-book style, and check whether he had left anything out.

'Welcome to *Managing Interdepartmental Change*, a booklet that has been produced for you by the Radio Production Management Resources Directorate, of which I, Colin Cross, am Acting Head.'

He paused here and held up the pamphlet. To the left of the page was a small black and white photograph of someone who looked a bit like Cyrano de Bergerac but was in fact him. He pointed at it and said, 'There I am. In the picture.'

Perhaps this was done to persuade us that he is not a robot. If that was the idea, it failed. I am now convinced that *he* is the man who hates me. He went on to tell us that all of the B B C is now to be divided into Sound and Vision, two departments that, initially, sounded as if they were completely separate. I wondered, for a moment, whether all newsreaders were going to be instructed to mime or whether peak-time television was to be given over entirely to programmes for the deaf. It turned out that although these two departments are called different things, they are in fact the same. All that has happened is that, since there are now two departments instead of one, the people in charge of them are going to be even more important. Cross went on to tell us that he was going to be 'not only Head of Sound, but also hands-on executive producer of all radio soaps, including *General Practice*' (here he gave Karl a meaningful look) and that Ashley Ramp, himself and Karl would be taking 'a close look at the direction the department was taking'. The last sentence in the masterpiece from which he was reading went, 'The Radio Production Management Resources Directorate will now work directly to the Core Directorate Policy Unit which will work in parallel with Head of Sound and will obviously be "sizing down" to accommodate this change. We are anticipating that anyone not part of the new "flatter" Directorate Structure, will be relocated to Scotland.'

Where they will presumably be shot. This may well be me, I suppose. If I am not made redundant or fired I will be forced to adopt a Glaswegian accent and take part in appalling regional rubbish about the Clearances, etc. All I really want to know is – who is on this sinister-sounding Core Directorate Policy Unit, who, according to rumour, were the people who first suggested I should be run over by a lorry? Are these the mysterious people who Karl said were out for my blood?

They do seem to be the only people capable of putting a brake on the obvious megalomania of the man Cross. But who are they?

## 12.45 p.m.

Writing this in Surinder's office. We are about to go into a conference about my suicide. She told me last night that she had prepared 'a bombshell' on the subject. She said I would have to wait until today to find out what it was, adding, 'Karl will do what he is told. I will let him know that I am prepared to reveal the truth about him.' When I asked her what the truth about him was, she said, 'I couldn't possibly tell anyone that!'

A man who I have never seen before has just walked into the room. He is carrying a tape-measure and he seems to be measuring the distance between each desk and the window. Is this perhaps a new Birt initiative to try and make it more difficult for us to run to the window and hurl ourselves out of it? Or perhaps to make it easier. Judging from what Colin Cross said this morning, auto-defenestration is going to be an increasingly popular option within the BBC. There is something very sinister about this man. I do not like the look of him.


## 1.15 p.m.

Have just had a long chat with the mysterious stranger. He is actually rather nice. He tells me that he is from a firm of design consultants. 'Apparently,' he said, 'all the people in these offices are going to be sent to the West Country.' When I asked him what was going to happen then, he said he thought they were going to knock down all the walls. I asked him who was going to be put in here and he said, 'God knows!'

'At least,' he added, 'they'll be better off than the poor bastards going to Scotland.' He said that he thought that the people who were going to be sent to Scotland 'would probably never come back'. I asked him whereabouts in Scotland they would be going and he said he had heard it was 'somewhere quite high up' because he had been told they were 'all going to be given special clothes'. I can hear Karl's footsteps in the corridor outside. Prepare to fight for your professional life, Esmond Pennebaker! Let's see what Surinder has up her sleeve!

## 3 p.m.

I am writing this in a basement room, without windows, in which I have never been confined before. I have the strong impression that it has just been carved out of the insides of the building by the same team who are busy dismembering Surinder's office. It is called M42. Surinder whispered to me as we went in that she thought it was very witty of them to name a room after a motorway.

With me in this hell-hole are Karl, a woman called (I think) Fudge, who is his Planning and Coordinating Assistant, an accountant called Nerys, Surinder, Steve Witchett, the Writer Who Never Expresses an Opinion, and about twenty crab sandwiches arranged in a circle round a samosa that is almost as wrinkled and uninviting as Karl's Planning and Coordinating Assistant.

The accountant called Nerys is reading from a report she has compiled. This, in the current style of such reports, assumes that we are in a world of profit, loss, surplus, etc., and other things that have absolutely no relation to an organization run out of public funds for no other reason (if my memory of the BBC Charter serves me right) than to tell the truth, speak peace unto nations, etc.

Karl opened the meeting by saying that he had never felt so confident about *General Practice*. 'Even Bleriod listens in!' he said. I assumed at first that I had got the composition of his household wrong and that he could not possibly be talking about his dog's response to the programme. I was wrong. He is either madder and/or more desperate than I had thought. Apparently this mangy labrador comes up to the radio and nuzzles it whenever the signature tune starts. During the programme it sits, rapt, staring at the receiver and, when the closing music begins, it howls for two or three minutes. I suggested it might be howling for joy. This did not go down well with Karl.

## 5 p.m.

Writing this in Main Reception, waiting for Surinder. She has, I must say, been superb this afternoon.

She began by projecting an indecipherable sheet of acetate, crammed with graphs and lines of figures. We were all pretty impressed by the fact that it occupied a screen as big as a billiard table, and, although it took her some moments to realize it was upside down, she recovered well, clicked her button and moved on to a second sheet, headed, in bold letters, ESMOND'S FEBRUARY PERFORMANCE. On it was a gigantic, phallus-like obelisk of a height and width I had never yet glimpsed in a bar chart. I had no idea what it meant but I felt positive about it. 'These,' she said, pointing to it with a modified conductor's baton, 'are the responses of a focus group in February. The fact is – Esmond's nervous breakdown is working. We asked them the following questions –

1. What is your mental picture of Esmond Pennebaker?
2. How do you think he dresses?
3. If he were a restaurant what kind of food would he serve?

To 1 – in January we were getting answers like "long-nosed", "probably going grey" and "looking worried all the time and who can blame him". After the push towards the mental breakdown – and especially the scene where he threw the specimen bottle at Lola – we got answers like "probably blue eyes", "a big, big man with strong hands" and "like a fighter pilot". Forty per cent of listeners in the sample thought that February Esmond was in his early thirties, even though much of his dialogue related to the problems of being middle-aged. In January most of our sample thought he wore "old tweeds" and "baggy trousers", whereas in February quite a lot of people visualize him in "trainers and jeans" or "Armani suits". And similarly, whereas in January many people saw Esmond as a "bangers-and-mash sort of person", he is now clearly associated with things like "radicchio" and "polenta". One woman even described him as having "a sort of wild mushroom quality about him".'

Surinder stared round at the group and said, 'I think Esmond should survive his mid-life crisis and undergo a radical personal transformation. I think he should contemplate suicide but reject it. Which would be an enormously positive message for our listeners. I think he should be hipper, younger in feel. I think he should discover contemporary music – bands like Oasis, for example. I see no reason why he shouldn't actually go into private practice and treat Noel Gallagher – and I think he should have a blazing, passionate affair. I want him to be raunchy, vital and having a lot of sex with a lot of people. Maybe even other men, I don't know. I think he could be gay or bisexual. I think he could get involved with someone from an ethnic minority – a young Asian man or woman, for example.'

There was a long silence after this speech. Eventually Steve Witchett, the Writer Who Never Expresses an Opinion, said, 'There may be something in that. There may not. But we can't rule out the possibility that it might work. Although of course, it might not. At the moment there is no way of telling without doing it. And then, of course, it would be too late. If it didn't work. Although I am not saying it wouldn't.' Nerys said, in a deep, fruity voice, 'I don't think Esmond bowls from the gasworks end!' Does this mean what I think it means?

Eventually, Karl, who, unobserved by anyone apart from me, had been writing the words 'SHIRLEY WEARS A BRA' in large letters on his pad during all this said, 'There's a lot that's interesting here, Surinder. I think we had better refer it to Colin as Executive Producer! He is very hands-on with anything sticky!' Surinder did not give up at this point. 'And what will he do?' she said. 'He . . .' said Karl slowly and heavily, 'will almost certainly have to refer it to the Core Directorate Policy Unit.' 'And who are they?' said Surinder, quickly. 'There's no secret about that,' said Karl. 'We don't know. We are not yet quite sure who they are going to be. They, like everyone else, are being restructured. And by the time we know who they are they may have been fired or made redundant. But as and when we know who they are we will pass on our thoughts to them.'

Steve Witchett, the Writer Who Never Expresses an Opinion, said, 'We could run it by Sylvia I suppose. Depending on whether we think Sylvia is a factor. She may be a factor. But on the other hand she may not. She may be completely irrelevant. It's hard to tell whether to show it to her until we know quite what her position is. Although of course given the fluid nature of things with the restructuring and so on, we may never find out what her position is. Which isn't, of course, to rule out the possibility that we might.'

As we went out, Nerys came up to me and said, in an even deeper and fruitier voice, 'No way is Esmond Pennebaker a bit light on the carpet!' When I asked her straight out what this meant she said, 'It means he does not know all the show tunes!'

# February 27th. 5 p.m. Gales, sleet, snow, etc.

*Estelle at Craftgirls Sales Conference. Edwin 'in rehearsal for his play'. Jakob in Lucerne. Ruairghry playing 'Lemmings 3D' (a computer game) downstairs. Me in my study.*

Have been trying to do the De Witjerer breathing exercises. Ruairghry, who says he has definitely decided to leave the University of South Wimbledon (how will they be able to tell?) shouted upstairs to let me know that the noise was distracting him as he was 'nearly at level eight'. He spent a lot of time on the phone to Norman Proek this morning, during which time I heard him say several uncomplimentary things about Jakob.

Six fridges arrived today. They are, so the man who brought them informed me, the property of Mr Jakob Slippery. I do not know what they are doing here. I do not know how Jakob got the money for them. I do not know when they will be taken away. I am a very unhappy middle-aged man. I called Jakob on his mobile and got Oliver, who was in the middle of a meeting of something called the Vodka Society. He said Jakob was in Lucerne 'for a meeting'.

## 5.30 p.m.

Message on machine from Estelle. She will be late. She is 'buying turnips'. Why?

## 6 p.m.

Relations with Surinder are at crisis point. I think she may be merely playing with my affections, i.e. unwilling to shag me. She seems willing to look as if she is prepared to do a lot more than this. But has some girlish prejudice against actually embarking on any of the steps that might lead to sexual intercourse. I think if I could just get her started there would be no stopping her.

What makes things especially difficult is her unrestrained enthusiasm for my marriage. I don't think I have ever met anyone so keen on the marital happiness of Paul Slippery and Estelle Thwaites. She refers to Estelle as 'amazing' and 'an incredible mother' and 'one of the most remarkable women I have ever met'. She has only talked to her on the phone, once, for about one minute and thirteen seconds. Mrs Slippery clearly made a big impression on her. When I asked Estelle what she thought of Surinder she thought for a moment and said, simply, 'Who?'

But we are working on saving my life. She says the dirt she has on Karl is 'fantastic'. And we have a few more clues about the Core Directorate Policy Unit. We know who they used to be. Which may be the first step to finding out who they are now.

There is a rumour that nobody is going to be sent to Scotland. Colin Cross is reported to be writing a life of John Birt.


## 6.45 p.m.

I think Edwin is in danger of losing direction. I do not want him to end up like me. Bozz, Scagg and Snozzer are also in danger of losing direction – although I was pleased to hear that Scagg had got a weekend job on the fish counter of Waitrose. They were all waiting for me in the bushes as I pulled up outside the school. Scagg has had a new haircut. I am not sure whether he paid for it but whoever did it seems to have pulled it out in clumps. Snozzer was smoking a small clay pipe which he thrust into his pocket as the car drew up. Just at the top of Wimbledon Hill he burst into flames and we had to drag him out of the vehicle and beat him with an overdue video until he was only smouldering.

When I got Edwin home I asked him to do some Spanish homework. He said, 'I have to watch *The Full Monty*.' I said, 'Do you mean you are obliged to watch it? You are being forced to watch this film by somebody? Who is the person who is forcing you to do this on a night when you only want to do your homework so that you will not fail all your GCSEs and have to go and work in Sainsbury's?' He told me to fuck off so I did. He is now downstairs making himself a cream cheese and turkey sandwich.

# February 28th. 11 a.m. Rain.

*Jakob in Lucerne or Oxford. Ruarighy gone out to shops 'to buy paper and look for job'. Estelle at Craftgirls. Me here. Edwin at school.*

I have just got Surinder's draft of the episode that takes me off in a new, exciting direction.

It is new. It is exciting. It is decidedly bonkers. I am going for therapy with a woman called Flora. I talk a lot about my urges. She says in the note that goes with it that all this may have to be rewritten but that if we can smuggle it past Karl I am well on the way to avoiding death. I was pleased to hear this. If Ronnie Pilfrey ever gets to deliver his speech at the Service of Thanksgiving for the Life of Esmond Pennebaker, it is almost certain to be the making of his career.

Estelle is on the Turnip Diet. The idea, as far as I can gather, is to choose a vegetable you don't particularly like and then make it the sole element of your diet. A friend of hers went on an Aubergine Diet and lost a stone in a week, as she cannot even bear to have an aubergine in the room with her. I think Estelle may have cheated slightly and, in fact, be fonder of turnips than she is prepared to admit. Yesterday she ate about a kilo of them. She has about half a ton in store in a room downstairs.

The doorbell. I have peered out through the study window. Jakob is outside with a tall, thin girl with blond hair. I don't know why but I think this may well be Laura Proek. She is wearing a skimpy jumper and very tight jeans. When she talks to him she puts her head to one side like a bird soliciting food. Can one tell just from looking at people whether they are doing it?

## 11.03 a.m.

Yes.

And they are doing it. I had better let them in. Otherwise, from the look of them, they may start doing it in the road.

Jakob, standing a little behind her, nodded coolly and said, 'Hi!' 'Hi!' I replied, trying to look equally cool. Laura shook her hair experimentally, as if she was testing her shampoo's ability to impart bounce and sparkle. 'Hi!' she said. 'Hi!' I replied. 'Laura!' said Jakob. 'Hi!' I said. 'Hi!' she said again. She has a slightly nasal, sing-song voice. But curiously attractive. Not that this was a problem. We were just people talking to each other. After a pause I said, very lightly and casually, 'Fridges!' Jakob looked evasive. 'Where?' he said. I said, 'Fridges! Here!' Jakob took a pair of dark glasses out of his top pocket and slipped them on. 'Is it cool?' he said. 'Sure,' I said. 'Sure! Are they like . . . paid for and stuff?' Jakob gave a weary little smile. 'Oh, they're paid for,' he said. 'The answer to that would be a "yes". We're moving them out tomorrow.' 'Right,' I said, 'cool!' 'Cool!' said Jakob.

I think Laura was pretty impressed by my performance. I am a fairly young-thinking dad. Even though, to my horror, I found I was developing a slight American accent.

Laura smelled sensationally pleasant. I had to make a pretty determined effort to drag my eyes away from her breasts. But she managed to keep her eyes on my face. She was probably, I decided, unused to the company of artists and intellectuals. Certainly, if her father was anything to go by, she had spent her youth in the society of humans closer to the Missing Link than anything else. Hitching my jeans up and imparting a slight, but not too effortful spring to my walk, I showed them into the hall and said, 'Beer?'

This seemed to impress her a lot. Jakob gave one of his small smiles and nodded slowly, keeping his eyes on the floor.

'We're like . . . tired . . .' he said. 'Right!' I said. 'Cool!' 'Up all night!' he went on. 'Cool!' I said. *And I have a pretty good idea of what stopped you getting to sleep, young man!* He smiled again and nodded. 'So . . . we're like . . . going to bed!' 'Cool!' I said. There was a slight pause into which I very nearly said, 'With each other presumably!' Jakob gave a slow, thoughtful nod. I found myself thinking, for some reason, of his performance of the slow movement from the Dvorak Cello Concerto at Cranborne School, Wimbledon. 'Cool!' I said, a slight squeak in my voice, 'Cool!'

They are up there now. Shagging presumably. I suppose I could have made an attempt to show her to the guest bedroom. Except we haven't got a guest bedroom. It only seems like yesterday that I was explaining to the lad exactly what Tamla Motown was. And now . . .

A car has just drawn up outside. A small, heavily built man in a fruit-salad shirt has got out and is squinting up at the house. He looks a little like a bailiff. But I somehow do not think he is. He has been joined by a woman. A woman in a sensible skirt, sensible shoes and the kind of haircut I last saw advertised in the window of Mr Toni's in Wimbledon High Street in 1956. She is glaring up at the house. I have a horrible feeling I may be looking at Mr and Mrs Proek.


## 12 noon.

I was. Close up and personal, Mrs Proek is even more of a problem. She has a nose that looks as if it has been professionally sharpened and a chin as emphatic as the prow of an ocean-going liner. She is a seriously mean woman. Her first action was to hold out her hand to me and say, 'I'm afraid your boys have been up to no good!' Then she took up a position some yards to the rear of Mr Proek and folded her arms. She seemed to be expecting trouble, although, if none arrived of its own accord, she gave the impression of a woman only too pleased to supply it herself.

'Laura not in her hall of residence!' said Mr Proek. Mrs Proek nodded. 'Maybe,' I said brightly, 'she just isn't answering your calls!' 'Only a humble traffic warden,' said Mrs Proek, with the same air of having paid for each word she pronounced, 'not a Radio Personality! But can spot an absent daughter!' 'Indeed!' I said. 'Called the police!' said Mr Proek. 'Good!' I said. Mrs Proek sniffed contemptuously. 'The police!' she said. 'Only a humble traffic warden! But capable of placing simple calls!' 'Did nothing!' hissed Mr Proek, mysteriously, 'nothing!' Presumably this referred to the police. 'She's probably . . . er . . . tucked up in bed somewhere!' I said, brightly. I do not know why I said this. Neither do I know why I added, 'With someone!' They both stared at me. 'Someone nice!' I continued.

At this moment there was a long-drawn-out moan from the top of the house.

Mr and Mrs Proek simply stared at me. Perhaps the noise of their daughter's orgasm was simply an off-limits experience as far as they were concerned. Perhaps they were only programmed to register things like her first word or her G C S E passes. Before their little girl started howling like an in-season she-wolf, I showed them into the front room, muttered something about an urgent telephone call and fled up the stairs. I think I had some idea of jumping up and down outside Jakob and Laura's room in order to put both of them off their stroke. As I write this, in haste, at my desk (the only therapy) I hear the front doorbell.

It looks like Edwin. Can it be?


## 2.30 p.m.

It was.

Apparently he was on a cross-country run which 'finished early'. He smelt strongly of cigarettes. Mr and Mrs Proek were still in the front room. I peered at them through a crack in the door. They were both sitting, in total silence, on the sofa. The noise of lovemaking was now positively deaf-making. Jakob was doing quite a lot of 'Woah yeahs' and I think I once heard him say, 'Tighter baby! Tighter!' As all this was going on – still ignored completely by the Proeks – Edwin, who was winking and leering at me, said, 'Monster shag in progress!' I grimaced, shook my head and put my finger to my lips. There was one last juddering sigh from the upstairs bedroom and Laura Proek subsided for what was (surely? please God?) the last time. I couldn't help, however, but feel a quiet sense of pride in my middle son's achievement. Not only a brilliant instrumentalist, not merely a place at Oxford University and a keen analytical brain – but also an ability to reduce his brother's girlfriend to a quivering heap of jelly.

'Some very seriously deep dicking is going on upstairs!' said Edwin. I pointed, crazily, at the front room. 'In there as well?' said Edwin. I shook my head at him but before I could make the position any clearer he said, in a loud, clear voice, 'It must be that Laura Proek girl! She is apparently a monster shagger. Ruairghy was giving it to her every night apparently but then she got the taste for old Jakob's little pet snake!' As I turned towards him – I think I had some idea of smashing him in the face, or draping him in a cloth of some kind – he went on, with equally perfect diction, 'She sounds so rough, that Laura Proek! She is the ultimate in rough! She is a beast!' Suddenly, Mr and Mrs Proek appeared in the doorway of the front room. Edwin was bent over his school bag and did not realize there was anyone else with me. 'I mean,' he went on thoughtfully, 'I take a pretty dim view of people shagging Laura Proek or whatever she's called practically outside the door of my room. I have to go up there and bone up on the Arab–Israeli War with all that going on. I mean, my God! It sounds like the Six Day War up there! And according to Ruarighry she can do it for *hours*!'

I finally found my voice. 'Edwin,' I said, 'have you met Mr and Mrs Proek, Laura's parents!' Slowly Edwin's hand crept to his mouth. He looked, for the first time in his sixteen years, seriously thrown. 'Ooh er missus!' he said. I turned to the Proeks. 'This is my son Edwin!' I said. 'He is taking GCSEs this year!' Mr Proek's eyes narrowed. 'He sounds like a real chip off the old block!' he said.

At this point, Ms Proek made a noise like a Lilo being rapidly deflated. 'What's that?' said Mrs Proek. I didn't answer. 'Only a humble traffic warden!' said Mrs Proek, 'But know when the daughter is . . .' She stopped and a troubled expression crossed her face. 'Is what?' said Mr Proek. 'Is missing!' I said swiftly and, followed by Edwin, beat a retreat upstairs.


## 2.45 p.m.

For some reason, when I got Edwin into my study the first thing I said to him was, 'What is happening with these fridges? Does it have anything to do with Lucerne? And is Jakob smoking "white goods" or whatever you call it?' He didn't reply. I went on, 'I am fed up with all this!' 'So am I,' said Edwin, 'I am completely fed up with it! Do you think I *like* people shagging when I am trying to do revision!' 'I am not talking about shagging!' I said. 'I really do not want to discuss shagging with you, Edwin. I am actually fed up with the way people in this house talk about sex. I am beginning to have a certain sympathy with your mother on this issue.' 'That's a relief,' said Edwin, 'considering you have been married to her for nearly twenty-five years!' 'Will you stop talking about sex!' I screamed, conscious that downstairs Mr and Mrs Proek were probably taping this conversation with the intention of forwarding it to the Director of Public Prosecutions. 'I am talking about people buying fridges and calling up sex-chat lines in Florida!' 'Why would they call up a sex-chat line in Florida?' said Edwin. 'Are they better or something?' 'As you well know,' I said, 'they are apparently immeasurably superior!' 'You seem fairly well up on it!' said Edwin. 'Admit it,' I yelled, 'you have been calling a sex-chat line in Florida! I found the number on a piece of paper in your room, 0019 something or other! Eh?' 'That,' said Edwin, 'is not a number in America.' 'Oh,' I said, 'then what is it, may I ask?' 'It's your credit-card number!' said Edwin. 'We used it to buy the fridges. Fridges are white goods. I thought everyone knew that. Don't you know anything? Where have you been all my life? Are you the most unobservant person in the universe? But they are good fridges. They are a bargain. You will make money on the deal, honestly, and you're not to be angry!'

I started to jump up and down like Rumpelstiltskin. I said, 'We need to have a really serious talk about the things that go on in this house!' Edwin said, 'I agree. The wind really howls round my window at night and keeps me awake. It's really spooky!' Then he left the room. I am now alone, writing this. Downstairs, the Proeks are waiting for me. The front doorbell has just rung. I hope it is the fish man. But I have a horrible feeling it is Ruarighy. He is due back about now.

## 3.15 p.m.

It was.

The Proeks rushed to the door as soon as he pressed the bell and let him in. Mrs Proek embraced him. She took out of her bag a crumpled length of knitted wool and held it out to him. It was, I realized with horror, a hat of some kind. Mr Proek said, 'Ro-Ree how goes? Old son of a gun doing OK?' Ro-Ree, I noted with some annoyance, looked genuinely pleased to see him. He was carrying a magazine. On its cover were the words 'GREAT COMPUTER GAMES AND OFFERS INSIDE'. 'Norman, hi!' I heard him say. 'I got to level eight! And I think I have cracked "Duck Colony".' Mr Proek turned to me triumphantly. 'What a boy!' he said. 'What a boy!' 'Yes,' I said, tight-lipped, 'he has been my son for around twenty years and I, too, rather like him.'

Mr Proek curled his lip elaborately. 'In the which case,' he said, 'moves on the Laura-Ro-Ree situation? Appropriate for caring father?' 'What do you mean?' I said. 'What am I supposed to do about it?' 'You must use your influence,' said Proek. 'Must tell Master Jakob to lay off our daughter!'

57

At this moment there was a long, satisfied groan from upstairs. 'Laura!' said Norman, as if criticizing her table manners. Ruairghry looked up the stairs, clapped his right hand to his temple and started to pace around the hall muttering to himself. 'You tell him to stop it!' I said to Proek. 'You go upstairs and turn a fire hose on them if you think it'll help!' Proek took a step forward. For a moment I thought he was actually going to try and implement this idea. Then he went to the foot of the stairs. 'Laura,' he yelled, 'this is Daddy! You are to come home now!' There was no reply. He then marched into the front room and announced that he was going 'to wait until they had finished and then take his daughter home and give her a good seeing-to'. Edwin said he thought that that was precisely what she was getting. I retreated upstairs. If Edwin was right about Ms Proek's sexual appetite the Proeks could be with us for a fortnight.

All we need now is Estelle to walk in.

I hear her car. I think that is exactly what she is going to do.


## 4.15 p.m.

She did.

She was dragging a gigantic bag of turnips behind her and when she caught sight of the Proeks she turned to me and said, in an accusing tone of voice, 'Who are these people and what are they doing in our house?' 'They are the Proeks!' I said, 'Mr and Mrs Proek. They are the mother of Laura Proek –' 'Who is upstairs shagging Jakob!' interjected Edwin, who seemed determined to normalize his *faux pas* by keeping the rest of his conversation at the same level of offence. 'Who used to shag Ruarighy, or Ro-Ree as we are now calling him! Mr Proek has come here with his wife, who is a humble traffic warden, in order to get you and Paul here to tell Jakob to stop shagging Laura so that Ro-Ree can continue to shag her and go and spend Christmas with these lovely people! Who knitted him –' here his voice mutated into a near-perfect impression of Julian Clary – 'that beautiful hat!'

There are moments when Edwin is my favourite person in the world. This was one of them. There are also moments when my wife is my favourite person in the world. And I had the feeling that I was about to experience one of *them*.

She lowered her head and looked at the floor for a good thirty seconds. She started to bite her lip. If Mr and Mrs Proek had known her for longer than about one minute and fifteen seconds, this would have been their cue to steal quietly away, or rather to run screaming for the cover of their V W Microbus. Instead, the male Proek said, 'Your Master Jakob! Cat among the pigeons! Needs a good talking-to!' Estelle nodded slowly. 'Why,' she said with ominous quietness, 'do you think this is anything to do with you?' The Proeks gaped at her. 'Are you trained Jungian analysts perhaps, or a picked detachment of outreach social workers?' Proek folded his arms. 'Rodent Operative!' he said, with what I thought to be misplaced pride. 'I don't really care, Mr Proek,' said Estelle, holding up her hand like a teacher who has had a very hard day, 'if you are a nuclear physicist. The point I am making is that only spectacularly insane busybodies would ever dream that what two young and healthy people do together in between the sheets is any of their business!'

'Listen!' began Mrs Proek, moving in for what she thought was going to be the attack. 'No, you listen, Mrs Ratcatcher,' said Estelle. 'Apart from your inability to knit I haven't yet got anything against you as you have wisely decided to keep your mouth shut! But I am afraid your husband has so far demonstrated that he has rather less intelligence than –' here she delved into her bag, 'this turnip!' She moved closer to Mr Proek and held the turnip up to his face. 'In fact,' she went on, 'I think that this turnip has the edge on him in almost every department I can think of. If you cannot think of a more civilized way of attempting to influence your daughter I suggest you leave her here with us for the foreseeable future. And if you are not out of our house in the next five minutes I am telephoning the police!'

She doesn't like people criticizing Jakob. She thinks, for some extraordinary reason, that he is highly sensitive. She has now dragged the turnips through to the kitchen and is pretending to phone the police. I know that she is pretending because she is standing as close to the hall as possible, talking in a loud, clear voice to an obviously invented character called Inspector Lewis. 'Right, Inspector, that's great!' she has just said. 'So you'll send a man round right away! Excellent! Two men! Excellent!' The Proeks are in the front room. Edwin is watching them through a crack in the door, and from time to time, emitting a throaty laugh. Ro-Ree is sitting on the stairs with his head in his hands. Jakob and Laura are still at it.

All we need now is for them to drift downstairs and talk Mr and Mrs Proek through what they have been up to for the last hour or so.

I hear a noise on the landing. I fear this may be them. And that that is what they are about to do.


## 5 p.m.

As I heard them pass my study, I crept out on to the landing. I watched from the top of the stairs as, arm in arm, they walked down into the hall. Jakob's face was a study in immobility, and, as they reached Ro-Ree, he flicked his elegant black hair back as if facing a crowd of paparazzi on his way out of the VIP lounge at Heathrow. But beneath the gesture I suddenly saw that he seemed embarrassed and defensive.

Maybe Estelle is right. Maybe I have got my middle son all wrong.

'It's the way it goes, man!' he said. Ruaighry started to walk in small circles beating his head with the flat of his right hand. 'How could you do this to me?' he said. 'You are supposed to be my brother for Christ's sake! Are you my brother? Or are you some kind of monster? I mean I am trying to make sense of my life here for Christ's sake! They will not let me into the People's Republic of China for Christ's sake!' Jakob shrugged. 'Look,' he said, 'you and Lucy –' Laura snaked her head forward and said, with what seemed like genuine concern, 'How is Lucy?' 'I don't care about Lucy!' said Ruaireghy. 'I really don't. I know I did but I don't any more. It's you I care about, Laura. You know I do!'

Mrs Proek nodded. 'You know he does!' she said. 'Does!' chimed in Mr Proek, 'Loves you! One of the family, Laura! Walks Mr Pedersen! Helped me lay the patio!' He pushed his face closer to his daughter's as I wondered about this hitherto undiscovered side to my eldest son's nature. Who, for God's sake, was Mr Pedersen? A snake perhaps. 'Son I always wanted,' said Mr Proek, turning towards me, adding, for some unknown reason, the words, 'karate certificate!'

'Taking daughter home now!' he went on. 'Jakob near her! Big, big trouble! Pin down! University! Not paying her to lounge! Master Jakob! Valentines!' Mrs Proek was nodding furiously. 'What are you going to do?' I said. 'Send her to a nunnery? Isn't this nearly the end of the second millennium?' By way of answer Proek turned to his daughter. 'Come, Laura,' he said, 'home! This house? Don't think so!'

At this point Estelle came out of the kitchen. 'Your absence! V. good!' she said. 'Detectives on way! Big van! Handcuffs! You leave! Yes? Do I make myself clear?'

Laura Proek, in whom I was beginning to conceive a more than fatherly interest, followed her father, hopelessly, to the door. She turned to her parents one last time. 'Ro-Ree really likes Lucy! Deep down it's her he wants! And she really loves him!' she said plaintively. 'It's your fault all this has happened! It really is!'

And then she, the ratcatcher and the traffic warden went out into the chilly February street.

## March 1st. 12 noon. Cold but with clear sunshine.

*Jakob and Ruairghy in bed. Estelle out buying more turnips and/or in Craftgirls meeting. Edwin on cross-country run.*

Or is he?

Edwin walked past with Bozz, Scagg and Snozzer. All were in running shorts and T-shirts. They were also smoking. I think Snozzer may have been smoking two cigarettes simultaneously. I ran out into the street and asked them what they were doing. Edwin said they were on their cross-country run but lost. I was about to scream at them until I realized I was desperate for someone to talk to. I invited them in and offered them all a lager. I think they were rather horrified by this. Snozzer blushed and said, 'We have to get going!' and even Scagg, who was in the middle of a discussion about the only subject that interests him – drugs, jumped to his feet and followed his comrades out into Mafeking Road at a speed that might have satisfied Mr Kroeger, their sadistic P T master.

They are all writing a play, written by Bozz and Scagg with 'additional dialogue' by Snozzer. Edwin told me he thought it was 'deeply flawed but not bad for someone of sixteen'. I do not think he intends to be in it. He told me, in confidence, that 'it was not right for the direction his career was taking at the moment'. Mr Hotchkiss, the English master, has agreed to direct it. It is called '*Fit as a Fiddle*', and, according to Snozzer, is 'all about sex with some drugs. Not many drugs but some.' Hotchkiss is, I think, mad. When we went to see him about Edwin's G C S Es he said,

'Edwin is a big, thunderous boy with many exquisite features.' There are rumours that he lives with a Chinaman called Hong.

Ruaurighy and Jakob spent the evening drinking a bottle of Scotch. I listened at the door to some of their discussion. There was a lot of shouting. Then Ruarigiury did a lot of incredulous laughter and Jakob became very calm and quiet. At one point I heard Ruairghy say, 'He will kill you, Jakob. Norman will kill you. He is a very passionate man. And if he doesn't kill you I will kill you.' I am very worried about this. What will fratricide say about my parenting skills? I have found out a little more about Laura and Lucy. They are, or were until this situation developed, best friends, and, according to Ruairghy, always sat next to each other in class at school. At one point Jakob used the word 'a bit of a goer' but I do not know to whom this was meant to refer. In a minute I am going to wake them up and have a real, in-depth emotional discussion with them.

Jakob is supposed to be back in Oxford. It is a little stricter than the University of South Wimbledon. They do expect you to turn up from time to time. I must wake them up.


## 2 p.m.

I finally woke them both up. I was amazingly patient and restrained until about 1.45 when I suddenly turned into a wild animal. I ran into Ruairghy's room and screamed, 'Have you any idea what time it is?' To which Ruairtghy replied, 'Sorry. Lost watch!' And went back to sleep. Is he going to start talking like Mr Proek?

I woke him up again. Then I used him to wake up Jakob, which he did with almost unnecessary zeal, screaming, 'Repent! It is the Day of Judgement!' about six inches from his younger brother's ear. I told them Jakob had to go back to Oxford.

They are both expert at feigning ignorance of the public transport system and after half an hour trying to explain to Ruairghy that the Metropolitan Line was not 'the turquoise one' I gave up and ran Jakob to Victoria Coach Station. Ruairghry insisted on coming as he said he had to settle this thing 'once and for all'. There was a lot of muttering in the back about the mysterious Lucy, none of which I was able to hear. Somehow or other, my children seem to have perfected the art of talking in a manner that is only audible to persons under the age of twenty-five.

God knows how this situation will be resolved. Must now go into work to try and find out whether self will still be alive at end of month.

## 6 p.m.

Writing this at home.

Script conference this afternoon. Karl said that the Core Directorate Policy Unit had now been appointed. It apparently consists of him, Colin Cross and someone called Howard Porda. When he mentioned this name he gave Surinder a heavily significant look. 'As you know, Surinder,' he said, 'I am totally behind the idea of Paul surviving. It's not a fixed thing with me that he should die. That's just one of a range of options I'm looking at. And I am prepared to convince Colin, who I think trusts me on this. But the . . . person in the woodpile is . . .' here he gave her another deeply significant look, 'our friend Howard Porda!' Surinder said, 'Howard has John Birt's ear!' adding under her breath, 'And I have his right buttock!'

I caught Karl writing 'SHIRLEY HAS LOVELY BLACK PANTIES' on an empty sheet of file paper.

Surinder told me afterwards that, as a result of the restructuring, it is not now definite that Karl or Colin will go to Scotland. There seems to be a feeling that Scotland has got a bit above itself. A senior adviser called Hoad, who got his job after writing a seven-hundred-page biography of John Birt, has suggested broadcasting the Burns Night Special from Maidenhead 'to show them we mean business'. I asked Surinder about Howard Porda and she said, 'Howard Porda is an unknown quantity. There is some doubt as to whether he does actually exist. But it isn't something you need to get involved with.'

I am not sure that she is as keen on me as I thought. I am not entirely sure that I am as keen on her. But she and the mysterious Mr Porda are obviously crucial. I suspect she knows more about him than she is saying. She did give me an encouraging smile as I left.

63

# March 5th. 10.30 a.m. Raining.

*Estelle downstairs with Craftgirls personnel. Ruarighry at Jobcentre. Jakob back in Oxford. Edwin doing mock GCSEs. Me in study writing this.*

Started a new series of breathing exercises this morning called the Klohn System. Had to stop after ten minutes as the man next door started banging on the wall. I am underemployed in *General Practice*. It is no longer the challenge it once was. My diary is about the only thing that seems to matter.

Edwin had a letter this morning, which, fortunately, arrived after he had left for school. The envelope was clearly marked THE WOLVER-HAMPTON SEX SUPERMARKET – EVERYTHING FOR YOUR LOVE NEEDS. LINGERIE, RUBBER, VIDEOS. BIGGEST COLLECTION OF TOYS IN EUROPE. IN-FLATABLE WOMEN, ETC.

Estelle, helped by me, steamed it open. We have been getting on rather better since Surinder's attitude to me has cooled, or rather, since I have become slightly puzzled as to what it actually is. Inside was a letter which read —

Dear Edwin Slippery,
 Thankyou for your inquiry about LOVEJUICE.
LOVEJUICE is a one hundred per cent laboratory-tested solution based on a rare South American herb. It has proved in tests that it is capable of stimulating the growth of feromenes and of the Boerg gland – thereby making the user 'phenomenally attracted to any person in the vicinity'. Here are some testimonials from LOVEJUICE users . . .

'I administered LOVEJUICE to Derek, a boy on whom I have been keen for eighteen months, but who has not responded to my advances. I sprinkled it on to a Chicken Korma that we were sharing with other members of our creative writing class, and, in accordance with the

instructions, positioned myself in his line of vision.
The results were extraordinary and we are now married
with three children. Thankyou!'
A. S., Crewe (name and address supplied)

LOVEJUICE works equally well on men and women since the
Boerg gland is present, in a rudimentary form, in both
sexes. But beware! Stimulating it can prove explosive!
If you give it to the one who loves you, you had better be
ready, willing and able to rock and roll all night!

'I gave LOVEJUICE to Annabelle, my on/off girlfriend
by injecting it into a meat bun that we had bought from
our local doner kebab van. I think I must have given her a
double dose because she practically dragged me into the
bushes and we made hot love all night – so much so that we
missed our bus! Although that was one delay that I
certainly didn't regret!'
'Gerald', Kidderminster (name and address available on
application)

I am afraid we have run out of supplies of ANGIE our
popular inflatable woman. We can, however, supply you, on
receipt of cheque or credit-card details with the videos
in which you expressed interest – *Eating Out Regularly*
and *Norwegian Women at Play*.
   We are also enclosing our series of pamphlets, written
by qualified medical experts on penis enlargement. If you
think you may be interested in the steel counterweights
or PHALLKRIM, the ointment mentioned in the
course-plan, do not hesitate to write. The twelve-part
audiotape guide to Dr Piuntchsli's exercise programme
may also be of help!
Thankyou for your inquiry,
Lorna (Sales and Merchandise)


Estelle wanted to burn this. I told her that we should keep it in a safe
place and discuss it with him. 'Oh sure,' she said, 'you and he can sit

down to a cosy evening in watching *Eating Out Regularly* and *Norwegian Women at Play*.' I said all this was no different from *Health and Efficiency*, a magazine which I and Herbert Green used to hide under the carpet in his bedroom around forty years ago. Estelle said she thought I was either stupid or criminally naïve or both.

I am now almost positive we have had sex at some time between now and January 6th. I think it was in early February, but cannot be more specific than that.

In the end I hid Edwin's letter in my desk. I was helped by the fact that there was also a letter addressed to Ruaighry in what Estelle said was 'obviously female' handwriting. She didn't dare open it – although I could see that she wanted to – but held it up to the light several times.

Whoever has written it has spelled his name Rory. Which is what we were going to call him before I got the idea that we should make a gesture to my (largely notional) Celtic heritage. I wonder who she is. Lucy perhaps?

There is much laughter from downstairs. I think I will go down and try and join in.


## 11.30 a.m.

Stella Badyass was entertaining the company with an account of her first marriage. Everyone stopped talking when I came into the room. I did manage to gather that she had been married to some guy she met in Sri Lanka. He could only make love to her if she was covered in yoghurt, but as far as I could tell that was not the only reason for the divorce. I asked Estelle whether the Craftgirls spent a great deal of time discussing the men in their lives and she said they had better and more important things to do.

She was biting her nails – a familiar, though long dormant obsession – and I gained the impression, I don't know quite how, that she was in charge.

I also met Gillian, who turns out to be a small, rather fancyable blond woman. She said she was a keen fan of *General Practice*. She asked me whether Esmond was going to survive his mid-life crisis and I told her he was going to 'come out of it a stronger and wiser man'. She seemed impressed by this, although she did say that Dr Pennebaker 'had never struck her as fully human'. I think I may have a chance with her.

Then Surinder rang and asked whether she could drop the new script round. I said there were about twelve women here and she said, 'That's not a problem for me, Paul!' Then she gave me another dose of the glockenspiel laugh. Estelle said, 'Who's that?' and I said, 'Just someone I work with.' I noticed several of the other women looking at me with interest. I think she may suspect. I am clearly an object of some interest to these women.

I seem to have got Edwin's guide to penis enlargement out of my drawer and am studying it. It is actually quite well written and tasteful.


## 1.30 p.m.

Gustave rang.

There is interest in my doing a voice-over for a natural-history film about slugs. Apparently my voice 'suggests insects'. I told him that I was concentrating full time on Esmond Pennebaker, who was 'not dead yet'. When Gustave said he thought that that was only a matter of time, I put down the phone on him.

I do not know whether the Boerg gland exists but the idea of Lovejuice is also attractive. After all, Viagra seems to have done wonders for many of the over-fifties. And I am almost sure someone once told me he had got hold of a herb in Buenos Aires that had an amazing effect on his groin. I am thinking of writing off for it and trying to get some into Estelle's cornflakes. Or possibly into Surinder's gin and tonic. I am not really bothered which of them ingests it, so long as I am in their line of vision at the time. I suppose all love is associating sexual desire with whatever or whoever happens to be in view at the time you experience it. It is a shame they are out of inflatable women.

The doorbell. It is Surinder.


## 3.30 p.m.

The Craftgirls were all eating open sandwiches when Surinder came in. She seemed keen to join in. She put her head round the door of the front room and said, 'This is nice!' 'It is!' said Stella Badyass, giggling foolishly, and asked Surinder in to join the group.

I thought at first this might be because of her first marriage and wondered whether they were going to have a cosy chat about Tamils but in fact it proved to be sheer girlish exuberance. Surinder went into raptures about the little dough men and said she had never seen little dough men like them. She placed an order for twenty-five. I cannot work out what she thinks she is going to do with them. Perhaps she is going to teach them to talk and give them parts in *General Practice*.

At this point, Estelle, who had been giving her a suspicious look from under her fringe, asked her whether she was interested in craft. Surinder said she was and that she 'would love to come along for a session'. They all started to discuss something called petit point and then Surinder and Melanie Feinstein began to talk about loose covers. I was excluded from this discussion. At one point I said I had done some crocheting at school, but was not made to feel welcome.

The effect of all this was to make Surinder more, not less erotically challenging and exciting. Stella Badyass, who had been giving Surinder very peculiar looks during all this (does she suspect how much I fancy her?), asked her about my mid-life crisis. She suspects what is going on. But what is going on? Please?

The script she brought with her, together with outlines for *General Practice* through the summer, is to be sent to the Core Directorate Policy Unit. When I asked her whether the dreaded Howard Porda would be on it she said she didn't know. But she did say that Colin Cross was on our side. In fact she showed me a memo from him that went:

```
To:        Surinder Blake
From:      Colin Cross
Subject:   Esmond's Death
Yes let's go with Esmond not dying – if the upswing in
viewer response is sustainable with 'normal' Esmond. I
don't think he can be constantly on the verge of a
nervous breakdown. What has to emerge from this crisis
(by the way a superb episode when he tried to bite the
malingerer!) is that a new and really changed Esmond has
to be our target. We'll obviously have to carry the Core
Directorate Policy Unit with us on this one. And, as Karl
Rhws Davies will have told you – Howard Porda is no soft
touch!
PS. I am at work on a book provisionally entitled
Liverpool Leader about the life and work of John Birt. I
```

am looking for people in the BBC who have met John Birt
and Karl said he thought you might be able to help me.

I asked Surinder whether she knew John Birt and she was distinctly
evasive. According to her, Cross is losing his marbles. Being made Head
of Sound has pushed him over the fine line between truth and falsehood
constantly walked by senior BBC executives. She showed me a pamphlet
he has sent round to all staff. It has yet another picture of him at the top,
with a duplicate of his signature underneath it, and is printed on the kind
of quality paper usually seen in prospectuses for merchant banks.

Hullo, I am Colin Cross.
   I am Head of Sound.
   As of today.
   Yesterday I was Head of the Series and Serial Sound
Documentary and Drama Continuing and Occasional Home
and Overseas Department.
   I was also Head of the Radio Production Management
Resources Directorate.
   I still retain these important posts.
   And am still involved with the Core Directorate Policy
Unit.
   Although we are not quite sure what that is yet. Or who
precisely will make up its team.
   But now I am Head of Sound.
   May I take this opportunity to welcome you to Sound.
   Sound, as we all know, is crucial to radio. Without
sound there would *be* no radio.
   Our aim is to make sure we in Sound are heard.
   And heard clearly.
   But Sound will be working closely with Vision.
   Because, sometimes, it helps to be able to see who
you're talking to.
   I have been in the BBC for thirty-five years.

Under this, someone, presumably Surinder, has written, 'In a sound-
proof box. Stark naked.' After which Cross continues –

That hasn't stopped me feeling that I am raring to go.

There is an awful lot of paper to read in the BBC at the moment, isn't there? Most of it coming your way from people like me!

*Who are paid hundreds of thousands of pounds for hiring people to write it, you horrible, talentless, time-serving little oaf!*

The script is unusually lively.

I start to have an affair with my therapist. There is a scene in which she takes off my clothes, ostensibly to give me a massage. On my suggestion, we read it aloud. This gave me a lot of opportunity for the kind of eye contact that has been missing, recently, from our relationship. Flora (read by Surinder) says things like . . . 'Oh you are so good . . . so good . . . so hot, so good . . .' At one point she says, 'Feel my breasts!' to which I reply . . . 'Yes! Yes! I will feel your breasts!' It is only a first draft but, in my view, well on the way. Although there was a little too much about breasts for my liking. I have always been a leg man.

Unfortunately as we were reading it Estelle came in from the landing. She laughed coarsely and told Surinder to 'make sure I kept Percy well out of sight!' Somewhat to my chagrin, Surinder seemed to find this amusing.

She is an orphan, it appears, and Surinder is not her real name. She got it off the credits of *Filmnight*, which apparently employs a girl called Surinder as an assistant floor manager. So my Surinder is doing rather better than her! She got the Blake from *Blake Seven*. A nice touch, I thought.

## 6 p.m.

Ruairghry returned from Jobcentre. He says there are no jobs.

## 7.30 p.m.

Ruaierghiry left for Gordon's with Leopold, who emerged from the bathroom. I had the weird feeling that he has been in the house, unknown to any of us, for the last few weeks. Ruairghry also announced his intention of 'killing' Jakob!!!!!!

March 7th. 12 noon. Fine clear day with a strong
north-westerly wind.

*Jakob in Milan (according to E-mail; see below). Ruairehgy at Gordon's.
Edwin in bed pretending to be ill. Estelle at work.*

It may not be north-westerly. In fact it sneaks round corners and comes
out at you from all directions when you are least expecting it. It may be
Wimbledon's answer to the sirocco – a local suburban wind designed to
bring pain of a unique kind to the inhabitants of south-west London.

But I like the word north-westerly.

Tried to talk to Estelle about the nail-biting. She said, 'I can either bite
my nails or smoke. Which do you want me to do?' I said, 'I want you to
do neither.' She said, 'Fine. You want me to drink sherry for breakfast?'
I said I did not understand this. She agreed.

Two more letters have arrived for Rory – which is how I feel I ought
to describe him since this is how they are addressed. They are all from
the mysterious Lucy. Estelle opened the first one 'by mistake'. She said
she thought it was addressed to her. She did not attempt to explain why
she had steamed open the sealed flap. I told her this was a low trick but
one to which I am now an accomplice. I simply could not bear sitting
there while she read the first one. She did not make my life any easier by
emitting a series of low whistles as she read. We have now steamed open
all three.

The first one read –

THE 'GOOD GEAR' DRIVING SCHOOL
WIMBLEDON, LONDON, SW19

Darling Rory,

You send back all my letters unopened. It must be more
trouble than throwing them away since I have already
written you thirteen. Does this notepaper remind you of
those long hot afternoons driving down Murray Road? Do
you remember that disastrous three-point turn on Skeena
Hill? Or the time we jumped the lights on Wimbledon Park
Road?

71

Do you do this to hurt me? Is it because our love
has taken one of those turnings from which it is
impossible to emerge, even with skilful use of reverse
gears?

I am not clever like her and cannot always put things
into words. Or rather, when I put them into words the
words do not always seem to be . . . What? You see? I
cannot think what the words do not always seem to be.
Which sums it up really. To me it has always been enough
to look both ways at junctions, remember the correct use
of mirror and signalling when drawing away from the kerb
and to observe lane discipline.

A mere driving instructor! What chance do I have
against a girl studying English at Leeds University? But
when we were at school together, Rory, Laura and I shared
everything. We were as perfectly 'in synch' as the
gearbox of a 7 series BMW – in spite of all the things I
ever said about its repeat transmission pattern, still a
great car in my view.

Forget her, Rory. Come back to me and let us rebuild
trust between us. You and Laura Proek are, literally, 'a
non-starter'.
Your darling,
Lucy

PS. I am writing this to you at home in the hopes that
when you get back after the end of term you will have
mellowed.

PPS. Have you completely forgotten about what happened
at the Chessington World of Adventures?

Estelle looked pretty grim when she had finished reading this. 'She is
completely wrong for him!' she said. I said I thought she sounded
completely wrong for anybody. There was then a silence while we looked
at the other two letters. After a while Estelle said, 'A driving instructor!'
I said, 'There's nothing wrong with driving instructors!' Estelle's eyes
narrowed. 'No,' she said, 'but you wouldn't want your son to marry one,

would you?' I said I would have no objection so long as she was a nice driving instructor. Estelle told me not to be completely ridiculous. I said the most important thing in life was to be happy. Estelle said that that was why she was opposed to her son getting involved with a female driving instructor.

Then we steamed open the second letter. It was headed —

MULDOWNEY'S ABATTOIR
WIMBLEDON

1 p.m.

My darling Rory,

You do not write you do not phone! I am alone with all this 'meat' and yet I do not have access to the 'meat' I crave, which is part and parcel of you. Must break off this letter now as I have to behead a chicken.

3 p.m.

As I was saying – I need your meat. Another boring day here. Today I have been put in charge of shooting cows in the head, a dull and unrewarding task. Every time I raise the barrel to their ears they look up at me and I think of you. Their eyes (as opposed to their ears) remind me of Laura, which makes squeezing the trigger more than usually pleasant.

I suppose it is not her fault that you have fallen in love with her. But it is something I could well have done without. We were, as I think I said in my last letter, always sharing things at the Ursuline Convent, Cheam – condoms, prayer-books, tubes of Vaseline – but I don't think we ever shared boys. And she, as you may have noticed, has fallen in love with a boy who bears a middle name that has a worrying amount in common with Bovine Spongiform Encephalitis.

83

This afternoon, as I am sawing through the legs of a consignment of donkeys, just in from Sicily, I shall be thinking of you and your doomed passion for Laura Proek. Her father, who seems to have managed to convince you that he is not about as dull as the lights of the average horse, will certainly do all he can to make sure your passion is consummated.

But it is tearing me apart, my darling! I feel as if my thighs were being given the kind of treatment I am even now dishing out to a particularly photogenic piece of Living Veal, who, judging by its age and general air of cuteness should be romping around in the Young Cows equivalent of a Montessori Playgroup, not being hacked to pieces by your loyal, betrayed, but still faithful . . .

Lucy

PS. Have you no feelings? Do you not recall the morning we dismembered the geese? Or the weekend spent braining heifers with my own father's steam hammer?

Estelle and I read this one together. When we had finished, as one man we ran to the third letter and practically tore it apart. It read —

My horrible room,
Oxford

Dear Rory,

I have tried being funny the way you used to say you liked me being funny. I have tried being angry and hurt and desperate and sad and alone and all the other things I feel. But you return my letters.

Well, you haven't returned the last two (they probably wouldn't have made you laugh anyway since you seem to have completely lost your sense of humour) so I am sending this one to the same address in the hopes that it will lie there or even, perhaps, be opened by your rather wonderful-sounding Mum. I wish I had had a Mum like that.

I don't think mine ever cared enough to be that
inquisitive. And, oh, intelligent. Didn't you say she
had a first-class degree in physics, which she gave up to
look after your pleasant but totally self-obsessed
father? (Sorry, I have still not managed to sit through a
whole episode of *General Practice*.) Isn't intelligence
the most important thing?

   As for her being short-tempered – so what? She sounds
honest. I'd rather have that than anything. Passionate,
open feelings please . . .

   Yes I hope she reads this. I think people should open
the letters of the ones they love. And then feel guilty
about it. If there are things you want to keep secret
from the ones you love, you probably shouldn't be doing
them. And if you don't love your parents you might as
well shoot yourself.

   Poor Laura. Is that why you are so nice to her
appallingly ignorant father? Because you want her to
feel better about him? You are sweet enough to try and do
something as foolish and hopeful as that.

   All my (unrequited) love . . .
   Lucy


Estelle and I read this together. There was a quite amazingly long
silence when we had finished. Then Estelle said, 'I think she sounds really
nice.' I said, 'Yes.' There was another pause. Then I said, 'I don't think
I am *totally* self-obsessed!' Estelle said, 'Don't you?' I could not find a
ready answer to this question. 'I think,' Estelle said, 'that she might be
the one!' I nodded slowly. 'I suppose,' I said, 'that *General Practice* is
aimed at a slightly older audience.' Estelle looked up, briefly, from the
letter. 'Yes!' she said, without showing emotion of any kind, and started,
with considerable skill, to reseal the envelope.

I am still not entirely sure about this Lucy woman. She sounds too
clever by half for me.

Estelle then left for work. Just after she had gone I found this E-mail
from Jakob.

```
Subject:       My willy
Sensitivity:   High
Priority:      Urgent
```

Dear Father,
   I have got a willy. What do I do about this?
Am going to MILAN!


It is easy to think of Jakob as older than he actually is. I suppose that is true of all of us.


## 12.30 a.m.

Estelle in bed. Snoring. Not safe to go in yet. When she came back from work she smoked three cigarettes. And she bit her nails. I offered her a sherry. She shouted at me.

Edwin upstairs playing chord of E minor very, very quietly.

Am I really self-obsessed? If so, what can I do about it? Shagging Surinder would help, I think, because then I would be obsessed with her instead of myself. If I am obsessed with myself. I don't necessarily think I am. Although I may be. Why else am I wondering whether I am or not? My God, I am beginning to sound like Steve Witchett, the Writer Who Never Expresses an Opinion!

Perhaps I should just be nicer to Estelle. Am I threatened by her job, intelligence, etc.? I keep forgetting she has a degree in physics. Is this fear? Perhaps she is dying to talk about things I know nothing about like String Theory. I must get a book on String Theory and bring it up at the dinner table.


## March 12th. 11.30. Sunny and clear.

*Estelle at Craftgirls. Edwin at rehearsals for* Fit as a Fiddle. *Jakob at Oxford. Me in BBC. Ruairghry at Chinese Embassy (possibly).*

Was late for rehearsal this morning. Writing this in the break. I took Ruairghry in with me hoping I could introduce him to Karl, who might give him some work experience. He did not seem keen on this idea. 'I need work, not work experience!' he said. He has decided he wants to be a chef. When I suggested a catering course he said 'not that kind of chef'. As soon as we got into Broadcasting House Reception he said he had 'a very bad feeling'. We had a brief row. He accused me, once again, of being 'blind to people's feelings'. He also went on about Jakob. Then he stormed out into Upper Regent Street, saying he was going to the Chinese Embassy.

Am I blind to people's feelings? What does this mean for me and Estelle? Is this why she comes back from work so late? Shall I start biting my nails? Would this draw us closer together?

Since I sent away for three bottles of Lovejuice I have had to wait in every morning in case it arrives. I do not wish Estelle to find it. Although it will be addressed to Edwin I have no desire to land him in it. In fact I feel rather guilty at horning in on his party, as it were.

He asks plaintively, most days, whether he has received any letters from Wolverhampton. Estelle is ruthless about winding him up on this subject. She usually says in tones of elaborate surprise, 'No! Wolverhampton? Good Lord! Wolverhampton did you say, darling?' Then, turning to me, 'Have you seen any letters from . . . Wolverhampton, darling? What kind of letters? Business letters? Postcards?' Etc., etc.

I have also requested a copy of *From Behind, Eating Out Regularly* and *Norwegian Women at Play*. They are all very reasonably priced.

The script and outlines have been approved by both Karl and by Colin Cross. But not, apparently, by the Core Directorate Policy Unit. Karl says they have to 'wait for Howard Porda'. Karl looked furtively at Surinder as he said this. Surinder herself was rather odd when I asked if she could tell me who Porda was.

Until the mysterious Porda has pronounced, I have been granted limited survival rights. I am definitely being allowed to live until mid-April, although, apparently, I am to have 'pretty constant suicide potential' until then. Surinder is having to do a lot of rewrites, about which she is not very happy. 'If we could get Porda!' she said this morning. 'If we could utterly destroy him and all he stands for then we might be able to start living!' She seemed to think, however, that this would be about as easy as getting rid of Dracula.

I am going to do a bit of detective work on my own account. I shall start to track down the man Porda during my lunch-hour. I think he may be an invention of Karl and/or Cross's. Since they spend their days inventing jobs for each other I imagine they are perfectly capable of inventing an executive who they can blame for all their unpopular or unpleasant decisions. I have always thought that John Birt was probably a really nice man. It is probably simply that his subordinates feel the need to blame him for every lunatic decision that is made in the organization.

I think this blaming thing happened with Stalin. Although of course, come to think of it, Stalin did turn out to be a morally warped mass murderer.

## 2 p.m.

Writing this in the canteen. Have just eaten its version of beef stifado. Do not feel well. I also had a glass of retsina as it is Greek Week in the canteen. This made me feel even worse.

Everyone on *General Practice* has gone on a seminar to teach them how to deal with danger in the workplace. I asked if I could go and was told I couldn't. Apparently each place costs four hundred pounds. I said that, since I still had only a fifty-fifty chance of surviving the spring, I thought I was probably in more danger than anyone else in the building. Karl told me 'not to be silly'. I was told that 'if I was good' I could go to the one on stress, which is held in a hotel in Devon and is, according to Mabel, our new PA, 'a shagathon'.

Listener response to mad Esmond continues to be favourable. Yesterday I received a proposal of marriage from a woman in Huddersfield. I have managed to find a room number for the mysterious Howard Porda. Perhaps I will throw myself on the floor of his office and tell him all about Edwin's school fees.

## 3 p.m.

In Surinder's office. The Danger in the Workplace Seminar is being held in a Conference Room next door. I can hear grunting noises. A small weasely man is trying the handle of the door and looking furtively up and down the corridor. I don't like to tell him that there is a Danger Seminar going on. He may be part of it. Perhaps he is about to stage a simulated terrorist raid on the Series and Serial Sound Documentary and Drama Continuing and Occasional Home and Overseas Department.

I have to pluck up courage to contact Porda.

## 5 p.m.

In Surinder's office. Waiting for the Danger in the Workplace Seminar to finish. Surinder did emerge, briefly, a few minutes ago. They spent the morning being taught how to sit down. Apparently there have been a lot of back injuries because people have been lowering their behinds into BBC furniture without having read a pamphlet called *Posture in the Workplace*. After they had been taught how to sit down, they watched a recording of a recent BBC TV children's programme. A firm called All Kinds of Beasties had let loose the wrong kind of cobra into a discussion programme in Studio Eight. They had forgotten to remove the venom from one fang. 'Slithering Charlie', as the trainer is apparently known, had 'been getting careless' and, the week before, had allowed a python to nearly asphyxiate Richard Griffiths. I went to Porda's office. It was weird.

It was one of those rooms that you cannot reach directly from the corridor – always a clue to the level of megalomania of the inhabitant. In the outermost office was a very small girl who looked about twelve. She said, 'Mr Porda works from home a lot. And he's also abroad. Or in Scotland.' Mere mention of his name seemed to give her the shakes.

I left a message for him to call me at home. It is somehow appropriate that the man who holds the key to my future at the Beeb seems to be almost impossible to get hold of.

Still waiting for Surinder. I cannot imagine what they are doing in there. But, as Edwin is off doing 'group revision' with Scagg (who is now Head of the Waitrose Fish Counter), Bozz and Snozzer, and as Estelle is working late, I really don't want to go home.

## 8 p.m.

Message on machine from Edwin. He, Scagg, Bozz, Snozzer and someone called Plonker are 'revising the Arab–Israeli War'. From the background noise they seem to be doing it in a pub. At least they are enjoying it. Someone who sounded a bit like Scagg was screaming in the background.

Edwin said he was pretending to be Yasser Arafat. I also heard female voices. Edwin said, 'Lulu is here. She's got G C S E too, although she's a girl.' I think he was being satirical.

Surinder is suddenly distant.

Is she a prick-teaser? Not that there is much to tease these days. I should have gone ahead and ordered the Phallkrim. Noise of car. Sounds like Estelle. I must remember to be calm and ask her interested questions about her workday.


## March 13th. 10 a.m. Sunny but cold.

*Estelle at Craftgirls. Ruaiuerhy in bed. Jakob in Milan. Me in front room. Edwin doing Community Recreation, i.e. in bed.*

Asked Estelle interested questions about her workday. She accused me of 'being a phoney'. She bit her nails, smoked two cigarettes and drank half a bottle of sherry. When I asked her, lightly and unthreateningly, whether there was anything stressful in her life she said, 'It is five feet eight and wears a green cardigan!'

I have a green cardigan! 'Nuff said!

Tried new breathing exercises. They are called Loebli Breathing and do not seem to have disturbed the neighbours. They have, however, given me a pain in my side.

Two men in a removal van arrived this morning to take away the fridges. I asked them for money and they said, 'Mr Jakob is taking care of the cash side.' I called Jakob's mobile and got Oliver, who told me Jakob was in Milan 'transferring some money'. Oliver is *definitely* on drugs. In the course of a ten-minute conversation he said, 'Oh the lights! The pretty, pretty lights!' no less than four times.

Estelle almost obscenely cheerful this morning. She went out singing, 'Hey ho! Hey ho! It's off to work we go!' I said, 'Glad to see the back of me?' She thought about this for some time. Then said, 'Glad to see the back of *me*!' And walked off down the garden path, wiggling her bum. It is, actually, a rather attractive bum. I do not think she is having an affair. But am increasingly worried about our relationship. I think she feels my interest in her work is faked. (It is.) And I am pretty positive that we have not done it since early in February. Maybe that is why she is so cheerful. Sex does not make women happy. Not sex with me anyway.

## 1 p.m.

The rewritten script has arrived from Surinder.

I am, I think, a little too irritable. I am not sure this will be good for my focus-group response. I feel the 'polenta/wild mushroom quality' I had acquired is in danger of evaporating. If she had been allowed to really go with my new 'youthful' character I could have made something of it. The only consolation is that Ronnie Pilfrey seems to have caught a potentially fatal disease. He has quite a lot of coughing to do, however, of which Pilfrey is sure to make a meal. Especially as his row with the Inland Revenue is being heavily featured over the weeks ahead. Jimbo, the gay practice manager, looks as if he is on the way out. I must get to Porda.

## March 14th. 9.30 a.m. High winds. Dry.

*Edwin at school. Estelle at Craftgirls preparing for expense-account lunch. Ruairghry in bed. Jakob probably in bed too, whichever country he is in this morning.*

Writing this before I go in to the BBC. Have just dropped Edwin off. He tells me that *Fit as a Fiddle* is not now going to be performed. Instead, a boy called Loomis is going to be allowed to write and perform his own work – 'a touching love story' called *Boris and Jane*. I am not surprised Hotchkiss backed out of *Fit as a Fiddle*. The first page, which was all I was allowed to see, began –

> *The street. Enter Niggah and Pussylips.*
> NIGGAH: Yo! Wadd up, Muthafuckah?
> PUSSYLIPS: I bin wit' my bitches!
> NIGGAH: Yo! Yo' all wan' smoke?
> PUSSYLIPS: Want it hot as a niggah's ass?
> NIGGAH: Yo Muthafuckah, you be cool wit' my bitches!
> *Enter Crack, a dealer, and Loretta, a transsexual prostitute.*

*81*

PUSSYLIPS: Yo Loretta! Y'all in my hood.

LORETTA: I be no in yo' hood, boy. I be in no muthafucka's hood. I
be doin' it fo' myself.

NIGGAH: Yo! Hear dat niggahbitch talk!

Etc.


Edwin, Snozzer, Scagg, Bozzer and Plonker say they are going to disrupt Loomis's play.

I am desperate for the post to arrive, but am not sure how long I can wait. I think I can see the postman now. I will pick up the post on the way to the car.


## 1 p.m.

Writing this in a pub round the corner from Broadcasting House. The postman, a small Irishman, handed me a large parcel, clearly marked SEX PRODUCTS. He leered and winked heavily, saying, 'This should keep you going nicely!' I said, 'For my son, I fear!' Even though it was clearly addressed to Edwin Slippery, it made no difference. The man was still winking and leering as he staggered off down the road, listing badly to port under the weight of his Post Office bag.

They have enclosed a 'free trial offer' of Phallkrim together with a list of instructions. I am not even going to bother to look at it.

I managed to scribble over the legend 'Sex Products' and, so far, no one has commented, although there was a nasty moment when I was examining the VHS of *From Behind* in Surinder's office. Steve Witchett, the Writer Who Never Expresses an Opinion, asked me what it was. I said, 'Oh just something for the kids!' and stowed it away. I hope he did not read the words on the casing – 'Ever "had it" from behind? Ever been "shunted" by something that won't take no for an answer? You'll love this candid look at rear-entry situations and may not be able to contain your excitement as some pretty big stuff gives it up the backside, long and hot and strong!'

I am not sure I want to look at it after all.

The three bottles of Lovejuice are in my pocket as I write. A pale liquid. The label says it contains 0.61 grammes of Aurea Genifera. The South American herb, I suppose. Does it work? Some of these things do,

I'm sure. I put a little on my finger and licked it off. Just as I was doing this Karl put his head round the door. I do not think I found him any more erotic than usual. But I had only had a very small dose.

A dull morning in the studio. A new receptionist, called Clare, has arrived in the surgery. She and I are flirting pretty heavily – although all conversations between men and women in *General Practice* seem, for some reason, laden with innuendo. 'It is,' as Petra Fisher, who plays my disabled mother, points out, 'the only way we can breathe any life into the dialogue.' This morning's dialogue went –

ME: Hullo there!
CLARE: Well, hullo!
ME: How are you enjoying life from where you sit?
CLARE: The view isn't so bad. I have more confidence.
ME: I'm astonished at how much you've opened up!

Apparently Clare's first 'hullo' was 'a blatant come-on' and I delivered the word 'sit' in an 'unhealthy, suggestive manner'. Clare's line 'the view isn't so bad' suggested that one or both of us was naked, while the words 'I'm astonished at how much you've opened up' was spoken in a way that took it 'beyond innuendo into midwifery'. We tried doing the scene again. It came out even filthier.

Could this be to do with the Lovejuice?

I think I will examine the booklet on penis enlargement that the people in Wolverhampton have so kindly sent me. It seems to involve a course of exercises. There is also a rather worrying-looking metal contraption, a little like a miniature frame tent.

This afternoon I am off to see Porda. Or, rather, to try to see Porda. Surinder seems to continue to be against my trying to do this. And Karl is behaving even more shiftily than usual.

4.45 p.m.

Writing this in Surinder's office. She is in with Karl. I put my ear to the door and heard what I thought was a row. It sounded pretty heavy stuff. Karl was saying, 'You can't do this! You'll be discovered!' and I thought I heard Surinder laugh. Then they both said something about Cross. I think they said, 'Would he find out?' but I am not certain. Then the mysterious Mr Porda's name came up once or twice.

## 5 p.m.

Just been into Karl's office. To the left of his desk is an art object cunningly designed to look like an important media award, although in fact it was made by his wife at an evening class in Finchley. On a sheet of paper next to the phone I read the words 'SHIRLEY HAS STOCKINGS AND LOOSE, FILMY PANTIES'.

Who is this Shirley?

Perhaps she is Porda's girlfriend. He has to do something with his time and very little of it seems to be spent in the BBC. Perhaps he is one of those executives who is paid to stay away from the building in case he makes a stupid decision. Is he the one who wants me dead? Someone, certainly, is after my blood and people are too scared to say who it is.

Had palpitations this morning. Almost certainly embolism of some kind. But, as usual, too scared to go to the doctor in case there is something wrong with me.

## 7 p.m.

Estelle is downstairs eating turnips. Edwin offered to eat turnips with her but she declined, saying she 'did not want his pity'. Edwin then said there was nothing wrong with being fat. 'If I had a huge bum like yours,' he said, 'I would make a feature of it!' He is the only person in the world who could get away with a remark like this. If I had said it she would have killed me.

She seems to have given up cooking anything apart from turnips. I suppose I will have to make Edwin some food.

When I got back home I could not find Edwin anywhere. I called up the stairs and screamed several times, but it was not until I was on my way up the third flight of stairs to his room that he answered. I yelled, 'What are you doing?' He answered, 'Revising! Don't come in!' I knew he was up to something, and, when he finally emerged at around five thirty I leaped out on to the landing. He was coming down the stairs, looking flushed, accompanied by a very small girl with bright red hair.

'This is Lulu!' he said. 'She is helping me revise!' I said, 'Thank you, Lulu!' Lulu grinned. 'That's O K!' she said. She seemed rather sweet. I said, 'You have a hard job on your hands!' She looked momentarily nonplussed and then gave a little silvery laugh. 'Oh,' she squeaked, 'you mean with the revision!' 'That's it!' I said.

Then they went off down the stairs. It is not possible that they are doing it. I refuse to believe this. It is against the law. It is unfair. All I have got to show for nearly fifty years' experience with women is three bottles of Lovejuice and copies of *From Behind*, *Norwegian Women at Play* and *Eating Out Regularly*. And, of course, Estelle. She is, as it happens, the only woman with whom I have ever slept. I dare not think what will happen to me if this truth leaks out. Think I will go downstairs and try and interest her in a bit of wild intercourse.


## 7.30 p.m.

She seems cheerful. We are going to collect Jakob in a few days. But she didn't look like a woman about to whip off her clothes and adopt interesting positions. In fact sitting down with her head in her hands staring at a bowl of turnips seemed about the only position of which she would ever be capable. I felt almost sorry for the poor old bag.

I thought I would try and make a slightly more subtle approach than usual – when in the kitchen my standard technique is to poke my tongue out and point towards the stairs. I thought about mentioning Phallkrim and, via that, trying to rouse a bit of enthusiasm for the subject of penises in general. From there it should be possible to work the conversation round to mine. This was not super subtle, but at least a few steps ahead of President Clinton's technique.

In the end I decided to bring up the subject of Surinder. It is a well-known fact that women only start to get interested in you when other women are forming an orderly queue to get into your pants.

Estelle, however, seemed remarkably unthreatened by my line of approach. At one point I even said, 'I think Surinder may be . . . a little bit keen on me!' Estelle gave an offensively coarse laugh and said, 'Hot diggety!' I said, with as much dignity as I could manage, 'I have to say I find her . . . very . . . attractive!' Estelle gave me a most peculiar look at this point and said, 'You mean you haven't spotted it?' I failed to grasp the significance of this remark. 'Spotted what?' I said. Estelle shook her head in simulated pity. 'There's none so blind as will not see!' she said.

I suppose she is trying to tell me that Surinder is a lesbian. It takes one to know one is all I can say.

Anyway I didn't get a shag. Might as well make Edwin's dinner.


## March 16th. 10 a.m.

*Ruairghy in bed with Leopold and Gordon. Jakob in Oxford (I assume). Edwin at school. Estelle in 'important meeting' at Craftgirls.*

I am here. I am always here. I am here alone. I have the house to myself. Ruarighy, Leopold and Gordon will be comatose until three, and even then showing only limited signs of life. Leopold and Gordon are now going to China without Ruairghry. He has announced his intention of 'going on the stage'. He has also found and consumed the latest consignment of Luxury Seafood Goujons. I hate him.

I am going to watch *Norwegian Women at Play*.


## 11 a.m.

Life is cruel.

*Norwegian Women at Play* was a film about a group of Scandinavian women at a tiddlywinks festival. It was, actually, quite interesting, but not what I had in mind. It was certainly not worth fifteen quid. *Eating Out Regularly* was a guide to 'Wolverhampton's finest bars and brasseries' and, most depressing of all, *From Behind* was a documentary about traffic accidents in which vehicles collided with the vehicle in front. The most erotic thing in it was an articulated lorry accelerating into the rear end of a Mini Metro. I watched it five times and by the fourth viewing the sequence was beginning to seem positively steamy.

Have been doing some research on Porda. He is Core Directorate Policy Adviser (Sound) and am told he is on 221 000. It is not clear whether this is his telephone number or his salary. As he has never made a programme in his life it is almost certainly the latter. One man I called said he thought he ran 'the Cockumentary Department' i.e. late-night programmes about sex. Robbie Fisher from the Series and Serial Sound Documentary and Drama Continuing and Occasional Home and Overseas Department said he thought he was John Birt's brother-in-law. Several other people said he was 'a hard man'.

He's in the BBC staff list. He has even been quoted in newspaper articles apparently. But as far as I can tell no one has actually seen him for two years. When I told this to Robbie Fisher, Robbie said that Porda could very well be dead. 'That wouldn't necessarily stop the BBC paying his salary or giving him an office.' Leonie Freeman thought he might be the invention of a syndicate, who were even now dividing his salary between them. 'The thing is,' she said, 'we've all been reorganized and restructured so many times everyone's forgotten who everyone is. Who are you?'

I am determined to discover the truth about Porda. Hilary Speed, the woman who did not get Marjorie Forbes's job, said she had heard that 'he sometimes sneaks in after office hours to pick up his expenses'.


## 4 p.m.

Just got new script from Surinder. I show no sign of being interested in Oasis. As far as I can tell it's back to being boring old middle-aged Esmond Pennebaker. I even start droning on about the closure of St Bude's, the neighbouring hospital. This won't get us any listeners. There's only one thing more boring than the closure of a real hospital and that's the closure of a fictional one.

At this rate I will be dead by the beginning of the summer term.

Talking of which – had palpitations again this afternoon. The nearest accident and emergency to us is about six miles away. And I think it closed down last year. I think I should have a private medical health check-up. If only I was Edwin's age again! He probably thinks High Cholesterol is a Clint Eastwood movie.


## 6.30 p.m.

When I went to pick up Edwin, he and Snozzer and Scagg (who has been promoted to the Cheese Counter) and Bozz were talking to Lulu. Plonker was watching them from the other side of the road through what looked like a telescope. I think this was intended to be some kind of street theatre. They all smelled strongly of drink. I couldn't work out whether Edwin was talking to her more than any of the others.

Near by, an enormous boy with ears the size of an elephant was talking to Mr Hotchkiss. Snozzer told me later that Hotchkiss is in love with this youth. I do not think much of his taste. Have now read the end of *Fit as a Fiddle*, retitled *Muthafuckas*. Think it has real talent and will send it to Royal Court.

Edwin is now upstairs 'revising' – which tonight takes the form of playing the chord of F major seventh very, very loudly. He has also announced his intention of 'having a nose job which will make him look like Noel Gallagher'. I told him he was welcome to have as much plastic surgery as he liked provided he paid for it.

Finally got through to Surinder at her flat. (Why have I never been invited there?) She had been engaged all afternoon. She was very odd when I told her of my plans to track down Porda. Why are all these people so scared of this man? Seeking to uncover more about her sexuality, I said, in a deliberately casual, unthreatening manner, 'Purely as a matter of interest – how do you spot a lesbian?' Surinder said, 'With binoculars usually.'


March 17th. 9 p.m. A clear, cold night. At least thirty days without sex.

*Ruarighy at Heathrow seeing off Gordon and Leopold (hope he does not get on plane by mistake). Jakob in Oxford. Edwin watching video. Estelle on eleventh phone call of the evening. Me in study.*

Tomorrow we go to pick up Jakob. Estelle seems very cheerful, although as far as I can make out we have still not had any sex. Apparently Craftgirls have landed a huge order for little dough men. They have managed to sell 15,000 of them to the Czech Republic. I said I did not understand how a country as small as the Czech Republic could accommodate that many little dough men. Estelle said that it was a faraway country of which I knew little.

I really should try and get hold of a book on String Theory. It may be my only hope of getting a shag before our twenty-fifth wedding anniversary (assuming she comes across in honour of this momentous occasion). I have totally given up on Surinder who, I have now decided, *is* definitely a lesbian. She spends more and more of her leisure time over at Craftgirls. I think she is having an affair with Stella Badyass.

Perhaps I should try and locate Karl's mysterious Shirley. She sounds like hot stuff. The other day I caught him writing, 'SHIRLEY HAS PEACH-COLOURED SUSPENDERS' on the back of a BBC envelope.

I lay in wait for Howard Porda this afternoon and, to my surprise, actually caught a glimpse of someone who may have been him. I went up to his office, and, instead of trying either of his secretaries, waited in the office opposite until they had both gone home. About ten minutes after they had gone I heard footsteps. A man in a heavy coat, wearing a trilby hat and a scarf over his face, came carefully along the corridor and, looking furtively this way and that, opened the door to Porda's private office. You could not see any of his face.

He went into his office and re-emerged carrying some envelopes and computer discs. Then, after another quick glance up and down the corridor, he stole away into the night. It is possible that it was not Porda at all but a high-up member of BBC Internal Security, investigating the misuse of BBC equipment. They are very hot on this at the moment. Karl droned on for hours about his equipment only the other day. Although, to judge from his doodling, he may have been talking about a kind of equipment very different from envelopes and computer discs.


## 11.30 p.m.

Estelle, still horribly cheerful (why?), spent the evening quizzing Edwin about his GCSEs. He says he does not wish to take any. We told him he had to. He said, 'Chemistry! What's the point?' I was unable to answer this question except by telling him that if he did not take GCSE he would have to go and work in Waitrose. Edwin seemed worryingly keen on this idea. 'Scagg,' he said, 'is well into the woodwork at Waitrose! He has . . . like . . . a future there! They locked him in the fridge the other day!'

Ruarighy returned from Heathrow and said he wished he was going to China. He then announced his intention of coming to Oxford to pick up Jakob. I asked why he wanted to come. Ruairghy said, 'I am going to kill him.' I told him I did not want any trouble. Ruairghy said, in an ominously calm voice, 'There will not be any trouble. But if he is there with Laura I am just going to kill him. Very quietly. Possibly with a brick.'

His spiky pale face gave him the look of Jack Frost as he said this. This is not going to be as easy to sort out as the famous incident of some fifteen years ago still known as Who Really Owns the Galactic Space Station?

## March 18th. 9.30 a.m.

*Estelle in bath. Edwin in bed. Ruarighy in bed. Me in bed, hoping for uninhibited sex.*

Writing this while Estelle in bath. Been to have a look at her but she does not seem in the mood for uninhibited sex. She is lying staring at the ceiling with a large, blue flannel over her face. I would not be surprised to discover that there were a few turnips in there with her. As I went out she said, 'What in God's name did I have against disposable nappies?' She is going through some kind of crisis, I think.

We are about to set off for Oxford. Hopefully we can sneak out before Ruarighy or Edwin wake.

## 1.30 p.m. King's Arms, Oxford.

Ruairghy woke at 9.45 a.m. At least three hours ahead of his usual schedule. I kept sneaking glances at him on the way up here, to make sure he was not suffering any ill effects. He still has a jet-lagged look about him. Edwin said he had to stay behind.

Appalling scene outside Jakob's college. Oliver, a tall, effete youth with curly hair and a smile that (I thought) was probably chemically induced, leaped up to Ruairghy, whom he seemed to know well, and said, 'Like Jakob has like run off with Laura . . . to a like . . . unknown address. Which is . . . like . . . heavy!' Then he turned to me and with a lot of public-school charm said, 'You must be Mr Slippery. I am so pleased to meet you! I am such a fan of your show. I loved the bit when Jimbo came out to your wife!'

I must say I was warming to him, although he was, rather distressingly, a fan of Pilfrey's. I was able to tell him, with some satisfaction, that in fact he has a rare, and fatal, lung disease called Moeran's syndrome. He is due to die in screaming agony at the end of June. Ha! Oliver got quite alarmed by this. He had been taken in by Ronnie's smoothie-chops voice.

It was then that I remembered that, a few weeks ago, this boy had not even heard of *General Practice*. I began to suspect him of creeping to me. And Ruairghy, who had started to walk in small circles, banging his forehead with the flat of his right palm, looked as if he was about to hit him. 'How can he do this to me?' he said. 'How can he do this to any of us? How can he do this to Norman?' I was about to say that I didn't think this was anything to do with Norman when Oliver laid his hand on Ruairghy's arm and said, in soothing tones, 'Shall we all go and have a . . . like . . . joint?' This provoked a strong speech from Estelle on the dangers of marijuana. To which Ruairghy, who was looking even more pale and spiky than usual and, now, quivering like a dog, said, 'You ought to know. You smoked enough of it.' Estelle said, 'I stopped in time. You have to stop in time!' Oliver put his head in his hands and started to wail. 'I'm . . . like . . . so sorry!' he said. 'I thought you were cool!' I said, 'We are. We are extremely cool. We would just like to know where our son is. Is he in Milan perhaps? Or attending a meeting of the International Monetary Fund?'

Estelle said we would have to call the police. At the mention of this word, Oliver, his smile wider and more fixed than ever, made his excuses and left. I think he said he had a meeting of the Lager Society. I cannot believe there is such an organization. I persuaded Estelle that the police would not be necessary. We were about to go and call Jakob's mobile when I saw a small, plump, very pretty girl come out of a doorway some way down the street. She had a raffia bag slung over her shoulder and I saw her glance, briefly, in our direction. There was such a forlorn look about her, as she tossed her long black hair back off her face, that I found myself giving her an encouraging smile. Ruarigthy was looking at her too, but the sight of her seemed to distress him even further.

It was only when we got back here, to the pub, that he told me. The girl was Lucy. She is, to use a phrase of Aldous Huxley's, pneumatic.

Estelle has been phoning Jakob's mobile for as long as it has taken me to write this. She has, as far as I can see, only just got connected.

## 2.30 p.m. The Raj Restaurant, Oxford.

Ruarighy has just eaten five poppadums, three onion bhajees, a kebab, a murgh muglai, two portions of rice and three portions of aubergines. He has also drunk four pints of lager. This seems to have calmed him – although he still talks of killing Jakob. Jakob has told Estelle he is 'somewhere in the country trying to sort things out with Laura and we are not to worry'. He says it is better for none of us to know where he is 'until Ruairghy calms down'. Ruarighy has left a message on Jakob's machine, some of which Estelle overheard. It began, 'You are going to suffer for this!'

They have both gone for a walk, leaving me to pay the bill.

Where is Jakob? Has he left the country? Will he ever return? Will Ruaighry ever calm down? Who is the mysterious Lucy and why did I find her so attractive? Was it simply that she was thirty years younger than me? Why does Ruyairghry not find her attractive? Why are the wrong people always in love with the wrong people? Why is life more like a soap opera than *General Practice*? What on earth does Oliver see in Ronnie Pilfrey? Why am I not more famous? When am I going to have sex? Should I have had the chicken vindaloo?

No.

## 10.30 p.m.

Ruarighy and I had a pleasant evening at the pub. Now he is back at home he has calmed down somewhat. He drank thirteen pints. I was a little concerned at this but he told me not to worry. Apparently this is very moderate compared to most members of the Lager Society – which turns out to be a very real organization, to which both he and Oliver (a classics student, who went to Eton) both belonged when he was there.

He seems still very hung up on Laura Proek. I tried telling him that I thought Lucy was a nice girl. In fact, after my third pint I became quite eloquent on the subject. He accused me of being a dirty old man.

Estelle has sold a large number of little dough men in the Boston area.

Apparently they go down well at Christmas shops – especially a small, pot-bellied one with a big nose and a bald head, called Mr Slippy Sloppy. They have attached a device for drawing corks to his trousers and are selling him with the slogan HE ONLY SCREWS WHEN YOU WANT TO. Craftgirls is opening an office in the West End, and they are all giving themselves important-sounding jobs. Serafina Wiles – who must have been studying events at the Beeb – has made Estelle Senior Liaison Officer of the Core Production Team. Stella Badyass has been made Head of Marketing. They are all going away on a management training course to learn about sexual harassment. I said that from my knowledge of them the Craftgirls were already pretty good at it. This did not go down well.

Every time Stella Badyass or Surinder is mentioned Estelle winks and leers. I am almost sure that she is having a lesbian affair with one or both of them. I feel she has stolen Surinder from under my nose.


## March 20th. 11 a.m.

*Ruarighy and Edwin in bed. Estelle at Craftgirls. Me at home. Jakob God knows where.*

I am not featured this week. And soon I will be dead. I wish I was asleep.

Edwin told us last night that 'the pain had come back'. When Estelle asked where it was he said 'all over and in my groin'. I suspect this may be Lulu's fault.


## 12 noon.

Good Old Steve rang. Suggesting lunch with Peter Mailer. I accepted eagerly.

I think, as women seem to be determined to give me a hard time, I shall spend the rest of the year with men. I shall do more manly things – such as potholing, etc. I will look up all my male friends and spend more time in the pub. I will learn jokes off by heart and punch selected males, carefully, in the upper arm, in order to emphasize my feelings of closeness with them.

## 5 p.m.

Life can be good to fifty-year-old men. Had lunch with Peter Mailer and Good Old Steve. Good Old Steve and I drank three bottles of 1993 Fronsac. Peter Mailer drank four bottles of Badoit. Good Old Steve consumed three packets of Nicorettes. Mailer told us he thinks that Nobby is 'at risk' and that he has an 'addictive personality'. 'Worrabout ush?' said Steve and I. Mailer shook his head. 'You are not alcoholics!' he said pityingly, making us, I thought, sound like failed suicides.

Good Old Steve said, 'You and Estelle have a great marriage! You really talk to each other!' God knows how he knows this, unless he has been hiding in the bedroom cupboard. He went on to tell us that he hadn't had sex since November of last year. He said he would be prepared to pay for a shag, he was so desperate. When we asked him how much he said, 'Up to two grand.' Peter and I said that for that money, we would be happy to oblige. He said that that wasn't the point.

We discussed Nobby. He is now shagging a twenty-two-year-old Brazilian girl, who, according to Good Old Steve, has 'breasts like frozen blancmange'. For his fiftieth they are going to Bangkok for the weekend. We agreed that Nobby is a rather shallow person.

Clearly they both think that because I am married I am more or less permanently on the job. I did not tell them that I cannot remember when I last had sex. I am now not even sure I had it in February. My memory is shot to pieces. Good Old Steve is fifty next week. He says he does not want a party. In honour of this he said he would pay the bill and told us he would put us on his expenses (he works for Rupert Murdoch). We raised our glasses to the absent Australian, after which he realized he had left his credit card back in his flat. Mailer and I split the bill.

I asked them both about potholing. They gave me an odd look.

Bill was £214.34. Tomorrow I am going to get hold of Howard Porda. I must sort out my future.

# March 21st. 11 a.m.

*Ruairghery in bed. Estelle at work. Edwin at school. Jakob somewhere with Laura. Me here.*

Estelle hideously cheerful. Craftgirls have bought her a black Mercedes coupé. I suspect she has been having secret conversations with Jakob. Ruarighy rang his mobile last night and left a long abusive message.

I asked Estelle, straight out, for a shag this morning (I have decided that a firm, manly request for sex, accompanied by a firm manly look into her eyes and use of the word 'please' is the only approach that will get results) and she said, flicking through her diary, 'Call me at the office and I'll try and block you in some time in June.' This was supposed to be a joke but I did not find it funny and told her so. She said, 'Don't take everything I say clitorally!'

Still no script from Surinder. What is happening? I called Steve Witchett, the Writer Who Never Expresses an Opinion, and he said, 'It could be that there's a crisis of some kind. Although of course it may be that nothing has changed at all. But from what I can see – and I don't really know anything at all – there is a possibility that the entire series may be scrapped. If it isn't scrapped – and, as I say, I can't say whether that is what they're thinking – it may well be expanded. Or of course contracted.'

There goes the phone.

# 11.15 a.m.

That was Karl. The first time he has ever called me at home. He says there has been a 'really tough memo from Porda'. I am summoned in immediately to meet him and Cross. In Cross's office. I sense a determined effort to end the life and career of Dr Esmond Pennebaker. Help! Will phone Gustave before I go, to try and find out what my rights are.

## 11.30 a.m.

Called Gustave. He screamed at me. Apparently I was supposed to go and do a voice-over for a film about snails. I completely forgot. In fact I can't remember whether he ever told me about it, but, as I am unable to remember things like the first name of the woman who plays the sister of the patient who has got Alzheimer's (I cannot remember his name either) or the date when I last had sex, I suspect Gustave may not, for once, be lying.

I asked him what my rights were and he said, or rather, shouted, 'No one has any rights at the BBC. We are not going to deal with the BBC. We are not going to allow any of our actors to work for them!' He first said this in (I think) 1975.

## 12.15 p.m.

Writing this in Surinder's office. I have been desperately trying to find her all morning but no one seems to know where she is. June Rabstein, who plays my half-sister, said, 'She kept saying she had to go and see these dough men!' I can only assume she is somewhere in Craftgirls. Which is not really where I want her to be when the anti-Esmond forces are massing. Here comes Karl.

## 12.45 p.m.

In the canteen. Cross is too busy to see us until after lunch. He is in a meeting to discuss the problems of bad language on the radio. 'It is awful!' said his secretary, a small, dim girl called Rita: 'Someone wanted to do an adaptation of a book called *The Cunt of Monte Cristo* the other day!' We listened at the door and heard Cross shouting, 'No one is fucking saying cunt on my fucking channel, you arsehole!'

## 4 p.m.

Just come out of the meeting with Cross. He has an office the size of a football pitch and we had tea in real china cups – a sure guarantee of status in the Beeb. On his desk was a huge colour photograph of a woman in a white dress, standing under a tree with two small children. They were obviously intended to reassure us that he is a human being/family man, etc., although of course there is no guarantee that any of them are related to Cross. Even if they are, that doesn't rule out the chance that he and Karl are part of a ring of senior BBC deviants. The people in the picture may well be part of it.

The 'tough' memo read as follows –

```
From:      Howard Porda
To:        Colin Cross
Subject:  Esmond Pennebaker

Well done! Dr Pennebaker is really working!
   He feels much warmer to me and I like the way he is
handling Jimbo. His attitude to Pamela is obviously very
delicate but there is a real sense he is a man doing
medicine for the nineties in a nineties way. If we have
to kill someone why don't we finish off Pilfrey? The
disease works for me I must say and people I have talked
to here feel it works for them.
   I am at a Strategy Meeting in Cornwall but you can call
me on my mobile.

PS. John Birt really liked Karl's 'Underwear'.
```

Cross sighed and looked at Karl. Something very complicated indeed was going on between them. Karl said, slowly, 'We can't guarantee that that is what Porda really thinks. He will wait to see how it all turns out and then blame us if it goes wrong. It is standard BBC practice. He is just covering himself.' I said, 'What do *you* think, Karl? Should I be allowed to live or not?' Karl sucked his teeth. 'If I could be sure Porda was one hundred per cent with us then I would go out on a limb for you, Paul. But I'm not.' 'In that case, Karl,' I said, 'I think I am owed a meeting with this guy!' Cross nodded. 'I think he is!' he said. Karl started to twitch wildly. He seemed terrified. 'If that is what you really want, Paul,' he said, 'I will try and fix it.'

He gave me his weirdest look yet as he said this. Maybe Porda really is the Invisible Man. Maybe the whole of the BBC has been taken over by aliens – or, to be precise, a different lot of aliens from the ones who are usually running it.

'Underwear' is, it turns out, a one-off play by a boy of Ruairghry's age. During the meeting Karl wrote, on a piece of scrap paper, 'SHIRLEY HAS SMOOTH SILK PANTS THAT ARE LOOSE AROUND HER BOTTOM.'


# March 22nd. 11.30 a.m.

*Estelle in Paris. Ruairghy in bed. Edwin at school. Jakob God knows where.*

Estelle off to Paris for the day on Eurostar. First class. *Les petits hommes fabriqués en farine* are, apparently, going down a storm on the other side of the Channel. Especially the bald one with a big nose. To cap it all she has gone with Stella Badyass and Surinder, who seems to have lost all interest in *General Practice* and is allowing Steve Witchett to write all the episodes. I have got a long and incredibly boring speech about traffic calming, although even this subject is treated with kid gloves. I say that I have heard there is going to be traffic calming in the street outside the surgery and Clare, the receptionist, asks me how I know this. I say, 'I am not sure. I think I had a letter from the Council. They are usually good about telling us when they are doing things like that. Although there have been times when they have been less good, they are certainly better than they were, although I am not, of course, saying that there couldn't be room for improvement. Not that I am saying they were bad before, of course . . .' etc., etc. When I suggested I should actually say something about traffic calming Witchett gave a kind of shudder and said, 'We don't want to rub people up the wrong way about this. This is an incredibly controversial topic, you know, and I am really sticking my neck out by even mentioning it!'

He has gone over the rest of the episode and carefully removed anything that might be construed as dramatic. Which gives it a rather uniquely upmarket feel. I have the sensation of being in a late play of Samuel Beckett's.

A ring at the door. Who can this be?

## 5.30 p.m.

It was Lucy.

The first thing I noticed, as she stood there on the doorstep, was how amazingly nice she smelled. Of soap and apples and honey, I thought. Then I noticed that she had very full red lips. Then I noticed that her eyes are almost black. Then I noticed that my tongue was hanging out.

'I'm so sorry to bother you!' she said. 'You don't know me. I'm called Lucy. And I wondered if Ruairehgy was around?' She has a high squeaky voice that makes her sound like a (rather appealing) cartoon mouse. 'He is,' I said, 'asleep at the moment.' She grinned. 'In fact,' I said, 'he will probably be asleep for the next few hours. But we could go up and throw a slipper at him.' She grinned again and said she thought that might not be a very good idea. Then she said, 'I so liked it when you were bitten by that dog!' For a moment I couldn't think what she was talking about. And then I remembered. About five years ago Esmond was attacked by Jimbo's pit bull, which had to be put down by Morag, a local vet whom Esmond obviously fancied. It was a very strong episode.

This was no mere attempt to 'curry favour'. She obviously knew her stuff. We went into the front room and had quite a long conversation about my affair with my secretary, on which she was sound. She even seemed to know who the writers were, and said, 'Witchett is talented but I think he needs to relax as a writer!' She must be the only person apart from his mother who has heard of Witchett.

I must say I was glad to meet her properly. She seemed pleased to be meeting me. Eventually I said, 'You haven't come to see me, have you? You want to see Ruarighry. Except he's still in bed!' At which she burst into tears. 'Not with Laura,' I went on quickly, trying to calm her, 'although of course I'm afraid I think he'd like to be!' She was sobbing furiously now and in an attempt to calm her I went over to the sofa and in a perfectly proper, paternal gesture put my arms round her. 'Laura is in bed with Jakob,' I said, 'and likely to remain so for some time!' This made her sob even more. She smelled better than sensational. Do women only stop smelling nice when you have lived with them for twenty-five years?

Do men?

Eventually we decided to wake Ruarghry up, and went, together, up to his room. He was lying with his mouth open and his knees drawn up.

His head was flung back over the pillow, his spiky blond hair, devilishly sharp, upon the pillow. Spread open on his chest was a large paperback copy of a book called *How to Get a Job*. As far as I could tell he was on page four or five. Lucy beamed at him fondly. 'Isn't he lovely?' she said. 'Yes,' I said. 'But he doesn't seem to need me any more,' she said. 'Me neither,' I said, and, for the first time, the two of us grinned.

'He once told me,' she said, 'that, years ago, he wanted to be a marine biologist. And then he suddenly realized he was no good at biology!' 'Or maths!' I said, 'Or physics! Or chemistry! And he gets seasick!' 'He wants to direct . . .' squeaked Lucy with an apologetic grimace. I said, 'Direct what?' She looked down at him, her eyes softening. 'Don't be hard on him. Even if he is much too nice for showbiz!' she said, and then put her hand to her mouth. 'Does that sound awfully rude?' 'No,' I said. '*General Practice* isn't showbiz. It is the audio equivalent of a convict ship.' She threw back her head and laughed. She shook all over when she laughed. It was not an unpleasant sight.

I think it was then that I suddenly saw she was the right girl for him. It wasn't part of a conscious thought process, more a sudden flash, like coming on a building as the mist clears and you see, clearly, what has always been there for the first, glorious time. The mere thought of her makes me able to write out his name correctly. Rory. That's who he is. A decent, practical, rather moral person who should be doing something useful rather than thinking that, like his father, he ought to be involved in the arts.

Lucy attempted to stop me but I threw a slipper at him.

He did not seem very pleased to see either of us. He made a croaking noise in the back of his throat, blinked rapidly and said to Lucy, in an accusing tone of voice, 'What are you doing here?' I said, in as bright a tone as I could manage, 'She has come to see you, Ruarigehry!' Ruairghry snarled slightly. 'Why?' It was at this point that I caught sight of no less than four empty packets of Luxury Seafood Goujons on the floor by his bed. I said, rather more harshly than I had intended, 'Maybe she has some advice on careers to give you!'

'I came,' said Lucy, 'to try and make it up.' I could see she was on the edge of tears. Sounding, I realized, a little like Norman Proek, I said, 'You see? She's come to make it up!' Ruarieghy put his head under the duvet. 'Good!' he said. 'As you are so friendly with her perhaps you would tell her she can go now!' At this Lucy did burst into tears. I heard myself say, 'Now look what you've done!' Lucy said, 'I only came because Laura suggested I try and make it up with you. She doesn't like to see you and Jakob like this.' At the mention of Laura's name Ruairhruy sat bolt upright in bed. 'Laura!' he said. 'Have you spoken to Laura?' 'I told you I had!' said Lucy. 'Where is she?' said Ruaighry, his eyes insanely bright. 'She's in your aunt's cottage in the Lake District,' she said. Raurighy leaped out of bed and ran for the clothes cupboard, tripping over the Luxury Seafood Goujons as he did so.

'For God's sake,' I said, 'Lucy has come all this way to see you!' Ruairghry was trying to disentangle a Luxury Seafood Goujons packet from his left foot. It seemed to be stuck to his skin. 'What do you care?' he said. 'What do any of you care about me? You can't even spell my name!' I said, 'That is a ridiculous thing to say!' 'Spell it then!' said Ruairghy. 'It may be ridiculous, but it is true. Plenty of ridiculous things are true. You have spent the last thirty years pretending to be Dr Esmond Pennebaker. No wonder Mum went out to work. To get away from you, probably!'

I didn't think it safe to offer Ruaighrerhy an off-the-cuff orthography for his Christian name. Instead I said, 'No wonder Gordon and Leopold didn't want to go to China with you!' Ruaighry rounded on me. 'You have never understood me, have you?' he said. 'You have never understood what I feel and what I am going through. That was an amazingly hurtful thing to say about Gordon. And about Leopold!' By now I was losing my temper. 'How about a job,' I said, 'instead of chasing all over Britain after a girl who has made it perfectly clear she can't stand you?' Ruairghry drew himself up to his full six feet two inches and, with as much dignity as is possible when you are still attached to a packet of Luxury Seafood Goujons, said, 'I am looking for a job. It is not easy to find a job. They do not want people like me. I do not fit in.' 'We noticed!' I said.

By now he was fully dressed and heading for the door. Lucy was sitting on the bed with her head in her hands. She seemed to be sobbing and saying, 'I am so sorry! I am so sorry!' I was not sure who she was addressing. I went out on to the landing after my eldest son, who was by now in the hall groping through his anorak pockets. 'You cannot just walk out of here and go to the Lake District,' I screamed at him, 'you have no money! You do not know where it is!' Ruairghry looked up at me, suddenly self-righteously calm. 'It is in the north,' he said, 'I will find it! And I have money. I still have the money I earned when I was in the circus.'

I had absolutely no idea what he was talking about. What circus? How much of a double life, I thought, has this boy been leading? 'Is this drugs?' I said. 'Has Oliver been selling drugs? Are you and Jakob and Oliver part of a ring?' 'What Norman says is true,' said Ruaighry in dangerously level tones. 'You never did hang my karate certificate on the wall!' And with this chilling criticism he went out into the March afternoon without so much as a spare pair of underpants.

'He'll be back,' I said. 'He has trouble finding Notting Hill Gate let alone Cumbria!' Lucy burst into tears again and wandered out on to the landing. I got her down to the front room, and a few minutes later I heard the front door slam and then the thump of Edwin's bag hitting the floor. Edwin said he would take her downstairs and comfort her. The last girl he tried to do this to ran out of the house screaming but she seemed quite happy with this arrangement. In fact Lucy seemed surprisingly well informed about him and his friends. I thought I heard her say something about Snozzer. When they were downstairs I put my ear to the floorboards. I am going to have to get used to doing this kind of thing if I am going to be able to get my children through important emotional crises.

I didn't hear a lot of what he said but he began by saying, 'Rory is not worth it. He is *so* fat! You are the only person in the world who seems to want him. I can't think why he wants Laura. Who is pretty rough in my view. And as for Jakob, he is completely grotesque. If you want any of us, I'm your man. I'm only sixteen but I am extremely mature and I play the guitar. Shall I play you a song? I have a girlfriend at the moment but she is for the chop and I am prepared to take you on at very short notice indeed!'

To my surprise this seemed to cheer Lucy up considerably. He is still downstairs – playing her the chord of C sharp minor.

## 9.30 p.m.

Lucy still here. Tried to contact Estelle re Ruairghy situation. She now has a mobile phone. I rang what I thought was the number and was connected to someone called Kevin. He seemed rather nice. She will not be in until twelve. Rang Jakob's mobile which, as it has been every time I have rung it since Oxford, was on answerphone mode. I said, 'Ruaighry is on his way up to the cottage. I think he may be violent. Please be careful!'

## 1 a.m.

Lucy still here.

Estelle got back about an hour ago. To my horror she had Surinder and Stella Badyass with her. Their behaviour was flagrantly lesbian. All three of them strode about the kitchen mannishly, behaving very like Mary Hopkinson (Cambourne Girls' School, Wimbledon, 1960–67) in her school production of *Murder in the Cathedral*, in which she played Thomas à Beckett. There was a great deal of placing of hands on hips with arms akimbo and once, I am almost sure, Badyass slapped Estelle on the back. When I said, 'May I share the joke?' they all subsided in giggles.

It occurs to me that the only reason Surinder ever expressed an interest in me was so that she could penetrate Craftgirls and link up with other lesbians. I have a good mind to tell Mr Badyass, although he is probably the kind of unworldly creature who thinks a muff dive is an incompetent method of getting into a swimming-pool. When they had gone I told Estelle about Ruarighy. She snapped, 'Why didn't you tell me this earlier? He could be lying dead on some railway line!' She suggested we get in the car straight away. At one point I thought she was going to insist we drove parallel to the Great North Western Railway in the hopes of catching a glimpse of our son. I said, 'Estelle – he is twenty-one years old! He is perfectly capable of taking a train up to Cumbria to try and kill his brother!' This, I realized, was not a tactful thing to say. 'Why are you so stupid?' said Estelle. 'Why do you walk around like an ostrich with your head in the sand?' 'Ostriches,' I said, 'do not walk around with their heads in the sand. They put them in the sand and then stay there. If they tried to walk around they would fall over or bump into things!' This remark seemed to make her completely hysterical. She then phoned Jakob and – as she always seems to manage to do – was connected to the man himself. I heard her say, 'If he becomes violent or attacks you, just roll over! You hear me? Just roll over!' I was not allowed to talk to him.

After this she seemed calmer. She started to talk to Lucy and, after a brief chat, was embracing her warmly. She suggested she stayed the night. Once I would not have paid much attention to this but I now see it as an extremely sinister move. I asked if she would like to call her parents and she said, 'They don't really notice if I'm there or not!' I do not think she meant they are partially sighted or neglectful. Perhaps they are simply absent-minded. She said she would love to stay over. Edwin said, 'I only have a few more days of school. Why don't all four of us go up to the Lake District and knock their stupid heads together?' He didn't say whose heads he meant but he seemed, as he often is, quite excited by his own notion. 'I think that is an extremely good idea,' he went on. 'I am at an impasse in my songwriting and the landscape may inspire me!'

## March 23rd. 11 a.m.

*Jakob and Laura in Lake District. Lucy in Ruarighy's bed. Ruarighy in Glasgow. Edwin 'trying to find crampons'. Estelle in Mafeking Road, shouting. Me in study.*

Ruarighy got on the wrong train and spent the night in Glasgow. He rang to tell us this but only got the machine. He did not say where he had spent the night. He sounded, I thought, potentially dangerous. Have not told Estelle he called.

Estelle packing car. I packed it at nine thirty but my packing is not good enough. She has taken everything out and is putting it back in a different order. I can see her from my study window. I asked her last night, straight out, when we had last had sex and she refused to tell me on the grounds that it might incriminate her. I think it may be even longer ago than I first suspected. Perhaps we have not done it for a year.

Perhaps we have not done it for two years! I am bringing the Lovejuice with me!

Lucy is amazingly well informed about *General Practice*! She can remember the electrocution of my wife's mother and the day I misdiagnosed legionnaires's disease while on a family holiday in Malaga. She even notices the odd inconsistency – most notably my saying, 'But I am bald, Jimbo! As bald as an egg!' in 1989 and then, in the autumn of 1993, remarking to Pilfrey, 'I must have my hair trimmed, Pilfers! It's getting in my eyes!'

Edwin and I have packed our walking boots. We both did a bit of walking practice round the garden. I fell over a bucket and hurt my knee.


## 2.30 p.m.

Writing this in a service station on the M1.

Edwin is eating something called a Megaburger. It is his third. When I asked him what was in it he gave an answer in a form that reminded me of an old Norse riddle: 'It's like chicken but it isn't chicken. It's beef-like but it is not beef. Neither is it fish of any kind, although if you didn't know you might think it was fish. Taste it yourself and you will find out what is in it.' I declined this offer. It is about the size of a ladies' handbag. Edwin has drenched it in ketchup.

Tried to slip some of the Lovejuice into Estelle's Diet Coke but failed. She is engaged in animated conversation with Lucy. Lucy seems to be some kind of scientist. I think I heard her say 'Quantum Theory' – although I suppose this could be the name of a rock group.

When she laughs, which she does a lot – she not only squeaks but claps her hands. I find this very engaging.


## 3 p.m.

Exciting development! Managed to get a small quantity of Lovejuice on to Estelle's Tastee Bun. She swallowed it almost immediately. I then made sure I kept in her line of vision for the next fifteen minutes. This wasn't always easy – at one point I walked backwards into a glass door – but I think I can definitely see signs of an awakening interest in me. Am writing this in the car, waiting for her to come back from making a telephone call to Craftgirls' Head Office.

Apparently the Japanese are going mad for the little dough men. Especially Mr Slippy Sloppy – the pot-bellied one with a big nose. Here comes Estelle. I must keep up as much eye contact with her as is compatible with road safety.

## 4.30 p.m.

Writing this on hard shoulder after near-collision with articulated lorry. Estelle is walking up and down outside to calm herself. I think I should abandon all experiments with Lovejuice until we get to the cottage. It has started to rain, as it always seems to do in this part of the world.

Lucy is outside with Estelle. I am getting more and more worried about Estelle's lesbian tendencies. She has put her arm round the young woman and occasionally she looks back in the direction of the car in a way that suggests she is talking about me. I do not think that what she is saying is necessarily favourable. All this to a girl who, it turns out, is a member of the *General Practice* fan club! Lucy asked me last night about how Norman Bartam was getting on. I had not the faintest idea of what she was talking about. It turned out that he was the manager of an off-licence who tried to get off with Esmond's wife in the summer of 1989.

A hideous thought occurs to me. Does Lovejuice have a delayed effect? Might I be facing a situation where my wife is shagging the best friend of the girl with whom both her sons are in love?

## March 24th. Slackbottom Cottage, Cumbria. 11 a.m. Raining.

*Estelle, Laura, Lucy, Edwin, Jakob and me all here. Reuairghy in Crewe.*

'Raining' doesn't really do justice to the thousands of different ways in which water has descended from the skies over the last few hours. It is never enough just to have good honest liquid falling in continuous straight lines – they like to vary the routine by sending it in cloud form, frozen or semi-frozen. Sometimes it comes in flailing tangles, like noodles, sometimes in large, well-spaced blobs and, from time to time, in consignments about a hundred metres square that make you feel as if someone had just emptied a swimming-pool on your head.

At the moment it is doing stealth-bombing rain. A brisk shower is going on at the bottom of the garden. Over by the dry-stone wall that separates us from the road a precision hail demonstration is in progress, while, on the patch of gorse that rises up sharply behind the house, it appears to be a bright spring day.

Riueirughy got on the wrong train from Glasgow. He rang Jakob's mobile to tell him he was taking the bus. 'I will have a lot of time,' he went on, 'to think how I am going to kill you while I am travelling in your direction!' Jakob seems very calm about this. Lucy said, 'He doesn't mean it really! He's very gentle!' Edwin said, 'He isn't when it comes to who is going to sit in the middle if we're all in the back!' I thought about Luxury Seafood Goujons and said nothing. Estelle gnawed her lower lip.

Everyone apart from me is still asleep. I have got up early and decided that I am going to give Estelle a mega-dose of Lovejuice. I am frightened that otherwise I may not be responsible for my actions. She too is asleep.

## 12.30 p.m.

A whole bottle of Lovejuice now emptied into a bowl of cornflakes on the breakfast table. I have placed it in front of Estelle's favourite chair, and am watching proceedings from a 'hide', i.e. a carefully placed chair in the next room.

I am still the only one up.

## 12.45 p.m.

Jakob has just come into the room. He has not seen me. But he has seen the cornflakes. Should I go in and tell him that –

Oh my God! He has just eaten the maximum recommended dose of Lovejuice! I have never seen anyone eat cornflakes so fast. All I can say is that if the next person to walk through the door is –

## 1 p.m.

The next person to walk through the door was Lucy. What have I done?

## 1.05 p.m.

Lucy and Jakob have just shared a near-fatal amount of Lovejuice. They consumed the bowl of cornflakes on a team basis. Their eye contact throughout was nearly one hundred per cent.

I am very worried indeed about this.

## 1.15 p.m.

Still in hide. Other people have come into kitchen, including Estelle, who, needless to say, did not go near the (by now empty) bowl of cornflakes. She is probably allergic to Lovejuice anyway. I am watching Lucy and Jakob carefully for signs of reaction. So far there has been none. If nothing happens between them I am writing to Wolverhampton for a refund.

What am I saying?

## 3 p.m.

Writing this in bedroom. I have removed my trousers in case Estelle should walk in but I do not think this is very likely. I hear someone at the door. Can this be Ruairehgy?

## 3.15 p.m.

It was. He did not look in any shape to offer violence, although he managed to glower at Jakob once or twice. Apparently he got on the wrong coach from Crewe and ended up in Wolverhampton. He became quite animated about geography and about the service available on the denationalized British train service. At one point he expressed interest in a job in the Virgin buffet. Then, after sneering at Jakob, he fell asleep in his chair.

Only two tubes of Lovejuice left. I am thinking of trying to get Estelle to swallow it while sleeping. Although, of course, this may choke her. I do not want her to die before I have had a chance to shag her, but cannot think of any other way of getting it down her throat.

## 3.45 p.m.

Back in bedroom. Have removed trousers once again in hopes Estelle should decide to have a sleep. In which case I could prime her with Lovejuice.

## 4 p.m.

Estelle did not materialize. I have suggested that we all go and look at Lord Leigh's Bottom (it is rumoured in the family that Estelle's sister chose this cottage purely because of its proximity to mountains and spots of natural beauty whose names are also rank *double entendres*) but no one seemed very keen. It is, as Jakob pointed out, 'only a rather dull hole in the ground from which you would not know your arse'. He is not, I think, very pleased that we have arrived. Edwin, however, agreed to come, on condition that he could bring his guitar. It is still raining. I told him he could bring Estelle's sister's microwave if he wanted.

Ruaierhgy had to be shaken for two minutes before he awoke. His first words were, 'Where are we?' Then he said, 'Is this the London train?' Then he went back to sleep. Edwin and I finally roused him by walking him round the room a few times.

## 6 p.m.

Am (I think) halfway up Old Man's Nob. We got to this via (I think) Mabel's Crack, Long and Narrow Hole and a near-vertical thing which Edwin swears is called Four Skins. As he said, when we were on the home straight, 'Why don't they just have done with it and call all these mountains Bum and Willy or Big Red Prick? They'd have a lot more people up here to see them! It would be good publicity!' He is a true child of the age.

He managed, however, to continue to play the guitar even when ploughing up scree at angles of about forty-five degrees. At one of the most tricky passages, just before the summit, he managed what I think was D minor diminished.

I do not think he knows I am writing a diary. I have told him this is a topographical report. He did, however, say one thing which I found alarming. As we were crossing an outcrop of rock known, locally, as The Piles, he said, in conversational tones – 'That Phallkrim is really good. I am going to end up with an absolutely colossal whanger if I go on at this rate. In fact I may need to send away for something to get my tackle down to manageable size!' I am not entirely sure he said this as there was a force eight gale blowing at the time, but if he did, I think I am going to have to have a serious talk with him. At one point I thought he said, 'Have you tried going down on an inflatable woman?' But I am almost sure I imagined this.

Have not yet even dared to use any of my supply. Could he have been stealing it and, by saying this, seeking to cover himself in some way? Or is this a cry for help?

If it is I do not think I should respond.


## 9 p.m.

How peaceful to be miles away from the tensions of the BBC! How nice not to have to worry about Howard Porda!

A violent argument broke out this evening over Monopoly. Edwin landed on Park Lane, which, like all the rest of the board, was owned by Jakob and, like all the rest of his properties, had two hotels on it. Edwin said he refused to play. He went on to say that he was a socialist and that 'everyone should be equal'. Jakob said, 'People are born equal until they play Monopoly!' – at which he gave Lucy what looked like a leer. I am very worried that the Lovejuice is having an effect on him. Edwin then said that no one should stay in hotels, and got up to leave the room. Lucy, who didn't seem to enjoy Jakob charming her, got up and followed him out. To my consternation, Jakob got up and followed her. Laura said, 'What's got into him?' I did not like to give her the correct and bitterly relevant answer – 'a proprietary brand of erotic stimulant which has caused him to fall in love with your best friend'.

Reiuerhy, Laura, Estelle and I were left alone. Laura announced that she was going to bed. Reirghriuy said he, too, was going to bed. He added that he wished he was going with Laura. Laura said, 'Why can't you give me more space? What are you and Jakob playing at? Have you set him up to come on to Lucy?' Reuairy replied, 'My brother is sex mad. He isn't really interested in you as a person!' Then Laura left. After a long silence Rueighry said, 'I was going to kill Jakob!' Estelle said, 'Can't it wait until tomorrow?' Rueighry said he was going to bed and that, at least here, he hoped I was not going to try and police the fridge. I was left alone with the Policy, Design and Marketing Executive of Craftgirls UK. Tomorrow I am going to slip a whole tube of Lovejuice into her sandwiches. This time there are going to be no mistakes. By this time tomorrow I am going to be wheeling her round the bedroom floor – her forward progress ensured only by her hands and the propulsive force of my genitals.

## March 26th. 11.45 p.m. Raining.

*Everyone in Lake District. If this rain continues we may be stranded here.*

I miss my study. I am peering out of the blackness that crowds in at the window of the spare bedroom (where I am sleeping tonight) as if hoping for a spectral glimpse of either Porker, Wickett or their local Cumbrian equivalents. I can see nothing, not even a sheep.

I have virtually no Lovejuice left. I smeared a great deal of the South American herb on to a cheese roll which I then carefully placed in Estelle's rucksack. Then all seven of us got in the car and drove a few miles away from the cottage, to climb a hill called, simply, Harrison. It is nothing spectacular but at least, as Edwin said, it is not called Pubes.

Estelle does not like walking. She likes the *idea* of it. She can often be heard to announce that she is, in the very near future, going to be going for a walk. Sometimes she comes back claiming that she has been on one, but it is some time since an independent observer has been able to confirm that she put one foot in front of the other for any longer than it takes to get from our front door to her car.

For the first few miles everyone kept vaguely together, although I could see that Jakob kept trying to get close to Lucy, which did not seem to please her. She is probably the fastest walker in the group. Ruarighy attempted to pull off the same trick with Laura, who, every time he got within striking distance of her broke away and tried to catch up with Jakob who, in turn, put on speed in order to try to catch up with Lucy, which, in turn, only made her go faster. By the time we reached a thousand feet we were all running like demented SAS men out on a training mission.

I said – at about altitude five hundred feet – 'Would you like a sandwich, Estelle?' She gave me an odd look. 'Why should I want a sandwich?' she said, accusingly. 'Are you trying to make me fat?' She has a paranoid fear that people – often quite innocent bystanders – are trying to make her put on weight. 'Of course not my sweetness!' I said. 'I just thought you looked a little . . . peaky. And a sandwich might perk you up!' She looked at me even more suspiciously. 'What's in the sandwich?' she said. 'Nails? Strychnine?' 'Tasty cheese!' I said, quickly. 'Crisp, crunchy Jarlsberg from Norway on a bed of freshly washed lettuce with a smidgeon of low-calorie mayonnaise, enclosed in a wholemeal bun!'

I got it out and waved it around in front of her. 'Mmm!' I said. Estelle grabbed it from me and held it aloft. 'Who wants a sandwich?' she cried. 'Who fancies some *delicious crisp, crunchy Jarlsberg from Norway on a bed of freshly washed lettuce with a smidgeon of low-calorie mayonnaise, enclosed in a wholemeal bun!*'

For one hideous moment I thought Jakob was going to grab it off her and wolf it down while gazing into his mother's eyes. Things are bad enough as it is without having people round here wanting to shag their own parents. In fact it was Ruairghy who got there first and, before I could stop him, commenced munching what is probably the largest dose of a love potion ever administered in the British Isles. For a brief, and horrendous, moment I found myself in his line of vision. I threw myself to the ground in a panic.

Ruarighy chomped through about six pounds and twenty-eight pee's worth of sexual stimulant. And as he did this, Lucy moved across the rough moorland grass until she was directly in his line of vision. For the next few minutes, from a distance of not more than three or four yards, she gazed straight into his eyes as if she had been primed to do so by Eros himself. I think she finds Ruairghy eating a turn-on. Which must be one of the best guarantees of a marriage I can think of.

As he was chewing the last of the cheese, she said, in tremulous tones, 'Look . . . I know what you think about me and if you think I am going to spend the rest of my life worrying about it you have another think coming.' Ruarighy didn't reply. 'That time . . .' she went on, her eyes moist with unshed tears, 'at Chessington World of Adventures I thought you meant the things you said, but I can see now you only said them to get me to . . . you know . . .' I was just beginning to wonder what *had* gone on at Chessington World of Adventures when Ruairghy began to tremble violently. 'I am going to get over you, Rory Slippery!' she said, 'I am going to go out and get a life and I just want you to know that I don't think you are clever or funny or nice – I think you are *pathetic*!'

This, of course, is just what your average bloke needs in order to get him in line and down on one knee with the bunch of red roses. We love being told what worms we are. If she had tried it a little earlier it might well have worked, even without the help of a dose of Lovejuice that was probably large enough to get an elephant going.

As it was, of course, its effect was electric.

Not that Lucy was aware of the fact. The tragic thing about people in love is that they say things that they think they mean. In fact being in love probably means simply that you are stupid enough to believe the things you say. She thought she was 'getting over' Ruairghy, although it was blatantly clear from looking at her that she was as far from that position as Juliet was from thinking that Romeo had arrived to mend the balcony.

As she turned to walk away from him, Ruairghy said, 'I don't know what Jakob thinks he's playing at. Actually, Lucy, I think I still feel it for you. More than he does anyway.' Lucy gave a very quick, almost undetectable, glance over at Laura and Jakob and her mouth shut like a steel trap. 'Oh,' she said, 'do you indeed? You and your brother both, eh?' Jakob started to say something but Lucy wouldn't let him finish. 'Or are you in this too, Laura?' she squeaked. 'Is this something you've cooked up between the three of you? Is it "let's have a laugh at good old Lucy" time? Because she's short and fat and good at science. Is that it?'

I was beginning to wonder whether it wasn't time I came out publicly and let everyone know that they were under the influence of a drug that, as far as I could see, made Spanish Fly look like Ribena. Unfortunately I was not/am not sure whether administering love drugs to people without telling them is something that can lead to a lengthy prison sentence. Instead I said, 'I don't think you're fat!' Lucy glared at me. I must have said it wrong. I certainly always say it wrong when I say it to Estelle. It is the kind of thing that is very hard to say to women convincingly.

Are there side-effects of Lovejuice? Is everyone going to start keeling over with stomach cramps? Will the only effect of trying to get my wife to shag me be that I have murdered my sons?

'It isn't that,' said Ruairghy, 'but I've been thinking, you see, and . . .' This only had the effect of making Lucy even more angry. 'I know what you think of me!' she said, marching ahead of us towards what looked like a large issue of mist, 'I know I'm a bit of a joke and just because your brother decides to pretend he wants something you have to –' 'No, no, no,' said Ruairghy, 'I think you're a very attractive and nice woman and I suppose the sight of Jakob trying to –' The Lovejuice was now clearly working through his system. It was, I thought, eating its way through the Boerg gland even as we watched. As Lucy, still unconvinced, stormed off across the heather, I wondered whether Estelle had had her Boerg gland removed. Is it something, I asked myself, that happens to women at the menopause? Biting down an urge to discuss the menopause I set off after Lucy, and everyone else followed. It started to rain heavily. Edwin, who had brought his guitar and was wearing only a T-shirt seemed quite unfazed by all this.

For the rest of the day we all blundered around, up, down and all over Harrison. We explored its crevices and gulleys, immersed ourselves in its bogs and, once or twice, very nearly fell off its extremities. I don't think we got to its top, although we saw a very great deal of its bottom, and, for most of the day we were so close up to it that we didn't really ever perceive it as any more than an agglomeration of holes, weather-beaten stone and grass as tough as the hair on an old wig. It was, I thought, as bits of the landscape started to become recognizable again, a bit like my relationship with Estelle. We would not really have any idea of what it was like until we and Harrison were far enough away from each other to take a slightly longer view.

All the time, Lucy stayed well out ahead of all of us, not speaking to Ruairghy or Jakob, who pattered after her through the mist, like desperate dogs. Laura chased them, and Estelle and I, heads down, sweated to keep pace. Eventually Edwin strode out ahead of all of us, occasionally shouting out, 'I remember this bit from a previous life!' He played the chord of E major until we reached about two thousand feet, when he switched to D sharp minor with an added seventh. He was adding a ninth to this chord when he very nearly walked over a cliff. As we started our descent he began to sing. I don't remember the words exactly but I think they began –

Why do you walk over Harrison's Bottom?
Why do you drown in its streams of pain?
Where is your map and where is your shelter?
Where is your four weeks' supply of cocaine?

He never seemed to lose breath once in all this performance, and as we hit the beck that leads you down off the mountain he acquired quite a large and enthusiastic following of sheep. We had to chase them away when we got to the car and Edwin said, 'It's just like Knebworth!'

When, finally, we arrived back at Slackbottom Cottage, Lucy locked herself in her bedroom and Ruaurighy and Jakob started to shout at her through the door. Then Laura started to shout at them. That was when Estelle and I retired to the kitchen. We poured ourselves large gin and tonics. I said, 'This is great! So now they're both hitting on Lucy! What have we raised here?' Estelle glared at me. 'Sex maniacs!' she said. 'I wonder where they get that from!' Then she added, 'I must go upstairs. I must put some time in with those poor girls!'

*Put some time in with the girls, eh?*

Somehow this was the last straw. I have not had an easy year. I may well be run over by a lorry, forced to drink poison or to place my head in a gas oven, at any moment. I am a mere sixty or seventy days away from being fifty. As far as I can make out I have not had sex since January 6th and, very possibly, not for a long time before that either. I had had to spend the day watching my children argue about which women they wished to shag – rather in the manner in which they once discussed whose turn it was to pretend to be Darth Vader. And now, it appeared, my wife was going to dash upstairs for a bit of lesbianism.

All I could think about was trying to get some Lovejuice down her. I went over to her glass, emptied the last of my supply into her gin and was rewarded by the sight of her lifting the glass and draining it in one gulp, with her eyes on my face.

She was definitely flushed. Her eyes were definitely brighter. Her neck seemed pleasantly mottled. Her hair was getting as close to shiny as it ever does. It was time to move in. I stepped towards her. She did not move away. Her lips parted ever so slightly. Now, I thought, now! The Boerg gland was soaking up Aurea Genifera or whatever it was called and passing signals out to the skin, the fingers, the toes and other parts of her anatomy which I did not, for the moment, even dare to think about.

I grabbed a buttock in each hand and started to squeeze it vigorously, peering at her upper body as I did so. It was possible, I reasoned, that the more one got the body sloshing about, the more easily the Lovejuice would insinuate itself into bits of her to which, for an unspecified amount of time, I do not appear to have had access. It must be well past the throat by now. It was probably seeping into the stomach, preparing to be pumped back into the system and arousing her to an unbearable pitch of desire. I started to roll her around a bit in order to make sure she was fully saturated.

As I did so she drew back her right arm and punched me full in the face. 'You pig!' she said, 'You horrible, slippery pig! I hope they do run you over with a lorry! I hope they pour liquid lava up your arse! I hope you never work again except as a voice-over insect! No wonder your boys don't know how to treat women! What kind of father have you been to them? What kind of role model are you? All you do is moan and fart and drink lager! I am no longer part of your agenda! I want a divorce!'

With which she left the room.

I do not think she has a Boerg gland. Or else, possibly, she needs a larger dose. Maybe middle-aged women need industrial-strength Lovejuice to get them going. Either that or a blow over the head with a baseball bat is the only thing that will get me laid before June 24th. Assuming I ever get that far.

Tonight I sleep alone. I am in deep, deep despair. I look out at the blackness of the night and, once again, I call on Porker and Wickett, my only friends. I come, my friends! Down the dark tunnel of middle age! I come to join you!


## March 27th. 10 a.m.

*Everyone still here.*

Lucy announced her intention of going home this morning.

I said I would run her to the station. She said, 'There's a station?' I do not think she has enjoyed this trip. I do not think she wishes to be a part of our family. I can't say I blame her. I'm not sure I want to be a part of our family.

Estelle (who ate half a pound of turnips for breakfast) sat, totally silent, at the table, glaring at the floor. Edwin, Laura and Ruarighy did not appear. I did not ask where everyone slept, but as far as I can tell no one slept with anyone else, since there are rugs and pillows all over the house.

I am not sure how long any of us wants to stay. Estelle and I will presumably have to go back to Mafeking Road to work out the divorce arrangements but after that the future is uncertain. I am pretty sure that I want Edwin although I am not sure that he will want me. If it comes to a legal battle I think Estelle's lesbianism will count against her – although, of course, I have, as yet, no hard evidence of this.

I have decided to write away to Wolverhampton for other sex products.

## 1 p.m.

Everyone still here in even worse temper than earlier. When Lucy said she was going, both Jakob and Rurarighhy said they would come with her. Jakob said to Rurughy, 'What's your problem?' and Ruaughry said to Jakob, 'What's yours?' I thought at one point they were going to come to blows.

Lucy does have very beautiful, lively black eyes.

Laura and Lucy have hardly spoken all morning. At about 11.30, Laura said, 'Lucy was always very competitive about men. Which I am not!' Lucy rolled her eyes and squeaked a lot at this. At around twelve she announced that she wanted to stay 'for a couple more days! Till the rain stops!' When she said this Ruairghy and Jakob both said they would stay. Jakob said he would 'show her around a few peaks' – at which Laura burst into tears. Lucy said, 'What's got into you?' Laura said, 'I think you have a very good idea!' Lucy said, 'I don't actually, Laura Proek – why don't you tell me if you're so sure!' At which Laura said, 'If you don't know, then I'm not telling you, although I think it's pretty obvious!' 'Obvious!' replied Lucy and the two of them continued in this vein for about an hour. It is clear that all this goes back to when they were at school together. They do make a rather well-contrasted couple – one short, plump and dark, the other tall, blond and skinny.

What Lucy doesn't realize of course is that the rain will not stop until July. My game plan at the moment is to take the lot of them up Harrison's Bottom and lose them there.


## 3 p.m.

Still no decision on what we are doing. Estelle is having whispered conversations with Lucy and Laura and Rouaighry and Jakob are muttering to each other like a couple of red deer trying out their antlers.

I am writing this in the kitchen staring out at a wall of rain as it moves in off the moor above the cottage. I hate the English countryside. I hate the fact that I have spent so much of life in cottages in the middle of it, with nothing but a few board games and some people I want to kill. I would rather be in Airport Boulevard, Los Angeles. Or the bus station in Johannesburg. Or – God help me – in studio 6 at Broadcasting House, Portland Place, London.

I am going next door. I am going to talk, passionately, of how I really feel. Of what it is like when you are fifty (or at least forty-nine and nine twelfths) and a man, and your wife does not love you and is a lesbian, and your children are having sex with girls and not even the right girls and you are about to have a nervous breakdown and/or be run over by a lorry because someone up there doesn't like you. I am going to talk, openly, of what goes on between Estelle and me. I am going to discuss our sex life. I am going to tell the truth.


## 6.30 p.m. Happy Eater. A1(M).

We are on our way home.

I have been put on a table by myself.

Everyone else is at another table. They are not talking to each other but at least they are allowed to eat together.

My speech was not a success – especially the bit about my sex life. I think I brought Surinder into it for some reason, which provoked Estelle into gales of lesbian laughter. In which, to my horror, Lucy and Laura joined. I am clearly a laughing-stock.

I have been coming on to a lesbian. I know no greater shame. No wonder I am such a flop with women. No wonder my acting range is limited to sound-only interpretations of the smaller invertebrates.

I kept saying, 'We have shared a bed for twenty-five years!' and Jakob kept shaking his head over the table and muttering, 'No, no, you haven't!' I spoke of my hopes for the future. I spoke of my career and Edwin said, 'What career?' He managed, as usual, to make this sound curiously inoffensive. I spoke also of the divorce. Estelle became quite animated. 'You want a divorce, do you?' I said. She seemed to have forgotten she wanted a divorce. 'Well,' I said, 'just wait! Just wait!' 'Wait for what?' she replied. I started to wag my finger at her. 'I want a divorce too! I am starting proceedings,' I said, 'I am contacting a lawyer.' 'Which lawyer?' she said. I named a lawyer, who turned out to be dead. I then said I would get one through the Yellow Pages. 'If you don't like it,' said Estelle, 'you can move out!' 'Oh no you don't!' I said. Jakob raised his elegantly floppy hair from off the table and looked me straight in the eye. 'She wants the CD player!' he said. 'She does,' I said, 'but she is not getting it! You can move out!' I screamed at Estelle.

Estelle said she didn't want to move out. She hadn't time, she said. She added, 'You could camp at the BBC. As you and Pilfrey have been doing for years, darling!' At this I started to make a noise resembling the sound of a wild animal being skinned alive.

This about sums it up really. We may not want to shag each other. We may bore each other rigid. We each may find the other physically repulsive, dull or self-obsessed. But we want to live in the same house. This seems to sum up twenty-five years of marriage.


## 1 a.m. Mafeking Road.

I had to sit in the back all the way home. I was, however, between Lucy and Laura, which I found quite exciting. There is something pleasantly pneumatic about women and cars. Estelle drove. It rained all the way back. Serve her right.

The next two months are going to be the toughest of my life. If I can get to the other side of them I think I will try and get early retirement and go and live in a small cottage by myself. So long as it isn't in the Lake District I will be fine.

Edwin can come if he's nice to me. As can Bozz, Scagg, Snozzer, etc. But not Lulu. We are not having women.


## March 28th. 10.30 a.m.

*Estelle at lesbian club (probably). Jakob and Ruairgehry with Lucy (maybe). Edwin and I here.*

Lucy left early this morning. Jakob and Ruaighry both said they would give her a lift. They almost came to blows over who should be accorded this privilege. In the end they both drove her off to wherever she lives. Laura, who had been in tears during all of this, was 'comforted' by Estelle and, in her turn, driven off to a secret lesbian destination.

Edwin came into my study and asked if he could have twenty quid 'for guitar strings'. I said he could have fifty if he wanted it. I am desperate to curry favour with him as he is the only one in the family who seems to like me and I am hoping to form the nucleus of a bloc. The trouble is, of course, he may be playing this game with Estelle, Jakob, Ruairghy, etc. Knowing him, he almost certainly is.

I was able to tell him that, in the batch of post that arrived while we were away, was a letter from someone called Gavin Sweep of the Royal Court who said that he had read *Muthafuckas* and been 'deeply moved' by it. I gave Edwin the letter, which read –

Dear Wesley Jones,
    This is to let you know that there is enormous interest here at the Court in *Muthafuckas*. It has already been read by myself, Tristram Leary and Kurt Vogel, our literary manager, and is now being read by the catering department.
    You write very powerfully about your dilemma and your passion for the black experience and it seems to me that we may well want to present this play at the Theatre Upstairs in the near future.
    One question – as a young black British man, why do you feel the need to set your work in the Bronx? The roots of

its inspiration – in black politics here – are crystal-
clear. Leslie 'Kwa Zulu' Jones, who is one of our
directors here, felt you should have declared yourself
and your material more openly!

   Do get in touch. Wimbledon must seem like the other
side of the moon to a young black man like you, searching
for his identity! The last time I was there it was full of
snotty boutiques and the fag end of the English middle
class . . .

Regards,
Gavin Sweep


'Who,' said Edwin, 'is Wesley Jones?' I told him that I had used this pseudonym in my carefully constructed covering letter that had accompanied the script. He seemed to understand this perfectly. 'They're not going to do a play by some middle-class snot in Wimbledon, right?' he said. 'Right!' I said. 'Especially if it's about black people and stuff, right?' 'Right!' I said.

'Did you actually say you were black?' said Edwin. 'No,' I said, 'the name was enough. That and the fact that I wrote the letter on a torn-off piece of exercise-book notepaper.' Edwin seemed quite pleased by this deception but said he wanted to 'set me right on a few legal points'. He went on to say that Bozz, Scagg and Snozzer had already worked out the exact status of their shared rights in the work (for UK only) but that he, Edwin, was prepared to negotiate for a one-off buy-out (theatrical) which would give the Royal Court limited rights 'on an option basis'. 'You will have to deal with me separately!' he went on. When I said I didn't realize he had written it, he said the concept was his and that until the concept rights deal was done I could not talk to anyone.

I think he was joking but I am not sure.

He went off to see Lulu after this. I had thought he had mock GCSEs. When I said this to him he said, 'I do not mock GCSEs. I take them extremely seriously.' I think we are losing control of him.

And now to play my messages.

## 12 noon.

There were twenty-three of them, nine from my mother, all of which, as far as I could tell, had been placed on the same morning. My mother is ninety and lives in Croydon. She always insists on talking to the machine as if it were not one. Which gives her monologues an eery, late-night-horror-film quality. 'Hullo, Paul! Are you there?' (*Silence.*) 'Paul, is that you; Paul, are you there?' (*Silence.*) 'Paul, it's me here; Paul, are you there by any chance, Paul?' (*Long, sinister silence.*) 'Paul, it's me; I wondered if you were there?' (*Immensely long and sinister silence at the end of which is even more sinister click as she signs off in a manner suggesting she is alone in the room with an armed man.*)

Three were from Laura Proek's father. All threatened legal action if we did not tell him where his daughter was. Once his wife made a guest appearance and cried, briefly. I imagine she is going to cry even more when she hears that Ro-Ree is no longer going to be around to help mend the Teasmade – a detail from which I derive some grim satisfaction.

One from Gustave. I have been offered the chance of the part of a cockroach in a low-budget animated film. Apparently my voice is perfect for the part. I rang Gustave back immediately and told him I would do it. When he asked if I wanted to see the script I said, 'Not until the morning of the recording.' Gustave said, 'It looks good if you sound a bit involved.' I told him to send it to me but to make sure that they knew that I was very excited about playing another insect. 'So you should be!' said Gustave, and rang off.

There is life after *General Practice*. If they do not resolve the Pennebaker question soon I am going to tell them that I want to go while I am still hot. I will not tell them about the cockroach but will mention that there is other work coming up. I am going to make one more sustained effort to get in touch with Porda.

If only I knew what role Porda has in all this. Today I strongly suspect it is Ashley Ramp who is my enemy. He knows I know what I know about the snail programme.

All the other messages, apart from one from Scagg (who revealed he told a cheese-counter customer that *fromage de chèvre* was made 'from the sperm of goats'), were for Estelle and most concerned Craftgirls business.

One from Stella Badyass concerned me greatly. She sounded drunk and she said, 'Estelle, my darling, it's Stella here . . . I've had a . . . a . . . a bottle of wine . . .' (*Long silence. Bar effects.*) 'I don't want you to tell Surinder about me . . . it isn't right . . . it doesn't even seem right calling her Surinder when she's a . . . she's a . . .' (*More long silence. More bar effects.*) 'What is she, Estelle? What has she become? Is it my fault? When he was born I . . . oh my God, Estelle, I can't believe I am saying this . . .' (*Amazingly long silence. Bar effects. Distant ambulance siren. Muted sobbing from Badyass.*) 'Estelle, are you there? . . . Are you there, Estelle? . . . Estelle, are you there for me? Do you love me, Estelle? . . . Estelle, you mustn't tell Surinder about me no one must know she is . . . she is Surinder now!' (*Massive sobbing from Badyass, with tutti of sirens, bar effects and traffic atmos. End message.*)

What does this mean? Is her name not really Surinder? What is her game? And is Estelle really mixed up in it? Isn't this final proof positive that she, my wife and probably the whole of Craftgirls UK are fully paid-up disciples of Sappho?

The final message was from Steve Witchett, the Writer Who Never Expresses an Opinion. He said, 'Hi! I suppose this machine will record what I have to say but if it doesn't I will try to get it through to you in some other form. I may send a fax or I may write a letter or I may come round and see you personally. I'm not saying I will do any of these things but it's possible that I might. I just wanted to pass on the news that you may have heard already while you've been away if you've been away. You may not have been, of course – I may have been misinformed. I can't think of any other way to put this and Surinder and Colin and Karl and Porda obviously have their own agendas and I do not know which, if any, of them, is telling the truth or what that truth might be. But . . . (*Long pause; muffled sob*) the show may be off the air by next week if something is not done! (*Howls of grief, noise of Witchett's friend, Nigel, in background, comforting him. Renewed sobbing.*) Goodbye Paul!'

In spite of his judicious use of the word 'may' this is the nearest to expressing an opinion Witchett has ever come. I must go in at once.

## 5 p.m. The George Bar.

It was in this very spot that I once met a man who had met a man who said he had worked with Louis MacNeice. During the course of the evening I met another man who claimed to have worked with a man who had worked with Dylan Thomas. Later in the evening I met three people who claimed to be Dylan Thomas, all of whom were paralytically drunk.

The great days of radio. How long would any of them last nowadays, I wonder? When the place is run by accountants who wouldn't know a poem by Dylan Thomas if it leaped out at them from a dark alley and hit them over the head.

I like to think they are with me in spirit. I like to think that, if they were to come back and stand with me, here in the bar, they would say, 'We are with you, Paul Slippery! We are fighting with you! This is what happened when they tried to demolish the Third Programme! We stand behind you and *General Practice* and integrity in public-service broadcasting!'

I hope this is what they would say. I have to say I am not entirely sure. It is possible that Dylan Thomas would simply honk all over my shoes and tell me that *General Practice* was about as dull as Swansea station at 3 a.m. on a Sunday morning and that all radio in the Britain of the 1990s was brainless rubbish. They did away with the Third Programme, didn't they? They did away with *Children's Hour*, didn't they? Whatever happened to the threepenny bit?

There is no such thing as integrity in public-service broadcasting any more anyway. A bloke Surinder met in the TV Centre, from Outside Broadcasts, said that they spend their time working for Sky Television. I am not quite sure how a publicly funded organization works out the ethics of this, but as nobody (including me) gives a stuff about ethics any more, I suppose we shall just have to put up with it.

All I care about is trying to keep Esmond Pennebaker alive. They can flog the whole thing (including world rights in *Muffin the Mule*) to the Japanese for all I care, so long as the doings of the Ashbourne Hill Practice are still allowed to be beamed out to a grateful nation. I cannot get hold of anyone, however. There is no script for next Tuesday's recording. Karl, Cross and Surinder have disappeared off the face of the earth.

I have pieced together the elements of the crisis. Apparently they played the programme to a new focus group because the Core Directorate Policy Unit (is Porda playing a double game?) had said that the first focus group was 'an unreliable sample'. It did include two schizophrenics who both really liked the show. The new focus group all said they thought that *General Practice* had run its course. Esmond was 'trying to be trendy and failing'. The only character they seemed to like was Ronnie Pilfrey – one woman burst into tears when she was told about his Moeran's disease. All of them, when asked how they would like the series to develop said they would like it to turn into something else. Four people said they wanted to see 'more about fishermen' and every single one of them complained about 'the amount of sex in the programme'. As there is no sex in the programme I can only assume they want lashings of sex.

The upshot of all this is that Cross has sent out a memo asking for ideas to replace *General Practice*. In the interim it has been decided that I should die. The favourite option at the moment seems for me to be shot by a man whom I wrongly diagnosed back in 1982. The thinking is for him to burst into the surgery with a shotgun and wipe out several of the principal characters, including Clare, the receptionist, Jimbo, the practice manager, Suzie Bee, the perky thirty-year-old ear, nose and throat wannabe and Dirk, my long-time buddy and senior partner.

But no one can find Surinder. I am going in to Broadcasting House and I am going to confront Porda face to face. If necessary I will go to his house and break down the door. If he has a door.

## 10 p.m. Mafeking Road.

This is all getting very mysterious.

I went up to Porda's office at around six thirty. Both secretaries had gone. But I put my ear to the door of the inner sanctum (which has a locked door giving on to the corridor) and heard someone moving around inside. I somehow knew that it was Porda.

I ducked into an office a little further down and waited.

After a while I heard footsteps. He came out into the corridor and clattered off towards the lifts. When I was sure it was safe to do so, I slipped out and followed him. He didn't see me. He walked towards the fire-escape stairs and, as soon as he was through the doors, I ran after him.

I got a look at him from about three floors up. He was wearing the same brown trilby hat and the same all-encompassing mac. He looked like some sinister figure from a forties movie and, for the first time, I felt almost scared. It occurred to me that there might be something corrupt or actually criminal going on between him and Cross and Karl. The upper echelons of the BBC are, after all, simply awash with public money. I think the licence fee runs into a revenue of billions. I don't think I have ever, in all the glossy pamphlets they churn out, seen a simple and straightforward explanation of where it all goes. Perhaps, unknowing, I had stumbled into some serious scandal involving lesbians, the licence fee, drug money and *General Practice*. I could not yet quite see how *General Practice* fitted in to all this but I was fairly sure that it was involved in some way.

I still think this may be possible. The dialogue of a typical episode is often so far away from anything one would recognize as English that it may well be some form of coded signal to an offshore Mafia boat or an elaborate series of cyphered instructions to some hostile foreign power.

I was close behind Porda when he came out into Reception. I don't know whether he was aware that he was being followed but, just as he came through the swing doors, he looked behind him. The scarf was still high up on his face and he still wore those sinister dark glasses. I dodged behind a pillar (of which there are a surprising number in the Reception of Broadcasting House) but, when he reached the pavement he started to run. I ran after him.

It was raining outside – a thin drizzle, and there were large black limousines of the kind that are used to ferry senior BBC executives to important lunches where they discuss how many people they are going to fire.

I thought Porda was going to get into one of these cars. If he had done that I would have lost him. Instead, still moving at a run, he dashed off across towards the Langham and turned up Portland Place, heading towards Regent's Park. He was clearly a lot fitter than me. But I was determined not to let him go. I ran up the other side of the road – the Broadcasting House side – and, as he turned left into the road that runs into Wimpole Street I saw him turn once more and look over his shoulder.

The scarf was flung out behind him and you still couldn't see his face.

I had the idea – I don't know why I had it – that this was some very famous or well-known person. I started across the road and made one more determined effort to draw abreast of him. That was when I saw the car. I didn't recognize it at first. All I saw was a blue VW Golf pull out from a parking space about fifty yards down the road and position itself in the middle of the road. The rain was falling more heavily now and I, after more than a minute's running, was becoming uncomfortably aware of the pounding of blood in my ears and the dragging pain in my lungs. It was only when I saw the back of the driver of the car – a woman with long black hair, wearing a jumper as black as the dark around me – that I realized that Porda was about to get into Surinder's car. And then, just as I realized this, the girl at the wheel accelerated out into the street, gunned the engine and the car was gone.

I may have got all of this very wrong. It may be that Surinder is not a lesbian. It may be that she is having an affair with Howard Porda. I think, on balance, this is a good thing. It means that Esmond is still in with a chance. It is possible that the poor girl is sacrificing her virginity – one of the reasons she advanced to me for not letting me shag her – for the sake of the show. This scenario would suggest that Porda, outvoted on the Core Directorate Policy Unit by the scumbags Cross and Rhws Davies (who are only pretending to support me) and possibly wavering on the subject of my future, is now being heavily pressured by Surinder.

Go it, girl! Offer him your body! I am right there with you! Make sure you get the polaroids!

I don't know, though. I did rather fancy her. Am I simply part of her career plan? As she is a thirtysomething it is a safe bet that that is the case. Oh God!

The other possibility of course is that Surinder and Porda are teaming up to send us all to Scotland. I wish I knew who to trust. I wish I could tell the difference between a lesbian and a number nine bus. I wish I was not so old and short of breath and so unable to remember when I last shagged my wife. I wish someone would offer me a part that is not an off-screen insect.

Estelle still not home. Where can she be?

## 11.30 p.m.

Estelle still not home. Edwin and I went out for a Chinese meal. Edwin spent a lot of the time with his chopsticks up his nose or sticking them at right angles out of his ears. He drank three pints of lager and ate about £95 worth of food. Towards the end of the meal he said, 'I might give Lulu the elbow.' When I asked why he shrugged and said, 'Three months is a long time.' A little later he also revealed that they argued a lot. What can they find to argue about? Do not they live in Paradise?

Their existence certainly compares favourably with that led by the sixteen-year-old Paul Slippery in the year 1965. My memory of it is of trudging round Raynes Park with a boy called Morris and a list of parties to which I had not been invited. In order to get into these houses – all of which seemed larger, better run and lived in by happier and more interesting families than mine – I had various cryptic instructions such as, 'Say you're a friend of Joanna's!' or 'Peter Webstein said it was OK to let me in!' Normally Morris and I would be turned back down the garden path but if we did get in we usually ended up in the kitchen with half a can of lager and a boy called Hughes.

I told Edwin this and he said, 'You must have been really sad!'

When we got back we both worried, briefly, about where Estelle might be and then Edwin said, 'She's probably in a meeting!' He then went upstairs 'to set up a meeting of his own'.

## 1 a.m.

Estelle, Ruairghry and Jakob finally showed up. It took me some time to work out how they had all ended up in the same car, but it appears that Lucy lives one street away from Laura in Cheam. Estelle had seen the two of them hanging around after she had delivered Laura to Mr and Mrs Proek – with whom she now seems to be firm friends. 'She's been having electric-shock treatment!' she said of Laura's mother – as if this excused the woman's behaviour.

It also appears that Mrs Proek is on a modified form of the turnip diet – in which you are allowed to eat any root vegetable that is not green or yellow – and the two of them had had a long conversation about this. Unsurprisingly, everything turns out to be Mr Proek's fault. I was told –

in tones that suggested I was in some way responsible for this – that the forty-seven-year-old rat-catcher failed to satisfy Mrs Proek's sexual needs.

Ruairghy and Jakob snarled at each other for a while. Estelle is now snoring next door.


# April 3rd. 12 noon.

*Estelle at work. Edwin at school. Ruirghy and Jakob lurking.*

After two days of more or less continuous sleep, Ruairghy and Jakob finally surfaced the day before yesterday. I tried, as I have often done, to broach the subject of work with both of them. Ruairghry – as he always does on these occasions, asked me if there was a job 'about to come on the market' at *General Practice*. 'Yes,' I said, a little querulously, 'mine! Unless the surgery acquires a talking insect!'

Estelle said I was not to be defeatist. She said it was important to maintain dignity in front of the children. Then she went on to discuss Mr Slippy Sloppy – the pot-bellied dough man with a big nose. I think he looks rather like me. When I tried to suggest that that might be the secret of his success, Estelle gave a mirthless laugh. Just before she left she prodded my left palm with a fork. When I asked her why she had done this, she said, 'I know you like to have a little prick in your hand when I'm not here!'

The boys seemed to find this amusing. I shouted at them and told Jakob to go and get a job in Waitrose. He said, looking straight into my eyes and giving me some of the sincerity he doubtless uses on countless women, 'I really would like to get a temporary thing on the cold-meat counter! I think I might learn a lot.'

While I was waiting by the phone to find out whether I still have a job, Ruairghy came in and asked to borrow the Volvo. I said I would think about it. A little later Jakob came in and asked if he could borrow it. I told him that I would think about it. I thought about it.

I suspect they both want it so that they can go and see Lucy. Not the sort of thing either of them should do. Doing it together would be insane. I am going to say that neither of them can have it.

## 1.30 p.m.

They have gone off in the Volvo together. Perhaps they are going to take turns on her. Edwin – who is finally on holiday – did not surface until one o'clock. He says he is going to Snozzer's house with Scagg (who has been moved to the fish counter) and Bozz and Lulu. Then he is taking Lulu 'on to the Common'. When I asked him what he was going to do with her, Jakob said 'Shag!' Edwin said, 'Actually we talk. Then we shag.'

## 4 p.m.

A depressing afternoon. I did discover, however, that Sex Products of Wolverhampton have a home page on the Internet. I logged on to it and, after scrolling through about ten pages of frilly nighties and full-colour photos of their in-house leather boutique called Going for a Thong, I found no less than ten listed love potions. Lovejuice is bottom-of-the-range stuff. They also market Passion Pills, a 'discreetly gold-wrapped lozenge with a delicate nougat-based aroma', that, according to R.F.W. of Wimbledon (could this possibly be Porker?), set his wife 'wiggling and groaning in a way she had never done before in twenty years of marriage'. Working on the assumption – as I do with wine – that the most expensive is likely to be the best, I am drawn to Liquid Love, a 'fragrant blend of guava juice, mineral water and Borrereiro, a South American herb known to the Amazon Indians and valued by them for its astonishing ability to arouse'. What is it with South America? They did not include any testimonials from tribesmen.

But it sounds just the stuff for me. At £25 a 100 centilitre bottle, it has got to be a state-of-the-art, top-of-the-range substance. I bought two bottles and requested the 'Discreet Delivery' option.

The phone is going. Perhaps this is Gustave with news of a role for me. I will not complain even if it is only another insect.

## 4.30 p.m.

It was Lucy's Dad.

He sounded really nice. He is called Bert. He asked me to come over. 'The thing is,' he said, 'it's like . . . this thing with Lucy and . . . like . . .

your lads . . .' There was then an immense pause, during which, at the other end of the phone, I could hear sounds of inhalation. 'They're like . . .' 'Bothering her?' I said. 'No, no, no . . . not . . . well . . . they're like . . . *outside*!' he said. I said, 'I am really sorry about this!' and he said, 'It is cool . . . it is totally cool but . . . like . . . could you . . .' There was another immense pause and then he said, 'like . . . *come over*!'

I said I would be delighted to come over. It is getting increasingly hard to find people who want to see me at all, let alone individuals in urgent need of contact. I spent twenty minutes looking for the car keys before I realized that Ruairghy and Jakob have them, and the car.

I cursed for some moments and then called a cab.


## 8.30 p.m.

Bert's house is in a long, straggling suburban street. 'We're in East Cheam,' he had said on the phone, 'where Tony Hancock used to live!' All the houses seem to be slightly smaller than their garages. If the owners had not been able to afford a garage they had constructed lean-tos, hides or awnings to shield the most important member of the household – the car. Where they had not even been able to afford this the citizens of Drumnore Gardens had built little nests for them on the pavement.

Bert's was the only house in the street not to have a car. His front garden, I was pleased to observe, although only about five yards square, managed to evoke the word 'wilderness'. About the only design feature of the house was a huge stuffed gorilla, cunningly placed on the window-sill of the upstairs bedroom.

The Volvo was parked about a hundred yards down the road. I think I caught a glimpse of Jakob pacing up and down next to it but did not, at this stage, have the nerve to confront him. As I was taking the first of the two long strides that took me up the garden path the door opened and a small man in faded blue dungarees opened it.

At first I thought he was immensely old. This was partly due to the fact that his hair was snow white, partly due to the fact that he stooped as he walked but principally because his face had the confused, weather-beaten aspect of someone who has been stoned out of their brain for the last ten years. As if to confirm the accuracy of this diagnosis, in Bert's left hand was a joint about the size of a small umbrella. He waved it at the street in an amiable fashion.

This is presumably why he does not notice whether his daughter is there or not.

'Hi!' he said, peering at me like a tortoise. 'Hi!' I said. He waved the joint around some more. 'Lucy,' he said, 'is like . . . upstairs!' 'Right!' I said. Bert offered me the joint. I took it and inhaled deeply. I took one last look at East Cheam as an invisible hammer got to work on my medulla oblongata.

He took me into the front room. There were no chairs, only cushions and in the centre of the carpet, a large hubble-bubble with an elaborate series of hoses and pipes leading off it. One of these was being inhaled by a small, ferrety woman in what looked like a blond wig. She turned and smiled at me amiably. 'Betty!' she said.

Over by the window was a large tin bath in which was a small jungle of plants. They all had the same type of leaves. I have never actually seen a marijuana plant but I am fairly sure that this is what was in the bath. Most of the books on the shelves, as far as I could see, were about marijuana or marijuana-related subjects and on a low shelf to the left of the door was a row of neat glass bottles. Next to it was an official-looking sign that read 'PLEASE KEEP OFF THE GRASS'.

Bert handed me the joint and I inhaled manfully. 'The thing is,' said Bert, 'both of your boys are . . . like . . .' 'Right!' I said. 'Lucy is really confused,' said Bert, 'because they both seem to be . . . like chasing her . . . and before . . . like it was Laura had . . . like taken Rory and . . .' This sentence was too much for him. He shook his head slowly and sadly. Mrs Bert started to shake her head too. 'The thing is,' she said, 'we know the Proeks . . . quite well . . .' – here she gave Bert a short, sharp look, '. . . and . . .' 'Right!' I said.

At this point we all started to laugh. I said, 'Is this stuff OK to use in East Cheam?' Bert said, 'Anything is OK in East Cheam!' I handed the joint to Mrs Bert, who managed to draw on both it and the hubble-bubble at the same time. 'I work,' said Bert, indicating the sign, 'for the Council. So tell no one I nicked that!' I found myself wondering what his area of responsibility was. Parking? Housing Benefit? Whatever their field I couldn't help thinking that Bert would bring to it a kind of latitude and tolerance often not seen in minor civil servants. *Parking? Why not? Where do you wanner go? Benefit? Yeah — we got benefit! You want benefit? Have benefit!* 'I am, in fact, working with rats. I am in the same department as Laura's Dad!' said Bert. Mrs Bert grinned at me seraphically. 'But Bert *likes* rats!' she said. 'He doesn't want them to die!' 'Right!' I said. 'But that's not the way Norman sees it!' said Bert. 'Right!' I said.

Bert gripped me by the arm and stared into my eyes. 'What are we going to do about Lucy?' he said. 'What are we going to do about this . . . situation? Why can't the love be . . . you know . . . like . . . shared?' 'Right!' I said. At which point he handed me the joint. We had all been sucking on it like demented toddlers with a lollipop.

These were nice people. They hadn't wasted time on the usual social nonsense. No one had asked me whether I had had trouble getting there or whether the roadworks on the A3 were still there. No one had discussed the weather or asked me how things were at the office. We had got straight down to basics. Human feelings. Drugs.

I felt I could trust Mr and Mrs Bert.

'The thing is,' I said, 'I gave them a love potion.' Mr and Mrs Bert nodded slowly. They looked, suddenly, like those small figures you used to see bouncing up and down on bits of elastic in the back windows of a certain kind of car. 'Right,' said Bert, everything at last becoming clear, 'a love potion!' Mrs Bert nodded. 'Right!' she said. 'Only,' I said, 'I gave the potion to the . . . like . . . wrong person . . .' 'Right!' said Bert. We all nodded slowly.

After an incredibly long pause, Mrs Bert said, quickly, throatily, 'We have to give the potion to the right people!' 'We do!' I said, equally swiftly, 'we do!' There was another long silence. 'I have run out of potion,' I said, 'but I am getting more potion!' Bert nodded. 'Where do you score?' he said. 'Like . . . Wolverhampton!' I said. 'Wow,' said Bert, his eyes wide, 'cool!' I passed the joint to him and Mrs Bert offered me some of the hubble-bubble. 'Could you get us some?' she said. 'I'd love to!' I said.

At some point both of them said they had to go to work. I was a little worried about this. Mrs Bert said I wasn't to worry. She went out into the kitchen and re-emerged in a traffic warden's costume. At first I was convinced this was some kind of fancy dress, and for a chilling moment thought it might be that I was expected to indulge in some form of group sex. They had to explain to me, gently and carefully, that she really was a traffic warden and she was going out to see where people had parked illegally.

'Wow!' I said. 'But . . . like . . . be nice to them!' Mrs Bert embraced me warmly. 'I'm always nice to them,' she said, 'that is why I became a traffic warden!' 'Right!' I said. 'It *isn't the parking,* 'she said, '*it's the people!*'

I can't remember quite how I got out of the house but I know it took an enormous amount of time. As I said my final farewell, Bert said, 'Remember! The right potion for the right people!' I thought this was about the most profound thing anyone had ever said to me.

Rory (he was definitely Rory) and Jakob were sitting in the front of the Volvo, eating a McDonald's. I tapped on the window and said, 'It's great to see you!' They looked, I thought, embarrassed. 'I love you guys!' I said. 'I really love you, you know that?' They looked even more embarrassed. 'I remember,' I said, 'when you were in short trousers.' 'Would you like a lift somewhere?' said Rory. I got the impression they did not like being seen with me in public. 'Let's go home,' I said, 'let's go home and talk about our feelings!' 'Let's not!' said Jakob.

I attempted to embrace him through the gap in the window. This was not a success.

Somehow or other I got into the car. When I was in the back seat, I said, 'I remember when you had a rabbit called Hoppity! And it died!' Rory started the car. 'I think,' said Jakob, 'he has been at the hubble-bubble! And the bhang!' 'I remember,' I said, 'when Hoppity escaped! He ran down the road and hid under Mr Samuel's camper van!' We drove, at speed, past Lucy's house and, as we did so, I saw both of them look up at the window of the upstairs bedroom. I looked out at the bleak shopping parade at the end of her street. A woman with a pushchair was battling her way forward through the bitter wind. Her face was pinched and white and sad. '*It's all right!*' I wanted to say to her. '*It's OK. East Cheam is all right! And all mannere of thynge shall be welle! The rose and the fire are one!*'

As we threaded our way through the traffic, back towards the A3, I groped for a single sentence that would express my deep need for inner harmony and my passionate conviction that Mr and Mrs Bert had brought me closer to it. They had shown me the way. They had lighted up my path. And these magnificent boys in the front seat were – I was suddenly sure – going to find true love. '*Jack shall have Jill!*' I muttered, aloud,

'*Nought shall go ill! The man shall have his mare again! And all shall be well!*'

Jakob screwed himself round in the seat and gave me a quizzical look. 'What are you on about, oh Slippery one?' he said. I looked straight into his eyes. 'We must give the right potion to the right people!' I said. 'That is what it is all about!' After which I closed my eyes and gave myself up to sleep.

I'm only now just coming round.


## April 5th. 11 a.m.

*Estelle at Craftgirls. Ruairghy, Jakob and Edwin all in bed.*

Estelle still horribly cheerful. Apparently someone wants to make an animated film, using Mr Slippy Sloppy as the central character. Estelle has written a storyline. I asked what it was and she said, 'He loses his willy and his wife finds it.' I said I thought this sounded cheap.

She has come off the turnip diet. Apparently a surfeit of turnips can cause 'severe personality disorders'. A man in California who ran amok with a shotgun is basing his defence on the fact that he was on the turnip diet for ten years. Estelle seemed worried that she, too, might be about to run amok with a shotgun. I had to reassure her about this. 'You've only eaten a few tons of turnips!' I said. 'This guy had been eating nothing but turnips for years. He was probably unstable anyway. No one other than a madman would live off turnips for ten years!'

She gave me a suspicious look when I said this, and then left for a Craftgirls meeting, barking over her shoulder as she went, 'Get Edwin to revise!' A bit like telling your loved one to discover a Unified Field Theory while you're out at the shops. I have left a trail of textbooks near to places most frequently visited by Edwin – the fridge, the lavatory, etc. When asking him to perform household tasks, I will speak to him in French.

With things at the Beeb still in limbo I have decided to devote today to confronting Porda, since Surinder seems to be trying to avoid me. I can't think why. I rang her twice yesterday and got her answerphone – something I've never heard before. It sounds as if a man has recorded the message, and I find myself wondering whether this is Porda.

If she is shagging Porda, then why are Cross and Rhws Davies pretending that he may not be sincere in his support for the show? The only explanation I can think of for this is that Porda, although trying to do us a favour because of Surinder, finds himself genuinely convinced of the show's awfulness and therefore feels it is his duty to get rid of it, even though he is shagging its principal writer.

This cannot be. It would mean that a senior BBC executive had genuine and unshakeable views on a programme that went against his personal convenience. Porda must be tracked down.

I also have a letter from the Royal Court to deal with. They are going into production with *Muthafuckas* and request meetings with Wesley Jones, rewrites, etc. Should I black up Snozzer?


1.30 p.m.

In the canteen. It is Spanish Week. I have had BBC paella, which bears about the same relation to the celebrated dish of Valencia as does the BBC week to the real week. The BBC starts on Saturday — perhaps to celebrate the day on which Lord Reith shagged his secretary. All the staff are wearing Spanish outfits and the lady on the cash till clicked a castanet in my face.

I have had three glasses of BBC Rioja. I do not feel well.

I have just had a very weird conversation with Karl. He is trying to get Steve Witchett, the Writer Who Never Expresses an Opinion, to write the episode (planned, now, for the week of my birthday/twenty-fifth wedding anniversary) in which I am shot by a madman. 'Your *friend* Surinder,' he said, with an evil sneer, 'refuses to do it!' 'I am not surprised!' I said, with as much dignity as I could muster, 'It is not true to the character. Esmond is not the kind of person who would be shot by a madman! He would reason with him! Talk him down!'

Karl started to thump the desk at this point. 'There is no reasoning with this madman!' he said. 'He is a complete madman!' He went on and on about this. 'Can't you see?' he said. 'You drove him to it! You are an incompetent!' I started to say that I was a highly regarded actor who had recently been signed up for a feature film (I did not mention that I was playing an out-of-vision cockroach) and then I realized that Karl was talking about Dr Pennebaker. I said, 'You hate Esmond, don't you?' His eyes glittered insanely. 'I think Esmond's day is over! He has swaggered around the place for long enough! We need new blood!'

'So,' I said, 'you *are* behind all this. And Cross presumably. I don't know why you didn't say so in the first place. All you ever do is write grubby little notes about Shirley!' The word 'Shirley' had an electric effect on him. He started to twitch and the bald patch on the top of his head grew little beads of sweat. 'You and your friend Surinder are in trouble!' he said. 'I can play dirty too. And I will blow the whole "Howard Porda" thing wide open. Don't rely on the "Invisible Man", my friend, because I will have no compunction about revealing his true identity!'

After he had said this he started to twitch even more. 'Are you taping this conversation?' he said. I said I wasn't. Karl said he always taped conversations. I said, 'I'd love to get hold of the transcripts of you and your dog. You and people like you are what is wrong with the BBC. You are a spineless time-server whose only wish is to crawl on your hands and knees to a man you've probably never even met, i.e. John Birt. I loathe you and people like you!'

Then he threw the first draft of Witchett's episode at me, which I am about to read.

At least we now know where we are. Cross and Karl have something on Porda – perhaps the fact that he is shagging Surinder, although I cannot see that this is a sackable offence – and are hoping to challenge him in this Core Directorate Policy Unit. Surinder has something on Karl (Shirley?) and perhaps on Cross too, but none of them seem prepared to reveal what it is. I have to rally Porda to put up a fight on my behalf. I will try once more to track him down this afternoon.

## 2 p.m.

I have just read Witchett's first draft. He, like everyone else around here, seems to have had a nervous breakdown, perhaps caused by being forced to write a scene in which something happens. The opening page reads –

CLARE: All well with you, Dr Pennebaker?
ESMOND: Mustn't complain. Although it could be better. I am not quite sure how. It's possible it couldn't be better. I don't really know.
CLARE: Are you feeling cheerful though?

ESMOND: It's hard to say. I thought I was and then I wasn't sure.

CLARE: But you slept OK?

ESMOND: As far as I am aware, yes I did.

CLARE: What kind of bed do you have, actually?

ESMOND: It's one of those specially designed ones.

CLARE: Good for the posture sort of thing?

ESMOND: That sort of thing, I think. I am not sure, actually. I usually get a good night's sleep in it though. But not always.

> Clare seems alarmed.

CLARE: Not always . . .

ESMOND: I mean I do sometimes of course. Sometimes I do sleep. As well I might. It cost £450.

CLARE: My, oh my! That's quite a lot for a bed!

ESMOND: It depends on the bed, I suppose.

CLARE: It does. It depends on the bed. I mean some beds are obviously worth a lot more.

ESMOND: Indeed. A four-poster, for example.

CLARE: Oh yes! A four-poster!

There are four more pages of this. After which Witchett has written

> Enter madman with loaded gun.

At this point he has abandoned the text. I am thinking of sending the whole thing to an archivist at the University of Texas. I think it has some historic value.

I have just seen Ronnie ('Very Nice Man') Pilfrey in the corner of the canteen. He does not look like a man who is about to die in agony of a rare disease. In fact he looks, as usual, sickeningly pleased with himself. There is a rumour that he has been offered the lead human being in a feature film. He has not the depth, subtlety or inner pain to portray an insect. Before he comes over here and starts boasting (or rubbing his legs together, something that it amuses him to do in my presence) I am off to track down Porda.

# 7 p.m.

Haunted by thoughts of death. Insurance makes the prospect slightly more palatable, however. I am slightly comforted by the fact that, when I stiff I will be worth £350,000 pounds. Estelle will be able to buy a lot of turnips with that. I really must finish my will. I bought a do-it-yourself one from W. H. Smith's but every time I try to start it I am overcome by emotion.

I am going to leave Edwin my supply of sex products. I feel we have bonded this year.

Edwin, Jakob and Ruairghy have gone off to buy food from the garage. I pointed out that I was making *agnello ai carciofini* – a peasant dish from northern Italy or a Jewish dish from Sardinia depending on which recipe book you are looking at – and they said, 'We do not like your food. You make the kind of food that Italian peasants throw back at their wives. We want tinned spaghetti and lots of it.'

Laura called, twice, and Jakob said he did not want to speak to her. I spoke to her instead. You can't smell her over the phone but her voice is pretty seductive. I said that I thought this was 'simply a phase' and that I was going to talk to Jakob very seriously. I did not, however, say that I was also going to slip a mega-dose of a rare South American love drug into his evening meal the next time Laura was anywhere in the vicinity.

The Porda business gets more and more mysterious. After I left the canteen I went up to his office, and, as usual, was told he was 'in a meeting'. I hung around the corridor for a few minutes and saw Karl come out of the lifts. I dashed round the corner and watched while he crept up to the door that leads directly into Porda's inner sanctum. He looked carefully up and down the corridor before tapping very delicately on the door. It opened, no more than a fraction, and Karl slipped inside. There was something immensely furtive about all of this.

Perhaps Karl and Porda are having an affair. Perhaps Karl, Porda and Surinder are having an affair. Perhaps Karl, Porda, Surinder and Shirley all regularly do it together in the Internal Affairs Conference Room. Perhaps Cross glues his ear to its keyhole while stimulating himself digitally. There is certainly not much else to listen to on Radio 4 at the moment.

They were certainly in there long enough to do it three or four times

– although my memory of the sexual act is so blurred I could not, now, reliably say how long it takes. All I know is that the next time it happens for me it is going to be very fast indeed. Eventually the locked sanctum door opened and Karl emerged, looking very red-faced. Once again he looked up and down the corridor and scuttled off towards the lifts. I didn't follow him. For some reason – I could not have quite said why – I was sure that Porda would emerge.

Which in the end he did.

He was, as usual, wearing the scarf and the hat (was there, I wondered, something wrong with his face? Did some frustrated BBC staffer throw acid at him?) and, as usual, behaving like a man who is keen that his style of walking should not betray the fact that he has just perpetrated an important crime.

Once again, I kept on his tail. But this time he did not see me. When he got to Reception he went out into Portland Place and turned left down towards Regent Street. There was a bitterly cold wind and, as he walked, Porda lowered his head and wrapped the scarf even more tightly around his face. This made my job considerably easier than last time.

He turned left into Mortimer Street and set off, still with his head down, due east, towards Charlotte Street. After a couple of hundred yards he turned left into a dark, featureless alleyway that led into a road I don't think I have ever been down before. There was a block of red-brick flats at the far end and Porda seemed to be making for them. Although I dodged into a doorway, there was no real need to do so. He went up to the main entrance and disappeared from view.

Seriously afraid I might have lost him, I ran across the road and to my relief found, to the right of the heavy wooden doors, a row of flat numbers with names printed clearly next to them. The one at the top read 'HOWARD PORDA'. I gave him a couple of minutes and then I pressed the bell hard. There was no answer at first. I pressed the bell again. A voice that was so distorted as to be unrecognizable, said, 'Who is this?' 'My name,' I said speaking clearly and slowly, 'is Paul Slippery and I play the part of Dr Esmond Pennebaker in the serial *General Practice*!' There was absolutely no response to this.

I am not a well-known name. But I would have thought that I was reasonably well known in broadcasting circles. I was not expecting Porda to hurry down and ask for my autograph. But some indication of the fact that I have been at the cutting edge of radio drama for nearly twenty-five years might have been nice. Even if he didn't make reference to my great moments – the day Madge Pennebaker was drowned, for example – even if he had temporarily forgotten who I was, even if, like many senior executives in the place he had never listened to a BBC programme, he might at least have pretended to care. But all that came out of the metal grille of the entryphone was static. I continued to talk into the machine. 'As you must be aware,' I went on, 'there is a move afoot to end my life. And I am anxious to talk to you about it!' Still no answer. 'I feel Esmond has a great deal still to give,' I went on. 'I do not feel he is ready to die. I do not feel people want him to die. I think they want him to live.' There was still no answer. At any moment, I thought, the man is going to cut me off. I found I was raising my voice. 'I do not want Esmond to die!' I said. 'I do not feel he is ready to die! I think if he is shot by this madman it would be crazy! The whole of his life will have been in vain! I am begging you, Mr Porda! I am beseeching you – please do not have Esmond Pennebaker shot!'

I became aware that a small fat woman was listening intently to my one-way conversation. She was looking at me very oddly. I glared at her and she moved away. 'Are you there, Mr Porda?' I said, 'Howard? May I call you Howard? Are you there?' And then, clearly through the crackling, came Surinder's voice. 'Paul, I can't talk to you now!' she said, and the line went dead.

So she was up there with him!

I realized, suddenly, that I would have strongly preferred her to be a lesbian. Stella Badyass did not seem to be such a threat as the man who had power of life and death over Esmond Pennebaker.

I think it was that that made me storm in through the doors and take the lift to the top floor, where Porda's flat was located. *You have never really told her what you feel about her*, said a voice in my head. *Tell Surinder what you feel about her, Slippery!* In order to do this, of course, I would have to work out what I felt about her. As the lift jolted to a halt on the top floor, I examined myself closely in the mirror facing me, trying to work out whether I looked like a man in love.

Not at first sight perhaps. The casual observer might take me for a man who had come to mend the drains. But closer inspection revealed a haunted, driven quality – a man driven by mysterious inner needs. I went to the door and leaned on the bell. There was no answer. I pressed it again – this time for nearly a minute. No answer. I leaned down to the letter flap and pushed my nose through it. 'Surinder,' I said, 'it is Paul here! I need to talk to you about our relationship! I need to talk to Howard as well! I need to talk to you both!'

Eventually the door opened a few inches. It seemed to be on a chain. I saw a little slice of Surinder's face – and although she was wrapped in a towel there seemed to be something very different about her. What was it? It wasn't simply the fact that she was wearing no make-up. It was as if I was looking at a different person. 'Howard can't talk to you,' she said, 'he is in the bath!' 'You're in the bath!' I said accusingly. 'Yes,' said Surinder, 'I'm in the bath!' 'Has he been in the bath with you?' I said. 'He goes everywhere with me,' said Surinder. 'He's there when I wake up in the morning. He's there when I go to sleep at night. He's there when I brush my teeth. He's there when I go to the –' I suddenly found I did not want to know any more of the places to which Howard Porda accompanied Surinder.

'It is obviously a very intense relationship!' I said, somewhat sourly. Surinder's face softened. 'Paul,' she said, 'I want to tell you something in complete confidence. Can I trust you to tell no one what I am about to tell you?' 'I am,' I lied, 'a very discreet person! Some people have told me things that are so secret that I have forgotten I have even been told them!' She gave me a slightly maternal look. 'I *am* Howard Porda!' said Surinder. I did not, at first, grasp what she meant by this. She gave a faint smile. 'As a man, I am Howard Porda. But I will not be Howard Porda for long!' Who, I wondered, was she going to be next? Robin Hood perhaps? Mother Teresa? For a moment I thought I was looking at the kind of personality disorder rarely found outside TV mini-series. Then Surinder said, 'When I have had my operation Howard Porda will no longer exist. I will be a woman, Paul!' I found I was gulping. 'You mean,' I said slowly, 'that you are not one at the moment?' 'Not at the moment,' said Surinder. 'You mean,' I said, 'that you've got a –' 'Yes,' said Surinder gently, 'at the moment. But not for long!' 'Right!' I said.

And then she closed the door, very gently, in my face.

I have been pursuing someone with a willy! My God! I still have not yet thought through the implications of this one! I must not let Ruarighy, Jakob or Edwin discover this fact or I will lose all parental credibility!

11.30 p.m.

Message on machine from Estelle. She sounded as if she was in a restaurant – offensively cheerful and friendly. She says she will be back late, adding, 'We're all celebrating! They love my storyline for Slippy Sloppy! Lift the lavatory seat to my success, lads!' The awful thought occurs to me that she has known all along that Surinder has a willy. This could account for her and Stella Badyass's behaviour. It is probably an expensive restaurant. And they are probably making jokes at my expense.

## April 6th. 9 a.m.

*Estelle at work. Edwin, Ruarighry and Jakob in bed. Me in study.*

Tried new loosening-up exercises called the Andersen System. Hit my head on side of desk.

Estelle came in at three in the morning and left the house at six. I do not know where she has gone. I did not sleep. Haunted by thoughts of Surinder – or Howard as I am going to have to get used to calling him, at least until he/she has it chopped off.

My God! I could easily have made a move towards her and found myself clutching another todger! I might even have got to like it! Perhaps I, too, would have been persuaded to have mine removed and start a new life as Lorna or Melanie.

I think Melanie would quite suit me as a name, actually. It has a robust quality that I think I would bring to life as a woman. In fact, the way things are going round here I might as well be a woman. I do the shopping, and cower at home waiting for tradesmen to call while Estelle is out at meetings/on planes/in expensive restaurants, etc. If I was a woman there is no way I would be one of those ones who wiggles her bum while men open doors for her. I would be one of the ones on Valium, standing over a pile of dirty dishes and waiting for her man to come home.

I did not realize this sort of thing went on in the upper reaches of BBC management, however. I thought it was restricted to airline stewards and members of the armed services. No wonder there is so much restructuring going on. The telephone is going. Perhaps it is an investigative journalist seeking to interview me about my sex life.

## 9.30 a.m.

It was Surinder. She was ringing to remind me that the fact that she is a chap is highly confidential. She said she was keen not to let her personnel officer find out. 'Which one?' I said. 'Presumably you have two!' I said I completely understood this and was anxious, for reasons of my own, to keep it under wraps. She said, 'Not many people know – apart from Estelle and Stella of course. And Karl.' I said I thought that telling those three people was equivalent to putting a full-page advert in the *Daily Mail*. Surinder said, 'Do you have a problem with my sexuality?' I said that as soon as I knew what it was I would have no problem with it at all. She said, 'I am a woman, Paul! I am a woman!' I said this was how I saw her.

I did not like to bring up the subject of her chopper. Instead I asked her whether anyone in the senior echelons of the BBC Home Serials Department had noticed that one of their most important male executives had breasts. She said, 'They wouldn't notice if I had four legs and a trunk!' It occurred to me, after I had put down the phone, that she is not only receiving two salaries but actually being paid to hire herself to acquire one of them. I think this is something of a coup – even at the Beeb.

## 11.30 a.m.

Everyone, apart from me, still asleep.

I thought of waking one of them up, just to have someone to talk to, but, after peering at all three of them, realized I did not have the heart to do so: Ruairghruy, as usual, lying flat out with his head back and his mouth open, the covers thrown back; Jakob curled up deep inside his duvet, only a small tuft of black hair visible; and Edwin fast asleep next to his guitar, his fingers, as far as I could make out, curled round the chord of G major.

Gustave rang about the cockroach film. Apparently they are having second thoughts. They have found someone whose voice has 'more of an authentic insect feel to it'. I was deeply upset by this. 'I think,' I said, 'that I am about the only actor in Britain who has made a speciality of this kind of role!' Gustave said that it was 'becoming a very competitive area'.

Another letter has arrived for Wesley Jones. It contains another request for a meeting and asks, among other things, for the name of his probation officer. I find this very strange. I cannot remember having given Wesley a probation officer. Perhaps he is starting to acquire an independent existence. Perhaps he will come round to the house and mug me for having made him (a) such a stereotypical black person and (b) the author of such an appalling play.

Although, in truth, I think *Muthafuckas* is really rather good.

## 12 noon.

Everyone still asleep. Although Edwin has just appeared in a towel. When I asked him what his plans were he said, 'I might go to France.' I asked if I could come with him and he said he 'would see'. He is now running the first of what are usually his three baths of the day.

Laura has telephoned and asked to speak to Jakob. I told her he was in bed and she said, 'With that bitch, I presume!' I think that – close up – Laura could be a difficult woman. In the background I could hear Mrs Proek screaming at Mr Proek. I think – although I am not entirely sure of this – that she was shouting, 'You never satisfy me!' I told Laura I would give Jakob her message and Laura said, 'Yes – do tell him Lucy is a bitch!' Then she hung up.

This is (I think) my sixty-second day without sex. Rang Good Old Steve. As he was out I rang Nobby. The phone was answered by his new thirtysomething. (He seems to have dumped the Brazilian.) She is, by all accounts, a lithe woman. She told me Nobby was at his therapist's – presumably being counselled about all this shagging he is being forced to undergo. When I said goodbye she said, 'Lots and lots and lots of love!' A standard pay-off from thirtysomethings talking to people they hardly know. I replied, in deliberately sneery tones, 'Lots and lots and lots and lots of love to you!'

She did not spot the satirical intention behind this. Like Americans, thirtysomethings are incurably literal-minded and nearly always assume you mean what you say. I rang Peter Mailer. His answerphone message goes — 'Hi! This is Peter Mailer. I am out but if you have an alcohol- or drug-related problem leave it after the tone! Jezza, if you call and you are in Leatherhead — remember *you do not need a drink*!' After the tone I said, 'I am Paul Slippery and I am an alcoholic. I have many other problems I would like to discuss with you, many of them of an intimate and sexual nature. I think my wife may be a lesbian. I think I, too, have strong lesbian feelings.' I was going into some of my other problems, not the least of them being the fact that I will be fifty in seventy-seven days when the machine cut me off. Presumably he has to keep a tight rein on these alcoholics or they would be droning on about their problems all night.

### 3.30 p.m.

Ruairghry and Jakob have taken the Volvo and gone off to sit outside Lucy's house. As far as I can make out, the object of the exercise is for each to stop the other from going in. Edwin has gone off to the Common with Lulu, Scagg, Snozzer, Bozz, Plonker and a new addition to the group called Wodge (I am not sure whether Wodge is male or female as he/she was only in the house for two minutes, did not speak and was wearing something that looked like a cross between a yashmak and a sleeping-bag.) I asked them what they were going to do and Edwin said, 'Meet with other young people and discuss issues.' I am, as I always seem to be these days, alone in the house. Estelle has recently given him a pager. I told him I would call him on it at the end of the day.

### 4 p.m.

Gustave rang again. It appears that the role of the cockroach will now be taken by Ronnie ('Very Nice Man') Pilfrey. I am consumed with hatred and spite. Gustave said that there might still be a chance of playing a 'slightly less important insect' in the show. I said I wasn't interested and put the phone down on him.

### 5 p.m.

The phone is ringing but I will not pick it up. I will listen and sneer as whoever it is leaves their message.

## 5.30 p.m.

It was Surinder. I picked it up. I had, in fact, gone to hide in the bathroom, as I find it almost impossible not to pick up the phone, and as soon as I heard her voice I ran back into my study, tripped over the waste-paper basket and fell headlong on to the floor. By the time I got to the phone she had hung up. Her message was as follows – 'Meet me at Broadcasting House at six thirty! Main Reception! I'll send a car for you!'

I am going to go of course. But I am not sure who I am going to meet. Sending a car is not the sort of thing Surinder usually does.

## 6.15 p.m.

Writing this in the back of a BBC limousine driven by a small fat man called Derek. He has just asked me whether I am 'a friend of Mr Porda's'. I told him that, in a manner of speaking, I was. He went on to say that 'Mr Porda was a wonderful man to drive'. I said I was sure he was.

This is all very confusing. On the way we stopped off at an off-licence and Derek picked up a bottle of champagne – 'for Mr Porda'. Later he pulled in at a laundry and came out with a pile of beautifully manicured clothes – 'for Mr Porda'.

If he knows that Mr Porda also doubles as one of his female employees he is keeping very quiet about it. I suppose these chauffeurs are trained to be very discreet.

Being Howard Porda looks like a good deal. I cannot imagine why he wants to be a female scriptwriter on *General Practice*. Especially when he seems poised to fire himself.

## 7 p.m.

Writing this in a posh bar somewhere behind Oxford Street.

It appears that Surinder had an affair with Karl before she decided to become a woman. Karl, too, apparently, wishes to become a woman but, according to Surinder 'is not really sincere about it'. It certainly has not stopped him thinking filthy thoughts about Shirley. Colin Cross also, it appears, has had an affair with Karl, although not with Surinder, and he too wishes to wear female clothing, although he seems to have some reservations about having his willy chopped off.

When they get into disagreements at work they all threaten to out each other.

I was absolutely staggered by this, and asked how many other members of the Home and Overseas Radio Documentary Drama (Occasional and Continuing) Department were considering gender alteration/cross-dressing, etc. She named three more people including Sylvia, Cross's assistant, although she seemed vague about what sex Sylvia actually was. Ashley Ramp, it turns out, is a rubber fetishist these days, but apart from that 'completely normal'. I did not tell her about the spanking. I asked her whether it went all the way to the top and she said she thought not. I questioned her closely about John Birt and she said that, as far as she knew, he had never shown the slightest interest in things of this nature. 'Actually,' she went on, 'he is a really nice bloke. I go to football matches with him. All the rumours about him are completely untrue.' When I mentioned that she seemed to have started most of them she said, 'It's funny. When I am a woman I do rather dislike him, but as a man I find him deeply appealing and sympathetic. It's probably because I work more closely with him as a man.'

She has now gone off to the Ladies in order to change into her Howard Porda costume. I did ask her whether she was worried about the morality of taking two salaries from the Beeb and she said she wasn't. 'It's a completely mad organization anyway. Beyond a certain level nobody actually does anything at all apart from go to pointless meetings. And without Howard's salary I wouldn't be able to finance the operation.'


## 9 p.m.

Writing this in the back of the limousine. Derek is about to take me home. I may not actually go home. When I asked him whether he minded going all the way to Wimbledon, he said, 'I exist to drive Mr Porda wherever he wants to go. And if he is not available I drive whoever he suggests to wherever they want to go. If you wanted to go to Addis Ababa I would drive you there, sir. I love driving.' I said I did not want to go to Addis Ababa.

I am thinking of where to go.

## 9.15 p.m.

Still thinking of where to go with Derek. I asked him if he wanted to go to the pub and he said he 'was not allowed but he would be happy to come in and watch me drink'. I said I did not fancy this and so he is driving round in circles while I think of where to go.

There is a colour television, a telephone and a fridge in this limousine. I think I will phone Edwin's pager.

## 9.30 p.m.

On the way to Wimbledon. The woman on Edwin's pager sounded guarded – perhaps because Snozzer has been ringing in every day for the last week and trying to persuade her to take down a message with rude words in it. Apparently she got so incensed about this that she refused to transcribe the word 'underpants' for Plonker and Plonker threatened her with the European Court of Human Rights in Strasbourg.

I have agreed to pick up Edwin, Lulu, Bozz, Scagg, Snozzer, Plonker, Wodge and someone called The Gremlin at the Eagle and Child, Wimbledon. I asked Scagg what he did at the fish counter. He said, 'I perch on it!' Then he gave a throaty laugh. Edwin has been buying them all drinks. He told me that one of the barmen questioned him about his age – but 'it was cool because I have your passport'. I said I was amazed that he could pass himself off as a man of nearly fifty. He said he had 'changed a few details on it – like the photograph and the date of birth'. When I started to argue about this he said, 'You never go anywhere anyway.' This is perfectly true.

I asked Derek if we could fit seven more people into the car and he said, 'Mr Porda once got twelve in here. Mind you, some of them were Japanese.'

## 11.30 p.m. Somewhere in Surrey.

This is so cool!

I am in the car. I have drunk the contents of the fridge. Plonker and I have bonded. Plonker, it turns out, is a Bob Dylan fan. Me, Wodge, Plonker and Snozzer have been singing 'Like a Rolling Stone'. So has Derek.

We are going to go to Brighton.

149

# April 7th. 12 noon. Clear and windy.

*Edwin and I here. Everyone else out.*

In bad trouble with Estelle. And with Ruairghy and Jakob.

Snozzer, Plonker, Scagg, Bozz, Edwin, The Gremlin, Lulu, Wodge and I got in at four in the morning and all started singing songs from the new Oasis album, accompanied by Edwin on the guitar. Derek came in too, as he said we were all 'wonderful people to drive'.

Estelle appeared in her nightdress and accused me of being irresponsible. She brought up the subject of Edwin's G C S E s. I said I thought passing exams did not necessarily mean you were successful. Estelle said, 'I presume you are basing that on your own experience. Matriculation is about the only complicated procedure you have ever been able to manage!' I thought I detected an attempt to sneer at my sexual prowess here.

I fell asleep, fully clothed, on the front-room sofa and when I woke I discovered that Snozzer, Plonker, Scagg, Bozz and Wodge had fallen asleep practically on top of me. Wodge is a girl.

Wesley Jones has had another letter. It says that he will shortly be receiving 'the money order as requested' through the post and asks if the assault charges have been dropped. It also says that they understand he will not be able to come to rehearsals while he is in prison but that *Muthafuckas* opens on May 14th. I am considerably freaked out by this news. Perhaps I have invented a person who exists already. If this is so, how come he is giving out his address as 52 Mafeking Road?

Perhaps he is here! Perhaps he is hiding in one of the cupboards upstairs!

I have been summoned into the Beeb by Karl.


# 4 p.m.

Been waiting for Karl for two hours. No sign of Surinder. Or indeed anyone – although we have a programme to record next Monday. Ashley Ramp put his head round the door and said, 'What are you doing in here?' I found myself possessed of a strong urge to say 'Rubber Pants!'

I am now sure he remembers that I know he is the man who took the credit for the programme about snails.

## 5 p.m.

Writing this in the George.

It is clear that Karl and Cross are planning some move against Surinder and me. Karl told me that he had definitely decided against the madman-shooting-me idea. He has also decided to fire Steve Witchett, the Writer Who Never Expresses an Opinion. I asked him what Witchett had said about this. Karl said, 'He's having a lot of trouble deciding whether he wants a leaving party.' They are going to have no less than three new writers, to whom I am to be introduced next week. When I asked what they were like Karl said, 'Don't get too fond of them. One of them may well be asked to kill you.'

I said I had had a very good meeting with Howard Porda. Karl twitched visibly. I said, 'He's a remarkable man!' Karl twitched again. 'And really on Esmond's side!' I went on. 'Howard Porda,' said Karl, 'is on the way out. Don't think of relying on Porda!' He sneered. I think when and if he changes into a woman he should go blond and have something major done to his nose.

And, while he is at it, stop drooling over poor Shirley's panties.

My only hope seems to be to persuade Surinder that she really does not want to be a woman. The longer she hangs on to her chopper – and the job that goes with it – the more chance there is of Esmond Pennebaker continuing to practise medicine.

I don't think I am just being self-interested here. I really like Howard Porda and in many ways feel easier with him than I do with Surinder. He also has a much nicer car.


## 8 p.m.

Estelle actually in when I got home!

I put my arm round her and kissed her on the top of her head. She said, 'What is this in aid of?' I said, 'Nothing! It's just nice to see you!' This was, as it happens, perfectly true. It is very reassuring to know that – although she may sometimes be a little short-tempered – she is a fully equipped female, inside and out. I went into the back sitting-room to have a look at Ruairghy and Jakob, who seemed to be in the middle of a conference call with Lucy. Then I went upstairs to check on Edwin, who was playing the chord of C sharp minor. The only person in the house wearing a dress is Estelle! And even though I can't remember when I last had sex with her I must have done it at least three times, even though the last occasion may have been seventeen years ago. This seems to be enough for the moment.

I asked Edwin about school and he said, 'In biology today we did the penis!' I said, 'How did that go down?' Edwin said, 'We all behaved like schoolboys, of course!' Everyone – including Estelle – snickered at this and I felt impelled to make a short speech about sex. This did not go down well. The only problem our family has with sex is when to stop talking about it.


## April 9th. 11.15 a.m. Dull.

*Estelle at work. Ruairghy, Jakob and Edwin in bed. Me trying to learn lines.*
I only have about three in this week's episode, and two of them are 'What?' But I do not seem to be able to remember the order in which they come.

An enormous parcel from Sex Products of Wolverhampton arrived this morning. I had, thank God, used Edwin's name and so was able to look genuinely shocked when Estelle opened it and found three frilly nighties, a thong, a pair of split-crotch panties and a box that looks as if it might contain an artificial penis. No love potion of any kind. They have clearly got my order muddled up with someone else's.

Estelle said, 'He has G C S E s in six weeks. Why does he need split-crotch panties?' I said I thought the two things might be related. Or, more likely, it was a present for Lulu.

After she had gone off to work I rang Wolverhampton and shouted at a man down the phone. It turns out that they had two parcels for Mafeking Road. One of them, it appears, was intended for Porker. I am going to have to pluck up the courage to cross the road and trade three frilly nighties, a thong, a pair of split-crotch panties and an artificial penis in exchange for South American love potion.

This may take some time.

**12 noon.**

Amazing development in my relationship with Porker!

On my way to post a letter to Surinder – telling her what a great bloke I thought Howard Porda was, how glamorous his moustache, etc. – I was waylaid by Porker and his whippet. Porker, who was wearing a kind of kaftan, fixed me with what I can only describe as a steely glare. There is something very military about him. 'I think,' he barked, 'that you may have my artificial penis!' I said I thought that that was possible. He stroked his moustache and said I should call round tomorrow morning, and 'we could exchange goodies'.


**12.30 p.m.**

A letter from the Beeb.

```
   Hullo.
   Colin Cross here.
   SOUND.
   First of all some facts and figures.
   Last year we set ourselves the objective of creating a
new top team to help us in the work of restructuring the
way in which SOUND is part of the wider Directorate
structure.
```

*i.e. we created even more executives. And paid them even more than the last lot.*

```
   We cut costs dramatically, all across the SOUND
   Directorate.
```

*By firing even more programme-makers.*

```
   We experimented with low-cost tape. We doubled up
   creative roles on the team. Elinor Fruhm, for example.
```

*Who?*

And at the same time we produced more programmes.

Many of these programmes were longer than ever. *Elf-stick*, for example, produced in the low-cost sound studio in the Isle of Wight, was a 'sound-weave fairy story' of immense technical complexity.

*I myself have not heard it. And do not intend to even try to. But — hey!*

How did we do it?

*We juggled with the books a bit. We employed a team of dodgy accountants to massage the figures. Sometimes we simply lied.*

Sometimes I find myself wondering what the answer to that question is. I know it took a deal of hard work. I know it wasn't always easy.

*For you poor bastards anyway.*

But at least we have now turned the corner and have got a clearer picture, at last, of where the Department is headed!

*Towards the abyss! But why should I care? My pension is five times the salary of the average producer so as far as I am concerned you can all just fuck off!*

Am thinking of sending my amended version of this prose poem to everyone in the building.

## 4 p.m.

Have been reading medical encyclopedia. I think I have got something called Prynne's disease. It is named after some bloke in a loony-bin who was on the job twenty-four hours a day in a desperate attempt to make up for the fact that he thought the last time he had had sex was thirty years ago. Even when in the middle of bonking — according to the book

154

– he experienced feelings of frustration and was 'unable to adjust to the idea that anyone was letting him do it to them'.

Apparently the therapists showed him videos of him at it with another inmate and his response was 'Who is that lucky bastard?' The outlook for Prynne's disease is not good. Indeed, judging by what happened to Prynne, it is a total nightmare. As far as I can make out, not being able to remember when you last shagged is the beginning of the end and invariably leads to hysterical fugue, paralysis, anomie, sleeplessness, irritable bowel syndrome and death.

A call from Ronnie Pilfrey, who rang to gloat about his spectacular entrée into the world of out-of-vision insects. I said, 'I was sort of offered the cockroach – but I feel I have done enough of that kind of thing. I don't really want to spend the rest of my life playing earwigs and so on!' Ronnie said, 'What do you want to spend it doing?' And I said, through gritted teeth, 'Who knows? There's an awful lot of mileage left in Esmond Pennebaker, I feel.' This is so untrue as to be laughable, but, curiously, Ronnie seemed impressed by it.

## 6 p.m.

Nothing else has happened. I went to Waitrose and spent £234.98. I seem to have bought enough beansprouts to feed the entire population of Taiwan. Edwin came with me. He bought seventeen packets of crisps, eight bottles of Ribena, thirty cans of Stella Artois, twelve cans of dog food and a gigantic packet of prawns.

I pointed out to him that we had not got a dog. He said, in rather sinister tones, 'Not yet, maybe!' I suppose I can always add some aubergines and a packet of curry powder and serve it up to Jakob and Ruairghy.

I have spent the rest of the time trying to think seriously about my relationship with Estelle. This is an acceptable substitute for talking to her/trying to shag her/having a row, etc. Do I love her?

Christ knows. If it means being lifted up on to a higher plane of spiritual awareness then I am certainly not in love and neither is she, since for the last twenty-five years we have both had our feet firmly on the ground and/or on each other's necks. Or rather, we don't make a habit of protesting love to each other. Is the love-story part of a marriage all over and done with after twenty-five years? What does a relationship mean after that amount of time? Is it just a matter of mutual convenience? Or, as Estelle would say, of my convenience? If all it means is that, then it is not worth having.

But if it means fancying someone and then finding out that you like them as well as fancying them and then finding out you like having children with them and then finding out the children you've had with them seem to like you and then finding out that what you feel for her and for them are part of the same thing which is nothing more or less than the knowledge that the world is or can be a very sweet and agreeable and amusing place then I am in love with her all right, in love more than any poet's pose of eternal vows because these vows, our vows – regular, in-it-for-the-duration long-service-medal vows – are not about what each or either of us think what we have might be but about what it actually *is* about each day, the way this diary is each day, and how each day adds up to the almost unfaceable mountain of days that make up your life but that is nevertheless something that's good and lasting and decent and true.

*Why has it taken me nearly sixty thousand words to discover this fact?*

*Why do I not sound entirely convinced by my own rhetoric here?*

Well, perhaps because I am the sort of man who cannot tell the difference between a transsexual and a number nine bus. And I'm an actor – used to speaking other people's lines – not mine.

## 7 p.m.

Have just read over my last entry – especially the long paragraph with hardly any punctuation. It has, I feel, a poetic quality to it. Almost, at times, like Joyce – and I don't mean Grenfell.

It has also clarified my mission in life. I have clearly not been attentive enough to her, told her I loved her, etc., and this is why she has been at home for about an hour a day for the last two months. Little dough men are, in a sense, a substitute for me! What I need to do is take a hold of my life – organize new roles – in film and television and theatre, solve my children's love problems and restore my authority in the home. I am a man and must act like a man. Not like some . . . insect!

Love! A real caring, exciting, romantic relationship! Passion! These things are possible – even for fifty-year-old men! And, of course, women!

Tonight, when Estelle comes home, I will prepare a tempting dish from the *River Café Cookbook* — wood-roasted ptarmigan I think, with a little sprouting broccoli and anchovy sauce — and I will buy a couple of bottles of white wine. Then, assuming I get rid of Edwin, Ruarughy and Jakob, Estelle and I will talk about our relationship.

Must go out now as no ptarmigan in the house.

## 8.30 p.m.

Estelle still not home. No ptarmigan in Waitrose so bought huge piece of beef instead. Ruairghy, Jakob and Edwin are circling it like buzzards. Put it in oven, finally, about a quarter of an hour ago. Suggested Edwin, Ruarighy and Jakob went out to pub and gave them twenty quid. They went, saying that Edwin was going to be driving. I think this was a joke but am not entirely sure.

Message on machine from Gustave. Apparently the animated film people weren't going to offer me the earwig anyway. I rang him back and asked him what they were offering and he said there was a chance of playing a worm. I asked what this involved and he said — in that lordly manner of his — 'Oh, a few lines and a bit of slithering, I think.'

Must wood-roast some vegetables. As far as I can gather from the *River Café Cookbook* this simply involves spraying them with olive oil and chucking them in the oven. I am going to wood-roast everything in the vegetable rack — apart from an aubergine that looks as if it has trench foot.

## 9 p.m.

Estelle still not home.

This is really too bad!

I have drunk one of the bottles of white wine. Am reading my diary. Particularly appalled by the long paragraph without punctuation. Love means wood-roasting about half a ton of fennel and then eating it yourself as far as I can see.

## 9.15 p.m.

Estelle still not back. Beef overdone. Going to pub. Have drunk both bottles of wine. I am sick of love.

## 9.45 p.m.

Writing this in pub. Have had two pints of Guinness. Edwin has, apparently, drunk nine pints of Kronenbourg. Apparently he drove them here and 'nearly missed a tree', which both Ruairghy and Jakob said was 'really great!' I have told them about my diary and read them some – edited – extracts. Ruairghry says he is consulting a lawyer. We have also discussed love at some length – particularly in relation to Laura and Lucy and Lulu. I think they felt that it wasn't an emotion that could be indulged after nearly twenty-five years of marriage.

All three of them said they believed in love. All three of them said there was nothing you could do about it. Edwin said, 'You just look at them and it's like your brain is not your own . . .' Jakob said, 'Right . . . and neither is your dick!' Ruairghy said, 'It's just weird!' I thought, but did not say, that this was another reason for thinking that Laura is right for Jakob and Lucy for Ruairghy. Ruairghy needs someone practical and Jakob is practical enough for two.

God knows what it means for Edwin and Lulu. They are, to me, like creatures from the forest. Edwin said, as he headed off for his tenth pint of Kronenbourg, 'Girls are just friends who give you erections!'

## 11.30 p.m.

Writing this in study. I have a good view of Porker. He seems to be pouring himself a nightcap before going upstairs to bed. Possibly to put himself in the mood. Judging by the speed with which Mrs Porker retired to bed he may well have slipped her a crafty dose of my South American love potion.

Estelle finally came home at 10.45 p.m., by which time all feelings of love had evaporated. She did not seem interested in the wood-roasted vegetables, perhaps because they resembled little pieces of anthracite.

# April 10th. 11.30 a.m.

*Estelle at work. All men in house and asleep. Apart from me.*

Just got back from Porker's. I have the love potion! He has the artificial penis! Liquid Love turns out to be bright green! I feel this is a good sign.

He was brought up in the Punjab by his uncle – who was an official in the old Indian Civil Service. He has a complete edition of the works of Kipling and, at ten forty-five, offered me something called a *chota peg*, which is a very weak whisky and water. I accepted.

We then talked about our health for twenty minutes. Porker said, at one point, 'My arse is practically dropping off!'

A good conversation all round, I felt. We managed to keep off the subject of parking.

# 12.30 p.m.

Three letters.

A letter from Surinder, most of which is about her need to wear tights, etc. There is, however, a key phrase, which has serious implications for my only real concern in life – to save Esmond from death.

```
. . . I must now put on the trousers and go, of all things,
to a Management Training Course in Swindon. At 'The
Hotel'. Just the place for odious, macho 'Howard' with
his sniggering repertoire of dirty jokes and his laddish
pranks that make him so popular with BBC Management!
    I suppose Esmond's future will be decided there!
    Surinder
```

Of course, nearly everyone goes through an identity crisis when they put pen to paper. But I had not expected something as serious as this.

## 1 p.m.

I am going to have to go to Swindon.

The second letter was a copy of a draft, embargoed press release that is due to be put out by the Department at the end of next week. It reads –

DEATH OF POPULAR RADIO DOCTOR

Dr Esmond Pennebaker, the star of the successful long-running series *General Practice*, will die 'some time in May', say the production team working on the show. 'There has been a feeling that Esmond needs to pass on for some time,' said the show's producer Karl Rhws Davies, 'but we are still debating the actual way in which his life comes to a close. Anything is possible! He may drown in a pool of his own vomit!'

   Paul Slippery, who plays Pennebaker, is said to be 'moving into films' and said, 'I am delighted! All I can say is that my death will be the high point of my time on the programme! It's what I have been building up to all these years – and it reinforces *General Practice*'s tough, gritty stance on the real world of medicine!'

The Press Officer has scrawled underneath this, *Obviously your reaction is only a suggestion at the moment. We would like any hints, Paul, on how it might be shaped. I left the vomit in because Karl said it but maybe it sets the wrong tone.*

   I scrawled out the paragraph beginning 'Paul Slippery' and substituted the following – 'Paul Slippery, a married man of nearly fifty with three children, said, "I DO NOT WANT TO DIE!"' Now I am going to climb into the Volvo and head for Swindon.

   The third letter was from Pilfrey, swanking about being a cockroach.

## 4 p.m.

Writing this in a service station on the M4. Edwin demanded to come with me – Lulu has gone to the Bahamas with her parents – and I could not refuse him. I am not sure how I am going to slip him into the BBC

Management Course — but he says he regularly passes for eighteen and 'in artificial light could easily pass himself off as forty'.

He is wearing a suit.

## 6 p.m.

Edwin and I have checked into 'The Hotel', Swindon. 'The Hotel' is part of a chain which includes 'The Pub', 'The Newsagent' and 'The Bakery'. They also run a 2,300-strong chain of Leisure Centres which are all called 'The Leisure Centre'. The secret of their success is that they all look so alike that you have no idea, when in one, whether you are about to buy a newspaper, jump into a swimming-pool or buy a loaf.

## 8 p.m.

Spent the last hour cowering in the room, raiding minibar, etc. I called home to see if it had burned down and was rewarded by a new answerphone message. It was Jakob. It began —

'Lucy, Lucy,
Give me a piece of ass . . .'

And then it got worse. Like some other very brilliant people — Mozart for example — there is a part of Jakob that shows no sign whatsoever of growing up.

Edwin says we must go downstairs — 'and get our noses up this guy Porda's ass!'

## 9.45 p.m.

Writing this in lavatory.

We got down to the Conference Suite between 8.30 and 9 p.m. From inside there was the noise of voices.

There was a little old lady in a red dress sitting at a table that looked as if it had been rented for someone's wedding. On the table were a pile of badges and clipboards.

Edwin, who was scrutinizing one of the clipboards, swung round —

'George Chattaquiras and Eamonn Pooley,' he barked, 'Management Application Systems.' The woman simpered. 'I'll give you your badges,' she said, 'You are . . .' Edwin did not smile. 'I am Eamonn Pooley,' he said. 'I thought they would have told you!' He leaned over the desk in a confidential manner. 'There are people,' he said, 'who will do anything to get a free drink!' Then suddenly he gave her a wolfish smile. She was impressed. 'Oh Mr Pooley –' Edwin became, suddenly, seriously confidential. 'In fact,' he said, 'we have had some problems. As has George. Jokers – if you know what I mean. If anyone rolls up claiming to be from Management Application Systems, call Security!' 'I will!' said the woman.

When we got inside there were about a hundred and fifty people – mainly men in suits, although the odd woman had been allowed to slip through – milling around a featureless, windowless, rectangular chamber. Over in the far corner, talking to a tall man with white hair, I saw Surinder. Or, possibly, Howard.

I must say that I thought the Armani suit, the Paul Smith shirt and the sharp shoes were a great improvement on the black polo-neck sweater and the miniskirt. Howard had never had very big breasts anyway and, as a woman, had always tended to wear too much jewellery. He looked seriously interested in the conversation he was having with the white-haired man who, I realized, as I got within hailing distance, was none other than John Birt, the Director-General of the BBC.

Edwin was right behind me. Fortunately we came up behind Birt's left elbow and I was able to point to my badge and jab my finger at my lips. Surinder/Howard was saying, as I pitched up, 'We've got to do something about 7 o'clock on Thursdays on BBC 2!' Birt nodded seriously. 'We've put in *Cook Your Heart Out*, but it isn't quite doing what we hoped. But there is this thing about sea lions . . .' Birt nodded. 'Right!' he said. I edged nearer and I saw Surinder/Howard crane forward to catch a glimpse of my badge. 'And how about radio? How about *General Practice*?' said Birt.

My heart was in my mouth!

Surinder/Howard nodded thoughtfully. 'What do *you* think of it, John?' he/she said. Birt pursed his lips. 'I love the show,' he said, 'I am an addict! And I am a particular fan of Esmond Pennebaker. He just gets that depressed middle-aged-man quality perfectly!' Surinder/Howard nodded thoughtfully. 'I'll tell them, John,' he said; 'they are thinking of killing him off!'

John Birt, a man for whom I was having an increasing amount of respect with every second that passed, shook his head, and, for the first time in the conversation, seemed to show real emotion. 'They are mad!' he said. 'On no account should we kill off Esmond Pennebaker! He is a major BBC asset! He's like . . . he's like . . . *Listen with Mother*!'

I did not like to point out that *Listen with Mother* had been killed off a long time ago. That did not seem relevant. What did seem clearer and clearer, as I listened to his small talk, was that John Birt was a man with an almost superhuman grip on programme quality. He seemed to have an ability to hone in on the essential point of an argument, digest it and then give an instruction, in clear and simple terms, that would help those below him to maintain the BBC as a name that was a byword for excellence.

At this moment the Director-General felt the pressure of my arm on his sleeve and turned to face me. He had a frank, manly, pleasing face and one to which I instantly responded. I said, with quiet dignity, 'I am a fan of *General Practice*! I think Esmond Pennebaker should live to a ripe old age!' John Birt said, 'My feelings exactly!' Surinder/Howard said, 'Do you know . . . er . . .' Her/his eyes flicked up to my badge once again and, in the same movement, took in Edwin's. 'Do you know George Chattaquiras and Eamonn Pooley,' he/she said, 'from Management Application Systems!' John Birt put out a hand and I shook it. He had, I thought, a handshake totally in keeping with the rest of him – firm, responsible and curiously reassuring. He was a man with whom one could go elephant-shooting – indeed, if elephant-shooting was what you wanted to do it was probably not wise to even think about doing it unless John was somewhere in the vicinity.

'George,' he said, 'I have heard all about you . . .' *And you are an impostor!* '. . . but we've not actually met, have we?' 'Indeed not!' Birt turned towards Edwin. Edwin shook his hand. 'And you are . . .' Edwin seemed to have acquired a slight Dublin accent. 'Eamonn Pooley,' he said, 'also with Management Application Systems. Here with George Chattaquiras. At the Conference. As you see.' John Birt nodded. If he was aware he was talking to a sixteen-year-old schoolboy from Cranborne School, Wimbledon, he showed no sign of it. 'I am looking forward to your talk, Eamonn!' he said.

If this news surprised Edwin, he, in his turn, was not going public on the matter. 'I am too, John,' he said. 'I am, too.' This seemed to provoke hysterical mirth amongst those around us. John Birt smiled amiably at him. 'And what are you going to be saying, Eamonn?' he said. Edwin laughed lightly. His accent, I thought, veered a little towards Swedish, as he said, 'I have no idea, John! No idea! I open my mouth and rubbish comes out and they pay me. That is all!'

This went down an absolute storm.

We were still laughing away when a small fat man leaped up on to a podium at the back of the room and said, 'Ladies and Gentlemen, we have with us tonight Eamonn Pooley of Management Application Systems. He's going to be giving a short pre-dinner talk which he has entitled, "Management Opportunity and Corporate Structure". Eamonn!'

Before I could say anything, Edwin had made his way through the crowd and was standing up, gracefully acknowledging the applause. To my left I heard Surinder/Howard hiss, 'What is going on, Paul?' I said, 'Later!'

'Management,' said Edwin in surprisingly forceful tones, 'is an Opportunity. And Opportunity –' here he paused dramatically – 'is Management. They are one and the same thing. They are . . .' – here he leaned forward and holding his right hand palm down bunched the points of fingers and thumbs into a cluster which he shook to emphasize his point – '. . . they are . . . *identical*!'

For a horrible moment I thought this was going to be it. But in fact Edwin was only just getting into his stride.

'In the part of Ireland from which I come,' he said, 'we have a saying. It's something that comes out when the Guinness is flowing. We say – and as I say we only say it when we're pissed . . .' – this got a laugh – 'we say – to each other and, indeed, to almost anyone who will listen – we say – oh will you listen to me wondering what the hell it *is* we say – we say – *if it ain't broke, don't fix it!*' This got a thoughtful murmur. It was as if the audience was beginning to get ever so slightly impatient. But Edwin held up his hand with sudden, almost schoolmasterly authority. 'But that's a cliché, isn't it?' he snarled, staring straight at the Director-General of the BBC. 'That's the sort of thing every Tom, Dick and Harry and Jim and Bert and Podger or whatever his face is called says when he can't think of anything else to say. That won't do, will it? That isn't the half of it, is it? That is just a load of old cobblers, isn't it? We're going to have to say something else, aren't we, if we are to get anywhere on the whole issue of Management Structure and Corporate Opportunity or –' he paused fractionally and went on – 'or Management Opportunity and Corporate Structure, aren't we? Aren't we?'

Everyone seemed riveted by this. Edwin's voice had acquired an easy, hypnotic rhythm. Next to me one man in a suit, who had clearly had a few too many glasses of wine, was nodding slowly, as if he was about to fall into a deep trance. Suddenly Edwin leaped forward and jabbed his finger at the crowd. 'What though, my friends, *are* we going to say? That is the million-dollar question, isn't it? That is, as it were, the one we can't dodge. No matter how light we are on our feet. No matter how close to the bone we take it. No matter how many times we run it up the flagpole and see if someone salutes it, we can't, and we won't, because we don't want to dodge what is, let's face it, inevitably, inescapably the thing that we are trying to avoid. Why else are we trying to dodge it, if it isn't the thing we are trying to avoid?' His voice rose in pitch and his eyes acquired a wild intensity. 'But why are we trying to avoid it? Aren't we trying to wriggle out of something here? I have to say I think we are!'

He looked round at them sternly. An elderly man next to me said in tones of the kind I have heard used by people during church prayers, in order to remind those around them that they are not just here for the choirboys, 'He has a point!' A few other people nodded. I thought I saw John Birt look pretty impressed. Aware that he was making headway, Edwin started to jab his finger at the audience and when he spoke again his voice was almost spitting with contempt. 'I don't have to look too closely at too many people in this room . . .' he began, 'to see why we are trying to avoid it!'

There were a few murmurs, but whether they were of self-disgust or of disapproval of the content of Edwin's speech was hard to tell.

'And not so much of the "we" perhaps!' he went on. 'I am talking about you. Yes, you. You and you and you. The people in this room. Who are management. Who are part of the Corporate Management Structure. Who see, perhaps, the Corporate Management Structure as their opportunity!' There was some sycophantic laughter here as well as a few worried glances over in the direction of the Director-General. 'But that won't do, will it?' Edwin snarled. 'That isn't good enough, is it? That just isn't bloody good enough! That won't get the dog washed! That is the kind of backward-thinking, stuck-in-the-mud, fuddy-duddy, limp-wristed style of management that cost this company or companies like it £22.4 million last year!'

There was more muttering here. But, also, a strong sense that Edwin had not come to play softball. A sense that, although he was not yet being specific, although he had not yet come out with a coherent English sentence, he had one somewhere up his sleeve and when he did finally reach it out of the bag, quite a lot of people were going to have nasty things done to them in basements.

There was total silence in the room. Edwin raked the crowd with his eyes. 'My father,' he said, 'was a poor man. He was an illiterate man. He was in many ways a disgusting man. He beat us. He beat my mother. He beat the animals we had, savagely. He was, if you like, a textbook example of How Not To Manage. He was an alcoholic. He was a pervert. Of sorts. I won't specify. But he knew the meaning of words. A table. A bench. A jug. It was a world of concrete objects. A blade of grass. A knife. A fork. A pair of pyjamas. A pair of . . . woman's silk stockings . . .'

Surinder/Howard shot me a quick, nervous glance. But Edwin was leaning forward into the audience, who, as far as I could tell, were completely enthralled by what he had to say. '*Corporate Management! Management Opportunity! Management Structure! Corporate Opportunity! You do not begin, as yet, to know the meaning of these words! You are at the shallow end, my friends! And there are people out there who know them backwards!*' He paused. 'But I haven't just come here to spout platitudes,' he said, 'I am going to be very specific!'

I must say I was rather alarmed to hear this. But Edwin showed no sign of slacking.

'I am going to go through your outfit, department by department. I am going to give you figures, broken down by unit and by team and by group, and I am going to target specific groups and structures with detailed analysis of their cost per unit in relation to their output.' He paused. I saw quite a few people look nervously at each other. Edwin shook his finger again. 'I am going to talk about Scotland,' he said. There was a sharp intake of breath immediately behind me. 'I am going to talk about Wales as well,' he went on, 'and I am going to do an in-depth analysis of the cost parameters per hour of broadcast television together with a summary of cash flow, staff costs, overheads, heating bills and so on!'

The man next to me clutched his neighbour's arm. His mouth was as wide as a goldfish's.

'But,' said Edwin, with a sudden, brilliant smile, 'I am not going to do it now! I think this can wait until tomorrow. Let us now, as the Irish say, eat, drink and be merry. I have little Irish, but *Cead mille failte* to you – a thousand welcomes from myself and George Chattaquiras of Management Application Systems! God bless, and may your God go with you!'

There was tumultuous applause. When Edwin came off the platform he was mobbed by eager executives. I am almost sure, as we went towards the doors to go in for dinner, I heard the sounds of a scuffle outside and a high, squeaky voice protesting that he was Eamonn Pooley and that he demanded to see someone in charge. But by the time we got out into the lobby there was no one there.

Edwin is on a table with John Birt. I have managed to get myself next to Howard/Surinder. I just hope Edwin manages to steer the conversation round to things he really knows about – like Oasis, GCSE Biology and types of lager.


## 11.30 p.m.

My head!

I do not know where Edwin has gone.

It was clear, from the second pint in, that Howard is a bit of a lad.

He also has a comprehensive knowledge of football. He talked for hours about someone called Grobblehour (I am not sure if I am spelling that correctly) and displayed an encyclopedic knowledge of almost every aspect of the game – even down to varieties of boot.

Then we got on to the subject of women. We had three more pints. 'Getting any?' said a man from Sport. 'The closest I have got to any kind of hole this year,' said Howard, to enthusiastic guffaws, 'is watching the US Open on TV!' More laughter and backslapping. 'The furniture in our bedroom,' he went on, winking broadly, 'is not the only thing that is handmade!' This got even more laughs.

I went back to bed and rang Edwin's room. A woman with a foreign voice answered. I asked if Edwin was there. She said, 'He sleeps now!' I have much to think about. There is a knock at the door. Who can this be?


## April 11th. 6 a.m.

*It was Surinder. She said she was 'disgusted' with Howard, and 'sickened by his sexism'. She was wearing a dress.*

This is going to be a long job. I do not think Howard is your average, run-of-the-mill sex change.

Surinder also revealed that she is Stella Badyass's son (or daughter) by her first marriage. It appears that she has never met her father and puts her desire to be a woman down to this.

One thing she did say (which may explain Howard's personality and may turn out to be useful) is that she seems to have a plentiful supply of both male and female hormones. I don't know quite how she wangled this – presumably it is something to do with leading a double life at the Beeb – but if we can manage to stoke her up with testosterone I think that Esmond may be in with a chance.

I managed to go through her handbag and pinch her spare pair of door keys while she was droning on about Howard, etc. They may come in handy.

Off now to wake up Edwin. We need to slip out before Pooley and Chattaquiras expose us for what we are.


## 10 a.m.

Writing this in a service station somewhere off the M4.

Edwin is eating a triple-decker bacon'n'cheese'n'lettuce'n'prawn'mozzarella burger. I am having a cup of coffee. Apparently John Birt likes many of his ideas on management. I did not dare to ask what they might be.

I woke him at around seven. He was in bed with a Swedish woman called Gerda who turned out to be Head of North and South Regional Radio Resource Management. She seemed anxious for him not to leave, saying, as he hurried into his trousers, 'Ven I see again, Eamonn? You call?' Edwin said, 'I'll call as soon as I return to Ireland. I have to be with my children!' Apparently he had told her he was married with three children. 'Although,' he said, 'this did not stop her. She was well keen.'

I called home to make sure everything was all right and the answerphone message had been altered by Ruairghy. It goes, 'Hi! This is Rurighry! If Lucy calls – leave a message for me because we have to talk about this!' Judging from the number of pips, there are a lot of messages. I just hope none of them were from Laura.

## 3 p.m.

When I got home, found Estelle and Ruairghy and Jakob engaged in intense discussion about relationships. The sort of conversation that I am unable to have with them. In fact, the sort of conversation that ceases immediately I come into the room.

## 4 p.m.

There has been a large pile of underpants in the front hall. At first they were in two separate piles, but over the week or so since Jakob's return they seem to have blended. What am I going to do with my children? Why are they so out of control? How will they resolve this appalling love confusion? What am I going to do about the underpants? Not to mention my own love confusion . . .

Another letter from the Royal Court for Wesley Jones. They thank him for the photograph (which they return and promise to use in the publicity for *Muthafuckas*) and ask whether his girlfriend has been released from jail yet. They also mention an upcoming court case in which he is involved and give the name of a lawyer who, they say, is particularly good in assault cases. They ask, too, about his brother Torvill, his sisters, Charity and Prudence and his grandfather, Winston. Apparently his granny is about to be sent back to Barbados for a complex social security fraud.

This is really very spooky. I have a strong feeling that I vaguely recognize Wesley – although he has not exposed more than a square inch of his face to the camera. He seems dressed for burglary. He is wearing a woolly hat – in Rastafarian colours – well down over his eyes. He is also in dark glasses and wearing gloves.

Seventeen messages on the machine, most of them from my mother – all within the space of the same afternoon. She has taken to describing herself as Granny, even when addressing me – perhaps to remind me that she is not far off a hundred.

MOTHER ... Paul? ... Paul? ... (*Long pause suggesting that she is alone in a darkened house*.) Paul, it is Granny! ... (*Long pause suggesting that she expects this news to set hundreds of people rushing to pick up the phone*.) ... Paul, it is Granny here! ... (*Restatement of main theme, pause for reaction*.) ... Oh ... you're not there ... (*Long pause to give me a chance to contradict this obvious truth*.) ... It's Wednesday! (*Phone replaced on receiver*.)

There is also a message from Nobby. He sounds very drunk. All he says is – 'Paul – never sleep with anyone under the age of forty!' There does not, at the moment, seem much danger of my doing this. His message was explained moments later by another one from his thirtysomething, who gushed on about how I was such a dear friend to Nobby and hoped her lawyers hadn't been too difficult. She left me, and him, lots and lots and lots and lots and lots of love.

There is also a message from someone called Leo, who says he is working on the episode in which I die and would like to talk to me about it. He sounded hushed and reverent. Indeed his tone suggested I had already stiffed. I called him back and agreed to meet him tomorrow. In a pub in Richmond. He sounds even older and more tired than me.

Ruairghy, Jakob, Edwin and I are going to the pub.

10 p.m.

A pleasant evening. Nine pints of Hochschule lager. Estelle still out, however.

I think I have gone some way to solving the Laura/Lucy problem. All I really have to do is to get Ruairghy and Lucy alone together and give Lucy a reasonable dose of the Wolverhampton love potion. I may top up Ruaurghy while I am it, although from the way he has been carrying on he does not need topping up. What I have to do this time is to complete the operation under controlled conditions. We cannot afford any more mistakes.

Edwin says Mr Hotchkiss has abandoned Loomis's play and has decided to do a production of *A Midsummer Night's Dream* instead. Edwin has been offered the part of Puck. Snozzer has been asked to be a fairy ('Peaseblossom or Mustardseed') and has declined. Wodge is to play Hermia, Lulu is to play Helena, Bozz Lysander and Scagg has been offered Demetrius. Edwin said, 'Scagg said the fish counter is very demanding and has asked for time "to mullet over".' Hotchkiss apparently indicated Plonker to Mr Feuerstein, the gay maths master, and said, 'Look at that lovely, lovely Bottom!' Plonker hit him. I offered to help with voice coaching.

Why is Estelle still out? What were Jakob, Estelle and Ruairghry talking about this afternoon? And why did they stop talking about it when I entered the room? What exactly is she up to? Why have I not maintained the momentum in trying to rebuild our relationship? Is there any momentum there anyway? Am I a sincere person? Why have I let the failure of my wood-roasted ptarmigan damage my attempts to find romance in my marriage once again as in, I think, *On Golden Pond*?

I urgently need a spiritual dimension to my life. I know this sounds ludicrous but, somehow or other, I have to convince Estelle, not only that the last twenty-five years have been worth it — but also that the next (twenty? eighteen? sixteen? any advance on sixteen?) years will be even better.

## April 14th. 12 noon. Clear and bright.

Have not written in diary this week. Too busy trying to communicate my deep feelings of new-found spiritual awareness/love for her, etc., etc., to Estelle. This has been made difficult by the fact that she has been in Liverpool.

I have tried passing them on to her voicemail in the hotel — with no real success. Yesterday, for example, I left a message which went — 'Do you remember that little café in north Wales where we had tea-cakes, in the summer of 1973 and decided we wanted children and that if we had children we wanted the first one to be a boy and we would call him Liam? Do you remember that? Well I loved you then and I still love you now!' That, anyway, is roughly what I said. It was a little longer than that. There were even a couple of quotations from Shakespeare sonnets.

I signed off, hoping she would not play it back when there were other people in the room. I rang her later in the evening and asked her if she had got my message. She said, 'Yes.' She did not amplify on this response. When I asked her whether she liked it she said, 'I don't think they were tea-cakes.'

I fear she has fallen out of love with me.

Off now to meet the man who is to write my death scene. I need to implement the Porda Plan soonest.


## 5 p.m.

Leo turned out to be a small, shy youth – not much older than Ruairghy. He had a wispy beard and a small ring through the end of his nose. We met in a pub just below Richmond Bridge.

The spring has suddenly arrived. The curious sensation – I have it every year – that this really is the first time it has ever happened. The river rippling with light and the earth smelling, suddenly, as exciting as a bakery. On the opposite bank, a hawthorn tree circled by daffodils was decorated with green buds, tightly clenched against the day.

I think my prose style is improving. 'Tightly clenched' is good. A word combination usually applied to buttocks – but given new force in the above entry.

Leo said, when we met, 'I'm really sorry about this. I'll try to make it easy for you!' He spoke, as he had on the phone, with the sincere quietness of an undertaker. After we had got some way down our pints, he leaned forward and said, in a voice that I had to strain my ears to catch, 'I think I'd like a wall to collapse on top of you!'

I said that I rather liked the idea of Esmond having time to face the reality of death. I thought he should come to terms with himself – and with Jimbo, Dirk, Pilfrey, etc. An end to selfishness! Living on a higher plane! I got quite animated about this: 'We should see him . . . donating his body to science, making a will, having an out-of-body experience, possibly even converting to Judaism . . .' Leo said, 'I suppose he could be . . . *trapped* under the wall . . .' For some reason he is adamant that it has to be a wall. I think he originally trained as an architect before getting into radio soap opera.

We both got quite excited about this. I suggested he could dictate his will while under the wall. Leo said, 'To whom?' He is punctilious about grammar which I like. I said, 'To the firemen!' Leo nodded keenly. 'Yes,' he said, 'and to lawyers!'

I am not sure he is entirely stable. It may be hard to keep him on the show. But he is definitely on my side. Or, at least, so hopelessly inexperienced that I can bamboozle him into giving me a few more weeks to live while I try to persuade Howard not to have his penis pruned.

'Maybe,' I said, trying to look like a man feeling his way through excitingly uncharted territory, 'one of the firemen could be a lawyer!' Leo got very excited by this idea. 'Yes,' he said, 'he could make a relationship with you and talk about your life and so on, while they try and dig their way towards you!' 'It could be brilliant,' I said. 'It might take them weeks to reach me!' 'Yes!' hissed Leo, 'and when they reach you – *you're dead*!' I said I thought I should be *almost* dead. 'They could take me to hospital,' I went on, 'and I could make a relationship with this nurse. We could fall in love! And we could talk about my life and so on and then . . .' 'And then . . .' said Leo, his eyes shining, 'you could die!' 'Maybe,' I said, 'maybe! Or maybe I could sort of . . . hover on the brink of death . . .' 'And then die,' said Leo, who was starting to give me suspicious looks. 'Oh yes, Leo!' I said. 'Yes, I'm not afraid of dying! I have no fear of death! I just want to die at the right time!' Leo stared deep into my eyes. 'There is no right time to die,' he said. 'Death is always an unexpected pleasure!' 'Leo,' I said, 'I can tell you're a serious writer.'

We bonded pretty deeply. He is, of course, writing a novel. I asked what it was about and he said, 'Nuns.' But my death is now clearly a non-negotiable issue. Plan Porda here I come!

## 8.30 p.m.

Writing this in a coffee-house round the corner from Surinder/Howard's place.

Howard keeps his hormones in a large cupboard above the wash-basin.

There were two large bottles. On one was a label that read *Oestriol. 0.75 mg by mouth daily*. On the other — *Virormone-oral. Methyl-testosterone. As directed*. Both sets of pills looked virtually identical.

I simply emptied the female sex hormone into the male sex hormone bottle and poured the testosterone into the other container. I gulped down a bit of testosterone on the way — although I have not yet felt appreciably more butch.

I figure that, after he has had to do a bit of macho swaggering around the Beeb, Howard will probably up his dose of oestrogen — with the result that, by tomorrow morning, he may well be whistling at women in the street.

I am not proud of what I have done. But I think Howard will ultimately thank me for it — even if testosterone seems to bring him out in attitudes that are less than chic. But it is a small price to play for the continued survival of Esmond Pennebaker.


# April 17th. 1 p.m.

*Everyone asleep apart from me and, I suppose, Estelle.*

Easter has come and gone, without anyone noticing.

Estelle is still in Liverpool. I have given up trying to tell her I love her. I am not sure whether I do. Perhaps it was just relief that she is not a bloke.

Edwin, Snozzer, Plonker, Scagg and Bozz have gone off to a rehearsal for *A Midsummer Night's Dream*. It is to be an open-air production and Edwin said, 'You all have to walk around during it.' 'Ah,' I said, excited, '*en promenade!*' Edwin said, 'No — it'll be at the school.' He has to take GCSE French in not much more than a month!

I am now going upstairs to try and wake Rurighry without alerting Jakob. I have to dose him and Lucy with potion. Someone at the door. Who can it be?

## 2 p.m.

It was a policeman! Looking for Wesley Jones!

This is starting to get really worrying. Apparently Wesley was apprehended in Wimbledon village. I am not quite sure what he was doing. As far as I could make out he was just walking along the street being black – which is, as we all know, a punishable offence. 'We thought he looked suspicious,' said the plod, 'so we pulled him over. He gave this as his address and legged it!'

I must say if he looks anything like his photograph I see their point.

It will not be long, I fear, before he is round here, demanding accommodation, help for his grandparents, etc.

Must wake Ruaieurhgy!

## 3.30 p.m.

Placed wet flannel over his face in order to wake Ruaieurgy. He said he thought he was having an epileptic fit. Offered him money to come with me to East Cheam. Writing this in the car outside Lucy's house. Ruarirghy is pacing up and down on the pavement, wondering whether to accept the £20 I have offered to 'come in and say hullo to the Berts'.

I have a nasty feeling that Jakob followed us here. He has always enjoyed undercover work. As a child of eight he once packed a small bag and announced he was going to live on the Common 'in disguise'. One of his favourite games when he was even younger was called 'tracking'. He used to follow us to the shops, hurling himself into people's front gardens if either of us turned round. Any sighting meant he lost a point.

Once or twice, as we came down the A3, I thought I saw the same minicab on our tail – although it was hard to be sure.

I have rung Lucy's bell but there does not seem to be any sign of her. Although a familiar figure is just coming down the street towards us.

## 5 p.m.

It was Mrs Bert.

I am upstairs in Mrs Bert's house. Mr Bert is downstairs. So is Mrs Bert. She has been reading me some of her poetry. I am upstairs with

Ginger, who is in his cage. Ginger is a rat. But he is really nice. Every so often he runs to the bars, peers out and then retreats. I think he may be as stoned as I am.

We have all had a great deal of dope.

And Ruairghy and Lucy, have, at last, had a sensible conversation. Well – a conversation anyway. It went something like this –

RUAIRGHRIY: Hi!
LUCY: Hi!
RUIERHGRY: Hi!

This went on for about ten minutes. It was followed by . . .

LUCY: I was like . . .
RURIERGHY: I know . . .
LUCY: It was like . . .
RUGIUHRY: Right right right . . .
LUCY: Like . . . *no* . . . and then like . . .
RUEIRHGRY: Like . . . *yes* . . .
LUCY: Right right right right!

After another ten minutes of this, Lucy said, 'Look. I haven't changed or anything. I just . . .' And Rueirghry said, 'Right right . . .'

It was at this point that I got out the Liquid Love, poured generous quantities of it into two wineglasses and uncorked a bottle of Bert's Châteauneuf du Pape. Ruairghry and Lucy needed no encouragement to drink deep draughts of the stuff.

There was no room for doubt. They were looking straight into each other's eyes. They had seemed, as far as I could tell, well on the way to feeling erotic about each other, with or without a highly priced South American herb.

Bert and I had finished off the wine before I realized Bert had tipped the remaining potion into the bottle. I think we maintained eye contact during the drinking period.

I must say that I do find him a soothing and sympathetic character. He does have a rather noble face and, for a man of fifty, a fine manly physique. But I am in no way attracted to him physically. If this Amazonian love philtre was any good Bert and I would be shagging like rabbits by now.

I have retreated up to Ginger's room in order to think out my position.

It is true, I note, that I am becoming a little obsessed with Bert. I cannot stop thinking about him. He is such a calm, decent and cheerful person! He is so gentle and civilized in his attitudes! He does have very beautiful eyes!

His rat is nice too!

## 7.30 p.m.

I think I am in love with Bert.

I think. I am not sure. We will need time. I am very stoned.

But he is a wonderful man, I think. There is a purity about him that I find ennobling. His bookshelf, for example! He has a book on rabbits — which I have tried to read. It is called *The Private Life of the Rabbit*. It is full of beautiful pictures of rabbits. I would like to come back as a rabbit after I die. In fact I would like to go straight on to being a rabbit now. Never mind dying.

Why is there so much ugliness in the world? How am I going to get home? What will happen to me? What will happen to Bert?

## 11.30 p.m.

Fairly scary drive home.

Very, very stoned, Rueighry and I got into the Volvo at about nine. He and Lucy seemed, as far as I could see, to be getting on fine. At least, just as we were leaving they went upstairs to her room and Bert, Mrs Bert and I waited in the hall for some twenty minutes.

What were they up to? Had the potion worked? Somehow or other we got back into the Volvo.

We were driving, very, very slowly up the A3 when I heard a noise in the back of the car. 'Ruairghry,' I said, 'there is someone in the car with us!' Ruaierghy, who was even more stoned than I was, said, 'Where are they? Are they in the engine? Or are they on the roof?' I said, 'They are in the car — here, in the car, with us!' Ruairghry, transfixed by this news, whispered, 'Are they . . . like . . . on our side?' 'I don't know!' I said. At which point there was a low moan from the back seat of the car.

I very nearly drove through the crash barrier. I raised my eyes, very slowly, to the driving mirror and thought I saw in the darkness behind me, the pile of old clothes, newspapers, blankets and other junk that lies on the back seat move, as if some creature was nosing its way through them to the surface.

I decided that this must be something to do with the Mexican grass dispensed by Mr and Mrs Bert, and tried to focus on Rurighry. 'How did you get on with Lucy?' I said. There was a silence. 'A lot better,' said Ruaeiurghy, 'a whole lot better!' At this point, there was another low moan from the back of the car and a weird high-pitched voice – I couldn't decide whether it came from inside or outside my head – wailed softly, like the wind outside in the black night, 'No-o-o! Ohhh . . . no-o-o!' Ruarighry jumped in his seat.

As we came up towards the Robin Hood roundabout the voice came again. 'This must not be!' it said. 'Lucy is my creature! I, Beelzebub, Lord of Darkness, declare this to be so!' I must have been very, very stoned, because it was only when his mop of black hair appeared through an old copy of the *Independent* newspaper, that I realized the voice came from Jakob. I hadn't, as usual, locked the car.

He seemed really pleased with his jape – although Ruirghry was furious. 'That wasn't funny, Jakob, actually,' he said; 'you shouldn't do that!' 'What?' said Jakob, grinning manically. 'Go round impersonating the Devil?' For the rest of the journey he kept up a stream of lively, unstoned invective on the subject of Rurighy and Lucy.


## April 18th. 10 a.m.

*Not sure where anyone is. Is my life slipping out of control?*

When I went downstairs to the kitchen I found Estelle, eating cheese which she said had been given to her by Scagg. Apparently she got back from Liverpool late last night. I had no memory of this happening at all. Mind you, I also could not remember what I had been doing after nine thirty, how much I had drunk, who I had telephoned, etc.

I followed Estelle up to the bathroom and asked her, straight out, if she could remember when her last period was. She lowered her face towards mine and shook her black locks at me. Then she said, 'Life is just one long period at the moment!' I tried to start a discussion about our sex life and she did respond – but as she was brushing her teeth I could not make out anything of what she said. Then she left to discuss Mr Slippy Sloppy with someone called Franz. In Birmingham.

How can I decide what I feel about her when, every time I try to do so, she leaves the room, or indeed, the city in which we are both resident? It is like trying to have a relationship with an eel.

Ruirghy and Jakob are still asleep. How did Ruaierghy get on with Lucy? Where is Edwin? Has he, perhaps, left home?

## 10.30 a.m.

Not yet.

There were a lot of bodies in his room, one of whom was Snozzer. Someone had drawn a pentangle and the legend '666 THE MARK OF THE BEAST' across his forehead in Magic Marker. I woke Snozzer but did not tell him about his tattoo. It appears it was inflicted on him in his sleep. I also woke Scagg, who had gone to sleep clutching a can of Foster's lager. Scagg twitched and said, 'The hake is nice, madam!' I shook him again and he said, 'Cheese, sir?' I think he has been traumatized by work experience. When I woke Edwin he asked me if he could have a lift to Aldershot. I told him he could not.

Now off to a meeting with Leo. Must put a call in to Howard before I go.

## 11 a.m.

Got through to Howard. He sounded, I thought, reassuringly gruff. He picked up the phone and grunted, 'Porda!' and – during our short conversation – never once mentioned brassières or the soft touch of silken undies on his delicate skin. I don't know whether this is a result of the testosterone or whether he is always like this in the mornings.

Was followed out of house by Edwin, Snozzer, Bozz and Scagg – all of whom demanded a lift to Cranborne School. When I refused they ran down the street after me, thumping on the roof. I gave in.

## 11.45 a.m.

Writing this in the Hand in Hand in Wimbledon, where I have agreed to meet Leo. He is now fifteen minutes late. I hope he manages to be even more behind schedule when it comes to delivering my death scene. It occurs to me that I am in a position not dissimilar to Scheherazade's in *A Thousand and One Nights*. As long as Leo finds Esmond interesting he will live. The moment he loses enthusiasm for the fifty-year-old general practitioner, Dr Pennebaker will fall down a lift shaft/have a wall collapse on him/fall victim to legionnaire's disease and/or suffer some other building-related trauma. Leo's enthusiasm for architectural themes may land him in trouble, I fear. In the script he sent me last night, people keep discussing Frank Lloyd Wright, Piranesi and the use of the flying buttress in the Gothic cathedral for no apparent reason.

My mood not helped by overhearing the following conversation.

MAN BEHIND ME: You know that doctor thing on the radio?

HIS COMPANION: What thing?

MAN BEHIND ME: It's with Esmond . . . Pennybonker . . . you know the one . . .

*Long pause.*

HIS COMPANION: Who's in it?

MAN BEHIND ME: The real star is that Ronnie Pilfrey.

HIS COMPANION: Oh, Pilfrey. Why didn't you say? I've heard of Pilfrey. Pilfrey's brilliant. Brilliant. I didn't know he was on the radio. Apparently he's a very nice man.

I nearly turned round and let them know the truth about Pilfrey. A pale face has just appeared at the other end of the bar. It is Leo. He appears to be carrying a trowel.

## 3 p.m.

A beautiful day. Writing this on the Common, as I decided to walk back home. A chaffinch is hopping around on a tree near the bench where I am sitting.

At least I think it is a chaffinch. It may be a heron for all I know. Birds are not my strong point.

Leo showed me the scene. It does not look good for me. Apparently Karl has approved it. I am going upstairs at the practice – to look over some architects' drawings that have been drawn up for our proposed expansion (there are no less than nine pages devoted to architecture in the episode) accompanied by a new character, a thrusting young architect called Larry Loader. At the top of the stairs a wall collapses on top of me. At the moment the ep. ends with Larry (who is clearly intended to be a major figure in subsequent storylines) saying 'My God! I think he's dead!' I managed to persuade Leo to change this to 'My God! He isn't moving!' He also said I could groan – although he said I had to groan quietly.

We are due to record this at the beginning of May. At the moment I am due to die on June 20th, four days before my fiftieth birthday.

Keep taking the tablets, Howard!


5 p.m.

Back at home.

Rurighy tells me he is thinking of getting married to Lucy. He does not appear to have asked her yet. I am not sure I approve of this. It is certainly not going to make life at Mafeking Road any easier. If Jakob decides to kill his brother he will probably succeed. He always was an organized child. I asked Ruaieghry how he expected to pay for lager, etc., and he said, 'The Lord will provide!' I reminded him that I did a hundred and fifty episodes of *General Practice* before I got married. He said, 'You poor bastard!'

Must discuss this with Estelle.

Message on the machine from Good Old Steve who is in Zurich on some story. Apparently Nobby has had a heart attack. Good Old Steve described it as 'a really big-budget job'. He became quite ghoulish at this point, adding plenty of the kind of colour he is always being asked to add to his pieces for *The Times*. 'His eyes rolled up into his head and he gave a sort of ghastly croak!' he said – although when I asked him how he knew this he said he wasn't absolutely sure. You can tell he is the man who won Economic Correspondent of the Year two years running.

Anyway, poor old Nobby is in what Good Old Steve described as 'the big black box'. I cast about for a suitable epitaph and came up with – 'He was a really nice bloke!' Good Old Steve said that – if you forgot that business in the bus shelter in the mid-seventies – he was the best friend a man could wish for. We both blamed the thirtysomething. Nobby told Steve that he was shagging as much as five times a day – which is not right for a middle-aged man. Good Old Steve said, 'I am lucky if I can manage it once a month!' I said, 'Once a year more like!' We both laughed.

There is to be a memorial service. I offered to write a speech. Good Old Steve sounded cautious about this.

## April 21st. 11.30 a.m. Sunny.

*Estelle on motorway* en route *for Taunton. Rureighy and Jakob – when last seen – engaged in full-scale physical combat in front of the television.*

I think they were arguing about Lucy. But it is possible that Jakob wanted a go on 'Ninja Assassins Five' – Rueaierghy's latest PlayStation acquisition.

Tried to discuss Ruriehgy's marriage plans with Estelle. All she would say was, 'Well, I suppose it's some relief he's not a woolly woofter!' I think she is losing interest in the family and has substituted little dough men for me, Rurighry, Jakob, Edwin, etc. I was just starting to discuss the state of our sex life when her mobile phone cut out. It always seems to do this when I try to discuss our relationship. Feel we are moving towards some kind of crisis.

## 4.30 p.m.

Writing this at the back of the Lucien Freshman Memorial Hall, Cranborne School, Wimbledon. Mr Hotchkiss, wearing a bright yellow shirt and tight white jeans is leaping about the stage, apparently unable to bring his *Midsummer Night's Dream* rehearsal to a close.

Plonker seems to have accepted the part of Bottom. Snozzer, Scagg and Bozz started out as fairies and are being re-cast as mechanicals – perhaps because Snozzer delivered the line 'Mustardseed!' while scratching himself under the armpits and making a gorilla face. When Hotchkiss asked him why he was doing this Snozzer said he did not want to be 'an effeminate fairy'. He is now playing Flute although, according to Edwin, he has not yet read enough of the play to realize that he will have to dress up as a woman. He seems to have taken to the idea that Flute is a bellows-mender, and in the scene they were rehearsing – Act One, Scene Two – Snozzer had brought along what looked like a rubber plunger and a chisel. When Hotchkiss asked him what these were for he said, 'Mending bellows'.

The main problem seemed to be Plonker (who seems to have grown about a foot in the last month). He announced that he wished to be known as 'Nick' rather than 'Nick Bottom' and suggested that, after Quince's line, 'You, Nick Bottom, are set down for Pyramus,' he might say, 'Just Nick will do fine!' Hotchkiss tried to explain that it was not common to rewrite Shakespeare and Plonker said, 'Why not? Everyone else gets rewritten! They even tried to rewrite Quentin Tarantino!' Hotchkiss explained that 'Just Nick will do fine!' was not a line in keeping with Elizabethan speech and Plonker said, 'You could make it sort of old style. I could sort of say, "Call thou not me Bottom for I'll not Bottom be – I'd as lief be Nick i' faith." Or something along those lines.'

Hotchkiss argued but Plonker was immovable. 'I just don't think my character would allow himself to be called by a stupid name like Bottom!' he said. 'He's like a very conceited man. He's like a weaver – which was a good job in those days.'

Edwin, although not in the scene as written, had been instructed to leap about the back of the stage during it. 'You are eavesdropping!' said Hotchkiss. At one point Edwin dropped on to his stomach and wriggled around like a snake, making loud hissing noises the while. Hotchkiss said this was 'very telling' and 'superb'. Then he started to go on about Plonker's magnificent thighs. When Plonker threatened him with the Merton Social Services Department, Hotchkiss said, 'Come on! You love it really!'

It is set, of course, in Nazi Germany and all the mechanicals are going to wear S S uniforms. Hotchkiss has also now decided that Scagg should play Hermia, Bozz Helena, Wodge Demetrius and Lulu Lysander. It has the makings of one of the worst productions of this play I have ever seen in my life. I said to Estelle I found it a hard play to take, adding that I was 'worried about the fairies'. She said, 'I am worried about the fairies too. Especially the ones directing it.'

## 9 p.m.

Making pork in balsamic vinegar with red onions. Estelle still not home. She rang me from the mobile. I started to try and discuss my feelings for her. I said, 'Look. The other week, when I was preparing wood-roasted ptarmigan, I got these great feelings of love for you, which I realized I had never really expressed. It's so easy to lose sight of each other in a marriage – especially one that's lasted nearly twenty-five years – and not really share your feelings. And then – because you were held up in a meeting, those feelings sort of . . . evaporated . . . and I felt this hostility moving me towards a kind of real crisis in what I felt about you. And I think we need to talk about this in relation to you and me, and not just the physical side of our relationship but the whole deal . . . parenting and sharing responsibility and Ruairghry's . . . my God, I can't believe we haven't even discussed this for Christ's sake . . . *marriage*, or *proposed* marriage, to this girl his brother is in love with!'

Estelle said, 'I'm sorry, I didn't get that. I think it may be something to do with Stonehenge.'

Sounds of violence from upstairs. It could be youthful *joie de vivre*. Or else Jakob is strangling Ruairgherhy.

## 11.30 p.m.

Estelle returned. Back in study after consuming pork in balsamic vinegar with red onions. It was burnt. Estelle said, 'Why the balsamic vinegar?' I said, through gritted teeth, 'It was in the recipe!' She said, lifting her snout from the plate briefly, 'Yes. But why?' She is a disgusting individual. As soon as I can get my hands on another woman, I am off. Let us hope this time it doesn't turn out to be one with a complete set of male genitalia.

I tried to broach the subject of my feelings for her (whatever they may be) but this was not helped by Ruairghry, Jakob and Edwin, who, every time I got on to the subject of my feelings, began to do pig impressions. I sometimes find this amusing. Not, however, tonight. Ruairghry, perhaps with the intention of winding up his brother, began to talk of his feelings for Lucy. 'I'd like to marry her . . .' he said, as they were taking away the remains of the balsamic pork, 'and live in a little house in . . . like . . . Banbury or somewhere!' 'Great!' I said through gritted teeth, 'I wonder how much a "little house" in Banbury . . . sort of . . . *costs*?'

I said this in a very light and unthreatening manner — but everyone looked at me as if I was some kind of monster! And it was I who had cooked the pork in balsamic vinegar! I who brought to the table the sprouting broccoli with anchovy sauce! I who mashed the potato with olive oil, mustard, cream and a little white wine (evoking, from Edwin, the words — 'Why have you made it all sloshy?').

Only Jakob seemed to find my remark amusing. He is in many ways the most intelligent and perceptive of my sons.

Tomorrow Estelle goes to Berwick-on-Tweed. We must, however, continue to talk about our feelings.


# April 23rd. 10 a.m.

*Estelle in Berwick-on-Tweed. Edwin on 'alternative games'. Jakob and Ruairghry in Parkside Hospital, Wimbledon. Me just outside it in car.*

Just delivered my two sons at the door of this privatized, state-of-the-art, luxury medical facility. During the course of a row this morning — precipitated by Ruairghry's revelation that he has been 'seeing' Lucy — Jakob bit him.

They were both frothing quite a lot and I did not wish to take any chances so have dumped them at the (automatic) glass front door of this high-class joint, surrounded by Arabs' Mercedes. Might as well use the thousands I have been paying in for private medical insurance all these years!

Dramatic doings at the Beeb. Colin Cross is leaving! He is going to 'pursue a number of exciting options'. I hope they include shaving off his moustache and learning to speak English. Sylvia, his assistant, is being sent to Scotland. She told me she has always wanted to be near Ben Nahuilinn. When I said I had never realized she was a keen mountaineer, she replied, rather stiffly, 'Ben is Head of Scottish Regional Radio Resources!' They tried to send Ashley Ramp to Scotland but apparently he refused to go. There is a rumour that they are going to try to send him to Wales but that he is going to refuse to go there. When I asked Barry de Latto, the producer of the ill-fated series *Foghorn*, where he thought Ramp would go he said, 'Notre-Dame for preference!'

This has considerably weakened Karl's hand. If I can get Surinder to settle for being a bloke, I may be OK, since Porda and Birt seem to be on my side. Keep taking the testosterone, Howard!

Ruairghry and Jakob are waving at me from inside the glass doors of Parkside. I have no time. I have to go in now for a departmental meeting.


## 2.30 p.m.

Writing this in the George. All the dead spirits who haunt this pub! I think of George Orwell, who once described the BBC as 'a cross between a lunatic asylum and a girls' boarding-school'. It hasn't changed much. Except that the lunatics are more convinced than ever that they are the only sane people around.

I suppose collective memory is always having to be erased. Perhaps the world had to forget how to do algebra in order to learn to do it properly. Perhaps it is important to call the same things by different names every thirty years or so. What seems to have gone utterly from this place – where I have spent the best part of my life – is any sense of continuity at all. No one talks about ideas – or even suggests that these most mysterious and important products of the human imagination could ever be simply defended by, well, more ideas. Ideas, now, have to do something called 'work', i.e. make money.

And what do we do with this money? Make more money, of course. All there is is money now – great glittering imaginary piles of it, recorded intimately in balance sheets boasted about in glossy pamphlets put together by hideously deformed morons like Colin Cross – who never stay long enough in one job to defend the decisions they made while in it – and used to justify every single decision in life.

These thoughts – which may simply be the cry of the middle-aged from Juvenal onwards – are prompted by the departmental meeting from which I have just emerged.

I need do no more than quote from the piece of paper we were all given as we came in.

SOUND.

It's been an exciting experience.

Over the last few months I have learned an enormous number of things.

*Such as — I am in completely the wrong job!*

We have focused in on our core audience for the early evening with *Siobhan MacMurdo* and *The Chat Hour*.

We have broken new ground in the young-mothers-in-cars slot at 6.45 p.m. with the help of our new documentary soap *Ungarotti Mansions*.

*i.e. no one is listening to it apart from a few women who are so stressed by their babies they cannot be bothered to change the channel.*

*General Practice* has found new focus with a younger audience and slimmed down its 'middle-aged spread' – pushing forward with the forthcoming death of Esmond Pennebaker – who will die in an accident in the workplace in early May, chiming in with Safety at Work Week – (thanks Esmond!).

Sylvia is going to Scotland! What will she be doing there?

*I 'dinna ken' and nae more does she!*

Her role should become clearer as more and more people move 'north of the Border' to support her in whatever it is she will be doing. And meanwhile, I am developing a challenging new initiative which will lead me to a place which I am very excited about – although, of course, as yet I am unable to be much more specific than this at the present time.

*More specific than what, you horrible little bushy-faced, half-witted careerist weasel?*

187

He went on to say that about fifty people are going to be fired and that they want all programmes to cost less. He also said that a new Head of Sound was to be appointed and that this person would also take over complete control of the Core Directorate Policy Unit. This is clearly a move planned by Karl and the odious Cross to make sure that Howard/Surinder is given the boot before he/she sticks it into them. I asked who this new head was likely to be. Cross smirked and looked at Karl.

If it's Karl I am really screwed. Off now to try and see Howard Porda and check on his male hormone levels.


## 4 p.m.

Porda unbelievably butch. Almost disturbingly so. Have just come from his office and seen him shout at inferiors down phone, pinch secretary's bum, make inquiries about new Arsenal striker, etc. This bodes well for me. He did not even seem to recognize me – although he slapped me on the back and referred to me as 'me old matey'. While I was there a shy, sensitive arts producer called Naomi Feitch came in and tried to sell him an idea about Oscar Wilde. Porda said, 'Oscar Wilde? Wasn't he a bit light on the carpet?' Feitch had to be helped out by the secretary.

I am still not clear what this phrase means. Or rather, I know what it means but do not know quite why it means it. When I asked Nerys, the accountant, a month or two back she said, 'It means a person is more carpet than hairbrush.'


## 5 p.m.

Phone home. Estelle still in Berwick-on-Tweed. Left a message on her mobile answering machine which went, 'We need to talk about our relationship, my darling. I feel we are headed towards a very serious place and if one or other of us doesn't do something about it there won't be a twenty-fifth wedding anniversary. We don't talk, do we? We need to talk!' As I said this I realized this was a British Telecom advertising slogan and that I had just spent about three quid on confiding it to a machine. I threw the phone in Surinder's office against the wall.

Who was it said that it was very clever of God to let Mr Carlyle marry Mrs Carlyle, thereby only making two people miserable instead of four? Maybe it was Mr Carlyle.

## 6 p.m.

Called home. A very sulky Ruairghy answered. Apparently you cannot just walk into private hospitals and expect them to look at your bites. You have to have a letter from your G P. Ruaierhgy said, 'I told them I could have had rabies.' At which, apparently, Jakob did his Dobermann impression. Ruairehgy is now 'off to East Cheam to gather flowers with Lucy'.

According to him she is 'a natural home-maker'. Jakob has said he is going to follow him 'on all fours if necessary'. I got Ruairehgy to put his brother on and I said, 'Jakob, you must promise not to bite him.' Jakob said, 'I can't promise that.'

What about Jakob and Laura? Should I try and use potion on them? Will this stop Jakob biting Ruairghry? Has the potion made Ruairgehry unhealthily obsessed with Lucy? Should I have used it? Will he really propose marriage to her? What will happen if she accepts?

I do not think I want in-laws in East Cheam.

## 8.45 p.m.

In George. Had pint. Very depressing. Black man in trilby tried to tell me story of his life. Will go home.

## 9.30 p.m.

At home. No sign of Estelle. Found her mobile on kitchen table. Played back her messages and listened to self-expressing need to talk with her about our relationship. Threw her mobile in bin. No sign of anyone else. No one loves me. Will go to bed.

## 9.45 p.m.

In bed. Still no sign of anyone. Have they all been run over? Would serve them right.

## 10 p.m.

Got up. Rang Craftgirls UK. No answer. Rang Snozzer's home. Got answering machine. Rang Plonker's home. Got Plonker's father. Realized I did not know him. Asked if he knew where Edwin was. Plonker's father said, 'Are you the man who has been giving him drugs?' I rang off. Dare not ring Scagg, Bozz or Lulu in case of similar accusations.

## 10.15 p.m.

Back in bed. Hear front door. Noise of Estelle. Sounds as if she is accompanied by Jakob, Ruairghry, Edwin, Bozz, Plonker, Snozzer, Scagg, Lucy, Wodge, etc. They all sound drunk. This is typically irresponsible behaviour from her. I am going to pretend to be asleep.

Think there is a man with them called Hamish. He sounds, unsurprisingly, Scottish.

## 10.30 p.m.

Still pretending to be asleep. Estelle, Jakob, Ruairghriry, Edwin, Plonker, Wodge, Snozzer, Hamish, etc., are all playing the piano and singing old Bob Dylan songs. They have no consideration for the neighbours. I do not, of course, expect them to have any thought for a man of nearly fifty with palpitations, hair loss, an uncontrollable paunch and nothing to look forward to apart from a near-fatal domestic accident.

## 10.45 p.m.

Still pretending to be asleep. Estelle came in at 10.39 precisely. She turned on the light. I did a rather brilliant impression of a man roused from sleep, involving eyelid work, quick susurrations of head, stretching, puzzlement, etc. But it was lost on her. She reeled across the floor, fell over and said, in a loud voice, 'What are you still doing here, pinhead?'

She was smoking a cigarette. Then she got up and went out, slamming the door after her.

I am not sure whether she was talking to me or not.

## 11 p.m.

Given up pretending to be asleep. Have put on dressing-gown and am wondering whether to go downstairs.

Do not think this is an option. Will continue to pretend to be asleep. If I pretend for long enough I may actually go to sleep. There is nothing, at the moment, that I desire more in the world. It is the thought of waking up again that depresses me.

## 11.15 p.m.

Noise from downstairs still deafening. Estelle is now singing 'Sloop John B' at top volume, in close harmony with – I think – Snozzer. Bored with pretending to be asleep, I got up and walked round the room. I sat down on the edge of the bed for a moment and fell asleep. I have only just woken up.

## 11.30 p.m.

Am going downstairs. Will not shout or lose temper. Will pretend that I wish to join in jolly party and offer to sing 'Sloop John B', etc. What to wear though? Obviously the white towelling dressing-gown is not appropriate. Jeans and a casual jumper? Possibly a lounge suit? That would surprise them and also give me confidence.

## 11.45 p.m.

Went downstairs in lounge suit. Estelle said, 'What on earth are you wearing that for?' I said, 'It's my party outfit!' My arrival cast chill on proceedings. Snozzer was wearing a flowerpot on his head and Jakob was beating out time on the table with a packet of spaghetti. I suggested he used a spoon. Have been sent back to bed, as people said I made them feel self-conscious.

Hamish is a midget in a blue blazer. I do not think he is her lover but you can never be too sure.

## 12 midnight.

Estelle has bought a new jumper.

I am lying on the bed in my one lounge suit, thinking about my life. I want to explain, dear diary. I want to tell you about me and Estelle. I want to tell you how I came to be married to the woman with whom I am living. This is the story I must tell. This is the real theme of this diary. This is the mystery I wish to unveil. And when I say —

## April 24th. 8 a.m. A Saturday. Exquisite spring day. Sunlight on emerging leaves, birds nesting, etc.

*All family, Snozzer, etc., presumably in house. Hamish also?*

Just woken up, fully clothed, with my diary in my hand.

Horrible initial fear that Estelle might have read it — and taken offence to references to her being fat, irritable, careerist, etc. However, from the look of her — one leg is half out of the bed, she is wearing a tea-cosy on her head and snoring like a grampus — she was not in a fit state to notice anything by the time she finally staggered up to bed.

Just read last entry. Presumably I was about to tell the story of self and Estelle for first twenty-five years of marriage. Looking back at the two hundred odd pages of this diary I suspect this is not a good idea.

Anyway most of it is a blank.

Why does the process of marriage destroy your awareness of it? I think more of this diary should be devoted to serious, in-depth discussions of my relationship to Estelle — why we are still together, should we leave each other, etc. What does our marriage *mean? What would her diary say about me were she to decide to keep one?*

Maybe not.

## 10 a.m.

Everyone still asleep. Writing this in my study. Hamish, as far as I can see, not on premises. Unless he is in bed with one of the boys. I have also written a serious fatherly letter to Rugirhry about his proposed marriage. It begins —

> My dear boy,
>     I am not sure that I can give my permission for you to marry Lucy. I realize, as I write this, that I do not even know her second name!

I realize, as I write *this*, that he has not asked for my permission. There is someone down in the street, looking up at the house. They are wearing a sort of pixie hood and muffler so it is impossible to see their face. When they first passed — on the other side of the road — I thought it might be Surinder. Now I am not so sure.

I am going down to investigate further.

## 11.30 a.m.

Writing this in a coffee shop in Wimbledon village.

The figure in the street was Laura Proek, who has just left.

She really is an enchanting girl. More intellectual, slightly sharper in manner than Lucy. And harsher in her judgements — especially of people. Less of a homebody. But with a sly sexuality to her that is very appealing. The only criticism I have to make is that it is very difficult, when talking to her, to take one's eyes off the two large bumps in her jersey.

I particularly like the way she licks her fingers after eating croissants. Running it a close second is the way she moves her head from side to side while talking. And number three is the fact that she has buck teeth — something I have always found deeply erotic.

'It's about Jakob!' was almost the first thing she said. I would have preferred her to say something along the lines of 'I can't stop thinking about you!' or 'I am deeply drawn to middle-aged men!', but something I have learned with advancing age is that it is often easy to draw conversations back to oneself if you allow your partner to drone on about what they want to talk about first. In the case of Estelle I have let this get out of hand – almost all our conversations recently have been about little dough men. And, of course, people who are obsessed – with themselves, their work or anything else – do not thank you for catering to their obsession.

Estelle has always been obsessed with something. Smoking or biting her nails or me. I couldn't take it when she was obsessed with me. As I think I said to her at the time, 'We already have one partner in this marriage who thinks about nothing except Paul Slippery!'

'I know!' I said. 'He bit Ruairghry the other day!'

She seemed interested in this news.

'You see,' she went on, 'in a way Jakob is very . . . like . . . I don't know . . . he's sort of . . . oh . . . *contained*! But he is also very, very shy. And quite young really!' 'I know!' I said. 'And you see I really didn't want it to happen. It sort of started when the four of us all went to Chessington World of Adventures . . .' I leaned forward in my seat eagerly. '. . . and we all went on this ride. It was a water ride. You go up and up and up and then you go down this long chute and there were four of us in this one car. I was with Ro-Ree and Lucy was with Jakob. Well you go down and there's a moment, just a moment before you hit the water, when you're almost certain that it won't stop you because it seems hard to believe that it will.' 'I know!' I said.

'Well,' went on Laura, 'when the car was at just that point, I found myself, I don't know why, looking straight at Jakob. And suddenly I knew.' 'Knew what?' I said. 'Knew he was the one,' she went on, 'because you see I knew, from the way Jakob was looking at *me* that with him I wouldn't ever know. I would always be asking myself. It would be like taking the water ride, only the ride would go on for ever and ever and it was like we'd always be looking at each other and wondering and not knowing and wanting to know and that that was what love is or should be, you know?' 'I know!' I said. 'That was how I knew,' said Laura. 'I knew because I didn't know.'

She paused and looked down at the table, tracing patterns on it with her slender fingers.

'I love him,' she said. 'I can't see why he's suddenly got this thing for Lucy!' I gulped hard. 'Neither do I!' I said in a squeaky voice.

After that we talked about other things. Somehow the conversation never got around to me. But I think it is clear that I am going to have to give Jakob a pretty stiff dose of potion and make sure she is somewhere in the vicinity when he gets it down his face. I may be a self-obsessed beast but I have some human feeling left. And what she said about Jakob was more or less exactly what I feel about Estelle – even though I keep losing it and forgetting it and not believing it and even though time and circumstance have worn it the way the road wears the face of a wheel.

How do you hold on to that after all this time? I'm not sure whether I can any more. Should I have written, above, 'what I *felt*' about Estelle? Is this the story of this diary? How to rediscover – or fail to rediscover – what has been lost through familiarity?

I wonder whether Lucy fell in love with Ruairghry at Chessington World of Adventures. What is it about the place? Perhaps I should take Estelle there.

## 12.30 p.m.

Back in study. Tried new breathing-exercise programme called the Lubin Approach. Am thinking of approaching Lubin myself and sticking one on him. I think I have done my back in.

Another letter for Wesley Jones from the Royal Court.

They say they are very upset to hear about the arrest of his family and ask for more information about the fire in the Newline disco in which a friend of his called Bro appears to have died. They seem very pleased with *Muthafuckas* and hope very much Wesley will be there on the first night.

I think I am going to have to go. Do I dare to confront him with the charge of being a figment of my imagination? He is not going to like it. And from the sound of him he has very little to lose.

Estelle, before she left to take a train for Norwich, wanted to know where her mobile phone was. I did not dare to tell her. Edwin says I should balance the waste-basket on top of it. 'Then when she asks why you haven't called her you could say, "Bin on the phone!"'

Hamish, too, is taking the Norwich train. I think he spent the night in the garden. He says he is an accountant although I do not believe this. Estelle and I said goodbye to each other in an almost dismissive, formal manner and I did not show the tempestuous feelings I was undergoing. I think all I said was, 'Well, goodbye then. See you when I see you!' And she said, 'I suppose so!' I don't suppose she even noticed the little sneer I gave when she said this. She and Hamish (who has a squint) went to the front door. On the surface of it just a 'work colleague' going off with another 'work colleague'. I didn't even bother to try and discuss our relationship again. I don't think this was entirely due to the presence of Hamish.

That conversation with Laura had set me thinking. There has to be a moment, in any relationship, where, to use her words, you *know* that the person you are with is right for you. What she described so eloquently is something that I certainly once felt about Estelle. But time, as time does, has interfered with it. That doubt I heard in my protestations the other week – in this very diary – has rattled me. Since then I have started going over and over the last twenty-five years trying to find the certainty Laura talked about. But the harder I look for it the harder it is to find.

Yes, Estelle, it is in crisis. But it has already passed the crisis. It is over. It is a marriage in name only. I am going to have to look for a way out of my marriage. I am going to have to put myself, officially, on the market for sex. If only in the hope that if I have it with someone else I will be able to remember what it was like afterwards. You have brought this on yourself. A househusband can only take so much.

Edwin is listening to a Spanish conversation tape downstairs. Every time I go in the woman on the recording seems to be saying the same sentence. It begins '*Todas las personas trabajon . . .*' and then becomes incomprehensible. When I asked him why he was confining his attention to one Spanish sentence he said it was his favourite sentence and he was not going to go on to another one until he was bored with it.

## 1.30 p.m.

As I have decided to have an affair I thought I would fill a small hip-flask with love potion – in case I run across someone who looks as if she might be a suitable candidate. To my horror discovered it was missing from the place where I had hidden it – under my bed.

It is not the kind of stuff I would trust any of my sons to use responsibly. I have a horrible feeling that Edwin may be the guilty party. He has stopped listening to the tape and is singing in a suggestive manner. When I went downstairs he put both thumbs in the belt of his jeans, gyrated his buttocks wildly and said, 'Get a load of my love machine.' I am almost sure he is the one responsible.

## 4.30 p.m.

A slow afternoon in study. Making lists of people with whom I might have an affair. Not an inspiring bunch. There is Hermione Breen, who used to be married to Christopher Schwimmer, until he ran off with the man who came to mend the central heating. There is, I suppose, Christopher Schwimmer himself, although I do not think that is a serious option – especially since the hair transplant. All friends of Estelle's are more or less out of court – even though Gillian looked a bit of a goer. All too risky.

Chances are that all of the rest of *General Practice* are either contemplating, in the middle of or recently emerging from – surgical sex-change operations. As I look back through the pages of this diary, I see that about the only new females of around my age who I have recently met are the mother of Lucy Whateverhernameis and the mother of Laura Proek. Who, I seem to have decided, has a seriously mean personality. Is this necessarily a drawback?

## 4.45 p.m.

Well, I am not an easy person. I am weak, desperately envious of others and totally absorbed in myself. But they do say that sexual attraction often begins in violent mutual dislike. If this is the case, Mrs Proek and I should be shagging away merrily by the end of the afternoon.

Ruairghry and Jakob came into my room about ten minutes ago. They looked as if they were plucking up courage to ask for money but did not have the nerve. They both looked sullen, although I could see no bite marks on Ruairehgy. There seems to have been a mild truce in their relations. They went into the front room and then Ruarighry put on a Deep Purple CD. I heard him say, in gloating tones, to his younger brother, 'This is Lucy's favourite record!' After this Jakob went out into the hall and slammed the door after him. I went downstairs and said, 'Shouldn't you go in and talk to him?' Jakob said, 'Oh dear! I'm too busy!'

Adult angst does not, like that of children, lay you open. I hardly recognized the boy in front of me. His face wore the closed expression I thought was usually confined to parents. Ruairgerhy has now departed for East Cheam. Jakob, after trying to get through to East Cheam on the phone set off after his brother. I think I'd better get down there (a) because otherwise they may kill each other and (b) because the only two women currently available for me to have designs on live in East Cheam.

Edwin has consented to come 'if we can play Oasis in the car'. I have agreed to this.


## 5.15 p.m.

While he was loading the collected works of the Gallagher brothers into the car, I searched Edwin's room. The bottle was in his desk drawer. At least an inch is missing. This stuff is dynamite. It should not be left in the hands of a sixteen-year-old boy – especially Edwin. He is downstairs, singing a song the chorus of which goes – 'Gonner make you in my love-shack baby, ooh yeah!'

Should I confront him with the love-potion theft?


## 5.45 p.m.

Weird.

On our way through Wimbledon to Cheam, Edwin suddenly shouted, 'Stop the car! It's my love machine!' I thought at first he was referring to the Volvo – and then I saw Lulu on the other side of the road with Snozzer, Bozz, Plonker and Scagg – who was wearing a white overall and a white trilby hat.

It was, I realized with a small thrill, the costume worn by him when in the act of dispensing cheese – and possibly fish – in Waitrose. Had he, perhaps, stolen it?

Before I could stop him, Edwin had got out of the car and thrown himself into the arms of Lulu. Little does this innocent girl know that he is armed with at least ten milligrams of an extremely powerful love philtre. From the look of her, however, she does not need any encouragement. I got out to remonstrate with him but he and the others ran off down the road – Edwin shouting in a Chinese accent, 'Catch me if you can, Slippery!'

I returned to the Volvo to find a traffic warden in the process of writing out a ticket. There was a nasty little moment between us while we both attempted to pretend this was not happening. Then, as I looked up at her I saw that it was Laura's mother.

She looked a lot better in uniform. She seemed about ten years younger than the last time I had seen her. I said, 'Mrs Proek!' She said, 'Only a humble traffic warden as you see, but' – and here she gave a not unappealing if slightly sinister smile – 'there are times when everyone wants to be my friend!' She held her pen poised over the ticket. I gave her a smile that was described as 'winning' when I used it in the RSC's studio production of *A Winter's Tale*, and moved slightly nearer to her. She held up her hand. 'Do not,' she said, 'I beg of you, attempt to influence me in any way! I am a public servant!' 'I would not dream of doing so!' I said, 'I expect no mercy! No mercy whatsoever!'

There was now, I decided, a definite sexual component to this encounter. I am almost positive she licked her lips. 'You are in charge!' I said, following up my advantage swiftly. 'It is, as they say, your call! You are on duty! Doing your job! And – if I may say so –' I went on, 'doing it very well indeed.' She allowed a slight smile to play round her lips. 'Don't give me too much old soap, Mr Slippery!' she said, her eyes now positively twinkling. 'I know you are in one but that doesn't mean you have to dish it out to us humble traffic wardens. And we are, as I do not have to remind you, very, very humble!' She very nearly winked as she said this.

'Look . . .' I said, 'I'm sorry if I was . . .'

She had still not filled in the ticket. Then, suddenly, she seemed to remember who I was, and, perhaps more importantly, whose father I represented. 'Where are you off to?' she said. I said, 'Er . . . East Cheam!' She narrowed her eyes slightly. I decided not to lie. 'Ruairghry's gone down there to see Lucy!' I said. 'He seems to be . . . er . . . pretty keen on her . . .'

This was the wrong thing to say. Mrs Proek wrote out my ticket and slipped it under my windscreen wiper. All she said, before she turned to walk away, was, 'It's a mess. It's a horrible mess. And Laura's father . . .'

That was all she said. But her expression was not unamiable. I have the odd notion, however, that I am in with a chance with her. She is clearly something of a sadist and giving me a ticket has probably sparked off elements of sexual desire.

Must now get to the Berts to avoid hideous confrontation between sons.

April 25th. 11 a.m. Even more exquisite spring day. Mild zephyrs, blue skies, rabbits, presumably humping, etc.

*Estelle still in Norwich. Ruairghry and Jakob at psychiatrist's. Edwin and me at home. Me not humping. Edwin hopefully not also.*

I can hear Edwin and Snozzer upstairs. They are rehearsing *A Midsummer Night's Dream* – or rather their version of it – in which Mr Hotchkiss looms large. The rehearsal involves whacking each other with pillows and jumping on beds in the way they used to do when small. At the moment, Edwin, who is impersonating Hotchkiss, is shouting, 'You have big, big thighs, Snozzer!' And Snozzer is yelling back, 'Yes, Hotchkiss! Oh Hotchkiss, I am coming, Hotchkiss!' I must go upstairs and stop them in a minute, but for the present do not have the heart to do so.

Ruairgehry and Jakob came to blows again last night. Superficially this might have seemed to be an argument about whether they were going to watch *Deep Space Nine*. I had to intervene and told them that it was, of course, really about the fact that Lucy had agreed to go ten-pin bowling with Ruaierghrey and Ruairghry had announced that he was proposing to propose to her. They both turned on me and accused me of being 'like some trendy shrink'. I am sending them off for free counselling from a real-life trendy shrink – Hermann Schinn, a friend of Estelle's who is a partially trained Kleinian analyst. It is not entirely free. We are not paying Schinn but I am paying them to go and see him.

I am brooding over recent aspects of Estelle's behaviour. Rang her room in Norwich and was connected to a Turkish man who professed ignorance of her. What is she up to? The other night was not the only occasion recently when she came in at one in the morning, smelling strongly of drink. Neither was it the only occasion on which I pretended to be asleep. On the earlier occasion, in fact, I think I was asleep. Or at least I had been pretending to be asleep for so long that I can't remember whether I was awake when she arrived in the bedroom.

This whole memory question puts me at a serious disadvantage. If, for example, she had been canoodling with Hamish – would I have remembered? Assuming I had seen her at it? Perhaps she has spent hours telling me about how she has been given oral pleasure by a man called Jones – only I am unable to remember that she has done so.

She has taken to dressing and undressing in the bathroom. I do not know whether this is because she does not wish to arouse me. But in fact I find it even more tantalizing. Before she went out one morning I did manage to ask her why she was away so much, what she had been doing, etc. I also asked her why she undressed in the bathroom. She gave me a pretty sharp look and said, 'We must discuss it actually. The bathroom is a real problem.' Then she marched out back to the bathroom. I did get to see her partially clothed, however, which is about the nearest I am likely to get to a shag for the foreseeable future.

Has Hamish left bite marks on her neck? If so – can I remember seeing them?

Perhaps she undresses in the bathroom because of her weight – although I think she has lost weight – even if it is hard to judge in the half-light. If we carry on meeting like this I can allow my body to go to rack and ruin, since the chances of her getting a look at it are absolutely minimal.

No matter. We are moving into an open relationship. I am going to be starting an affair any day now. Am aware of pitfalls and will watch out for potential partner's penis, cross-dressing predilection, etc.


11.30 a.m.

Post. Late again.

A letter from Good Old Steve about Nobby's memorial service. It is to take place at St Barnabas's Church, Streatham – 'a place of worship of which Nobby was particularly fond'. I presume this means he once parked his bike against the walls. Nobby was the most irreligious person I think I have ever known. I had hoped Good Old Steve might have put together a sort of tasteless neo-pagan junket with readings from Walt Whitman, *Zen and the Art of Motor-cycle Maintenance* and other authors of whom Nobby had almost certainly never heard.

There isn't much about the content of the ceremony – although I have not been asked to speak, which I consider frankly rude. My speaking voice is particularly suited to large echoing buildings.

Good Old Steve ends his letter with the news that one of the pieces of music will be by Delius. I cannot think what this is about. Nobby was tone-deaf and the most appropriate musical tribute to him would probably be a sample tape of the muzak played in his local off-licence.

I must now go into the Beeb to find out whether I have any chance of surviving the collapse of the interior wall of my premises. Not to mention who the new Head of Sound will turn out to be. No sign of Ruarighy and Jakob.

The partially trained Kleinian is seeing them this morning even though his premises are, he tells me, 'only partially open for business'. What does this mean? Only half a couch? Must wake them.

Jakob should have been back at Oxford for a week. Jakob said, the other day, 'They won't notice. My tutor is senile.' I said this was no excuse. He went on to tell me that he had been reading this old idiot the essays of a boy called Chowdray, who is a scholar at Balliol. 'He really likes them!' said Jakob giving me the crooked smile that has attracted so many women, apart, of course, from the one I have chemically induced him to love.

Edwin said he was not going to school today, although it is supposed to be his first day back. I had not even realized this was the case. Things are really falling apart here. He said he wanted to come into the Beeb with me. 'I need to work on my album! I need work experience!' he said. I said he did. What he did not need was experience of watching other people work, since he had already had sixteen years of that.


## 12 noon.

Send boys to Schinn the Kleinian.

Message on machine from him. He wants me to come in for 'a chat'. He seems to think I have 'problems'. He also expressed an interest in Edwin. I did not pick up the call. I think I heard shouting in the background. I thought Hermann sounded more than partially stressed. Also message from my mum. It goes —

MUM: Paul? Paul, is that you? Are you there, Paul? (*Sinister footsteps. Pause.*) Are you hiding, Paul? Are you hiding there behind the machine, Paul? (*Distant sounds of screaming. Long pause.*) It's about Mrs Rusedski, Paul. Do you remember Mrs Rusedski, Paul? She was very ill. (*Long pause. Burst of singing in the distance.*) She wasn't expected to last the night, Paul. And she hasn't. Apparently. (*Long pause.*) She was ninety-eight, Paul. (*Even longer pause.*) Ninety-eight. (*Silence. End of message.*)

## 1.30 p.m.

In canteen with Edwin. On the way in I asked him about his album as this was the first I had heard of it. He said, 'We have the T-shirt and the promotional material all in place. All I have to do is write the songs.' I said I thought this was the wrong way to go about it and he said, 'With respect, you are from another era. Brand definition is the most important thing. Look at your career!' I said, slightly edgily, 'What about my career?' Edwin said, 'My point precisely!'

I need to ask him about Lulu.

I can see Karl Rhws Davies approaching with Cross. Leo is with them.

## 2.30 p.m.

Still in canteen. Edwin has eaten four helpings of goulash and nine dumplings washed down by four glasses of Bulls' Blood (it is Hungarian Week in the canteen and all the waitresses are wearing white aprons, bows in their hair, etc.). It seems that the final decision on whether I survive the collapsed wall will be taken by the Core Directorate Policy Unit some time at the beginning of May, which is good news. Unless, of course, by that time Howard Porda has turned into a gorilla.

I tried to tell Karl, Cross and Leo that John Birt really liked me. They looked at me as if I was mad.

Leo stayed behind and whispered his plans for the series. 'I think,' he said, in a low, tremulous voice, 'I want to play down the medical angle!' I told him that as the series was set in a doctor's surgery this might be difficult. His plan seems to be to build up a new character called Rupert, an architect who is called in to redesign the practice premises and gradually devote the whole show to him. He intends, eventually, to kill off all the medical characters in a series of industrial accidents. 'I haven't told anyone this yet,' he went on, 'apart from you!' I promised to keep it a closely guarded secret.

He is, I think, clinically insane. Edwin said, as he left, 'Where have they been keeping him?'

The bad news is that apparently they issued a press release on my accident in which they said I am to die of 'complications related to having a wall fall on me'. This piece of illiteracy came complete with manufactured quotes from me saying how I had always wanted to move on to other things. The good news is that this, according to Karl, has spawned a whole stream of letters expressing deep love and concern for me. Well, three letters anyway. Much talk of Cross's leaving party – to be held in a room called B34576. No one seems to know where this is. Or where he is going to when he leaves it.

I tried to work up courage to tackle Edwin on the subject of the potion. I am now sure he has stolen it to use on Lulu. I started a general conversation about love philtres through the ages. He gave me a very suspicious look and started talking about GCSE French. Quite clearly he is hoping to use it on this innocent girl in order to get her to come across. I am not proud of him. Off now to record the episode.


5 p.m.

In George with Edwin, who has just drunk three pints of lager. Dylan Thomas would have been proud of him.

I think he was pretty impressed by my performance this afternoon. Karl, who now that he thinks I am totally in his power, publicly announced as about to die, etc., is being rather nice to me. He allowed Edwin (who he called 'young feller me lad') to go into the control suite. I had a pretty strong scene with Ronnie 'Very Nice Man' Pilfrey, who was, as usual, trying to upstage me and failing hopelessly. We were discussing, among other things, fund management and the recent outbreak of meningitis at the Ashbourne School for Girls. Pilfrey's daughter (an appalling performance from Alison Thornby) looks as if she is coming down with the disease.

I did something today that I have been playing with over the last few episodes. I have given Esmond just the very faintest hint of a Russian accent. Nothing that you would notice. It is really only for myself. But I have decided, over the next few weeks, to push it as far as I can until someone notices. As soon as they do I will drop it. But the thought occurs to me that – if things go on as they have been – I may well be sounding like President Yeltsin before anyone spots what I am up to.

Edwin did say, however, as we went towards the lifts on our way out, 'How come you're making him sound like a mad Russian? Is it deliberate?'

## 7 p.m.

Estelle no longer in Norwich. The only reason I know this is that she rang her mobile phone, which I heard beeping away in the waste-paper basket. I retrieved it and the message, which went – 'This is Estelle Slippery here! I do not know where my mobile phone is but if it is at Mafeking Road perhaps somebody there would ring me and tell me it is. If it isn't I would like whoever is listening to this message to contact me on 0141–7776990000.'

This is a Glasgow number. What is she doing in Glasgow? Hamish perhaps? Although I am still very angry with her and about to start an affair, I suppose I don't want to put her through the fag of having to cancel and reorder her mobile. I will get Edwin to call her. She deserves worse but I somehow cannot provide her with it.

Trying to be good is about as complicated as being married and, somehow or other, related to it in ways I do not fully understand. This is not an explanation of why I am still with Estelle but it goes some way to explaining the curious phenomenon of our very long-lasting marriage.

## 11.30 p.m.

Dinner with all three boys. Veal with paprika and cream. On a rota system as Jakob and Ruairghry refuse to sit at the same table. Ruaierhgy said he would eat his in the scullery – although we do not, as far as I know, have a scullery. Good man-to-man talk, however – albeit on a serial basis. We do not need Estelle. Jakob still shows no sign of going back to university. He says he has 'a man in Magdalen who will read his essays for him'. As they are written by someone else this does not seem a totally bad idea. The only work he has done this vac is to study a short book called *The Homosexual Kings of England*, which, apparently, maintains that every single king, apart from George the Second – who was certainly suspect

— was a raving brown-hatter (a phrase I have picked up from Nerys, the accountant).

Queen Anne and Queen Mary were both lesbians and Queen Elizabeth the First was a man. It doesn't go up to Elizabeth the Second.

The reason Jakob is staying down, it now appears, is 'business commitments'. He will not say precisely what they are, but Edwin told me, when he was out of the room, that 'it's a major deal and could be worth a few K'. I have decided to actively encourage his entrepreneurial side.

Ruarigrhy, who ended up by eating his veal *en promenade*, said, 'The reason Estelle is away so much is to punish you for all the times you hung around the BBC bar with Pilfrey and the lads.' I cannot believe this to be the case. I may have had the occasional half of lager with Pilfrey to talk through a tricky point in the script but I think I have always been a good and conscientious father.

If I did hang around the BBC bar with Pilfrey, why am I now no longer doing so? Are they hanging around without me? If so, why are they doing this? Have I become dull, suddenly? Perhaps this would explain Estelle's continued absence.

April 27th. 9 a.m. More zephyrs, blue skies, sounds of birds shagging, etc.

*Estelle in Ireland. Edwin back at school, just. Ruarigeughy and Jakob asleep. Me in study.*

Edwin has finally consented to go back to school although Jakob seems still uninterested in returning to Oxford. Last night he revealed that Oliver has been sentenced to six months in prison for drug-related offences. Apparently he was using the funds of the Lager Society to buy heroin. Either that or he was using heroin to buy lager for the society. I said, 'He seemed such a nice boy!' Jakob said, 'Precisely!' Ruaigrhy then said, once again, that he wanted to go away and think about his life. I said, 'I wouldn't mind going away and thinking about mine, mate. What there is left of it. I would like to go away and do things.' Rueighry said, 'What things?' Which rather stumped me. Eventually I said, 'Live on a Greek island!' I knew this was a feeble reply. Greek islands are full of the kind of people one wants to avoid in Wimbledon.

Jakob has discovered Ruaighry is taking Lucy to the Wimbledon Odeon. He says if Ruairghry does this he, Jakob, will destroy Ruarighry's entire collection of Megadeth recordings – a truly colossal task. Ruriaghry said, 'I don't care about Megadeth any more.' This seemed to disappoint Jakob. Was this because Heavy Metal was an interest they once shared? Or, more likely, because Ruarighry was losing an area of vulnerability? When I tried to raise this point, they both turned on me. Ruiaghry said I was 'controlling' – a phrase I think he has picked up from the partially trained Kleinian, of whom both boys seem to have become partially fond.

On the way in to school Edwin gave me a stern talking-to about my career. He seems to think I have been allowing people like Cross, Rhws Davies, John Birt, Ashley Ramp, etc., to walk all over me. I said that the whole point of such people's existence was to walk over people like me. And if it kept them happy I was perfectly willing to let them get on with it. This seemed to annoy him. 'Dis them!' he said to me as we rolled down Parkside. 'Give them heavy pain, man!' His speech pattern seems to have completely altered over the Easter holidays without my noticing it until now. 'With my band, right,' he said, 'I do not take any shit, right? If people are no good I like fire them, right? I like give them a hard time, right? It's safe, right?' I asked him whether they had played yet and he said they hadn't.

I then foolishly made a speech about my sadness that he had abandoned the piano at Grade Three, to which he replied, 'Do not be old!'

Emboldened by his remarks I am going into the Beeb to kick ass.


10.15 a.m.

Writing this in canteen. There is, I fear, no ass here to kick. In fact the whole place seems completely deserted. Perhaps they have finally fired everybody.

Picked up a letter from home, addressed to me and marked PRIVATE, which I think is from East Cheam. Perhaps Laura or Lucy needs some fatherly advice. Lunch in an Italian restaurant? Have not opened it in case it is a solicitor's letter inspired by Norman Proek.

The only person I have found in the entire building is a man called

Wainwright who produces a late-night show on Radio 3. He has been here even longer than I have and is, after thirty years in the Beeb, very red and almost completely circular. He was wearing, as always, a green tweed suit. He tells me he thinks Colin Cross is trying to come back but has been told he can't. Ashley Ramp has refused to go to Wales, Scotland, Northern Ireland and East Anglia. 'Who,' said Wainwright, 'will be the new Head of Sound?' He seemed to think Karl stands a chance, as does Ashley Ramp, if he can avoid being sent to any of the places to which they want to send him. Both would be disastrous for me. My only concern is — whoever it is — where does he stand on Esmond Pennebaker? And how long will he last? Will he last long enough to repudiate the press release put out by the odious Karl?

I asked Wainwright about the Core Directorate Policy Unit. He confirmed that it will consist of Howard Porda and whoever replaces Colin Cross's replacement, and also include two other new bosses who have only emerged as a result of the latest round of restructuring. One is called Assistant Head of Drama Policy and the other is called Associate Head of Sound Drama. He also said that the two front runners for Head of Sound were Karl and Ashley Ramp.

When I asked Wainwright what he thought the two new appointments would actually *do* he said, 'This is very much up in the air at the moment. So far they have only invented the jobs. Now they have to invent people to fill them. I suspect their main role is try and slim down each other's departments.'

Just seen Howard Porda at the other end of the canteen, helping himself to a bowl of jasmine tea (it is almost the start of Chinese Fortnight). I think now is the time to go and ingratiate myself with him.


12 noon.

Writing this in Main Reception.

I am dealing with something far more complicated than a mere sex change! As so often (as, perhaps, in the case of the Ruaigrhy/Laura/Jakob/Lucy quartet), my intervention may only have intensified the state of play rather than altered its course! I do not know whether to feel smug or depressed about this.

I should, I suppose, have spotted this before.

It appears that Howard has a very rare disease of the pituitary gland which makes his hormonal levels liable to violent fluctuations. Even before I switched his tablets round he was pretty confused. 'The thing is,' he told me, in an alarmingly loud voice, as we strolled along the corridor to his office, 'I just can't make up my mind whether to be a man or a woman!' Some days he wants to drift around in black lingerie and soap his breasts, and on other days he wants to drink pints of lager, throw his weight about in corporate meetings and ogle young and attractive people of the opposite sex.

'Right now,' he said, 'I'm feeling very, very male!' I did not dare to suggest the possible reason for this. 'I cannot wait,' he said in a deep and decisive voice, as we entered the lifts, 'to get rid of these breasts!' The only other occupant of the lift was Ronnie 'Very Nice Man' Pilfrey. He raised his eyebrows slightly but affected not to be listening to our conversation. Howard seemed completely unabashed. Presumably his testosterone level is now so high that the thought of exposure holds no terrors for him. 'The thought of striding around in a bra and garter belt,' he went on, in the same authoritative, masculine tone, 'has absolutely no charms for me at the moment!' At this point Pilfrey stuck his long nose into the conversation. 'Join the club!' he said, in an offensively camp voice. Howard completely ignored him.

We went back to his office where he dictated five memos, fired eight people, arranged six lunches and shouted at his secretary. Then he shooed her out of the way, closed the door and said, 'This press release is out of order! I was very much against the wall falling on top of you! I argued strongly against it in the Core Directorate Policy Unit, but at the time I was in a difficult situation. I was planning to become a woman.' 'I know!' I said. 'It makes my flesh creep to think of it,' said Porda. 'Imagine having some guy take a billhook to your winkie! My God, I must have been mad!'

I wasn't, I have to say, altogether sure of his sanity at the present time but, once again, I nodded. 'I am totally against these new writers,' he went on, 'and I cannot understand all these references to buildings and architecture in the show. As soon as the wall has fallen on you we'll get you into hospital. I think you may meet a nurse to whom you respond sexually; she could give you a blow-job or something!' I said I liked this idea. Howard then rolled his eyes and flailed his tongue, graphically, against the roof of his mouth.

Then he went back to the telephone. In fact, during the course of our conversation, Porda managed to keep about three conversations on different phone lines on the go, as well as faxing a letter to John Birt, receiving and sending three E-mails to a man called Roger and handwriting a note to Ashley Ramp telling him that if he refused to go to Plymouth he would be sent to Norwich and not allowed to return.

His condition does seem to be related to some form of mania. But at least he is on my side. I need him to keep me out of the clutches of Rhws Davies and the equally insane Leo. 'I think,' went on Howard, 'that Pilfrey should die and die horribly.' I nodded. 'I am not against that!' I said. 'There's a disease,' said Porda, 'where your brain goes all mushy and you can't remember anything and your legs ache!' 'I know,' I said, 'I think I've got it!' Howard gave a big, booming laugh. 'I like you, Slippery!' he said. 'You have a nice dry sense of humour!' 'Yes!' I said. Howard laughed again and, suddenly serious, leaned across the desk. 'I love my mother very much!' he said.

The interview was at an end.

It's been a great year for chemicals, Slippery. Not only have you completely altered your sons' sex lives, you have also sent one of your colleagues round the twist. I would say you were a worm but we both know that you have not even the acting talent to portray one.

Must go now as have arranged lunch with Peter Mailer and Good Old Steve.


## 12.45 p.m.

In taxi. Just opened letter. It was from Gwendolen Proek, suggesting lunch at a Chinese restaurant 'to talk about the situation'. She says at one point – 'The situation between me and Norman and Lucy's parents is horrendously complicated. Perhaps I have been a little unfair to you, although you were parking in a Controlled Parking Zone outside the time when it was legal for you to do so!'

Gwendolen, huh? I think I am in there with a chance.

I have to meet her anyway. I have to get Jakob back together with Laura before he and Ruairehughry kill each other.

## 5 p.m. L'Abattoir Restaurant, Islington.

At least I think that is what it is called. It certainly specializes in gigantic hunks of meat, all done to three specifications – bloody, very bloody and bloody well bloody so up yours. Good Old Steve said they threw out some fairy who asked for it medium, and a gentleman who asked for the vegetarian menu was attacked outside by hired thugs and had to have nine stitches in the back of his head.

Peter Mailer asked for Perrier water and the waiter openly sneered at him.

Good Old Steve and I drank four bottles of Château Haut-Brion, for which Good Old Steve – or rather Rupert Murdoch – paid. The alleged purpose of the lunch was to discuss Nobby's memorial service, which is next week. I asked about the funeral and Good Old Steve said he thought that Nobby had asked not to be buried. 'Does this mean he is just rotting somewhere?' Good Old Steve said that that was what Nobby had done for most of his life. I said I thought you had to be buried because it was the law. Good Old Steve said he didn't know about that. The things Good Old Steve doesn't know about are amazing. Years of working for the Murdoch press have reduced his curiosity to almost zero.

It was agreed between us – I think I let them know, in a subtle manner, that as I am a professional entertainer, I should be asked to perform – that all three of us would speak. I said I would like to read one of Nobby's favourite poems. Steve reminded me that Nobby had not read a book since 1968. We agreed I would read something by Philip Larkin.

An extraordinary thing happened halfway through lunch. I was almost sure I saw Jakob sitting at the other end of the room. He seemed to be wearing a dark suit and talking earnestly to a middle-aged man. I looked back once and decided I was mistaken. But when I looked back again – by this time he and the middle-aged man were leaving – I was positive that it was my middle son. How on earth does he find the money to eat in places like this? Or am I simply hallucinating?

Will ask him when I get home. Must go now as have to pick up Edwin from rehearsal.

## 9 p.m.

Estelle 'somewhere in Connemara'. Edwin, who spoke to her on, or rather with, her mobile, says she is there to 'do music' for the animated film of Mr Slippy Sloppy, the pot-bellied dough man. Let us hope it is not full of cheap jokes about husbands! He said he had suggested me for the part but Estelle had said I was 'old hat'. There are times when I would like to strangle her. Even if, however, I could be bothered to fly to Shannon, etc., to do this, to have any chance of success I would have to sedate her first.

I made boned shoulder of veal stuffed with apricots and thyme, accompanied by broad beans with garlic – a dish that, according to the *River Café Cookbook* is a particular favourite of charcoal-burners of the Maremma region of lower Tuscany. It does not say whether these guys boil it up when they are out in the woods gathering charcoal or whether they only tuck into it when over in Hammersmith on their annual two weeks' holiday.

Edwin said it tasted 'soapy'.

Writing this in the front room while I listen to Elgar's marvellously evocative cello concerto.

## 9.15 p.m.

Or, as we say, Dvorak's marvellously evocative cello concerto.

## 9.30 p.m.

Message from Gustave on the machine. He says I have been offered a small part in a musical in Leicester. Apparently I play an animal of some kind but he does not like to tell me what it is over the phone. Perhaps I would like to call him to discuss it. It is possible, I suppose, that I am at last getting live-action insect work. Very excited about this, briefly, and then, of course, depressed again. It is probably the back end of a horse.

Also message from my mother. It goes

(*Tape crackle. Long pause.*) Paul, is that you? Are you there? (*Long pause. Heavy breathing.*) It's Granny here, Paul! It's the old Granny with the stick who lives in the flat on the hill! Do you remember her, Paul? (*Mad laugh. Long pause.*) I watched *Brookside*, Paul. It was disgusting. That woman died, you know. Did you watch *Brookside*? (*Heavy breathing. Sounds of thumping in background.*) That's my fridge, Paul, do you hear it? It makes that noise at night, Paul, like a spirit groaning in hell – do you hear it?' (*More thumping. Heavy breathing. Mad laughter.*) This is Granny here, Paul. I will see you Saturday if I'm not dead. (*Long pause. Then, thoughtfully.*) I'd be better dead really. All things considered, better dead. (*Long pause. More thumping. Mad laughter. Heavy breathing. Tape crackle. Silence.*)

I am thinking of dubbing off these messages and preserving them in some kind of archive. They have the makings, I think, of a powerful piece of drama.

### 11.15 p.m.

Called Gwendolen Proek. Luckily she, not Norman, answered. We have agreed to meet in a Chinese restaurant in Wimbledon. She said, 'I can't talk now because Norman will be in off the roof soon.' She is obviously falling for me in a big way.

Rang Gustave at home. The job in Leicester was a duck. It was a children's show. I said I didn't do ducks.

## April 28th. 11.30 a.m. Blue skies. Slight breeze. Cumulus cloud over Wimbledon.

*Edwin at school. Ruairghrey staying night at Berts'. Jakob, presumably, pacing up and down hall, biting nails. Estelle in the Arbour Hotel, Leitrim. Me in Beeb.*

We have just read the scene in which the wall falls on me. I am emboldened by the fact that I have heard that (a) the Core Directorate Policy Unit meets at the end of the week (or thereabouts) to make their 'final decision on Pennebaker'; (b) that the new Head of Sound is rumoured to be 'in the Porda camp'; and (c) that there have been rumours of a rumour that Karl Rhws Davies is to be sent to Northern Ireland. I have demanded, and got, several rewrites. Leo is rapidly becoming terrified of me, which is how I want him to be. Fight back, Slippery!

As we climbed the stairs, the first draft of the dialogue went as follows –

ARCHITECT: Well, Dr Pennebaker, this building is almost as old as the century!
ME: It was designed by Snueygens, the Dutch architect.
ARCHITECT: Really? I love his buildings. They are so full of light and space and spirituality.
ME: He died in a train crash in 1932.
    *FX wall collapse. Pennebaker screams. His screams fade away to silence.*

After some pretty tough talking I got this changed to –

ARCHITECT: This is an old building, Dr Pennebaker!
ME: You don't need buildings to practise medicine, my friend!
ARCHITECT: But –
ME: Care in the community is what my job is about. There are twelve patients on our list over the age of seventy who have serious asthma. Mrs Nuffield, for example, from Greenacres. My job is to make sure that she and people like her enjoy a dignified old age.
ARCHITECT: I suppose you're right.
    *FX wall collapse. Pennebaker's screams continue, hauntingly.*

Although Karl had been very against my screaming at all, in the end I also managed to get them to agree to my shouting 'Help!' in a faint voice, after my screaming dies away. (Karl was particularly unpleasant about my ability to scream convincingly.) At first he said, 'You can groan once after you scream and then let the *groan* die away.' I got round this by groaning so badly that they had no alternative but to let me speak. Karl said my groan had 'an unpleasantly constipated feel to it'. Which was, of course, just what I intended.

I called for help this morning in a manner that made it clear I expected it to arrive. Even if Ramp or Karl do get the job of Head of Sound, Porda and John Birt and I are an unbeatable combination! The trouble with the

BBC, of course, is that it has been set up to create an environment in which everyone can repeatedly unmake everyone else's decisions. I fear the debate about my death will be as long drawn out as that surrounding the end of Mary Queen of Scots.

That, needless to say, is where I trust my resemblance to the Scottish queen ends.

Must now get back to Mafeking Road. V. worried about Jakob, who was muttering death threats against his older brother when I went to bed last night. Lucy and Ruairghery do seem, to use Edwin's phrase, to be 'an item'. She has tidied his room and put up a large picture of a hamster on the wall. I asked her if she would do the same for my study. She squeaked, clapped her hands and shook in a delightfully plump manner. I think this means 'yes'.

Her surname is Rachnowski. This is presumably why Laura Proek (a German name?) said, glumly, the other week, that Jakob was completely up the Pole.

I have uncovered what Jakob was up to in L'Abattoir the other week. He is using profits on currency deals to set up, among other things, 'an electrical budget warehouse'. He tells me their 'operating profit' is likely to be in six figures. The most worrying thing about all this was that he kept reassuring me that none of the goods were stolen, which made me suspect that they all were.

If he has contacts in the underworld, perhaps he could arrange to have Ruaigerhgy topped! I am, I have to say, not best pleased with my eldest son at the moment – not least with his refusal to get a job, attend University of South Wimbledon, etc. But I do not think he deserves to die at the hands of a contract killer.

It turns out Jakob also has part share in a restaurant in Norwich.


## 12.15 p.m.

Just got home. No sign of Jakob. Called Berts. Mrs Bert said, 'They're still in bed.' They should be safe enough there. Call on machine from Gwendolen Proek suggesting we meet this evening as 'things are getting critical at this end with the Rachnowskis'. What can she mean by this?

## 1 p.m.

Jakob just returned. From where? He wouldn't say. He looked, suddenly, terribly young and vulnerable. I said, 'Look. It isn't that bad! I'm sure they won't get married or anything!' Jakob said, in a tight voice, 'Why not? I could run down the aisle shouting, "It should have been me!"' Then he said, 'It's probably to do with my willy! I think it's developing mange!'

He has the look, sometimes, of an abandoned goblin. At such moments I would like to take him in my arms but know he would freeze in puzzled shyness if I did so. So I don't.

I think I should make some attempt to get him back with Laura. Perhaps ask him to my tête-à-tête with Gwendolen Proek. Get her to ask Laura. Tip some potion into their meal. It is worth a try. And if this goes on much longer I am going to need a lot more than a partially trained Kleinian to keep them from tearing each other apart.

I don't think Jakob has any objection to Laura. And he is extremely fond of Chinese food.

## 1.30 p.m.

Called Gwendolen Proek (we are now on first-name terms) and put this plan to her, without, of course, mentioning potion. She was all for it. Slightly depressed at what may be a lack of interest in my body but strong feeling of virtue.

## 1.45 p.m.

Attempted to capitalize on virtuous feeling by telephoning Estelle in Leitrim. I was connected to her room and spoke, once again, to a Turkish gentleman. I was almost sure he was the same Turkish gentleman I spoke to in Norwich and so I said to him, 'Are you the same Turkish person I spoke to in Norwich?' He got quite offended at this and told me he had never been to Norwich. I then said, 'Do you know where Estelle Slippery is?' He put down the phone.

Am not, actually, sure either of them was Turkish.

## 2.30 p.m.

Ruarieghy came back from the Rachnowskis with Lucy, who brought with her a large furry rat which she is going to install in his bedroom. She shook out her black hair and squeaked, 'He's called Roger and the rodent operatives use him for training!' Think this was a joke but am not sure. I asked Ruiaerghy about the University of South Wimbledon, a job, etc., and he said, 'You can tweak Roger's nose if you like!' Then they both went upstairs.

Jakob sitting alone downstairs reading a biography of Maynard Keynes. He looks horribly lonely. Perhaps I should get him a fluffy toy for his room.


## 3 p.m.

Edwin seems to be using Estelle's mobile. He rang me from what sounded like a moving train. I asked him where he was and what he was doing and he said, 'Oh it's Tuesday!' When I said this did not explain why he was not sitting at a desk studying for his GCSEs he said, 'On Tuesdays we do Good Deeds!' I will find out more about this.

He also seems very well informed about Estelle's movements – which is more than I am. Apparently she is in Angmering-on-Sea. He said she would be home 'as soon as she has sorted out this Hamish thing'. Told Mrs Hamish perhaps? Do I even want her back at Mafeking Road? Do we need her? Her presence now, I feel, might only cramp my style with traffic wardens, kicking ass at Beeb, Tuscan cuisine, etc.


## 3.45 p.m.

Edwin home, smelling of tobacco smoke. I asked him what he meant by Good Deeds and he said, 'On Tuesdays instead of games we can do like social-work things, like visiting old people. So I went down to visit Granny.'

## 4 p.m.

Jakob in really bad state. Sitting listlessly on sofa on page four of the Keynes biography. Checked Liquid Love preparatory to booking the Jade Garden in the village. I am sure some more is missing. And Edwin is upstairs singing, 'Be my little love pump baby gonner let you suck me dry!' in a manner that I think the neighbours may find offensive.

## 4.30 p.m.

Lucy making high-pitched squeaking noises from Ruairghy's room. I do not think she is doing mouse impressions. The bed is also thumping against the wall in a rhythm faintly reminiscent of a Russian folk dance. I hope to God Jakob can't hear this.

## 6 p.m.

Writing this in the Chinese restaurant. Jakob 'on his way'. Driven out early by the noise from Ruaighry's room (which sounded to me as if Roger the Rat was joining in the proceedings), I left Jakob staring at the ceiling listlessly, saying he would be there but he 'had to think about things'. As I went out of the door, he said, in a voice of infinite pathos, 'Ruarghy took my Black Sabbath CD. And he never asked me.' No sign of Laura Proek or of her mother. I am deeply depressed. Especially as have not had courage to tell Jakob Laura is going to be here.

Suddenly depressed by the whole idea of the potion. I should never have started on it. Isn't love one of the few areas of the world left where we can operate free choice? And here am I trying to engineer it. One's desires for one's children are becoming easier to engineer than they were for my parents' generation – frighteningly so. In the 1960s my poor dead father tried to rely on threats, invocation of vanished authoritarian values and that tragic standby, duty. When we had children we boasted we were through with all that. But because what I still think of as 'our lot' – the fiftysomethings who once smoked dope, had Che Guevara posters and espoused anything that looked libertarian – pretended to abandon the right to control their offspring and gave them the illusion of a negotiated independence, Jakob and Ruairghy's coming of age has been deprived of significance.

I am behaving in exactly the way I did when I made sure to buy them the same number of Star Wars men. I think of them as children, not men. And, like all children, I am more cunning than my father was about my chosen methods of control. All four of the men in this family have to, somehow or other, grow up. And if I can't help my sons to do that, what kind of use am I as a father?

## 6.15 p.m.

Still alone. Have eaten three portions of prawn crackers. The enormous Chinaman who runs this place is smiling at me. The days when Chinamen were considered sinister are long gone, but their present mode – a sort of relentless, steely jollity that seems to say, 'We are Chinese! We are here! And there are a fuck of a sight more of us where we came from!' still has undertones of threat. He has twice approached the table and said, 'Anything else for you today, Mr Slippery?' but his friendliness is neutral enough to suggest that he expects me to ask for a few hundredweight of cocaine or for a considerable sum of money to be laundered.

## 6.30 p.m.

Still alone. Have eaten six portions of prawn crackers. Proprietor still smiling at me in sinister fashion.

Here comes Jakob.

## 6.45 p.m.

Writing this in Gents. Tension at table unbearable after arrival of Laura and Gwendolen Proek.

At first Jakob looked at his plate for about five minutes. There is nothing unusual about this. He usually does look at his plate for about five minutes whenever we go out to eat, only raising his head when he thinks it might be safe to do so. This is, of course, classic middle-brother behaviour.

Laura did a lot of soliciting routines, lowering her head almost to tablecloth level – which was what was needed in order to catch his eye – and nodding furiously at everything he said.

He has only raised his eyes, briefly, to order spare-ribs, seaweed, soft-shell crab, two portions of grilled dumplings, butterfly prawns, chicken satay, four bowls of chicken and sweetcorn soup, deep-fried oysters and sesame prawn toasts. He followed this with a request for a half Peking duck, hot sizzling beef, sweet and sour pork, sea bass with ginger and spring onion, kung po chicken with chilli, broccoli with oyster sauce, three portions of special fried rice, two portions of Singapore noodles and a dish of bean sprouts. Then he said, 'What are you guys having?'

I must go back in.


## 7.15 p.m.

Retreated to Gents again. Mrs Proek making concerned noises about my prostate.

She had been doing a lot of the kind of nodding and winking that certain women seem to think is only visible to themselves and the people for whom it is intended. Otherwise no communication between Laura and Jakob. It was, clearly, high time I got some love potion down his face.

Which was not as easy as I had supposed.

Liquid Love looks a bit like Green Chartreuse. There was no chance of slipping it into his wine. The best bet was to tip it into the broccoli. But I was not quite sure where Jakob stands on broccoli. In the end I decided on the seaweed. He is particularly fond of seaweed.

Too fond for my purposes.

When it arrived at the table, carried high by one of Mr Lu's Lovelies (as Jakob refers to them) sashaying across the floor in a tight turquoise silk dress, I seized it almost as soon as it hit the tablecloth, and waited for Jakob's attention to be drawn to some other dish.

It was not. He just sat there, staring hungrily at the seaweed, like a dog watching the dinner table. I put it next to my plate and waited for him to look away. He did not. I was sitting there, wondering what to do next, when Mrs Proek, beaming helpfully, reached over and passed him the seaweed. He started to shovel it down his face.

In desperation I pulled the small bottle containing the potion out of my pocket. 'Have you tried this?' I said brightly. 'They never have it! So

I always . . . er . . . bring my own!' They all looked at me very oddly. 'It's Mang Seng sauce!' I said brightly. It looked, I have to say, very green and very sinister. 'Why,' said Jakob, 'were you hiding it under the table?' In an attempt to distract him I started to wave the dish around, making aeroplane noises as I did so. 'Look!' I said brightly, as I seem to remember doing, about sixteen years ago, when trying to get him to eat an egg. 'Look Jakob! It's flying!'

He was now looking very suspicious indeed. As well he might be.

'It is delicious!' I said. 'Lovely Mang Seng sauce! Mmm! Yummy! Seaweed and Mang Seng sauce! What is it the Chinese say – *No field without rice! No seaweed without Mang Seng sauce!*' I waved the potion around wildly, widening my eyes in an attempt at guilelessness.

I am not very good at guilelessness. I had to do a lot of it in my Ferdinand in Patsy Stroud's ill-fated *Tempest* at the Donmar Warehouse in 1981. I opened my eyes very wide and parted my lips slightly which, according to Patsy, gave me the look of a male prostitute slightly past his prime.

Jakob was certainly not convinced. 'If,' he said, 'as the Chinese say – *No field without rice! No seaweed without Mang Seng sauce!* – how come these bastards have been keeping it from us for all these years?' 'It is,' I said, quickly, 'very expensive!' For a moment I thought this might persuade him to try it. It didn't.

Must go back to table or la Proek will have me sent away for a check-up. Memo to self – must check on prostate as soon as can bear to have doctor shove his finger up my behind. Tremendous fear that I may find it pleasurable.

How am I going to get this stuff down these two young people? If I don't, how long will it be before Jakob murders Rueiaghry? Why am I suddenly strangely drawn to Mrs Proek? Is it because I saw her in uniform? What was the Turkish man doing with Estelle? Is he connected, in some way, to Hamish?


## 8.30 p.m.

Back in Gents.

Very nearly locked into detailed urological discussion with Mrs Proek. Oh God! Oh God! Why did I decide to do this?

When I got back to the table Mrs Proek said, looking at me coquettishly, 'Do you know — I'd like to try some of that Mang Seng sauce! On my spare-ribs!' 'It doesn't go with spare-ribs!' I said, rather more brutally than I had intended. 'What does it go with? Apart from seaweed?' said Jakob. 'Er . . . sprouts!' I said. 'Does it go with green things?' said la Proek. 'On the whole it does!' I said. Just as I noticed the broccoli had arrived. Mrs Proek held up her plate. 'Well!' she said, 'You and I will have to share some, won't we?'

I was, eventually, obliged to pour some on her broccoli. Both Laura and Jakob, who seemed to have run out of conversation, told me I should have some. 'Oh,' I said, looking away, 'I don't like it that much.' 'In that case,' said Jakob, 'why do you carry it round to Chinese restaurants and try and force it down the faces of your dinner companions?'

I had no answer to this. I have now eaten an above-average dose of a powerful South American love herb while maintaining forced eye contact with a female traffic warden — who is also the mother of the woman with whom my middle son needs to be in love if I do not want him to kill his brother.

I have ruined my life. I am going to stay in the lavatory. What makes this situation all the more difficult is that, if I am honest, I would have to admit that I have had designs on this woman ever since she caught me on a single yellow line. If I go back there and allow myself to succumb to the herb (I swear she has been ogling me seriously ever since the first mouthful of broccoli), will I proposition her? Will she proposition me? If she does will I accept her proposition? What will her proposition be? If it involves sexual intercourse, will I remember it? Or does Prynne's disease only affect conjugal relations with one's wife?

## 11.30 p.m.

Finally got through to Estelle tonight. She was not in Angmering-on-Sea but in Wolverhampton. I thought of asking her to nip round to Sex Products to ask if they had an antidote but decided against it. She seemed only to wish to speak of little dough men. She was, I thought, very odd. I do not know why this should be. Is this to do with the Turkish man? Or Hamish? Or the two of them? Or does she suspect I am about to have an affair with a traffic warden?

Ruarighry still in bedroom with Lucy and the large fluffy rat. From some of the noises coming through the floorboards I think it may have been joined by a few real ones. I think they have a bottle of Macon in there as well. Edwin says they are going for the world record. 'If I fail GCSE,' he said, 'it will be because of the volume of noise coming from the next bedroom. How am I expected to revise Pliny's letters with her making a noise like a train going into a tunnel?'

Luckily Jakob announced, earlier this evening, that he was going to stay with a 'business acquaintance'. He did not say anything about Laura. I hope this business acquaintance does not have access to firearms, hit men, etc.


## May 3rd. 11.30 a.m. More blue skies, emerging leaves, tumescent buds, etc. A calculated insult to the Viagra-using classes.

*Estelle on her way home from Wolverhampton. Edwin at school. Ruairghry still in bed with Lucy. Jakob still here. Me here too.*

Jakob and I had what nearly amounted to a proper conversation. He has decided not to stay with this business acquaintance and is, for the moment anyway, managing his investments over the Internet. Every day about twelve E-mails arrive for him from all over the globe. A large number of them – they land on my machine as we have the same number – are from Sicily. I have not dared to open any of them. One of them is titled 'DOWNLOAD RUSSIAN GIRLS AND ORDER AN E MALE!' When he is not on the Net, Jakob sits downstairs, staring at the ceiling, his face pale.

His reserve, at times like these, is heartbreaking.


## 12 noon.

Ruarighry and Lucy still in bed. Laura rang to speak to Jakob. I asked him if he was in and he said he wasn't. Unfortunately I think Laura heard most of this conversation. She said, in vinegary tones that strongly recalled her mother, 'Is Jakob still mooning around after Lucy? And is she still

wobbling like a jelly and making mouse noises?' I said, 'Laura, look –'
at which she burst into tears. She wept for some time but I felt it rude to
hang up so stood there, listening to female sobbing at peak-time rates.

Noise from Ruairghy's room now deafening.

Still no news from the Beeb about the Head of Sound. But there are
rumours that Porda may be in some kind of trouble. Not good for me.


## 1.30 p.m.

Wainwright rang to say there is a rumour that *General Practice* is to be
wound down. Perhaps Leo has a larger architectural disaster in mind.
Ashley Ramp has been told he must go to Portsmouth and is refusing to
go. It is now definitely between Karl and Ramp. And apparently both are
planning to move against Porda. How though? Isn't he in a pretty good
position *vis-à-vis* Birt, etc.?


## 2 p.m.

Received conspiratorial message on answerphone from someone who
refused to give his name. He said, 'Have you read *Private Eye*?' Then
added, 'Karl Rhws Davies has made his move.' I am going out to buy
*Private Eye*.


## 2.45 p.m.

This small para in the *Eye* headed 'MORE BONKERS DOINGS
AT THE BEEB'.

> As the BBC slips into total chaos, Radio Drama – unable to provide
> anything worth listening to – is manufacturing its own real-life soap.
> Karl Rhws Davies, the 'drunken Welsh bastard' (*Eye*, 256) is fighting
> to save the ailing soap, *General Practice*. Even fans of the show (there
> are only two) have to admit that the uncharismatic Esmond Pennebaker
> (see IS HE A CROSS-DRESSER?, *Eye*, 315) is driving more
> listeners away with each day that passes. His attempt at a nervous
> breakdown has led to a lively debate inside the Beeb about whether to
> bump him off. Rhws Davies has received opposition (from the odious

Howard 'Blokey' Porda – see *Eye*, 311) to his plans for ending the life of the amazingly dull medic – but is fighting back and has called a press conference to be held in the canteen at Broadcasting House on the 16th. He promises 'spicy revelations' about the odious Porda and his cronies. Watch this space.

As usual with the *Eye*, nearly all the facts are wrong (I am many things but I do not think 'uncharismatic' is one of them) and the story, as usual, betrays its source in almost every line, but it does sound as if Rhws Davies is going to have a go at me and Howard.

I must get hold of *Eye*, no. 315, and see if there's any chance of a libel suit.

## 3 p.m.

Ruairehgy and Lucy still in bed. Must go now to pick up Edwin from rehearsal. Hotchkiss has asked me to give the lads some voice coaching. I asked what was wrong with them and Hotchkiss said they had runny vowel movements.

## 5 p.m.

Writing this in the Lucien Freshman Memorial Hall in a break from a punishing session with Snozzer, Plonker, Scagg, Bozz, Wodge, Lulu and a boy called Mingey. Not to mention Edwin Slippery. We did a few exercises and then Plonker said he was 'having trouble with his motivation'. Hotchkiss got really into this and said we all had to stand in a circle and hold hands. Apparently he does this at every rehearsal, always trying to make sure that he is standing next to Plonker, whom he fancies. Plonker cunningly substituted Wodge at the last minute. After this Hotchkiss said we all had to strip to our underpants and run round the room waving our arms. I was about to object, but all the lads seemed keen so I went along with it. We were all jumping about half-naked – Snozzer was standing on a chair with his trousers draped over his head, making monkey noises – when the new headmaster, Mr Steevens, walked in. He said, 'Good work, Lionel!' Which is the first time I have heard anyone call Mr Hotchkiss by his first name.

225

Scagg, I noticed, refused to take off his shoes as 'he might damage his feet and feet are important'. When we started running through a scene, Plonker and I had a bit of an argument. Partly about his Irish accent – which is not very convincing – but, more seriously, about the changes he has made to the text. Bottom – or Nick Hooley as he is now called – has a very long speech about reading books on the lavatory, which sits very awkwardly. It is, however, impossible to argue with Plonker. He just grins at you, which is most disarming.

I told them some pretty amusing stories about my time in fringe theatre in the seventies – including the time I broke Maggie Smith's leg – and I think they were all quite impressed. I did notice Edwin holding his head in his hands and crooning, 'Oh no!' But I am pretty sure he was being humorous. I think he may well be the one who turns out to be an actor.


## 8 p.m.

I am writing this in a break from preparing a dish of stewed lamb with artichokes and tamarind. In celebration of Estelle's return. Apparently it is all the rage among Iraqi Jews. I hope it will have the same effect on the Slippery household. Ruaierghry and Lucy are still in bed. Edwin suggested I take them up some soup.

Estelle came home very excited about her animated film and gave me a pep talk. Apparently I am in danger of becoming 'a defeatist bore'. I joined in enthusiastically with this – as it is the first time for at least a month that we have talked about me – and said, 'Yes yes yes! I am a defeatist bore!' 'That,' said Estelle, 'is exactly what I mean!' She then said I had to 'reinvent myself'. This fashionable piece of management-speak got me going. 'Next,' I said, witheringly, 'you'll be setting me Objectives! And Strategy! And telling me what my Core Competence is!'

No chance of a shag tonight I fear.


## 12 midnight.

How right you were, Slippery!

Message on the machine for Wesley Jones. Man with butch, gruff voice calling himself Pringle. It says the first night has been brought forward to the 5th. The day after tomorrow. Then says all at the Court send 'lots of love and best wishes'. They also say they were deeply moved to hear about the funeral of Bro. Very disturbed by this.

## May 4th. 11 a.m. Rain and suddenly cold.

*Estelle at home! Edwin at school. Jakob on the Internet. Ruairghry and Lucy in bed. Me writing this in study.*

In some ways it is not easy having Estelle under one's feet! She marched around the kitchen as if she owned it last night – and, at one point, tried to move my aubergines from the wicker basket where I have been keeping them. She also peered rather unpleasantly into my Kibbeh Tarooshiya (or whatever it is called) and, at one point, tried to pick bits out of it with a spoon and eat them before I was ready to serve!

This morning she has been lumbering around on the landing muttering about 'the state the house is in'. Really! Does she think things fall apart while she is swanning around the west of Ireland with Turks?

Must move saucepan with baked beans from bathroom. All boys disclaim responsibility for it. Snozzer?

### 11.30 a.m.

Ruarigrhery and Lucy still in bed. Estelle went upstairs and 'reasoned with him' through door. This had no effect. Edwin says he only got two hours' sleep last night, adding 'she squeaks more than the bed!' GCSE Spanish is only a week or so away. I sneaked a look at Jakob through a crack in the door as he stared at his computer screen. He looked, I thought, pale and too interesting for comfort. If only I had managed to get the potion down him!

I found a piece of paper downstairs with the words '*Come to me, Lucy, through this dark night of my soul*' written on it in Jakob's handwriting.

### 11.45 a.m.

Ashley Ramp has been made Head of Sound. Aaaarghhh! Oliver Plaque rang to give me the news. He suggests it is a piece of positive discrimination and points out that there are no other hunchbacks in positions of managerial

227

authority at the Beeb. I suspect it is because they had run out of places to try and send him.

What does this mean for Esmond Pennebaker? Can it be good? (I think not.) What does it mean for Howard Porda? Will Karl Rhws Davies go ahead with his plan to expose transsexualism in the department? If he does, how will this affect me? Will Ashley Ramp appear in a diving suit? Should I buy one in order to ingratiate myself? Will I survive the hospital? Will Ruaierhgy and Lucy ever get out of bed?

## 3 p.m.

Ruarighry and Lucy still in bed. Edwin (just back from school) suggests we 'luzz a few pizzas up to them from the street'. Message on machine for Jakob from Laura saying 'we need to talk'. She has also sent him an E-mail, which I am afraid I have opened. It is entitled – POEM BY A GIRL CALLED PROEK. It runs as follows –

Jakob's face is mask-like, secret,
Hiding where his feelings lurk.
Does he prefer plump, lively L U C Y
To his sad-eyed L A U R A  P R U R K?

Has the strumpet got his number?
Does she speak as well as squawk?
Is it just my stupid surname?
Yours sincerely L A U R A  P R A W K.

Is it that she bakes, sews, mends things?
Or is it just you like them dark?
If you could pronounce me could I
One day be your L A U R A  P R A R K?

I think the girl has talent. Jakob still uncommunicative.

Have just received, in the post, my first scene in the hospital, written by another of the new writers, a small woman with glasses called Christine.

She seems very keen on my radio wife, Pamela, who has been, for the past twenty years, a shadowy figure, mainly droning on about our children and how we ought to get the dining-room wallpapered. She came into

228

her own when I had an affair with my secretary ('It's so sordid, Esmond! So demeaning!') and was briefly lively when her best friend, Horst, fell under a train, but on the whole her dialogue has been of the 'I did shepherd's pie tonight just how you like it' variety. When I was shagging my secretary I got quite a lot of letters of support.

My accident has made her positively loquacious. I have a long bedside scene in which she talks about our marriage. (I can only grunt for the next three episodes.) Pilfrey (appalling performance, as usual) has told her that she has to keep talking to me in order to give me the will to live. What is eerie about the stuff she comes out with is the extent to which it feels like the kind of thing Estelle would say to me, if she were instructed to talk to me on medical grounds (which is probably the only way I will ever get her attention). Her opening lines went –

PAMELA: What does it all mean, Esmond? What does our marriage *mean*? I keep thinking of the day we met. Do you remember? By that little white house in Cornwall. I think it was Cornwall, anyway. And you were standing by the sea in that white fisherman's sweater – I've still got it – it needs dry-cleaning – and you looked sort of . . . tousled . . . you're still tousled . . . you're my tousled . . . rumpled boy, the one with whom I ate –

ME: Aieeroiughrrr . . .

PAMELA: What are you trying to say, Esmond?

ME: Aieeroiughrrr . . .

PAMELA: Are you trying to say 'Pamela' . . . ?

At this point I feel I should say, 'No. I am trying to say "Aieeroiughrrr . . ."' But in fact there are about ten more pages of appalling schmaltz. My only line in the whole thing is as she is leaving. I 'lift myself up on my elbow' (God knows how I am supposed to convey that on radio) and say, 'Mackerel!' Pamela comes back in and says to the nurse, 'What did he say? Did he speak?' and the nurse says, 'I think he said "mackerel".' At which Pamela bursts into tears and we go into the signature tune. I think this is probably the worst piece of dramatic writing in which I have ever been involved – even including my 1979 performance in the musical *Blair Peach*.

What is most disturbing is what this is going to do to Susan Vullermeyer, who plays Pamela. For the last twenty years she has been quite a biddable, mousy little thing. There will now be no doing anything with her. In the next episode, I hear, she has a five-minute speech about our first night together. I am going to talk to Leo and try to make sure I get physiotherapy as soon as possible.

## 5 p.m.

Rueiaiughry and Lucy still in bed. At least I assume there is no one else in there with them. 'Judging by the noise,' said Edwin today, when I picked him up from school, 'about thirty people abseiled in through the window late last night!'

I am seriously worried about their not eating and have just knocked and asked them if they would like anything. A cracked, hollow voice that (I think) was Ruairghry's said, 'Just slip something under the door!' This does not leave me much scope beyond pancakes or filo pastry.

## 7.30 p.m.

Estelle has been at home all day, wandering around tut-tutting to herself. She also criticized my ironing. As I haven't done any ironing I find this unfair.

She did, however, say something that suggested to me that we might have had sex on April 27th. I have gone back through this diary and discovered that she was in the west of Ireland with Hamish on this date.

She is thinking of offering Mr Slippy Sloppy to Ronnie 'Very Nice Man' Pilfrey. I was speechless with rage. I told her that if she offered Pilfrey the part our marriage was over and she said, 'Well I'll just have to risk that, won't I?' I then tried to have a rational conversation about Pilfrey's work. I wasn't bitchy or mean-minded about him. I paid tribute to his good qualities. He is very hard-working and conscientious and he can carry off certain things very well indeed (he's very good at saying 'goodbye', for example, a hard thing to do well on radio), but in the main he simply hasn't got the tonal range to be a really expressive radio actor. I said, 'I genuinely am very pleased that he has a following and that he is doing well. I want him to do well. It's simply that I find his voice grating and awkward, and his timing very inconsistent.'

Estelle said I was jealous.

I said, 'Actually, my opinion is shared by quite a lot of people. Donald Fleer, who plays the Oldest Patient, loathes him and so does Penny Uzbowski, the Practice Nurse.' Estelle said we were all jealous.

It is true, of course, that Pilfrey has shagged Uzbowski – but then, so have Martin Cunningham, the Osteopath, Willibald Glock, the Ambulanceman and the Man with Piles. I did have an argument with Pilfrey about ten years ago but cannot, now, remember what it was about. Par for the course really.

She also said she was going to be away tomorrow night. When I asked her where she would be staying she just said, 'Oh, some hotel.' 'Some hotel!' Does she think I am stupid? By her own admission – yes! I openly asked her whether she had a lover and she told me not to be stupid. Still no mention of any plans for my fiftieth or for our silver wedding anniversary. After furious row I had serious palpitations and went upstairs to consult the *Well Man Health Guide*. It said –

## PALPITATIONS

Sometimes your heart takes longer to pump blood through your system and you then experience a 'glitch' as the muscle works to continue its all-important task. On the whole this is absolutely nothing to worry about – although cf. Myocardial Infarction, Prachysmal Tachycardia and Blintz's Disease.

This is absolutely typical of the *Well Man Health Guide*. Their tone of relentless calm always reminds me of an air hostess trying to retain her smile as the Jumbo goes into a nosedive.

## *BRAIN TUMOUR*

*Sometimes you get a tumour on your brain, which can affect your speech or movement and, in certain circumstances, your ability to live. But, on the whole, this is absolutely nothing to worry about. It all depends where it is situated in your brain and, indeed, where your brain is situated in your body. If, as in the case of the authors of this manual, it is situated in your arse, it will be a comparatively simple matter to remove it – cf. Cancer, Death, Funerals, etc.*

She is up to something. Has probably been up to it all year. Why have I hardly ever been able to get her on the phone? Did she really go to Eastern Europe? What about the Turkish men? Hamish? Was Julian really Gillian? Are the little dough men really the big success she says they are? Could they really have taken off in such a big way quite so quickly? If she is having an affair – what am I going to do about it?

Kill the bastard.

First I have to find out who he (or she) is.

## May 5th. 11 a.m. Rain and sleet and hail. Total absence of spring, blue skies, etc.

*Estelle 'in a hotel'. Edwin at careers forum. Ruairehgy and Lucy eating cereal in front room. Jakob sitting in front of his computer screen. Laura on her way to 52 Mafeking Road. Aaaargghh! Me wondering whether to check into hotel myself.*

Ruairghrey and Lucy were up at nine. Ms Rachnowski looked invigorated from a marathon spell of intercourse. She wobbled and laughed, I thought, slightly more than usual. She makes a mean scrambled egg. She is doing a postgraduate in physics at Oxford. She is clearly super-bright – although when I asked her about String Theory she said she didn't really know about String Theory. She and Estelle did not discuss cosmology, quasars, white dwarves, etc., but giggled girlishly and talked about baking. Then Estelle departed to a destination she still refuses to reveal – presumably to shag Hamish, Turkish men, Julian/Gillian, etc.

Ruairghy says he is about to go 'picking flowers' with Lucy. I pointed out there was a force eight gale blowing. Ruairghry said, in rather simpering tones I thought, that that didn't matter. He spoke also, ominously, I thought, of marriage. Saying, in rather soapy tones, 'How long have you and Estelle been married?' I said, through gritted teeth, 'Twenty-four years, eleven months and nineteen days.' Ruarighry said, 'That's marvellous!' I said, again through gritted teeth, 'Is it?' He then put his arm round me, which I found rather offensive, and said, 'If I got married . . . I'd sort of like to get married in a . . . like . . . tent!'

I said, 'And what would you like for a wedding present? A Megadeth CD?' He smiled in an unpleasantly tolerant fashion and said, 'A Megadeth

CD would be really nice!' I said, hoping to provoke him into a less holy frame of mind, 'Perhaps you would like to leave your other requests in the form of a letter by the chimney, possibly next to a biscuit and a glass of whisky?' 'Oh,' said Raueighry, with what I thought might be assumed naïvety, 'why would I want to do that?' *Because Santa Claus is probably the only person who will be able to afford to grant them!'* I replied.

This made him even saintlier. It is easy to be saintly when a man has been shagging for two days non-stop. His only comment was to say that 'Love is ... like ... a beautiful thing.' When I said, 'So is a three-day bonk,' he said, 'Paul – you're a rather crude person in many ways, aren't you?' Felt strong urge to hit him but did not do so as he is bigger than me. I am increasingly worried about Riurghy's grip on reality.


## 11.30 a.m.

Edwin returned from careers forum. He told them he wanted to be a rock and roll star. Apparently the careers master said he had to be a lawyer or an accountant. Jakob still sitting in front of computer screen with his head in his hands. When I told him Laura was on her way round he leaped to his feet and said, 'I'm in Italy,' and ran from the room.

Worrying about Estelle's whereabouts. I asked Edwin, who seems to have taken the day off from school 'to revise', if he would follow her for me. He asked how much. I said £50 a day plus expenses. He said he would only do it if I threw in a car. Will ask Ruairghruy. Although do not think he is capable of following anything at the moment – apart, of course, from his penis.


## 12 noon.

Laura Proek has arrived, looking woebegone. Jakob is in hiding somewhere. I said, with perfect truthfulness, that I did not know where he was. I must say she is a very nice girl. She spoke, most interestingly, of the work of someone called Jacques Derrida, whom I think she is studying. I said I did not know any of his records but had heard he was a marvellous singer. She laughed and explained that he was, in fact, some kind of philosopher. She was wearing a low-cut woolly jumper and her upper chest made it difficult for me to concentrate on her account of this French sage. I have left her in the front room downstairs while I brood about the changes at the Beeb, my forthcoming accident, etc.

She asked about Jakob and I said I thought he would probably be back from wherever he was at any moment. Looking almost as pale and woebegone as Jakob – albeit for different reasons – she said, 'He can't have gone shopping. He never goes shopping. The thing he likes doing most is sitting there picking his nose!' I think she has a good grasp of the essentials of his character and is almost certainly the right girl for him.

## 3 p.m.

Ominous memo from Ashley Ramp. It simply reads, 'In order to discuss the new round of restructuring, programme proposals for the upcoming year and the Whirligig scheme, all members of SOUND are asked to assemble in the playground of St Barnabas School, Acton, at 2.30 on May 15th. VISION will have their own meeting on the roof of the NCP Car Park, Hounslow, at the same time. Do all make an effort to attend and bring some warm clothing.'

There is a rumour that we are all to be sent to Siberia. What on earth is the Whirligig scheme? Is there any significance in the fact that Ramp's meeting happens the day before Karl's press conference?

I rang Wainwright, who said that Ramp was going to make a pronouncement about *General Practice* at this mass meeting.

## 5 p.m.

Off now to the first night of *Muthafuckas*, accompanied by Edwin and Lulu. Lulu has a cautious, pregnant expression from which it is impossible to work out whether she has been granting or denying him sexual favours. To his credit, Edwin's demeanour makes it impossible to work this out either.

## 9.15 p.m.

Writing this in the bar of the Royal Court Theatre – greatly changed from when it was the scene of my great triumph in the 1980 production of *Scab* in which I played a Geordie trades union organizer. One of the major changes is that it is now in a completely different building, in the West End. *Scab* was actually premiered in the bar and never, in spite of much lobbying, made it through to a stage of any kind. I have never really liked Geordies. They seem to me a shifty lot. Opposite me is a man who, at first, I took to be Ashley Ramp in a large leather bag with armholes, but apparently it is Kurt Venning, the most vicious theatre critic in London. He seems to be wearing a flying helmet, although I have seen no sign of an aeroplane parked in the vicinity.

*Muthafuckas* is going down really well. I peered over Linda Bloomer's shoulder, and she, the least vicious critic in London, was writing, 'Young black man. Angry voice of new generation' in her little book. I thought about telling her it was written by Snozzer but decided against it. There may be money to be made out of this.

There is a figure right at the back of the crush bar who I think may be Wesley. He is tall and thin, wearing a balaclava helmet and the only bits of his skin I can see are black. He seems to be on his own. I dare not go up and ask him. It could be the ghost of Bro – or his brother – I think one of the letters said he had eight of them.

Venning is talking in an offensively loud voice. I think I heard him say 'Rubbish!' But apparently this is a good sign with him. He often says 'Rubbish!' when he likes something. What you have to watch is when he is grinning and laughing. That means he is going to be vicious.

Off now for the second act – which is, as I recall, set in a brothel in Las Vegas, a location that inspired Snozzer to produce some really fine writing. Lulu is being chatted up by Kurt Venning.


## 10.45 p.m.

In some pub up West. Near to where Lulu lives. I am dying to see the inside of her house, assess possible size of fortune, chances of any of it rubbing off on the Slipperys, etc. Don't know the name of pub. Edwin has just drunk three pints of lager. I am having a triple whisky. Lulu is having a Bacardi and Coke. I have found out more about her. Her father is, so she says, 'very rich', although she seems vague about how he made his money. This has raised her enormously in my estimation.

I have just seen Wesley Jones – a person I thought I had invented.

The second act went down a storm. From the opening sequence –

NIGGAH: Yo Loretta! Yo niggah bitch!
LORETTA: Who yo' cussin', Niggah? Who yo call a niggah bitch? etc.

– through to the final shoot-out and the powerful last speech: 'Yo go suck yo own pussy, niggahbitch!' – it held a hundred and fifty progressive intellectuals absolutely spellbound. I saw Colin Lindsey of the *Sunday Times* write the words 'Deeply moving account of black experience' in his little book, adding the words 'American influence?' L. Bloomer was equally struck. Edwin says she wrote, 'Voice of the street. Refreshing change.' Venning apparently wrote 'Bollocks' on his pad, but I am told that with him this is a very good sign.

I had my eyes on Wesley, who was watching from the back. He never removed his balaclava throughout the performance, which must have made viewing rather difficult, as the eyeholes were amazingly small. Immediately the show was over he made for the exit and, without waiting for the curtain call, I dragged Edwin and Lulu out after me and we gave chase.

As soon as Wesley was out on the street he started running. Edwin, Lulu and I gave chase.

Wesley ran down into St Martin's Lane.

The night was surprisingly warm and as we ran into more theatre crowds I could feel, all too clearly, that I am only a matter of weeks away from my fiftieth birthday. Edwin was well ahead of me. Lulu seemed to have disappeared altogether. Warm air on my face I stopped and, bent double, breathed hard. Opposite me a well-dressed crowd took the air on the steps of the English National Opera and, ahead, a dense queue of cars and taxis quivered away the minutes in a familiar London attitude – frozen, mulish patience. When I looked up Edwin was nowhere to be seen.

I'm a suburban person. My early theatre successes were nearly all at the Orange Tree in Richmond and I have always loved the quietness and order of the suburb. I once, actually, wrote a poem about it, which I do not think I have the courage to reproduce here. I know it had the line 'Oh lime tree, lime tree, sticky in the heat!' and, as far as I can recall, it rhymed. But I have always been faintly nervous of the centre of London.

I suddenly got rather scared.

Then I saw Edwin coming back towards me. Lulu was behind him. He didn't seem tired at all, although he, too, was breathing hard. He said, 'I lost him!' 'Where did he go?' 'Down towards Buckingham Palace,' said Edwin; 'maybe he's gone to petition the Queen!' Edwin slumped down on to the pavement. I followed his example and the two of us sat there for a minute or two as the crowd milled round us. Then Edwin said, 'Just before I lost him he took off his woolly hat!' 'Yes?' I said. 'Wesley,' said Edwin, 'is one big black geezer. He is like massive man. He is like . . . gigantic. He is well large!' I moistened my lips slightly. 'Did he seem . . . like . . . angry?' I said. 'He seemed well angry!' said Edwin. 'He seemed basically furious!'

I got to my feet and, looking over my shoulder slightly nervously, started back towards the car park.

'Of course,' I said slowly, 'we don't *know* it was Wesley Jones. It might just have been some black geezer who thought we were police following him . . .' 'It was Wesley Jones, man,' said Edwin dourly, 'that was like *the* Wesley Jones, no messing. My God!' 'How do you know?' I said. 'Just know! Just do, man!' said Edwin. I said I thought he was beginning to sound a little like Wesley Jones. Edwin shook his head. 'This is like scary, man!' he said. I agreed.

I suppose it is possible that I have invented someone who already existed. He may even have written a play called *Muthafuckas*. He also, as Edwin pointed out when we got into the car, knows where I live.

## 11.45 p.m.

Got back to find Ruairghery, Lucy and Laura all sitting round the kitchen table. Ruaieruighy had his arms round both girls. At first I was suspicious of his intentions towards Laura, who was no longer wearing the low-cut woolly jumper but a black cardigan. But it turned out he was in counselling mode. He seemed to be using a lot of phrases he had clearly picked up from the partially trained Kleinian. 'Jakob's feeling for Lucy . . .' he was saying as I came into the room, 'is a projection of his hostility towards me. He's experiencing sibling rivalry if you like, which I have dealt with in my own way, of course!'

By shagging the woman he loves! No sign of Jakob. Maybe he really has gone to Italy.

Several calls on the machine. One from Estelle which, delivered in her usual, close-to-the-chest tone, simply says, 'Estelle here. There are some men coming to take away some furniture tomorrow. Just let them get on with it. We're getting some new furniture, that's all. OK? Bye!' She did not say where she is.

I was rather devastated by this news. At first I wondered if it might be that Estelle is moving out and is trying to break it to me gradually. First, a few chairs, sofas, pictures, etc. Then the bed. Finally – when I am alone in an almost empty house – the solicitor's letter. I decided this was impossible.

## May 7th. 9.30 a.m. Blue skies, spring, etc. Lark, or possibly chaffinch, singing in garden.

*Estelle 'somewhere with Hamish'. Edwin at school. Ruairghrey and Lucy in garden (also singing). Laura on sofa downstairs. Jakob 'at Heathrow'. Me in study.*

Estelle finally came home about eight last night. She seemed very cheerful. As well she might be after a night of wild sex with somebody else. I said lightly, 'Er . . . where exactly did you go last night?' She looked up sharply. 'I had a meeting in Liverpool!' she said. 'Ah,' I said, with just a trace of irony, 'Liverpool! So much nearer than . . . *the west of Ireland*!' I said this with just a slight sting. She gave me an odd look. But I think she knows I am on to her. Definitely thinking of hiring a private detective.

She left early this morning to 'look at Hamish's thing' – her words.

I can hear Raurighrey, down in the garden, singing to Lucy on Edwin's guitar. I think on balance I prefer Edwin. Rueirghy has a faintly weedy voice.

## 11 a.m.

The men have just come to take away the sofa and two armchairs. I asked them where they were taking them and they said they had been asked not to say. Must challenge Estelle with this.

## 11.15 a.m.

Note from Gwen Proek (Gwen!). It reads –

Dear Paul,
  Nice to see you the other day! Under that conceited
'luvvy' act you are really quite a nice, kind person,
aren't you?
  The situation between us and Lucy's Mum and Dad is a
terribly complicated one. One day I will tell you about
us and the Rachnowskis!
  Come down here one evening! We can talk! Norman, I
fear, will be still up on the roof!

Love
Gwen

This, I suspect, is a blatant come-on. Found myself fantasizing about shagging a traffic warden in uniform. Not sure whether it had Mrs Proek's face or not. I am definitely going down there.

## 11.30 a.m.

Jakob has been cowering in his room all morning, having come in last night looking haggard – just after Laura went to sleep on the downstairs sofa. He has just come into my study and told me to tell anyone asking after him that he is 'at Baggage Reclaim at Heathrow airport after my trip to Italy'. I asked him if he was all right and what he had been doing. He has apparently been commissioned to write a piece for some weekly about the new EEC currency. I tried to get him talking about it and he said, with no sign of being pleased by or proud of his own joke, that it was 'a Euro paean'.

He has now gone out. But he will have to pass the room where Laura is still asleep on sofa . . . wearing very tasteful but not unerogenous nightie . . . if only I had the potion!

### 12.30 p.m.

Jakob met Laura in the hall and twitched at her for about five minutes. All this time – I was watching from the landing – I was acutely aware of Ruaieiughry's voice floating up from the garden singing his 'Song to Lucy', the words of which go –

> Lucy, Lucy
> Beautiful Lucy
> Etc.

It seems to be set to the tune of 'Lead Kindly Light'. I got Jakob and Laura into kitchen and offered various bits of (green) food, drink, etc., in the hope of slipping potion to the pair of them. They both refused my offers. I think tying them down and pouring Liquid Love down their throats through a funnel is the only thing that will get them together.

### 1 p.m.

Ruaighriury, Lucy, Jakob and Laura now all in front room. Ruaighry seems to be doing most of the talking. From the tone and content of his performance I think he may well have converted to Christianity. All Jakob has said, so far, is 'Yeah!' in a sort of low growl.

### 2 p.m.

Just back from lunchtime *Midsummer Night's Dream* rehearsal. Hotchkiss has decided that all the fairies must wear jockstraps. A mutinous mood. Scagg has resigned on a footwear-related issue. Peaseblossom said he would only wear boxer shorts. Edwin has decided to get about the stage on a pogo stick. Hotchkiss is very excited about this. Not a good rehearsal.

### 4 p.m.

Picked up Edwin from school. Fairly sensible conversation about Lulu. He told me he is thinking of dropping her. Neither of us, of course, mentioned sex. Funny. We talk about sex and we talk about relationships.

240

But never about the two at the same time. He said they argue a lot. I said, 'Estelle and I argue a lot!' He said, 'It's different for you!' 'It isn't different for me!' I said. 'I'm a person like you are! I have feelings! It isn't any different when you're nearly fifty!' Edwin gave me a narrow look. 'It isn't any different when you're sixteen,' he said. 'People think you can't be in love at sixteen but you can be!' 'Of course you can be!' I said. 'And you can be in love with someone for years and still argue with them.' 'Is that how it is with you and Mum?' he said. 'I think so . . .' I said. 'How do you mean?' said Edwin.

I suddenly felt very old and tired and frightened of saying what I felt. What I wanted to say was – 'I sometimes think I don't know any more.' But I somehow couldn't bring myself to say that to him. Does this mean that I stay with Estelle only because of the children? I certainly can't imagine a conversation where I say to them that we are separating. But I can imagine a conversation where I say it to her. In fact I have been saying it to her, on and off, for the last twenty-five years. What does this mean?

Fuck all, probably.

But I didn't like the glimpse of insecurity I saw in Edwin's usually confident, clear blue eyes, and just before we got home I said, 'Listen, Edwin. We all argue. But if you love someone you should be able to get through the arguments. That is what love means. And that's as true for you as it is for me.' Edwin gave me his beautifully clear grin and said, 'Does this mean that I have to . . . like . . . marry Lulu?' I told him to fuck off and we both laughed.

If anyone knew the work that there is in families! People think that all they are is weddings and funerals and Christmases. They're not. They are unrelenting labour. But the satisfaction that they give you – which is, I suspect, the only real satisfaction in my life, since I have put everything of myself into my family – is in the moment when, like a traveller reaching the brow of a steep hill, you talk your way into a clear view of open country in the company of someone you love so much that they are a part of you and will never be separated from you, even by death.

That's what happened this morning when Edwin smiled at me. It didn't make me any less angry with Estelle for moving the furniture out and/ or having wild sex/lying to me about the west of Ireland, etc. But, even though I was still angry with her, the happiness I felt in Edwin was still, somehow, connected to her.

Will I ever find a way of saying this to her? Or will I carry on carrying on like a prat until we split up?


## 5 p.m.

A phone call from Leo. Apparently my accident has been very good for the ratings. He said he was trying to persuade 'upstairs' to subject me to a series of punishing accidents, diseases, etc., and see if my popularity rises or falls. 'I could give you a skin complaint,' he said, glumly.

The main issue is still whether Porda remains strong enough to see off Ramp and Karl. Will Karl's press conference weaken him fatally? Or will it do serious damage to Karl? Where will Ramp stand in all this? In galoshes presumably.

The new writer's — Christine's — next episode is to be biked over to me this morning. Karl — who continues to be nice to me (worrying sign) — said, 'It takes the show in a completely new direction!' 'Ah,' I said, 'you mean — it's interesting?' He did not laugh. I telephoned Gustave. A mistake. He said, 'I'm so sorry — can I call you back? I'm in the middle of something' (i.e. I need time to think out my next lie about why I have found you no work apart from insect voice-overs for the last six months).

He did call me back and said, 'I think, Paul — this problem we have with you is to do with where you see yourself . . .' I said I saw myself in work and earning money. Gustave said, 'Good! That's good!'

I was thinking about how to get out of the long, uncomfortable silence that had developed between us when I heard a voice in the background. I recognized the voice. 'Have you got Pilfrey in there with you?' I said. There was a short, awkward pause. 'Ronnie dropped by!' said Gustave. 'All you do really, Gustave,' I said, 'is take 10 per cent of someone else's success, don't you?' 'That's the general idea!' said Gustave. 'Well,' I said, 'for what it's worth I don't feel my success belongs to you any more . . .'

There was a very long silence. Then Gustave, in that deep, mellifluous voice of his said, 'To whom your . . . er . . . success belongs, Paul, is a very, very hard question to answer!' I put the phone down on him.

I am going to get a new agent. I have had Gustave for almost as long as I have been married. It is time I got someone who will put my career back on track. I am unclear, at the moment, who they might be. Perhaps I could get Estelle to represent me? Or Jakob? Or Edwin? Or Snozzer?

I think Snozzer might be rather good. He would be very tough on the deals. And I would certainly far rather have lunch with him than with Gustave. The last time 'Flaubert' took me out he sat staring at me over his avocado prawns like a bulldog that is about to be emasculated. Gustave's success is due entirely to his red waistcoat, which he is rumoured to wear even when in bed. That and his posh voice, which is almost as much of an affectation. He was actually brought up in the East End, the youngest of nine children and, until the age of twelve, had never read a book, let alone seen the inside of a theatre. He taught himself to speak 'proper' with the aid of a Linguaphone record designed for foreigners who want to learn English – which gives his small talk that authentic rich fifties feel and suggests he must have known Noël Coward, etc.


## 6 p.m.

Christine's script has arrived and I have just read it.

I am convalescent. I spend a lot of time in the hospital garden with my wife Pamela (I nearly wrote 'Estelle' there) and Pamela says at least twice as much as me. I am not happy about this at all. At one point she says –

PAMELA: Where's it all gone, Esmond? Where is the youthful idealism we shared back in the sixties? My God! Do you remember that Vietnam demonstration?
ME: I think so.
PAMELA: We were out on the streets, Esmond. We believed in something. There was a working class, not an underclass, and no one felt the need to put the 'New' in front of the words 'Labour Party'. We were the generation that produced the Rolling Stones, the Beatles, International Socialism, Drugs, Fringe Theatre, and Real Ale. My God, Esmond! We had wings! We could fly! And now here we are with our *children* getting married and worrying about mortgages and there are still people in housing estates frightened to go out at night and nothing has changed except there is no hope and no idealism left any more, only money, money, money, everywhere you look.

Look at the Health Service for God's sake! And we just let it happen!
Why did we let it happen?

ME: I don't know.

I am very unhappy about this scene. I feel it lacks dramatic coherence.
There is also a very distasteful moment with the physiotherapist –
when I am in the swimming-pool. And Christine has decided that I am
to have a semi-permanent speech defect. I do not think that this will
endear me to the nation.

Pamela has also started to have an affair with Pilfrey – about which I
am very angry indeed. I haven't even been told about it. They get to stay
in a posh hotel and Pilfrey talks about his guilt. I think I have about ten
lines altogether in the whole show. Death would be preferable to this.
Have put in a call to Karl who is 'in a meeting'. I asked his secretary who
was with him. She paused and then whispered, dramatically, 'Howard
Porda!' What does this mean?

## 9.30 p.m.

Message on the machine from my mother. It goes –

Paul? Paul? Are you there, Paul? (*Long silence. Mysterious thumping
sound.*) It's Granny here, Paul! I'm sitting on my sofa! (*Long pause.
More unidentifiable noises.*) It's a hideous sofa, Paul! I hate it! Arthur
got it! I hate it! (*Sound of water.*) Do you remember Maud, Paul, that
went to Northcote Hall? She had that black bunny rabbit you liked
that was eaten. Do you remember? We came back and it was all
over the lawn. In bits. The foxes had got it. (*Water effects get louder.
Sound of distant screaming.*) Maud was very very intelligent. She got
a first. In Architecture. (*Long silence. Wheezing.*) Anyway she's dead.
(*Silence. Click. End of message.*)

May 8th. 10 a.m. Blue skies and light breeze. The tree in the garden (whatever it is) is almost fully in leaf and the bird on its branches (whatever *it* is) is warbling.

*Ruighry and Lucy in Richmond Park. Laura still on sofa downstairs. Jakob on his way to Kensington. Estelle also, apparently, in or near Kensington.*

Violent confrontation between Jakob and Ruairghy this morning over whether they were going to watch a video of *Friends* or a live transmission of an American chat show focusing on people who have had sex with their neighbour's pets. Lucy squeaked at them to stop and offered to make everyone 'a nice cup of tea'. Laura snarled at her. Jakob put his head in his hands and Ruaighry said, 'This argument isn't really about television, is it? It's about your need to be a man. Melanie Klein would have been very worried by your phallocentricity!' Jakob said, in a joke African voice, 'De Klein is not just a synonym for slope!' Which seemed to annoy Ruairghry enormously.

I should never have sent them to the partially trained Kleinian. Although as I am now not even partially paying them for going, it has to be some kind of bargain. And children should be exposed to some of that kind of bollocks, if only to stop them taking it seriously.

Eventually Jakob stormed off to meet Estelle in Kensington and Laura had to be taken out in strong hysterics. She looked as thin and pale as Jakob. Plump and cheerful Lucy made a really very nice cup of tea.

10.15 a.m.

Much sympathy for Jakob. Ruairghry can be really infuriating. He has just turned off my CD player in the middle of the first act of *Ariodante*.

I did try to raise the subject of his job and he said, 'I don't want to discuss it with you. You wouldn't understand. I am going to be doing something that you will probably despise but I want to do it.' I asked him whether he was going to open a brothel or, perhaps, train as an estate agent and he gave me a pitying smile. 'There are things about me you will never understand!' he said, allowing a light smile to play about his lips. I resisted the temptation to smash him on the head with the nearest saucepan. I have a horrible feeling he may have become a Buddhist.

In the middle of all this there was a phone call, that, as usual these days, was not for me. It was an Oxford friend, ringing to tell Jakob that Oliver had escaped from prison. Apparently he is likely to turn up on our doorstep. I asked Ruirghry whether he was violent and Reuighry said, 'Only when he needs drugs!' He and Lucy then went upstairs 'to hang up a hamster picture'.

Downstairs alone with Laura. Just the kind of girl I like. Thin and needy as opposed to large and confident like Lucy or Estelle. Almost tempted to give her dose of potion and see what happens. She did say that she had been deeply moved by my perf. in the hospital episode. As far as I can see the speech defect is really working. But I do not think she is in the mood for hanky-panky.

Seriously, guys – she is in love with my sweet, gentle, trying to-be-cool but oh-so-lovable middle son. Why can't he see it? Why is the world so unfair?


## 12 noon.

Crawling message on the machine from Gustave, who suggests 'a spot of lunch'. His voice managed, as usual, to imply that there was a job in the offing. Perhaps this is the secret of his success. Like some senior Jesuit, he manages to give the impression of being in touch with the invisible engine of the universe.

Off now to Nobby's memorial service.


## 2 p.m.

Am in a pub in Streatham with Good Old Steve and Peter Mailer.

Good Old Steve has abandoned his role as Economics Editor. He tells us that 'people are not interested in economics any more'. I said it was nice to hear that, at last, Good Old Steve had something in common with his readership. He is, apparently, going to devote himself to writing profiles of the rich and famous. I suggested myself, to general hilarity.

Peter Mailer had more gruesome details of Nobby's heart attack. According to Mailer, Nobby was actually on the job with his thirtysomething at the time he stiffed. She thought, Mailer told us, that Nobby was in the throes of sexual ecstasy. Good Old Steve said, 'What a way to go!' He says he has not had any sex this year, although 'a girl on a plane looked at him'. I tried to look like a happily married man and, I think, succeeded. Off now to St Whoever it is's.

## 5 p.m.

Back in the pub.

The thirtysomething clearly fancies me. She has just gone round the corner to give lots and lots and lots of love to someone. Her speech was a classic.

She was wearing a minimal black dress, a black fur boa and wobbled up to the pulpit in a way that suggested that Nobby had come back from the grave shortly before the service in order to finish what he started. 'I've only just begun to find out about Nobby,' she said leaning over the rail and staring intently at Nobby's brother Jim. 'I literally had no idea, for example, that he was the author of a book on butterflies.'

This created consternation all round as the congregation wondered how many more revelations of this nature were forthcoming. 'How many of us here, for example,' she continued, 'knew that he had been, briefly, in the late sixties, a male model!'

Quite a few people began to look very worried here. 'Or,' she went on, 'a French-polisher!' This line created near panic in several rows of the church. Good Old Steve turned to me and whispered, 'Is she going to mention the bus shelter?' A lot of people looked at him.

'It is entirely typical of him,' went on the thirtysomething, looking suddenly girlish and stern at the same time, 'that he kept such things from me, because in many ways ours was a very simple, almost child-like relationship.' At which Good Old Steve whispered, audibly, 'With a lot of shagging!' 'When he went from me so suddenly . . .' she went on, '. . . and so cruelly due to . . .' 'A lot of shagging!' (This from Good Old Steve as thirtysomething struggled to retain composure. More people looked at him.) 'I vowed that, although I had only known Nobby three months, there was a sense in which I had known him all my life because when he went from me he was in the middle . . . just in the middle of . . .'

247

Into the silence, Good Old Steve said, rather louder than he had intended, 'A lot of shagging!' This did not go down well.

There was an appalling speech by his brother, who maintains Nobby appeared to him last Wednesday in Sainsbury's in the King's Road. All this stuff about people coming back from the dead. God save us. The whole point about being dead is that you don't come back from it. It's a one-off experience.

Must stop now as thirtysomething has reappeared. I think she has changed her costume. How did she manage to do this? In a bus shelter perhaps?

Must try and make it look as if I am writing poem/novel/short story/memoir of Nobby, etc.


## 8 p.m. Another pub. Clapham, I think.

Well in there with thirtysomething.

She has very long red hair, scraped back from her forehead, an intense expression and a lot of very large teeth. Her eyes focus on your face with a seriousness that suggests she is probably in need of contact lenses. She also, as is the way with thirtysomethings, is greatly in need of physical reassurance from men – something fiftysomething women have long since given up on. I got a lot of feeling and squeezing and kissing. In fact, after about half an hour of it, I had the distinct impression I had shagged her, which, I think, from both our points of view, was highly satisfactory.

She works, it turns out, for the BBC. Although, as she works in Vision she is now totally separate from Sound. I am pretty sure she is one hundred per cent female – although, of course, you can never be too sure. But I think Nobby would have drawn the line at that.

'I had the impression . . .' she said, lighting up her twelfth cigarette of the evening, 'that Nobby was like . . . someone on a raft . . .' 'Yes!' I said. 'A sort of huge raft,' she went on, drinking deeply of her vodka and tonic, 'floating out into the sea. And that although one could sort of . . . *call* to him from the shore as it were . . . he was on this raft . . . floating out to sea . . .' I said I thought that was a very good description of Nobby.

'Sometimes,' I said, trying to get into the spirit of this, 'I had the impression he was sort of . . . down a well . . . or up a tree . . . or in a balloon almost . . .' She nodded furiously at this. 'Yes,' she said, 'yes yes yes yes! A balloon!'

We have agreed to meet for lunch at a place called Mezzo. Since I was obviously supposed to have heard of it I pretended I was a regular there. Will have to look it up in *Guide*.

When we parted she embraced me with almost terrifying fierceness and I managed to get a squeeze of her buttocks (not much of them). As she turned to go through the door she said, 'I had split up with Nobby, as you probably know. And . . . when he died . . . we were having a sort of . . . brief . . . reconciliation . . .' I nodded gravely, wondering, once again, at the many, many different words that women can use to mean 'shagging'. I thought I might be about to get a coherent account of what it is like when someone pegs out while on the case. I must say that, as none of us are getting any younger, it is the sort of information that might well come in handy in the near future. But that was about as much hard information as I got about Nobby's closing moments. 'I hope I did right with Nobby!' she said, wistfully, as we finally parted. 'I tried to give him lots and lots and lots and lots of love. But he just wouldn't accept it somehow.'

## 11.30 p.m.

Estelle back at eleven. Jakob with her. More furniture missing. This time a writing-desk, two chairs and a sideboard. She was cagey about where they had gone, simply saying she was 'reorganizing'. I asked her whether this was intended to make me feel as uncomfortable at home as I am at work and she said 'probably'. Also worried about why she and Jakob should be at Kensington.

Convinced now she is planning to leave me. Jakob would certainly be the first person she would tell. I have to make some headway either with thirtysomething or with Mrs Proek (Gwen) before the end of the month. Which is it to be? A fifty-year-old traffic warden or a thirtysomething television producer? I think, at the moment, I favour the traffic warden, but that is probably only because I have seen the television producer more recently.

There is a FOR SALE sign up outside Wickett's house. Why? Are they fed up with me peering at them? I must say I hope they are not going to leave. I have been peering out of the window at Wickett and his wife for fifteen years. And, though I have hardly ever spoken to them, there is a degree of intimacy between us. New people might never open the curtains.

Ruairghry and Lucy spent the day making bread and cleaning the house. They had whispered chats with Estelle tonight. I asked Estelle whether she had any news about his job. She obviously has, but was not saying anything. Everyone in this house is against me. And I am fifty in a little over a month!

Suddenly cold and rainy. I feel depressed.

Will administer potion to Estelle at earliest possible opportunity. Not, however, until after tomorrow night, when I have my tête-à-tête with Laura's Mum.

## May 10th. 10.30 a.m. Still cold and rainy. There is a bird in the back garden but he looks almost as depressed as me.

*Estelle 'with Hamish'. Ruairehgy 'at work'. Jakob in bank in Wimbledon. Edwin at school. Lucy in kitchen eating toast. Me at home (surprise, surprise!).*

A letter from the Royal Court for Wesley Jones.

It reads —

Dear Wesley,

    I was very sorry to hear your reaction to Gavin's production of *Muthafuckas*, a play which all of us here feel is a seminal piece of the last ten years. In my view it is right up there with Jed Braynes's *Largo* and Winston Nkozula's *Bad Traffic*.

    I understand your hurt feelings, Wesley. But what you call 'the oppreshan' is in no way involved with us at the Court. I think to refer to us as 'pigs' and 'white dirt' is really not helpful. Neither is it really getting us anywhere to talk about a director who has worked long and hard on your piece as 'limp-dick, paleface scum'.

    I was as disappointed as you were by the reviews. But I

have to warn you that death threats are simply not an
acceptable form of artistic discussion and that all of
us at the Court refuse to be intimidated by them.

Yours,
Jim Baeldi
Artistic Director

PS. I enclose some more reviews.

I can see why Wesley is upset. They have all had a go at him apart
from Venning who describes it as 'a masterpiece'. Could they, perhaps,
have been copying out each other's notes? They also all seem to disagree
violently about what actually happens in the play.

Doorbell. Oh God. It is Jakob. And Lucy seems to be going to answer
it.


## 10.45 a.m.

Violent row between Jakob and Lucy. I heard most of it. She insists he
does not 'really feel anything for her' and is 'coming on to her for a bet'.
I must say, this did seem entirely possible to me. 'No, baby!' I heard
Jakob say, 'I need you! I need you!' Seriously thought of giving them
potion, and then remembered Ruairehgy may well have proposed marriage
to her. After about ten minutes they started throwing things at each other.
I rang Estelle on her mobile for sympathy, advice, etc. She was cold. She
said she was 'in a meeting with Hamish'. 'What kind of "meeting"?' I
yelled, to which she said, 'For God's sake, Paul, do not go all pathetic on
me!' 'What do you mean, pathetic?' I said. 'What on earth is pathetic
about me? I am just confused. What are you up to? What do you feel
about Hamish? Is Julian there? Are you having an affair? Are those Turks
there? Are you leaving me? Why is the furniture disappearing?'

She hung up. She is definitely leaving me.

## 12 noon.

New script arrived. I am hanging on there by a thread. Still in Intensive Care. Pilfrey has horrible scene with Pamela in which they make love. She says, at one point, 'Stroke my thighs!' I rang Christine and reminded her that *General Practice* goes out at eleven in the morning. She said, 'That is exactly the time you want your thighs stroked.' There is obviously more to this woman than meets the eye.

She says no one knows whether Porda will see off Karl and Ramp, i.e. whether I will live or die. It seems unbelievable that a man who has the confidence of John Birt should be countermanded in this way. Let alone J. B. himself. He is the boss, for God's sake! He has a pretty firm grip on programmes – especially radio soap opera as far as I can see. John really understands *General Practice*. Let him get on with it. Thinking of writing to him to express my support for his stand on various issues – digital, restructuring, etc. Would this look creepy?

## 4 p.m.

Just got back from trip to shops, which are full of old ladies and middle-aged men who have just been made redundant, gone for early retirement, etc. I met Porker, who was in Boots buying vitamin pills, some of which he offered me. I ate five.

I bought aftershave and new shirt for hot sex date with Mrs Proek. Must go now to pick up Edwin. Where is Ruaghry? What is this 'job' of his?

## 5.30 p.m.

Edwin only just finished rehearsal with Hotchkiss, who brought along Hong, his Chinese boyfriend, to 'advise on movement'. Hotchkiss himself has decided to play Oberon (who is in full SS gear throughout the piece) and has rejected Plonker's ass's head as 'too crude'. Instead, Plonker will apparently make donkey noises, eat hay, etc. Plonker very unhappy about Hotchkiss being on the same stage as him. I told him he was lucky Hotchkiss had not decided to play Titania. Plonker said, 'Right enough, Paul baby!'

252

For some reason he has given Edwin a machine-gun. It is, I think, the first time I have seen Puck leap on to the stage and spray bullets around the place. Edwin seems very pleased with it and asked if he could take it home as he wanted to show it to Lulu. We had a positively Elizabethan exchange about him showing off his weapon to the women in his life, but of course I told him firmly it had to remain at school.

Hong is a great fan of *General Practice*! He asked whether it was true that I was going to leave my wife. I said – speaking, I felt, for Esmond and my real self (whatever that may be) – that after twenty-five years it seemed rather pointless to go anywhere. Hong said, 'All relationships mus' grow an' change. Arter I leave Hotchkiss for the man in Woolworths, our sex life improve a ver great deal!'

## 7.30 p.m.

More furniture has gone missing. Two standard lamps, two easy chairs and a writing-desk from downstairs. Nothing of mine has gone. Called Estelle in office to try and talk about relationship, her leaving me, my imminent affair with traffic warden, thirtysomething, etc. Was connected to 'Julian'. If really Gillian then she either has a sore throat or a recent sex change, possibly both. He said, 'You really need to speak to Hamish if it's for Estelle.' I told him, with quiet dignity, that the message was not urgent. 'It's a family matter!' I said. He said, 'It sounds urgent!' 'No! No!' I said, lightly, ''twill pass!' Then I hung up. Think I won this encounter. Off now to East Cheam.

## 8 p.m.

Writing this outside the Proek's house in East Cheam. Think I saw Laura at upper window. She was wearing a tank top (I think).

It is rather more upmarket than the Rachnowskis. A Toytown cottage – clean white walls, a brilliant front lawn and a bright yellow car in the driveway, which looked as if its previous owner might well have been Noddy.

Have brought potion. In we go, Slippery. This is your only chance.

## 9 p.m.

Back in the car again.

Got this one badly wrong. She seemed to have completely forgotten about her note inviting me to turn up at her place. She and Norman were watching a programme about wildlife. She seemed surprised to see me. I whispered – peering over her shoulder at the back of Norman's head – 'Not on the roof, then?' She did not seem to understand this reference.

I tried rolling my eyes. It was probable, I felt, that she simply hadn't been able to phone me. He probably watches her like a hawk. The minimal front hall – no more, really, than a screen and a few coats – was, however, enough for me to get quite a bit of eye-rolling under way. Mrs Proek looked at me oddly. 'Are you all right?' she said, in a loud voice. 'You seem to have a squint!'

This was not a promising beginning. And the male Proek showed no sign of moving. For a moment I wondered whether to suggest the two of us nipped out for a curry. Anything, in fact, to get away from the back of Mr Proek's head. But, before I could speak, Mr Proek said, 'What does the greasy little bastard want now?'

This was, also, not helpful. I looked into Mrs Proek's eyes and tried to read the message that was within them. *Don't come now! He suspects! I tried to phone but I was frightened your wife might find out! You must go from here! He is insanely jealous! He will kill you! He will kill me! He will kill himself! He may well kill some of the neighbours!! Our love can never be! It is like the love Vronksy had for Anna Karenina or the love that other Russian bloke had for whatshername! Go from here! I beg you my darling! Leave!*

I decided that, on the whole, this was not the message that was within them. There was a message there but it was more along the lines of 'Who the fuck are you and what are you doing here?' Perhaps Liquid Love wears off after a few days. 'It's about Laura!' I said. 'You better come in.' I walked into the room.

Somehow or other she got me into the back kitchen. I could hear David Attenborough, next door, talking to Norman. 'It is time!' he was saying, 'for Henry's lunch!' Mrs Proek said, 'The thing between us and Lucy's Mum and Dad is horrendous. You wouldn't believe it, Paul. And Laura is so in love with your Jakob. What can we do about that?'

I did not like to mention potion. I think I heard Laura moving around upstairs. When I went out I finally made eye contact with Mr Proek. He looked as if he had been crying. 'She was so lovely when she was small!' he said. 'She was so sweet!'

What do I do about all these love complications? Eh?

## 11.45 p.m.

Estelle back and in bed when I got back. Presumably sated by Hamish. I went in to look at her. She was lying on her back, her nose in the air, snoring softly, black hair spread out behind her on the pillow. Her hands were arrayed on the duvet in front of her like fish on a slab. I went over to her side. How often have I seen that face: beside me in the car shouting directions; coming towards me across playgrounds when the children were little; at my side in the registry office all those years ago; looming up at me from behind the windscreen of her car! Above me below me beside me beyond me, always a little beyond me, unknowable, familiar, alien, cold, warm, sweet, sour, dazzling, dark. My wife.

## May 12th. 11 a.m. Warm again. Brilliant sunshine. Slightly hazy sky.

*Estelle 'on recce in Scotland with Hamish and Gillian/Julian'. Ruaghrury and Jakob at therapist. Laura and Mr and Mrs Proek downstairs in garden. Edwin at Irish dancing class. Lucy with Mr and Mrs Rachnowski (why is this anything to do with me?) in East Cheam Hospital. Me here.*

Lucy (apparently) took an overdose. We do not know what of. All we do know is that it 'wasn't serious'. She is in East Cheam Psychiatric Hospital. It appears that she was in deep distress about Jakob keeping on trying to shag her as well as Ruaighry. I know how she feels. He is a very determined boy.

I really do like both girls. Am genuinely upset about all of this.

Laura and her parents have somehow got in on the act and are (somehow) round here. Gwendolen Proek keeps dropping weird remarks about them and the Rachnowskis. What is going on? Jakob and Ruaighrey both had hysterics and I tried to get them to go to the partially trained Kleinian

255

but he has had to go to Wimbledon Magistrate's Court to answer charges connected with an accident for which the police say he was partially responsible. Left a message on Estelle's mobile, outlining these dramatic events.

## 11.23 a.m.

Have just found Estelle's mobile in fridge – while looking for prawns. There is a distinctly raunchy message on it from Hamish. Partially trained Kleinian left message to say he was now free 'although he couldn't give them a whole session'.

## 11.45 a.m.

Gustave on machine again, requesting lunch. I think I am going to call him and say that if he wants to give me food he can send it round in foil containers.

## 12.30 p.m.

Jakob and Ruaiehriughy completely back from partially trained Kleinian. Apparently he tried to suggest they had both been partially sexually abused. They 'left early'. I said, 'It's possible! You never know!' Jakob said, 'Who would have sexually abused us then?' I said, 'Well . . . me!' They both laughed – a little contemptuously, I thought. 'You would never have had the nerve!' said Jakob.

Lucy's half-hearted suicide bid (apparently she took Junior Aspirin) seems to have calmed them a little. They are now in garden with Mr and Mrs Proek and Laura – who is wearing a high-necked fawn cardigan.

## 2 p.m.

Called Estelle on her mobile. It was not until I heard bleeping sound from fridge that I remembered that that was where it was. Another crisis and she not here! I fear me and thirtysomething may well be an item if she is not careful.

### 3 p.m.

Off to pick up Edwin from Irish dancing, which he is doing instead of physics. He has equally little talent for either discipline but apparently he stands a chance of getting an A in Irish Dancing G C S E. The invigilators are, he says, 'often well pissed'. We will go from there to Hotchkiss's rehearsal and then to see Lucy at East Cheam Hospital.

### 3.25 p.m.

*En route* for East Cheam *avec* Edwin. Via rehearsal.

Apparently Hotchkiss now wants them to lose the jockstraps. I said I was relieved to hear this. Plonker said, 'My God! We have to hang on to the jockstraps!' I said, 'I thought you didn't like the jockstraps.' He said he didn't but that they were 'better than nothing'. Which is apparently what the insane Hotchkiss is suggesting they wear.

The men came round to take away more furniture as I left for Edwin. I asked Jakob whether this was anything to do with the fridges and he said, 'Absolutely not. We deal in good gear. We wouldn't touch the stuff in this house with a bargepole.'

### 5.15 p.m.

In Reception of East Cheam Hospital with Edwin.

Poor kid! She is so sweet! Thank God they were Junior Aspirin is all I can say! This is all my fault! If I had not given Jakob the potion this would never have happened! I have to re-administer it to Laura and get those two back together!

The Rachnowskis were there and really very sweet. But there is clearly some major problem between them and the Proeks. Have no idea what it is. Mr and Mrs Bert looked at me very oddly. Does Mrs Bert fancy me? They are, it occurs to me, the only people who know about the potion.

Estelle, also, clearly to blame as she is thinking only of career and not of her responsibilities as mother. Rang her mobile to give her an (edited) view of this *aperçu* and left message on her machine. Then remembered machine in fridge at Mafeking Road.

## 7 p.m.

There is a very strange man lurking around in the street opposite the house. At first I thought he might be something to do with the Wicketts (whose bedroom curtain seems, at the moment, to be permanently closed) but he seems to be keeping his eyes on number 52. He is in his early twenties, raggedly dressed and with wild hair. I have a horrible feeling he may be something to do with Wesley Jones. If he is there for much longer I am calling the police.

## 9.30 p.m.

Ruighry, Laura, Jakob, Edwin and Lulu are all watching the television. Sad events have made Riushury and Jakob a little closer. Jakob even punched Laura, gently, on her left cheek. Ruaighry (who says he is 'very tired after his job' – whatever it may be) keeps saying, 'She was such a nice girl, man!' This did not please Jakob who said, through gritted teeth, 'She is not dead yet!'

I think Edwin may have stolen a little more of the potion – which I have still not had time to administer to Mrs Proek, the thirtysomething, Laura, Estelle or any of the other women in my life. He is lying on the sofa with Lulu in an attitude I think inappropriate for a boy of sixteen. Occasionally he thrusts his hips forward and says, 'Gooja Mamma Hey Whaddya Say We Gonner Live it Large in My Love Coracle Baby!' I have retreated upstairs.

The view from my window offers little comfort. The strange man has just lurked past again. He does not, however, lurk for long enough for his lurking to be obvious enough to be reported to the police. He walks up to the Wicketts' house, lurks for a few minutes and then walks on briskly down the street, where, presumably, he lurks for a little bit before coming back to do more lurking outside number 52.

Is he, perhaps, a stalker? I am quite a modest, shy person but – let us face it – have a certain amount of celebrity. Articles have been written about me. I have spoken out on various subjects. I have been pretty frank about the N H S and the current state of arts funding, and have said some pretty uncomplimentary things about R. Pilfrey. I have described the theatre critic of the *Sunday Times* as 'an ignorant berk'. I have enemies.

I have alienated people at the BBC: Karl Rhws Davies and Colin Cross, for example. I know that Ashley Ramp did not really make the programme about snails. And many other people there, who pretend to be my friends, are probably working against me. Christine, for example, insists on giving my radio wife more lines than me. Not that one 'counts', but in the last episode she had two hundred and fifty more lines as well as a much higher strike rate of exclamation marks and question marks – all of which, as we know, make for higher performance impact.

I am starting to worry about John Birt. I still have gut respect for his programme judgement, courage and integrity but am fearful that those round him have 'got to him' in some way and turned him against me. Why has he not phoned or written to follow up his kind words about *General Practice*? Has he, perhaps, changed his mind?

## 10 p.m.

Called Good Old Steve to give him (edited) version of moan above. He was out – said an unnamed voice on his phone – 'with a woman'. Who can this be? Thought of calling Nobby and then remembered he was dead. Will call Peter Mailer.

## 10.15 p.m.

Christine had biked over next episode – in which I am still in Intensive Care. More dialogue for Pamela. I had a bit of a go at Christine on phone and she burst into tears and said she was an alcoholic. This will not help my recovery. Gave her Peter Mailer's number and suggested she call him. Will call him. Maybe he can tell me if Christine can be relied upon to keep Esmond Pennebaker alive.

## 11.45 p.m.

The first time I rang, Mailer was in therapy. Or, to be precise, dispensing it.

When Peter rang back he told me that he had had a five-minute conversation with Christine, who 'wanted to cut off his head with a knife'. I must say I have often found Peter annoying but I thought this was probably a world record in establishing zero tolerance as far as he is concerned. He then said, 'She isn't an alcoholic, Paul. She drinks a bottle of Scotch a day but she is not an alcoholic.' He is a real snob about alcoholics.

Apparently she has got something called 'co-dependent dependency' which is about the worst thing you can get short of a Nobby-style cardiac arrest. The reason she has been writing Pamela into the series so heavily, Peter told me, is because she wants to marry me. I was rather flattered by this. Apparently, however, she has the urge to castrate love objects. God knows how he managed to find out all this in a five-minute phone call.

## 12 midnight. All asleep.

Called Estelle on a number she had left with Edwin. Spoke to Hamish. He said, 'Your wife is a very remarkable woman.' I agreed. Message on machine from Howard Porda. He said, 'Paul — Karl and Ramp are determined to kill you. I hope we can keep you alive.' I am, I realize, determined to live.

Esmond is an ordinary Englishman like me. He is a little battered by time. He is not, and never will be, fashionable. He lives in the suburbs. He has a regular job which he tries to do well. He bonked his secretary in 1985 and then apologized for it like a white man. He is not a great doctor. He has misdiagnosed multiple sclerosis, breast cancer, angina pectoris and gout (twice). His bedside manner is brusque to the point of rudeness. He has little interest in events over which he has no influence. He rarely travels abroad. He has no post-colonial guilt; he is proud to be British. He thinks about sex a lot. He is getting older. He has started to have serious accidents. He is heading in the direction of his memorial service.

I am going to fight for him. He is Everyman. He is out there — from Düsseldorf to Kingman, Arizona, there are men like Esmond Pennebaker quietly fucking up other people's lives. And I make a solemn vow now, here, in my upper room at 52 Mafeking Road, Wimbledon, that I, Paul Slippery, actor, minor celebrity, family man and would-be decent neighbour, not being of sound mind since I am, it appears, unable to remember when I last had sex with my wife (assuming I ever did have sex with her) and am also, it would seem, unable to tell the difference between men and women, I (I say) yes I, Slippery, say that I (yes me) do solemnly swear by everything I hold holy, i.e. not very much, that Dr Esmond Pennebaker will live and that I, too, will continue to live since when I die he dies and he is not going to go before me and I, with luck, am not going to go before him so we will both, with luck, go on and on and on and on and on, which is what soap opera does and we never want it to stop because it is like life, dull sometimes and inconclusive and deeply ordinary but always (we hope) there.

May 13th. 11 a.m. Blue skies, white clouds, green leaves etc. Warm. Same bird back on tree in garden. Looking obscenely cheerful about something. Probably having sex with other bird.

*Estelle in 747 over Greenland. Jakob and Ruairy at therapist. Lucy and Laura back home where they belong. Edwin at school where he belongs. Me in Wimbledon.*

Just read last sentence and last paragraph of last entry – virtually the same thing. I think I may have potential as a novelist.

Just had spooky experience. Playing back answer-machine tape I discovered a conversation that must have been recorded (accidentally) a long time ago. Don't know how it surfaced or why I have not heard it before. It went –

ESTELLE: I am sure he doesn't suspect.
HAMISH: If he suspects you are stuffed.
ESTELLE: Paul has his head too far up his own arse to suspect anything.
HAMISH: Let's hope.

And this is the man who has now gone with her from Edinburgh to Los Angeles. She told Edwin (not me) that she 'needed to do some deals about the animated film'. Perhaps Pilfrey is there with her also! I did not know it was even possible to fly to America from Scotland. I hope the planes are reliable.

Off now to St Barnabas School, Acton, via the Old Stag Inn, Shepherd's Bush. Let us see what Ashley Ramp has to say for himself. If he thinks he is going to rub out Dr Esmond Pennebaker he has another thing coming.

## 1.15 p.m.

Writing this in the Old Stag Inn, Shepherd's Bush. Waiting for Wainwright, Steve Witchett, the Writer Who Never Expresses an Opinion, and Ronnie 'Very Nice Man' Pilfrey. If he is not in LA. I tried to phone Howard Porda but he was, as usual, 'in a meeting'. The Stag is a place normally full of people from television but, of course, as most of them are in Vision, they are all off at the NCP car park in Hounslow.

I am told of a rumour that, for some reason, religious programmes are in Sound rather than Vision. Perhaps they thought Vision was a controversial word to use in relation to religious matters. Also still in Sound, the word is, are programmes that are on very, very late at night. Whether they are not worthy to be in Vision because they consist of men in cardigans droning on from armchairs or because their potential audience is usually fast asleep or too drunk to see is not clear.

## 2.15 p.m.

Quickly scribbling this before we head off for St Barnabas.

Pilfrey (here) has been offered the role of a sea slug in a forthcoming film for children. It is, he tells me, a fat part in every sense of the word. Hearing him talk about it makes me feel so ill that I did not bother to ask for clarification. I asked Steve Witchett, the Writer Who Never Expresses an Opinion, whether he might be coming back to the show and he said, 'If I decide to come back, I may well write and tell whoever I need to tell that that is what I am doing. Or fax. If I am doing it, of course.'

## 3 p.m.

Writing this in the playground of St Barnabas School, Acton.

I am sitting on the edge of a climbing frame, at the back, as I have been for most of my life. Ashley Ramp is addressing the massed ranks of

Sound through a megaphone. I say 'massed'. I am amazed at how few of us there are left.

The programme about snails was made by a Dane called (I think) Knaedler. He had taped snails doing all the things that snails do over a period of nine years. Ramp, who for some reason was executive producer of the programme, had always opposed Knaedler making it. When he first heard it he said it was 'too slow'. But when it won nine awards at the Oregon Natural History Radio Festival Ramp started talking about 'our' programme. By the time it won the Golden Tongue at the San Francisco Sound Fest it was 'my' programme. Knaedler never worked for the BBC again.

'Restructuring', as Joel Farrago from Radio Continuing Features pointed out not long ago in this very playground, 'is basically about firing people.' And I am amazed at how many old Beeb stalwarts are simply not there any more. Rosie Jones, who made all those wonderful programmes about lifeboats. Ellen Weevis, who took three years to create her 'sound portrait' of Moreton-in-Marsh which won so many awards. Norman Brierly and Maxwell Cake, who lived together and did those marvellous programmes about ballet. Phoebe Jacques, who used to put her lipstick on back to front and wore a wedding dress to work for a whole week in the late seventies. Marshall Playnes, who was so decisive in meetings, and Jeremy Huelbetter, who wasn't. Julian Grayling, who despised us all and wore red velvet waistcoats. Arthur Klipstein, the American, who was not going to stay long but did.

Some of these people are dead, I suppose. But there are many, many gaps among the younger ones. Templeman Hume, a great voice-over artist, should have been there. And Sidney Poultrier, the Poulenc specialist – where was he? Most of the people here are younger than me – too young to know who Ashley Ramp is or where he came from.

But I know that Ashley Ramp has made his career out of bullying those below him and crawling to those above him. I could give you times and dates and places on the promises he has broken, the people he has betrayed and the ignorant rubbish he has talked. Once he talked Young Turk and demanded the right to include four-letter words in news bulletins. Then he talked Creative Responsible and talked about 'nurturing' and 'seeding talent'. And now he speaks a language that is a horrific mishmash of Carl Drucker and his successors, the American management gurus whose linguistic games provide the gloss on the smooth and unquestioned rapacities of contemporary capitalism. But even this management garbage he spouts now — 'objectives', 'strategy' and so forth — will give way, as did all his other previous languages, to the grammar and style of the next ruling class. He is, in his own way, as typical a specimen of his time as Andre Vyshinsky, Stalin's prosecutor, who squealed so loudly when he thought that it might be his turn to be shot.

But I didn't do anything to stop him, did I? I didn't speak up about the appalling mixture of New Labour modernity and old-style patriarchal complacency that pervades this place, did I? I didn't want his boring job, did I? So I didn't stand up to Colin Cross or Karl Rhws Davies or any of the others whose only concern is to make sure their next pay cheque arrives on time. Did I?

Political responsibility now begins and ends inside large corporations. Morality, for most of us — if we are lucky enough not to live in Nigeria or Iran — is something that happens at work or at home, two places over which we have less and less control. But what the boss says is not necessarily right. Have we lost the right to question him (or her)? To say that he (or she) has the duty to listen to you?

Ramp has started to jump up and down and shriek, waving his megaphone in the air as he does so.

'We have separated Sound from Vision! But Sound needs Vision!' he has just yelled. 'Without Vision we are simply a voice in the wilderness. We are what used to be called radio. We don't want to go back to that, do we? We need to find our way to Vision and work with them to integrate the broadcasting process fully and comprehensively. Our meeting, as you will have noticed, is here in Acton. Theirs is in Hounslow. We want to change all that and that is what this afternoon is all about.'

Behind me someone muttered that if that was what it was all about why didn't we all meet in the same fucking playground. But Ramp was now unstoppable. 'This afternoon,' he screamed, 'Sound is going to find Vision. Or try to. Vision are in Hounslow. Sound are in Acton. You have all been given a list of bars and open spaces where you are to informally link up during the afternoon, mirroring the "casual meeting" meetings of normal business life!'

Ramp started to jump up and down again.

'*General Practice . . .*' he began — and then, almost at once, his voice faded to a shrill whisper as something went seriously wrong with his megaphone. I heard snatches of what he said — as the amplification seemed to be going in and out of phase — but all I got was, roughly — '. . . audience share in the early evening . . . A B viewer share in the first half of the year . . . *General Practice* . . . lone mothers listening in . . . commuters who are also lone mothers . . . the death of Esmond Pennebaker . . . the *Guardian*. . . stealing light-bulbs . . . Norwegian film crews . . . how can we? . . . Pennebaker's death (*laughter here*) . . . in our terms . . . thankyou!'

This is a lot of help. Off now to reintegrate what my masters decided to disintegrate about six months ago.


## 4 p.m.

Ronnie 'Very Nice Man' Pilfrey and I (with some help from Steve Witchett, the Writer Who Never Expresses an Opinion) have captured the thirtysomething in a park in Acton. Witchett says we have made a good business decision.

It turns out she works for some documentary programme or other. I still have not managed to gather her name.

I am a touch low at the moment. Those nearer to the front in the playground have bad news for me. Apparently Ramp is determined to end, not only *General Practice* but also the life of Esmond. I am to die in Intensive Care and the whole practice is to fall to bits. Pilfrey is to become an alcoholic. My long-term buddy Dirk is to find out he is gay and leave to set up home with Jimbo. Meningitis will decimate the junior staff. And, finally, the building is to go up in flames.

The word is that Ramp is determined to fight Porda on this issue and, according to Pilfrey, Howard's behaviour has been so eccentric of late that there are rumours he is for the chop. He spends much of his time arm-wrestling and watching the Sports Channel. Some say he mooned at Linda Billington and has, thereby, lost the confidence of John Birt.


## 5 p.m.

In pub.

'What is wrong with Ashley,' said Pilfrey, 'is that he isn't getting enough. We need to fix him up with someone. But they have to be into rubber. Do you know anyone who is into rubber?' I said, hastily, that I didn't. The thirtysomething, looking rather tense, said she knew loads of people who were into rubber, but they were all already fixed up. Witchett said, 'I would like to get fixed up. But not with someone who was into rubber. Not necessarily anyway. I don't have very defined views on rubber. I can see its attraction but I also, in a sense, just see it as a method of waterproofing. Although obviously that is not all rubber is used for.'

We talked of love. I said all three of my sons were in love – two of them with the same woman. Pilfrey asked whether I was still in love with Estelle after twenty-five years of marriage. A typical Pilfrey question. He has been divorced three times. I said, 'It depends what you mean by love!' Which, of course, was a typical Slippery answer. The thirtysomething said we all knew what we meant by love. 'It's a feeling!' she said, staring at me intently. (Good sign?)

Then they all started on me. I had to say whether or not I was in love with Estelle. Why are people so curious about people who have been together for a long time? Is it because they want to *be* them or because they're glad they're not them? And why do they assume they know any more about their lives than anybody else? I can't begin to describe what I feel about her to them or anyone else. I'm either too far away or too close up to her to answer that question. She's just part of me.

## 8 p.m.

Estelle presumably landed in LA. More furniture missing. Strange man still lurking in road. When I mentioned it to Ruairghry (who is now seeing a Jungian called Bertram), he said, 'Oh God! It's probably Oliver!'

It turns out Ruairghry has got a job helping homeless people. I said I thought this was an admirable idea – especially as he was probably about to join their ranks. He was not amused by this. He talked – again – of marriage. Although, apparently, he and Lucy are having a 'cool-off period'. Presumably this means only shagging for twenty-three rather than twenty-four hours of every day. I said he couldn't possibly get married yet. Jakob came in from his therapist – who is still the partially trained Kleinian. All was well until he said that Lucy was 'taking time out because she was still very drawn to him'. Ruarighery said, 'In your

266

dreams!' Jakob said, 'Who's having Jungian analysis, then?' They chased each other round the dining table.

Ruaeroighy is cooking this evening. We are to have a dish of lentils from a recipe book called *On the Street*, all proceeds from which go to the homeless. I asked whether I could cook dinner at the same time, as we might need a back-up. Preferably from a recipe book whose profits and content were aimed at the rich, fat and greedy. I was told I could not. Am in my study, rehearsing my lines. Mostly grunts of pain I fear. I really am on the way out.

## May 16th. 8 a.m. Overcast. Quite cool. Spring on temporary hold.

*Estelle in west Hollywood. Edwin, Jakob, Ruaieiuerghy all asleep. Me in study.*

Was woken by call from Estelle. She sounded drunk. It is, of course, twelve midnight in Pinot Hollywood, the sickeningly trendy restaurant from which she, Hamish, Turks, etc., called me. I was unable to discuss our relationship, when we last had sex, etc., because she kept bursting into song. I said, with quiet dignity, 'I am glad you are having a nice time. I have to take Edwin to school now!' Let her shag Hamish. What care I?

A lot.

## 10.30 a.m.

Have not taken Edwin to school. He is still asleep. Will write lying note to Mr Brain, the awesomely titled discipline master.

Message on machine from Peter Mailer.

It runs as follows —

MAILER: Hi, Paul, how are you, are you well? I'm pretty well although of course it's hard to say these days but mustn't grumble in the main. I expect you're working pretty hard at . . . acting which is what you do and you're good at it and that's as it should be and it's good. It's what should happen. (*Long pause.*) I have made love to Christine. We need to talk. (*Long pause.*) It was good, Paul, it was very very good. It was passionate and very physically intense and it lasted a long time. (*Long pause.*) I'm as you may know very turned on by anal sex and we had plenty of that, Paul, as well as a lot of other kinds of sex. (*Long pause.*) We used ropes, Paul, and whips. (*Long pause.*) And hairbrushes also we used. (*Long pause.*) Call me.

I am damned if I will call him.

## 10.45 a.m.

Another message on the machine from Mailer. It runs as follows:

MAILER: Paul, hi, Peter here again hope all is well with you assuming it is well anyway although of course you are not there or at least not picking up for some reason. (*Long pause.*) We dressed up, Paul, in sort of . . . boots and a kind of cloak and we sort of . . . played various roles . . . (*Long pause.*) Have you heard of watersports, Paul? I am not talking about snorkelling here, Paul. (*Long pause.*) Call me.

I am thinking of taking the phone off the hook.

## 11 a.m.

I did not. There is another message from Mailer. It runs as follows:

MAILER: Paul, hi, Peter here again I know I keep ringing but I have to talk to someone and as you are not there I might as well talk to your machine we all talk to machines these days life is rather lonely don't you think, Paul? (*Long pause.*) You know I am an alcoholic, Paul? Which means that I respond badly to drink in any shape or form and so I shouldn't have one. (*Long pause.*) Which I have just had. One I mean. Don't call me.

## 11.15 a.m.

I rang him straight back but the phone seemed to be permanently engaged.

I think I may have to go round there. Will wait to see if he calls me first.

## 11.30 a.m.

He called at the one time I had left my study to go deal with Oliver (of which more later). He left a message on the machine which ran as follows –

> MAILER: I have just had three gin and tonics, Paul, and I feel great.
> I think I may not have been an alcoholic at all. I feel bloody
> marvellous. I feel really alive. (*Long pause.*) She rubbed me with oil,
> Paul. She has one of those things you strap on. And a cloak. And a
> . . . hood thing, Paul. (*Long pause.*) I have had a bottle of white
> wine. I feel absolutely fine. (*Long pause.*) Call me.

I have a damned good mind to get into a cloak, boots and hood, strap on a phallus and get round there without delay. I may actually do this. Although he does not make it clear whether this is an open party. Knowing my luck I would probably be greeted by Mailer on his own – pissed out of his brain, reeling around the room in wellies and a Batman outfit. One thing is certain. I am not going to call him. Ever again.

It is now twelve midday. Time for Karl's press conference. Going to leave boys in bed all day.

## 4 p.m.

Writing this in what used to be Surinder's office. Will we ever see her again, I wonder?

Karl Rhws Davies's press conference has just ended.

It was sensational. By the time he came into the canteen there must have been nearly two hundred people in the place. He was wearing a loose-fitting, green, sleeveless evening dress, which, I must say, rather suited him. He was well made up (although perhaps there was a shade too much mascara) and was wearing a very skilful blond wig which made him look a little like Dusty Springfield.

His voice seemed to have risen an octave but had a rather reassuring, Mumsy quality to it. The faces in the room — apart, perhaps, from Val Cheirley of the *Mail*, suggested they were in the middle of a rather tough funeral. In total silence, Karl read from a prepared statement, 'Hullo and thank you for coming to my press conference. My name is Karl Rhws Davies and I am the producer of *General Practice*, a long-running drama that, as you may have heard, is under threat of being discontinued.' Here he gave a meaningful look towards Ramp. 'It is my contention that the upcoming death of Esmond Pennebaker will give the show the added vitality it needs to survive into the Millennium — although that is not why I am here. I am here to announce that, from henceforth, I wish to be known as Shirley!'

There was a lot of scribbling. And quite a lot of super-sympathetic nodding from Louise Slay, from the *Express* Women's Page. I looked round for Porda. Not there. Karl continued. 'There are, as it happens, many of us in the BBC under great pressure. *General Practice*, as we all know, is losing listeners . . .'

Here Wainwright whispered to the man next to him, 'Not after this little lot!'

'. . . and those of us concerned with it inside the Corporation are doing what we can to put it back on track. Drama has to tell the truth. Those of us who make drama have to live the truth, which is why I have called this press conference! There are many people like me in the BBC who wish to wear women's clothes, although we may not feel the need for genital surgery. There are others . . .' — here Karl allowed his eyes to roam over the gathering. It was only then that I noticed that Howard Porda was standing right at the back; Karl's eyes rested on him. '. . . who, for one reason or another, are unable to freely admit to their sexual natures! Whatever their tastes . . .' — here Karl looked straight at Ramp, who squirmed in his chair and tried to scratch his hump — 'it is my belief that we should be free to be ourselves. My wife fully supports my stand on this issue. Thank you!'

Everyone wrote furiously in their notebooks. Fiona Stalker from a woman's glossy put up her hand and asked whether Shirley felt the need to grow breasts. Karl was pretty eloquent on this subject and went into some detail. Fiona, as far as I could tell, was looking for a lingerie angle. But after that the pack started. 'Are you saying,' said Tony Staunton of the *Sun*, 'that there is a "ring" of senior BBC executives who like to wear women's clothes? If so, are you prepared to name them?' Karl got a bit shirty at this question but it didn't stop Staunton – or Lewis Grassett from the *Express* or Val Cheirley from the *Mail*.

Has he told them something he was not prepared to acknowledge publicly? I have been seen with Surinder in public places, have I not? The last thing I need is RADIO DOCTOR IN SEX-CHANGE LOVE TRYST ROW. That is really going to improve my status at Mafeking Road. I will probably be put in a kennel in the garden.

What baffles me is how he got away with calling the thing in the first place. I can only assume that, like Hitler on the eve of an invasion, he simply didn't (officially anyway) tell anyone what he was about to do. It was certainly the most interesting Drama press conference I have attended in twenty-five years in the business. I think it may play well for him. But the implications are not good for me. He wants the series to go on with me dead or he will expose both Ramp and Porda.

## 5 p.m.

Still at Beeb. Can't get through to Howard. His secretary said he had gone to a football match. He does not, of course, invite suspicion of effeminacy at the moment. I think I am safe. But suppose Karl – or Shirley, as we are going to have to get used to calling him – has got photos, tape recordings, etc. In whose name is the flat registered? The car? What about Surinder's doctor?

The British press is not known for efficiency and hard work. But set it the task of tracking down a sex-change candidate in high places and it makes the Wehrmacht look like a bunch of slackers.

I finally rang Howard at home and asked him to call me tonight. His answer-machine message makes him sound like Tito Gobbi. Going out now to see if Karl's announcement has made the evening paper.

# 7 p.m.

In a pub near Broadcasting House. With Leo and Steve Witchett, the Writer Who Never Expresses an Opinion. It appears that Leo and Witchett are writing an episode together. I shudder to think what it will be like. An overly tentative mixture of medicine and architecture, I suppose. The curious thing, however, is that Witchett – when Leo is around – sometimes comes dangerously close to formulating an unambiguous point. Just now Leo asked him what he would like to drink and Witchett, whose response would usually take about half an hour, said, 'I might have a cider, although of course I am not a dedicated cider drinker. But if I don't have a cider, which I probably won't, I might have a beer. In fact,' – here his face brightened gloriously – 'I think I will have a beer.' This, for Witchett, is a world record in decisiveness.

We have managed to get hold of a late edition of the evening paper. Karl is headline news. The banner reads 'I WEAR A DRESS TO WORK SAYS THE MAN FROM AUNTIE BEEB.' There is a very fetching picture of Karl in his outfit and, on the inside, a photo feature assessing the reactions of the man in the street. Everyone seems very positive. A junior Labour Minister has revealed that he too likes to wear women's clothes and finds 'it helps focus'.

No one has pointed out that Karl is a venal incompetent. About the only thing going for him, it seems to me, is that he has decided to call himself Shirley. But it was clearly a good card to play. Someone else is going to be blamed for the fact that ratings are slipping.

The only dark note is sounded by another spokesman, whose name is Chitterling. Chitterling is asked about the figure the paper is already talking of as the Third Man. He starts, 'We are an equal-opportunities employer and are fully committed to respecting the rights of minorities. Last year, for example, in our pamphlet *Initiating Change* we promised to overhaul the disabled toilet facilities. In our pamphlet *Are You a Stranger?* we gave very clear signals to the Bengali community, in Bengali, that we were solidly behind the Bengali community and fully respected their right to listen to and understand television and radio programmes . . .', etc., etc. After about half an hour of this he says (always bury the key point where no one will spot it), 'if of course there was any impropriety in a BBC employee's conduct that would be a very serious matter', i.e., if we wanted to fire him, we would. All we need is an excuse. And employing yourself under a woman's name (probably a mild peccadillo by senior Beeb standards) would not look good in the papers. Looking good, these days, is what it is all about.

If Howard goes down I am finished. I put another call through to Howard. His phone was busy.

## 10 p.m.

A nerve-racking evening discussing the love lives of my two eldest sons. No one mentioned my birthday once. Or the fact that Estelle and I will soon have been married for twenty-five years. Not that that may be the case by Midsummer's Eve.

Reirghy spoke again of marriage. 'If I married Lucy,' he said, dreamily, 'I'd . . . like . . . do it in the open air!' Jakob said, 'Would that be before or after you married her?' Reiuerhgy said he was a crude and unfeeling person. Jakob said he wasn't the one who had stolen the girl he loved. Rueiguehry said, 'Lucy tried to kill herself, man. Because of you.' Jakob said, 'She didn't try very hard.' And the whole thing started all over again. Edwin, during this conversation, stood in the middle of the kitchen with one hand behind his head, gyrating his hips and thrusting his behind backwards and forwards in a suggestive manner. He sang a song which began, 'Do me in my lovea chopper woa yeah honeychile sexamachine-aoohyeah!'

I think he may have been at the potion. Must check level in bottle.

I am afraid I screamed at them. I know this is bad but do not regret it.

Am not complete ostrich. Let them know that fathers still do have feelings. Still do get scared and lonely and desperate, even though they are supposed to be the opposite of all those things – for their children's sake.

May 17th. 11 a.m. Sunshine and showers. Classic April weather in May. The bird on the tree in the garden has been joined by another bird. I think he may be displaying to her, as seen in David Attenborough's excellent show. But it is rather a low-rent display. He raises his beak rather feebly and sneers. Bit like me really. A sparrow.

*Estelle at Paramount Pictures, Hollywood. Ruaierhuighy gone to see Lucy. Jakob following him (oh God!). Edwin at Irish dancing gala. Laura downstairs on sofa (wearing tank top).*

Lunch today with thirtysomething. Have put on aftershave. Jakob said I smelled 'sort of rotten'. Estelle rang at four in the morning and left long message on the machine demanding to know where everybody was, why we weren't having supper, etc. I listened to it, in the darkness, gnashing my teeth the while. The animated film is going well. Think I heard Hamish in background.

## 11.15 a.m.

Smell effeminate. Have taken off aftershave. Still too smelly.

## 11.45 a.m.

Still too smelly. Have had bath. Now too moist.

## 12.15 p.m.

Edwin has reappeared from school. Has just taken GCSE Art. Why did no one tell me about this? Apparently he has created an installation called *Hate*, involving the traffic cone, a plasticine blob, a sheep's skull and some items that look like, but aren't, artefacts from Sex Products of Wolverhampton Ltd. Lulu is with him and they have gone upstairs for what looks like a pretty serious personal encounter. I asked him about the Irish dancing gala and he said, 'That was yesterday. I got 80 per cent!' I am losing touch with him. Have taken potion, and am now off to West End to shag thirtysomething.

## 1.15 p.m.

Am in West End. Am lost. Cannot find Mezzo. Cannot find thirtysomething. All possibility of shag now fading.


## 3.30 p.m.

Am on Leicester Square tube station.

I finally ran down the thirtysomething in Wardour Street. She was rushing along looking distracted, and, like me, half an hour late. We didn't go to Mezzo, so I suppose I will never, now, find out where this amazingly trendy place actually is.

We went to a small Italian joint on Old Compton Street.

We started out talking about Nobby. I have clearly been missing out on a staggering amount of sex. Not simply at 52 Mafeking Road but also in the great wide world where, it is clear, people are all at it like stoats. Nobby was not only shagging the thirtysomething but a girl called Louise, a married woman called Stevie and, as far as I could make out, a bloke called Hugo. No wonder he pegged out.

'What did he actually do?' said the thirtysomething over *prosciutto melone*. 'I never really found out!' I told her that none of us had ever really known what Nobby had done. 'He lived abroad for some time, of course!' I continued brightly, feeling that at least one of us should try and make it look as if we had done our homework. 'Did he?' said the thirtysomething, a look of wild panic in her eyes. 'He did,' I said. 'I think . . . I think he did . . . in . . . Belgium, I think!' 'Belgium!' said the thirtysomething raising her eyebrows elaborately. 'Maybe it wasn't Belgium!' I said.

'How did you meet him?' she said, breaking the silence produced by my last remark. 'Do you know,' I said, 'I'm not precisely sure. It wasn't at university . . .' 'No,' said the thirtysomething, 'I don't think he was at university . . . not in this country anyway . . .' 'Where did you meet him?' I said quickly, before we got down to where, when and indeed whether Nobby had received higher education. 'I met him,' said the thirtysomething, 'in a bus shelter!'

There was a very long silence after this. The thirtysomething wiped her lips very neatly with her napkin and sat up very straight like a good

275

girl in school. When she looked at you, I noticed, she looked straight at you.

'Something terrible happened to Nobby,' I said slowly, 'in a bus shelter!' To my surprise she threw back her head and gave an astonishingly coarse laugh. 'Well, not with me!' she said. 'No,' I said, 'it was ages ago. Ages and ages ago.' She nodded, seriously little-girlish again. 'Yes,' she said, adding, 'he never spoke of it to me!' 'No,' I said thoughtfully, 'as far as I can make out he never spoke of it to anybody. And no one, obviously, mentioned it to him. Because it was . . . you know . . . he never . . . you know . . . did it again . . .' 'Did what again?' said the thirtysomething. 'What he did in the bus shelter!' I said.

'Right!' she said thoughtfully. Then she said, 'What did he do exactly in the bus shelter?' I looked straight back at her. 'I don't know!' I said. 'I never liked to ask. I think it was fairly . . .' 'Fairly what?' said the thirtysomething. 'Fairly bad!' I said. 'I gather . . . although, as I say, this is totally hearsay . . . I gather that he was . . . ashamed of it.' 'And you don't know . . .' said the thirtysomething, 'what it was . . . you have no idea . . .' 'I suppose,' I said, 'I have speculated. We have all speculated. And those in the know, know what they know. People have used the word . . . "disgusting" about it. But . . . I really don't know for sure . . . and . . . it's probably better that way . . .' She nodded. 'Let the dead rest in peace!' she said. 'Yes,' I said. But could not resist adding, 'I have heard that the police were involved . . .' She blew out a slow, dry whistle. 'Wow!' she said.

We talked of other things after that. But I could see the bus-shelter question was troubling her.

She saved her revelation for when her pork chop arrived. It turns out that Good Old Steve, whom I didn't even realize she knew that well, is madly in love with her. Although she is not with him. Apparently he cries into his soup whenever she is near. A thing I have never seen him do.

'You see,' she said, 'I usually seem to fall for married men!' I nodded sympathetically. 'We're much the nicest, most attractive men around. Which is why we are married. Everyone wants us.' She laughed, briefly. I knew this was the cue for me not to talk about Estelle.

'What are you thinking about?' she was saying. 'I was thinking about my wife!' I said, a leaden feeling in my chest. I knew I was going to say something that was not going to help me get any further with the really very attractive girl opposite me. 'Yes . . .' she said slowly, 'and . . . ?' I didn't answer. 'What?' she said, a little more eagerly. 'What about her?' 'I can't stop thinking about her,' I said, 'I think about her all the time. I think about her when I get up in the morning and when I go to bed at night. I think about her when I'm waiting for a bus or running for a train. I'm in love with her. Do you see that?'

The thirtysomething was looking pretty gobsmacked. This was not, I think, what she had expected me to say. It was not what I had, in fact, intended to say. It was, I decided, the last thing I wanted to say in the world. But, like a man hypnotized by some evil scientist, I seemed unable to stop.

'I think about her all the time!' I said, aware that this was probably the worst chat-up line in history. 'When I'm alone out walking or when I am looking at my kids or listening to the radio or waiting for her to come home – which I do quite a lot these days because I haven't really seen her much this year – I can't stop thinking about her. I've been married to her for twenty-five years and I am completely obsessed with her. I love her. I love her so much I can't even begin to describe it to you.'

Why are you telling me this, the girl's face seemed to say. Isn't this something she would rather hear than me? I had no easy answer to this point.

'And you see,' I went on, 'I think I may be losing her. I don't know what to do, or why or what I've done wrong. She doesn't even seem to care about the fact that I am about to be fifty. She ignores me all the time. We seem to be at war. It's like she only cares about our kids. Our kids are all we have in common. I just feel she is slipping away from me and there's nothing I can do about it. I feel old suddenly. I can't tell you. I have started to feel really old. I feel I'm going to die pretty soon, pretty damn soon!'

There was a long pause. I think my eyes may have been slightly moist. 'Is there,' said the thirtysomething, with just a hint of sharpness, 'something seriously wrong with you?'

We suddenly found we were both laughing. 'You shouldn't have asked me about my wife,' I said. 'It always ruins my chat-up lines!' Why are the wrong people always in love with the wrong people? Why doesn't the thirtysomething get together with Good Old Steve? At least then someone would be getting laid. And why do I go around telling other women I love my wife? Is this my idea of a chat-up line? Why can't I tell her?

## 8 p.m.

Just remembered.

Called Estelle in LA. I kept waiting for an opportunity to tell her that I loved her. But she kept talking about the animated film. Pilfrey, she tells me, gave a very bad reading of Mr Slippy Sloppy. Is he in LA too? This cannot be. 'He sounded,' she said, 'like some kind of insect.' I did not feel it necessary to point out that this was because Pilfrey has been playing nothing but insects for the last few months. I waited for her to suggest me for the part. I, anyway, was at first-drink-of-the-evening stage while she was in let's-take-a-meeting-kick-ass-when's-lunch mode.

Poss. send her note of some kind? Do I love her anyway? That is the million-dollar question asked by this diary. Answer-machine message from Peter Mailer, who spent last night at Christine's house.

MAILER: Hi Paul, it's Peter here! Are you well? I hope you are well. You work so hard I know and so does Estelle! I spent last night at Christine's. With other people . . . a lot of booze, a lot of sex, a lot of drugs. It was intense, Paul. Very intense. She has this sort of . . . hose. (*Long pause.*) I am in love, Paul. I am going to marry her. This is the most important thing that has ever happened to me. I have just drunk two bottles of plum brandy. (*Long pause.*) I am going to marry Christine. Call me, Paul.

No way Jose.

## 9 p.m.

Ruaiugeruy phoned. He and Lucy are in a pub in Wimbledon. He sounded conspiratorial. He said, 'Listen. I can't talk now. But I think Lucy and I are being followed by this weird guy. He's . . . like wearing dark glasses. And a big black coat.' I said I was sure he was imagining it.

I am pretty sure this is Jakob, who left a few minutes after them this morning wearing precisely this kind of costume.

Oliver has finally been brought into number 52 by Porker. Oliver was sleeping in his garden it seems. 'He made rather good friends with our dog,' said Porker, not unamiably, 'but I think he belongs to you.' With him is a girl called Aphrodite who is, apparently, a founder member of the Lager Society.

To cap it all, Wesley Jones has left a message on the answering machine.

It sounds as if he is calling from a mobile phone on his way into, or out of, a tunnel. It runs as follows –

WESLEY: Me carn't believe it! Rass claat! Whiteboy Rule! Y'have trouble a plenty, Mistah Slippery! Yuh die soon bekars' yuh carn't unnerstan' how yuh mess wid me mind! Brothers comin' fo' yuh, Slippery! Brothers on the march, Slippery! Niggah make yuh bleed, bro! (*Car FX. Poss. sounds of gunfire.*) Be ready whiteboy! I am de real Wesley Jones!

This is really very unfair. I am prepared to give him the royalties of a play which, as far as I know he had no hand in writing – simply on the grounds of his colour. How far backwards do we white liberals have to bend, for Christ's sake?


# May 19th. 10 a.m. More spring. Blossom, etc. Blue skies, light breeze, sparrow not in garden, almost certainly shagging somewhere.

*Estelle in 747 over Atlantic, presumably with Hamish. Jakob in house somewhere. Riuiuoghry at work. Lucy, Oliver and Aphrodite in front room. Edwin 'cooking with Lulu'. Me here.*

Riuoighry off at eight to help homeless. Jakob in business meeting in front room with 'associates', two large men in heavy suits with Italian accents. They were very amiable and slapped me on the back several times. The smaller of them said, 'You are a good father. You spend time with your family.' I had the feeling that one of them was about to try to kiss me, so made an excuse and left. There was something ever so slightly sinister about them but Jakob says they are 'very reliable wholesalers'.

Apparently he has been let down on a few deliveries of electrical goods.

He told me, in confidence of course, that he followed Ruieruirhy and Lucy, and that they went to Laura's house. Very disturbed by this. Jakob said he peered in through the Proek's front window and 'all three were having an intense discussion'. I asked him what Laura was wearing but he was unable to tell me. He did say, however, that 'something weird was going on between Lucy's Mum and Dad and Laura's Mum and Dad'.

Satanism perhaps?

He was at his most sweet and vulnerable. And funny, albeit in a rather clinical way. At one point he described Ruairghry as 'Jung and in love'. And said he was worried that he 'might never get to feel that way again'. Ramp, Porda and Shirley (or Karl, depending on your mood) are apparently having 'a special Awayday' on June 3rd. They are going to have it, according to Wainwright, on a boat on the Thames. 'Why,' he said, 'can't these people think in bed or on the lavatory like normal people?'

Of course what is really going to happen is the showdown *vis-à-vis General Practice*. Karl/Shirley will try and keep the show on and get them to agree to have me killed. I am determined to find whereabouts of boat.

## 11 a.m.

Disturbing conversation with Oliver and Aphrodite (they seem to be sleeping on Ruoirughry's floor) on the subject of Laura. According to him she is being bothered by some middle-aged perve. This is all she needs!

I said that nothing made me sicker than middle-aged men lusting after young girls, and Aphrodite, drawing her legs up so I could practically see her knickers, said it was wonderful to talk to someone like me, who had a wonderful marriage and was so nice and kind and obviously didn't think about sex all the time. I said, smiling winsomely, 'I sometimes think about sex!' She and Oliver laughed uproariously. He is a nice lad. It is such a pity there is a warrant out for his arrest.

I have made it clear that I do not want any heroin consumed on the premises. Jakob said, 'Is it all right if he does it in the garden?' I said it wasn't. But apparently Oliver only takes it at weekends. I am amazed at this. I thought that once you started on heroin it was more or less a one-way ticket to crawling around the floor of the Gents in Piccadilly

Circus screaming about spiders on your face. Jakob says this is not the case. 'In small quantities,' he tells me, 'it can be quite therapeutic.'

## 12 noon.

Weird call from Leo and Steve Witchett, the Writer Who Never Expresses an Opinion. They rang to tell me that they have finished working on their joint episode and that they are 'very excited about it'. Trying to conceal the incredulity in my voice I said I was looking forward to reading it. Then Witchett said, 'We could bring it round this afternoon if you liked!' This is the most simply constructed sentence he has ever produced in the ten years I have known him.

## 1 p.m.

Estelle returned! She talked, boastfully I thought, of having jet lag. She also said, 'I can't sleep with Hamish next to me!' The nerve of the woman. She has now gone to bed. She also said that while in America she had had cocaine. I am very worried about this.

## 3 p.m.

Lucy has been talking to Laura (must ask her about this perve and offer to thrash him). She seems to think it would be good if 'we all got together. Perhaps with everyone's Mums and Dads as well! It might help!' More dark hints about troubles between the Rachnowskis and the Proeks. Perhaps there is an East European nationalism dimension to this business.

Lucy, who seems back to her old cheerful, home-making self, squeaked, 'Sometimes we all go to a themed evening in a Greek restaurant in East Cheam.' Include me out! Although I felt Laura (and indeed both girls) were trying to say they needed my social skills at such a gathering. And I grow increasingly fond of Lucy. She made me some really nice shortbread this afternoon. I asked, humorously, if Laura might be wearing some kind of toga. Lucy gave me an odd look.

Jakob has been in a meeting with his Italian associates all day. They went out for lunch – which seemed to take two hours – and when they returned the older of the two men was staggering slightly. Their car is about the size of a hearse. I pointed this out to them as I opened the door on their return and they seemed to find it very amusing. The younger of the two said, 'It's had a lot of dead people in it for sure!' Everyone laughed and I felt I ought to join in but made note to speak to Jakob about these people.

Oliver has retreated to the garden shed with Aphrodite. I do not know what they are doing in there but suspect the worst.

In the middle of all this Steve Witchett, the Writer Who Never Expresses an Opinion, turned up with the new episode. He looked completely different. He used to have a little wispy moustache which he has (in my view wisely) obliterated. He used to wear jeans and a T-shirt but now he seems to favour an expensive suit, which gives him a far more credible air. He tossed the script on to the table and said, 'It's far too good for them, of course. But it may do you a bit of good.'

I have never heard Witchett express an opinion, let alone express it confidently. But what followed was even more surprising. 'There's bags of sex in it!' he said. 'Sex is all anyone is interested in nowadays.'


## 4.30 p.m.

The episode is really rather good!

It's amazingly confident. There is lashings of sex. Although still severely damaged by the accident, I seem to have started an affair with Pamela's sister, which is amazingly steamy. Pamela has split up with Pilfrey (which pleases me) and Pilfrey is definitely making eyes at my long-time buddy and senior partner, Dirk. Clare, the receptionist, has started shagging a patient called O'Shaughnessy, while I treat no less than three cases in which I have to do an intimate examination. At one point I say to Mrs Abrahams – previously a rather cosy stock character who comes in with colds, rheumatism, etc. – 'I am going to have to take a look at your vagina, Mrs Abrahams!' To which she replies, 'Makes a change!'

It is electric stuff and for once the steaminess, amount of shagging, etc., has started to resemble what seems to be the experience of most ordinary people – apart of course from me. Karl/Shirley is not going to like me bouncing back from my accident like this!

Jakob and his business associates are leaving. I think I will see them to the door. Not that I think they would try and pinch the silver (if

they stole anything it would be a lot more substantial) but I feel it important to remind them that Jakob is only twenty years old and I am his
father.

## 5.30 p.m.

Mr Vanelli and Mr Scarrotto are both fans of *General Practice*! And were
particularly warm about my own role in the series. Mr Vanelli – the
younger one – said, 'It's nice to hear about a good man like that. Doing
good things and helping people. Like he was a priest. Doing people
favours. It is what the world is all about!' I said I heartily agreed.

I do not always like their manner – Mr Scarrotto pinched me on the
cheek as he left, which I found rather offensive – but they are a good-hearted
pair and seem genuinely fond of Jakob. Apparently the electrical goods
wholesale trade is a taxing one and industrial accidents are common.
Someone they work with called Benny the Greek recently had both his
legs broken. I asked whether this happened when he was carrying heavy
equipment and Mr Scarrotto said, 'That's what we told the judge!' We all
laughed about this but when they had gone I did say to Jakob that I
thought the Mafia was not really something to laugh about.

## 7.30 p.m.

Rueighry came back five minutes ago covered in vomit. He assured me
it was not his own.

He is having Lucy and Laura over for the evening while Estelle, Edwin
and I troop off to Hotchkiss's Indian buffet. Jakob seemed, for some
reason, not as opposed to this as I thought he might be. I left him poring
over a copy of a book called *Mexican Beans*. Have reminded them, as
I always do, not to burn down the house while I am out. Estelle woke
about ten minutes ago. Irritable. Apparently you rub cocaine into your
gums.

Rurighry made an amusing 'gag' of sprinkling the sideboard with
turpentine. I had to get a bit serious and told them that, as they were
responsible working men, they should really start to take a keener interest
in domestic matters. Jakob said that my interest in domestic matters was
limited to cooking elaborate Italian meals which nobody ate.

Off now, with Edwin and Estelle. She speaks of nothing but Hamish. Apparently he takes it up his nose (cocaine I mean). But I am not taking things lying down. Encouraged by the new episode I am fighting back. I have got some Liquid Love in my hip pocket. It is your turn tonight, Estelle Slippery!

## 11.30 p.m.

Writing this in my study.

Hotchkiss's Indian buffet was a sensation.

Snozzer and Scagg and Bozz ate all the onion bhajis in the first five minutes. Snozzer — whose appetite is legendary — went on to eat ten parathas, six naans, eight portions of rice and a whole chicken mughlai. Hotchkiss skipped around with Mr Pringle, the gay Latin master, Mr Ligetti, the gay physics master, Mr Sorensen, the gay biology master, and Miss Dawkins the lesbian. I don't know what she teaches but she is, Edwin tells me, famous for being a lesbian.

I do not know whether there are any straight teachers on the staff of Cranborne School, Wimbledon. I asked Snozzer about this and he said, darkly, 'It's the straight teachers who are the problem. Most of them are perves who are dying to get a look at your willy.' This is something of an obsession of Snozzer's, who fears most of south London is trying to get a look at his willy. He has, I am glad to say, never accused me of this.

At about eight thirty Edwin and Lulu disappeared into the school grounds.

I waited until Estelle had heaped her plate with what Hotchkiss calls 'Le Vindaloo de Hong!' and sidled up beside her. Just as Hotchkiss was getting ready to make an announcement (he loves announcements) I tipped the love potion into her vindaloo and, as she started to shovel it down I tried to get into her line of vision. But at that very moment, Plonker was propelled forward, the lights went down and Plonker gave us an extract from the forthcoming production. It bore, as far as I could see, very little relation to *A Midsummer Night's Dream* — since, according to Edwin, Plonker has been allowed to rewrite most of his part and has added several songs of his own composition.

Accompanying himself on the guitar he sang —

'When my head is full of cocaine wildness
And my hands are heavy laden
All my dreams are tortured salvoes
All my eyes are bearded weirdos
Who will take me home?

Who will take me home?
Who will take me home?
When my fucking eyes are bleary
And my mind is sad and dreary
And my breath is stale and beery
Who will take me home?'

When the song was over, several people were heard to mutter, 'Not me, squire.'

I did not, personally, object to the song. There is something about Plonker that is difficult to resist. His arms poke out of his school blazer in such a helpless way. His ears are so large and his nose so small. His eyes switch between gross self-confidence and the aspect of a startled rabbit. He has the look of someone who has been recently scrubbed all over with wire wool. I like the fact that his voice seems two octaves too low for his complexion. I like his spots. In fact, I like Plonker.

My problem with his performance was that Estelle was riveted to it. Her eyes never left the boy's face once. And all the while she was cramming a lethal erotic cocktail into her mouth. She was gobbling up the stuff, and as Plonker gave us the reprise of the last chorus I saw an extraordinary light dawn in her face. It was the sort of look you usually only see on the faces of people in Coca-Cola adverts. 'Oh Plonker!' I heard her whisper.

Women, unlike men, take a positive pride in their emotions. And Estelle was keen for the room to be in on what she felt about Plonker. If, to the uninitiated, what she was going through might look like the excessive politeness common among mothers determined to show their children's less talented friends every fairness, I knew it was something a great deal more serious. You do not mess with the Boerg gland.

'Isn't Plonker marvellous!' I heard her coo to Hotchkiss, who nodded gravely. 'Plonker,' he said, 'is remarkable. A remarkable performer. I found his song deeply moving.' 'I found it deeply moving!' said Estelle. 'I was absolutely knocked out by it. I thought it was amazing. And he wrote it himself, apparently!' 'He did,' said Hotchkiss, delighted to be discussing Plonker, 'he did! He wrote the words as well! Which are brilliant, I think!' 'They are amazing!' said Estelle. 'In a boy of that age they are so . . . so astonishingly mature . . .' 'They are,' said Hotchkiss, 'and witty too, I think. That line about his breath being beery is very, very funny, I think!'

'He has also,' went on Hotchkiss, 'magnificent thighs!' 'Yes!' said Estelle with the keenness of a real connoisseur, 'Yes!' Hotchkiss was now beaming paternally at her. They have always got on. Ever since Estelle made nineteen suits of woollen chain-mail for Hotchkiss's disastrous production of Henry the Fourth, Part One. Hotchkiss has always asked for her artistic advice. She has never given him the information he really needs – 'Stop doing it, Hotchkiss; now' – but, for some reason, he seems to rate her opinion rather higher than that of a seasoned actor like myself.

He is, I think, a little jealous of me. I suppose to him my lifestyle must seem intensely glamorous. I am rubbing shoulders, on a daily basis, with the presenters of the *Today* programme. I know what the senior management of BBC Radio look like – which not many people do. My name appears in the *Radio Times*. I have been profiled in the *Guardian*. And my voice, at ten forty-five on Tuesdays, Thursdays and Fridays, can be heard by millions. Well hundreds of thousands anyway.

He was starting to irritate me slightly. He and Estelle could not seem to stop singing the praises of Plonker to each other. When the evening was over, and Hotchkiss had made a short speech thanking everybody, Estelle dug Edwin in the ribs and hissed, 'Ask Plonker home!' 'You ask him, weird woman!' said Edwin. 'I can't,' said Estelle, 'I am a middle-aged woman! You ask him home! I think he's so wonderful!' 'You ask him home if you think he's so wonderful!' said Edwin.

Mr and Mrs Plonker were nowhere in evidence so, under pretence of offering Plonker a lift home, Estelle managed to get him into our car. Apparently Mr and Mrs Plonker are away in Spain. Estelle said Plonker was very welcome to stay with us. He seemed surprised by this, and, after thanking her profusely, said he had to be home to see his dog.

This conversation took place in the car and Estelle made strenuous efforts to catch Plonker's eye in the driving mirror, something which was, obviously, new to Plonker. He became, I thought, rather bumptious. Estelle said, as we went down Wimbledon Hill towards Mafeking Road – 'You are a really seriously talented songwriter, Plonker!' Plonker flushed with pleasure. 'Thank you very much!' he said. 'No,' said Estelle, 'you are going to be rich and famous! Don't you think he's going to be rich and famous, Edwin?' Edwin seemed doubtful about this. 'And you deliver the song so well!' said Estelle. 'I can't wait to see your Bottom!'

This drew quite a lot of hilarity from Snozzer, Edwin, Wodge, Lulu, Bozz and Scagg, who had also, somehow, been fitted into the car. Estelle joined in this, seemingly unabashed. 'Ooh, what have I said!' she screeched. 'What will you think of me?' Everyone, apart from me, found all this very amusing. Estelle seemed encouraged by the reaction of the youth. America has made her even more raucous than usual. 'What have I said?' she went on, giggling hysterically, 'I'm going on about Plonker's Bottom! My God! What will it be next? Where will it end?' There was more laughter. Estelle shot me a sideways glance. 'Paul doesn't like me going on about Plonker's Bottom,' she said, 'because Paul is a miserable old git!'

There seemed to be quite a lot of enthusiasm for this view. I could not, of course, tell anyone what was really troubling me. They obviously all thought this was a merry jape and have no idea that a fifty-one-year-old woman has just been made to fall head over heels in love with a sixteen-year-old boy by the administering of a sex potion from Wolverhampton. She does not know it herself! She probably thinks she is simply 'being nice to Edwin's friend'. Only I know that it will not be long before she is trying it on with Plonker. Which will lead to public scandal, prosecution by Mr and Mr Plonker and the kind of tabloid coverage only usually accorded to serial killers and dead or divorcing members of the royal family.

She will be lucky to get ten years. To say nothing of the effect on the children. MY MOTHER SHAGGED CLASSMATE, SAYS EDWIN SLIPPERY! MY SHAME WILL NEVER DIE!

When we got home they all went downstairs to play the piano and hear Plonker sing his other hit from the show, 'Gonner be a Bandit'. Rurighry and Jakob (who was wearing a black shirt with a white tie and natty black and white shoes) had set the kitchen on fire and the fire brigade had been called out. The damage is not serious – although the Aga is badly singed – and Estelle seemed positively cheerful about the fact that one of the cupboards had been incinerated. 'I never liked that cupboard anyway!' she carolled, winking broadly at Plonker as she did so.

Lucy and Laura are obviously trying to make things up between them. As a result, Lucy seems v. tense with Ruaierhgy. I regaled them with tales of my youth in the Communist Party, which I think they found pretty amusing. Laura wearing high-necked sweater. Both boys tense with me. I feel my relationship with both of them is heading for some kind of crisis. This can only be exacerbated by the fact that I have induced their mother to fall in love with a sixteen-year-old tone-deaf idiot called Plonker.

What have I done to poor Estelle (downstairs singing with Plonker)? Is she already trying to remove Plonker's Y-fronts? Has she offered him cocaine? If she goes to prison and Esmond Pennebaker is bumped off, how will we live? Will I survive the strains of this year much longer? Will I ever even reach the age of fifty? And if I do, will anyone throw a party for me? What is happening to all the furniture? Has Jakob really joined the Mafia? What means this sudden certainty in Steve Witchett? How will Ashley Ramp, Howard Porda and 'Shirley' decide my fate? Will I ever be able to tell my wife I love her? Do I love her, come to that? Or do I only really love these women I keep telling I love her?

And, most important of all – when did I last have sex? And if I have had it this year, why can I not remember when I had it?

Bed. Alone.


May 20th. 9.30 a.m. More summer than spring. A lot of leaves. Blue skies. Sparrow somewhere in bush in front garden, probably with other sparrow.

*Estelle 'at studios'. Edwin at school. Jakob and Rieugeriuy in bed. Lucy and Laura in garden, shouting at each other. Oliver in shed. Aphrodite somewhere in house. Me in study.*

In one month and four days I will be fifty.

Lucy and Laura's truce was short-lived. It appears Lucy is thinking of leaving Oxford – which would explain why she is always round at our house rather than at lectures in laboratories, etc. Anyway she tells me she is more interested in croûtons than protons. Ruaiehgy may even have proposed marriage to her. Very unhappy about this, as is Jakob. I think Lucy may have tried to say something helpful to Laura about Jakob. Or, perhaps, simply been a little too nice to him. At least he has cheered up a bit.

Laura, who graduated from Leeds, and has been looking for work, hopes to find a position as a fashion buyer. Tried to discuss tops with her but she did not seem interested. The two girls are now scratching each other's eyes out by the fish-pond.

Estelle woke early. She woke me to tell me what a marvellous creature Plonker was. Then, singing to herself, she went off to organize this animated film. The part of Mr Slippy Sloppy is still vacant. I did not dare suggest myself. I presume, if things go on the way they are going, she will offer the part to Plonker.

I ran Edwin into school. He said, 'My God, she wasn't half going on about Plonker last night!' I said, 'Wasn't she, though?' Edwin said, 'She is off her head!' I began to feel extremely guilty. 'I wouldn't say that,' I said, 'she is going through . . . a . . . difficult phase of life . . . and . . . er . . .' Edwin gave me sharp look. 'You mean the menopause?' he said. I did not answer this question. 'I mean,' went on Edwin, 'I am very sympathetic. I realize her hormonal balance is altering rapidly. I appreciate that. But I do not think that excuses her behaving like a loony with one of my friends. Does she fancy him or what?'

I still did not feel able to tell him the reason for her behaviour. In fact, as he talked on, I was so gobsmacked by the scope and detail of his knowledge of the inner workings of his Mum, I said less and less. At least, I thought, he stands a chance in GCSE Biology. If he knows as much about fruit flies as about human sexual reproduction he may get an A starred.

'You don't have periods, right?' he was saying. 'Your body temperature is variable, right? Especially at night, right? Because you are not like producing eggs, right? You're like a chicken without a head, right? But, you know, I am going through pretty intensive hormonal changes, right? I mean I don't walk around the house moaning because my willy has suddenly become like huge, right? I don't sort of go, "Ooh, er Missus I've got like . . . hair!" you know, do I, right?'

I had no answer to this.

I dropped him, a long way from the school gates, at Pizza round the Clock in Wimbledon village. He said he could not face the day without eating a pepperoni with cheese. I glimpsed Snozzer in the interior, smoking a large cigar.

The following items of furniture have recently disappeared:

A sideboard
Three dining chairs
Another sofa
Two garden tables
Two beds
A free-standing cupboard.

There is one comfort in *l'affaire* Plonker. If she was having an affair, Hamish is almost certainly to be chucked over for a sixteen-year-old boy. Ha! Serve him right! And at least I will not now have to lay out on private detectives and/or Snozzer.


## 11 a.m.

Oliver has been in the garden shed for days now. I do not know what he is doing in there. I have asked Jakob to get him his plane tickets as soon as possible. Jakob says he is waiting for Mr Scarrotto to get him some cheap ones. Apparently he has an arrangement with Alitalia.

Rurighry has asked if he can bring one of his 'customers' home for a few days. He is, apparently, very nice. His name is Alec and Rugihrgy found him in a park near Paddington. I suggested he could stay in the shed with Oliver but both Ruighry and Jakob said that that was not a good idea. Apparently Alec can be violent and he, too, as far as I can make out, is wanted by the police.

Jakob says if Rueiughery can have people staying here, he too wants 'a crew'. The names he suggests so far begin –

Benny Cammeroni
Toni Gerrasimo
Louie the Greek
Jackie the Horse

Jimmy the Knife
The Albanian
'Jodie' Sanzarotti and the Twins
Vittorio Spinetti and Family.

I was pleased to see some of his old friends from Cranborne – including Partha Goswami the physicist and Benjamin Wick-Forbes, who was unsure about his sexuality – have made the shortlist. But there is an alarming shortage of women. When I tackled him about this Jakob said, 'Women are good for the home. They are like bread and bread is good. Everybody needs a family. But business is for the men. You are my father. I love you. I have a mother. She is like a mother to me. What else do I need?'

I am pretty sure this was intended humorously. But he speaks in a Brooklyn accent for so much of the time that it has almost become a part of him. Is he giving up on Lucy? And, if so, is that only because Riusheiury seems more absorbed in his job, at the moment, than in Ms Rachnowski? It made him slightly easier with Reiurghry for a few days but now he spends a lot of time making cracks at his brother's expense. Today he said, 'Ruighry is part of the New Age. He's joined the Under-fives.'


## 4 p.m.

Writing this in the studio where we are recording Leo and Witchett's first co-written episode. They appear to be holding hands.

It is hot stuff. I have just had a very steamy scene with Pamela's sister, Julia, played by Helena Twist, who has not done much recently. In the words of *Practice Tales*, a nine-volume guide to the characters in the series, devised by Morton Cavendish and Henry Bude, two gay bit-part actors in it, 'Julia once talked of opening a wine bar with Esmond's half-brother Duhuig, but it came to nothing when Duhuig was beheaded in 1989.' At the end of the scene I had to have an orgasm – a physical response of which I have, at the moment, only a dim memory. 'Cheesey' Haworth, the new director, said I made it sound as if someone had dropped a heavy object on my toe. Then we all had to make orgasm noises. Tremendous fun. Pilfrey's (I noted with disgust) was voted the most convincing.

In spite of his hatred for me, Karl – as I have insisted on calling him today, in order to annoy him – pretended to like the thrust of the script. 'Thrust' is the operative word. There were no less than twelve acts of coition in a forty-five-minute programme.

Karl was wearing a sensible tweed skirt, clumpy shoes and a rather mannish blouse with pearl buttons. He also had with him a small billycock hat. I thought – though I did not say so – that he looked rather nice.

A worrying script note at the end. Pilfrey, looking slyly at Karl, said, 'I'm fascinated to think what Pamela will do when she finds out about Esmond and her sister . . .' Everyone joined in this discussion. I said I thought Pamela would forgive me. After all, she forgave me for bonking my secretary. She was understanding about what I did that weekend in Malaga. And, though she has sometimes complained of my sexual demands, she nearly always comes across, to use her own words, 'for the sake of a quiet life'. Pilfrey said, 'I think she would want to kill him!' No one said anything for a moment and then Karl said, 'She might hire a contract killer!'

He looked, briefly, at Leo and Witchett as he said this and Leo raised one eyebrow very slightly. None of this, of course, bears any relation to what will happen at the script conference, to which I will probably not be invited. Or to the fact that the script conference will act more or less on the orders of Ramp, Porda and Karl when it comes to deciding whether a major character will live or die. But it sounded chillingly probable. 'True' in the way fiction can sometimes be true – although, of course, it is really nothing but lies from start to finish. Is this how Esmond will meet his end? Death never comes when you are expecting it and almost hardly ever in the form you anticipated.


6 p.m.

Estelle there when I got home!

It turned out she had been to pick up Edwin from school. She managed to scoop up Plonker and insisted on running him home as well. When they got back here she said, girlishly, 'Perhaps Plonker would like to come in!' Plonker, who, according to Edwin, is getting more and more of a pain with every minute that passes, said he would come in and play her some of his songs.

This one goes –

Over hills and over vales
The cocaine nightmare stomps
Where are we? In Scotland? Wales?
Or some primeval swamps?
Who or what is standing at
The door beyond the stair?
Have they eyes or teeth or lips
Or bones or ears or hair?

CHORUS

Gremlins at the door
Gremlins at the door
Gremlins Gremlins Gremlins Gremlins
Gremlins at the door!

Estelle sounds pretty enthusiastic about this number. The words 'defin-itive' and 'stunning' have already been used. I have to find an antidote to this Midlands love drug.

She is now going off to buy Plonker shoes.

## 11.30 p.m.

Writing this in my study. Everyone in the family pretty concerned about Estelle's obsession with Plonker, who stayed to dinner and played us some more of his songs. Jakob has suggested that he get Mr Scarrotto to 'have a little talk with him'. It may well come to that.

I saw Porker this evening as I was on my way to post a letter. He tells me Wickett 'is moving to Lincolnshire'. And I never really knew him at all!

Message on machine from Good Old Steve. He says, 'I need to talk to you about the woman we must stop calling the thirtysomething. It's serious.'

I am perfectly happy to stop calling her the thirtysomething if I could think what else to call her. I suppose, at a pinch, I could use her real name, but there seems no chance of my ever remembering what it is.

293

May 24th. 6 a.m. Dawn chorus lively. Beautiful day in early summer. No sign of sparrow. In his nest? Read the other day that sparrows are dying out due to pollution, etc. So maybe he has croaked.

*Estelle in bed, snoring loudly. Jakob, Rueighry, Oliver, Aphrodite, Lucy, Laura, Edwin, etc., all presumably in bed.*

Although I think I hear noises from the shed that suggested that some, if not all, of them are in there. My boys have abandoned therapy since each of their therapists announced they could only see them in the morning.

A month away from being fifty. I woke at four and was unable to get back to sleep. A hot night. I am writing this in the garden, in the towelled dressing-gown that was given to me five years ago by a woman called Ulrike.

Still no sign of anyone wanting to give me a party.

What does love mean at fifty? Does it mean what it did at twenty? Or thirty? Twentysomethings and thirtysomethings and maybe even fortysomethings would like to think that it doesn't. I am not so sure. It's a word we use to stop ourselves thinking about all of the strongest things we feel. It's about need, certainly, and thinking the same as someone else – but it's also about being able to be different. My dream of a relationship is to be separate but permanently on the edge of complete togetherness. I don't like the idea of being absorbed in another person. I like the idea of permanent, if risky, companionship.

What was it Chekhov said? If you don't want to be lonely, don't get married. I have certainly never felt lonely in my marriage. Angry, yes. Suspicious, of course. But never lonely. Perhaps that is why I can't tell Estelle I love her. Because it is blindingly obviously the case. It is one of those things that don't need saying.

That won't work though. Everything needs saying. That's why they had the Declaration of Independence, for Christ's sake. Familiarity helps us to realize we are in love but doesn't help us to express it. I have to say it to her. I have to tell her how much I love her – even if she doesn't love me.

This is going to be tricky though. Especially as she has recently emerged from an affair with a Scottish midget and is now head over heels in love with a sixteen-year-old called Plonker.

## 8.45 a.m.

Went upstairs to tell Estelle I loved her. She was stomping around the bathroom in her dressing-gown. When I entered the room she left it for the bedroom. When I followed her there she went back to the bathroom. Finally she did start to get her knickers on while I stood by the wash-basin and leered. 'What's going on with you?' I said. She didn't answer. 'What's going on with us?' She didn't answer this either. Then she crossed over to me and, reaching up her hand, stroked my face very gently. 'Hullo!' she said. And walked out of the room.

Did we, perhaps, have sex last night?

This relationship business is all a question of timing, I think. That and drugs of course.

## 12 noon.

Reighry (home for the day – why?) has asked if he can bring home a person called Bolt, who, he says, 'will be company for Alec'. He is, apparently, fine, 'apart from the Special Brew'. I asked whether he would then want to bring home someone who was company for Bolt. He was exactly like this with his lizard. Reigurhry said that I lived a very protected life and did not understand what life was like for people like Bolt and Alec. I said I realized this. I also said that if he wanted to, he was welcome to offer shelter to the entire population of the Embankment, but not at 52 Mafeking Road.

Reuighriury looked hurt. Feeling guilty, I said that of course I would love to meet Bolt and Alec and, possibly one or two other homeless people. They were welcome to stay for a long weekend, perhaps joining Oliver in the shed. I did add, however, that even Good Old Steve, my oldest friend, got pretty tricky after a weekend. Jakob said Good Old Steve began to pall shortly after he had entered the room. We got a bit heated about this. I accused them of being intolerant. They accused me of lacking compassion. I reminded both of them that I, when young, had done quite a few socially conscious things. I was about to mention my membership of the Communist Party, but, seeing a warning light in Jakob's eye, did not. 'I know how to talk to people like Bolt!' I said. 'And as it happens I am rather partial to Special Brew.'

Reueighry said I would not know how to talk to Bolt, adding glumly that no one knew how to talk to Bolt. Then they started arguing with each other instead of me. About Laura. I said she was a nice girl, looking seriously at Jakob. Jakob seemed depressed by this news.

## 5.30 p.m.

Writing this in a pub in Barnes.

I have just left a meeting with Leo and Witchett, who are obviously passionately in love, and clearly having an enormous amount of sex. Witchett seems to be living with Leo or at least about to move in with him. They spent quite a lot of the afternoon talking about colour schemes, etc. Witchett's decisiveness grows apace. He expressed opinions about Tony Blair, Communist China, the Hollywood film industry, the pros and cons of charter flying and the best way to cook broad beans. By the end of the afternoon he was positively barking at poor Leo – who clearly loves being dominated. Leo has lost all interest in architecture and only wishes to talk of my contract killing. The point of the meeting. I think it is Karl/Shirley's idea.

I said I thought it would be better if Pamela hired a contract killer and he (or she) bungled the job. 'You mean,' said Leo thoughtfully, 'left you sort of . . . crippled! Like the wall but worse! You could go back to the same hospital! I always liked that woman who gave you physiotherapy!' 'No!' I said. 'I've already had physiotherapy for about ten episodes. They don't want to hear about physiotherapy any more. I mean the contract killers screw it up. They doctor the wrong car or use the wrong kind of gun and miss or something. And then I go after them. Vigilante style.' Witchett said he didn't see Esmond Pennebaker having 'a vigilante quality'. I said I was fairly well up on violence. I told them about Mr Scarrotto, adding a few, imaginary touches and they seemed impressed – especially with the bit about him shooting someone in Mafeking Road. 'My son,' I said, 'is pretty closely involved with the Mafia.' This too, I found myself believing more and more. In fact I rather worried myself.

Must ask Jakob whether he is a 'made man' or not.

By the end of the afternoon we had agreed that they would try out an outline on Shirley in which hired thugs tried to run me down outside the practice and, instead, drove straight into the practice garage – a building Leo has never liked. 'You can then go after them,' said Witchett, 'and if Ramp, Porda and Shirley decide to have you killed, we have a logical way of doing it. It's been led up to. If they decide you can live, you can wipe out the gangsters.' I feel this at least gives me a fighting chance.

## 8 p.m.

Stricken with conscience *vis-à-vis* self's role in potion, Edwin, etc. He was singing a song that sounded like 'Come into my loveachamber ooh sexamachinea baby oohpump it up baby bouncey!' I said, 'Love is an emotion that arises out of a complex mixture of things – closeness, hormonal changes, pheromones, biological necessity, mental and spiritual compatibility and so on.' He did not look impressed by this.

Jakob has gone out for dinner with Laura. Riueiughry behaving in positively Pandarus-like fashion in relation to this. Plus he spoke again of 'moving in' with Lucy. I said, 'Moving in where? The Embankment?' He said I was a cold, heartless man. Lucy has put up a large picture of a moose on his wall and this afternoon she made chocolate biscuits. Estelle still not home.

## 11 p.m.

Estelle not home for dinner. Hamish? Or Plonker? Another sideboard has gone missing. We now only have three chairs to sit on. I pointed this out and everyone laughed and sneered at me. When I talked of the other missing furniture they all looked away. Perhaps Estelle has told them she is leaving home and they are going with her. Edwin said he would stand as 'food doesn't make you fat when you are standing up'.

Jakob back from dinner with Laura. Apparently she is out of work and wished to ask 'his advice'. Or, as Jakob put it, 'to get into my pants'.

Rurighry said he was 'harsh – like your father!' Jakob said, with a worryingly dispassionate glance in my direction, 'Paul is basically a complete softy!'

Laura, as I suspected, is artistic and, according to Jakob, would like to go into the theatre. I said I would be perfectly happy to introduce her to some people. Much smirking at this. Edwin said he thought she already knew enough people. I gave him a tolerant smile and explained that, when you get to my age you have a network of 'contacts' – people who know and esteem you professionally and are only too willing to help your children get jobs in the media. Edwin's jaw dropped at this news. He said, 'Cool! Who are they?'

I found it curiously difficult to think of anyone offhand, and, in the end, said, 'I know the producer of *General Practice* pretty well!' 'Oh,' said Ruairgry, 'is that the one who dresses up as a woman and wants to fire you!' I had to admit that it was. Jakob said, 'I have talked to Mr Scarrotto about him. We know where he lives.' After this we had a lively conversation about the Mafia and Jakob's involvement in it. At about ten thirty Lucy, Oliver and Aphrodite suddenly came in. Then went out again.

Estelle has bought Plonker a suit and offered to help him with guitar lessons. The boys and I discussed Estelle and Plonker. Edwin said, 'She is in love with Plonker. It is disgusting!' Riuerhy, still in holier-than-thou mode, said, 'She just thinks he is a charming boy.' We all said that that was not one of the words anyone would use about Plonker. Apparently Estelle's attentions continue to make him insufferable. This morning, he demanded his school dinner be brought to his table. He was given a detention to which he replied, 'I do not accept your detention!' He then sang aggressively and was given another detention for 'aggressive singing'.

Writing this in my study. Where is Estelle?


May 26th. 10 a.m. Skies even bluer. Leaves positively tropical. Sparrow, however, not in evidence. Dead from sexual excess? Light breeze.

*Estelle at school 'helping with rehearsals'. Lucy and Ruighrty in bed. Edwin at school. Oliver, Aphrodite, etc., in shed. Jakob disappeared. Me in kitchen writing this.*

Estelle came in at three in the morning. I think she had taken cocaine. She tried to wake me up and spoke, glowingly, of Hamish and Plonker. I went to look for somewhere else to sleep and discovered Jakob not in his bed. Hope he is not in shed with Aphrodite. Must get him together with Laura. She is such a nice girl and so talented! Did the De Witjerer Exercises.

### 10.15 a.m.

Gustave on the machine. He tells me that Pilfrey is up for a part in a major Hollywood film. I thought at first there must be some mistake. But apparently he plays an insect. It is, to my intense chagrin, an insect from Outer Space, the sort of role I have always thought I would do rather well. The producers heard his sea slug and liked it. I asked whether it was a large part and Gustave said, 'I think he has to get inside the costume and wave his feelers about in vision so it could be quite large, yes. The movie is called *Creepy Crawly*.' I said it sounded perfect for Pilfrey.

Gustave said, 'Paul, I think we should have lunch soon. I think you are becoming bitter.'

I told Gustave I was firing him and banged down the phone. Felt good about this. Have asserted self.

Now have to find new agent.

Rang Snozzer. He was, of course, at school. But he is the man for me.

### 3 p.m.

To school to pick up Edwin. Hoping to see Estelle there but she has 'gone to a meeting about the animated film'. Edwin seems to have stopped taking GCSEs. I asked him when the next one was and he said, 'I think I may have already taken it.' I tested him on his Latin while we waited at the back of Hotchkiss's rehearsal. I got rather involved with the unseen, which was all about a man called Aulus who surprised his slave eating a chicken and ran him through with a sword. Or, at least this was what I thought it was about. It might have been about a man called Aulus who saw a chicken trying to eat a slave and was so surprised he ran himself through with a sword. Edwin thought it was about a chicken who ran through a man called Aulus with a sword and then ate his slave.

Middle age has really arrived when you no longer understand your children's homework.

Hotchkiss having tremendous problems with Plonker, who is now

299

objecting to the other characters' having lines to say. He kept saying things like 'Mrs Slippery thinks I should play it in a Welsh accent!' and 'Mrs Slippery particularly likes me to lift my chin in the air at this point!' You could see that Hotchkiss was getting pretty jealous. Hong, who was there to do movement ('Kicka harder! High in the air, boys!') was clearly delighted by this and kept winding Hotchkiss up. 'Plonker in love with Mlissis Slippery, no Lionel? Likee da older woman, no?'

Edwin was called up to do some slithering and I had the chance to have a word with Snozzer. I didn't actually say I wanted him to be my agent as I thought he might find that intimidating. I just asked if he needed to earn a little pocket money. Snozzer said, 'As long as it is not oral sex with strange men I will do it.' I explained that all he had to do was make some phone calls. He said, 'Good! Obscene ones I hope!' I said he just had to ring up various theatres, film production companies, etc., and see if they had any work. 'Oh cool!' said Snozzer, beaming. 'You want me to be . . . like your agent!' He is a sophisticated boy.

He seems to have no problems with the job as 'he once saw a film about it'.


## 7 p.m.

A message on the machine from Peter Mailer.

He seems to be proposing to marry Christine. There was a lot more about what great sex they were having. I rang Good Old Steve to complain about this and got his machine. I left a message and fifteen minutes later he rang back, sounding out of breath. When I asked him if he had been running he said, rather coyly, 'Actually – I was in bed.'

I did not ask him with whom, so he told me.

It appears that the day after I had lunch with the thirtysomething and droned on about my love for Estelle (which is oozing away with each piece of missing furniture and each new Plonker excess), she rang him up and asked him out to the theatre. They ended up back at her place and . . . 'It was amazing, Paul. I have never had such an intense experience. It was very, very physical and also very, very intense emotionally. My entire life has been turned around. I am feeling things I never thought I would feel!'

This is not surprising, from a man who last had sex about nine months ago in Amsterdam. But he was not content to boast about his bonking. He seemed compelled to talk about something which has never seemed to bother him in the past – his feelings. 'She likes the Impressionists. I like the Impressionists!' he said, as if this was something remarkable. I did try to tell him that most people liked the Impressionists. Almost the only people to dislike them were nineteenth-century French art critics. 'She told me,' Steve continued, 'she has never been to Spain! And you know what?' 'No.' 'I've never been to Spain! Isn't that amazing!' I said it was astonishing. Good Old Steve laughed tolerantly. 'It must be boring for you, I suppose,' he said, 'always married to the same woman!' 'What do you mean,' I said, 'always? Did I treat you like this when you droned on about how you had not had a shag for nearly a year? Why am I suddenly an object of derision? I mean you may marry this thirtysomething. Do people lose all interest and romance as a result of being married?' 'My feelings for her,' said Steve, 'are diamond sharp. They are tough and strong and real. They will never fade.' His voice suddenly became very serious. 'We're not there yet . . .' he went on. 'We haven't made it to the top of the mountain. She wants to get closer to me, Paul! She feels there is something . . . distant about me. And she's right. There is. She says it's like I'm . . . on a mountain . . . or up a tree . . . or on a boat . . . drifting out to sea!'

Something about this worried me. I don't know why. I said, 'Don't overdo the shagging, Steve. You are not a young man any more!' Steve laughed musically. 'It isn't just sex, Paul,' he said, 'there is more to life than sex!'


10 p.m.

Snozzer rang. He has got me a job opening a leisure centre in south Wimbledon. A hundred and fifty quid and all expenses paid. This is more than Gustave has done in the last five years. I told him he was a great agent. He said, 'I will take 10 per cent if that's OK.' I said it was fine by me.

## 11.30 p.m.

Estelle downstairs with Rueighry, Jakob, Lucy, Edwin, Bolt, Alec and Plonker, who is performing his latest song for them.

Alec is a lively individual. He has a pitch near the NCP car park in Wardour Street where he makes, on average, twenty pounds a day from begging. He was most interesting about his begging technique and showed us his sleeping-bag, which he had carefully 'roughed up' to give it the authentic feel. He does not, he said, usually sleep on the Embankment, which was where Rueighrhy met him, but he is saving for a deposit on a flat and does not want, to use his own words, 'to waste money on rent'.

He was vitriolic about the homeless in general, referring to them as 'losers' and 'spongers' and told us that there is a hierarchy almost as rigid as that of the BBC among this class of person.

Bolt, a large hairy man of about thirty, did not say a word all evening. I tried to suggest we might ask Laura round. This did not go down well. Estelle sucking up to Plonker horribly.


## June 1st. 11.45 a.m.

*Estelle 'with Hamish and Plonker!!' Jakob on the Internet. Rueighry with homeless. Lucy back in Oxford. Bolt, Alec, Aphrodite, Baldwin, Oliver, etc., in shed. Edwin doing GCSE Chinese. Me here.*

And determined to take new grip on life! Phone call from a travelling theatre company based in Bristol. They have clearly been talking to Snozzer. They seem to be offering me the part of Macbeth, starting next Tuesday. I thanked them for the offer and said that unfortunately I would be in the studio. They said, as we signed off, that they were great fans of my work and had greatly enjoyed my last TV appearance.

I have never been on television, unless you count my brief appearance in *Holiday '76*, talking about my experiences on a kibbutz. Clearly Snozzer is determined to make me higher profile. I hope all this is not affecting his schoolwork.

Jakob is talking to Laura! I found an E-mail from her to him and of course opened it. It read, 'Dear Jakob, I thought your last letter was remarkably sensible.' This is not passion but it could lead to it. He seems a little more cheerful and is, as he always has done, working extremely hard in a very organized way.

Apparently Lucy is leaving Oxford to work with the homeless alongside Ruairughy. When I said to him that this would be a waste of a fine physicist he said, 'Wherever did you get hold of the idea that she was a fine physicist?' Looked back through pages of diary. I am not quite sure where I got hold of it.


## 3 p.m.

A letter has arrived in the second post for Wesley Jones. It was originally addressed to 13 Carslake Road, Wimbledon and has been readdressed with the legend NOT KNOWN HERE printed on it in bold letters.

```
Dear Wesley,
    I am not sending this to 52 Mafeking Road as you tell me
you have moved. I am sure after what you have said about
what goes on in that house, you have made a wise
decision. I am therefore enclosing a royalty cheque,
and, as requested, I have made it out to Rudeboy
Productions. I am only sorry it isn't for more.
    Stay in touch. I was so sorry to hear about your uncle.
No one can choose the manner of their passing but his
sounds particularly painful and unpleasant.

All best
Jim (Baeldi)
```

## 7.30 p.m.

Bolt has gone missing. So have two CD players, forty pounds in cash and my complete edition of the Mozart Piano Concertos (Brendel and Sir Neville Mariner). I am very, very angry. I said to Rugighry, who was insufficiently moved, I thought, by my distress, 'I cannot imagine that a person like Bolt even likes Mozart!' Ruairghery said, 'What do you know about people like Bolt? All you do is wander into the Beeb occasionally

303

and get paid for impersonating a doctor. As a matter of fact Bolt is very fond of music. He went to the Royal Academy and played the tuba.' I said that that did not entitle him to take possession of my complete edition of Mozart Piano Concertos. Reighery said I was very lucky that he didn't take Byrd's 'Ave Verum Corpus' as 'Bolt is particularly fond of English choral music.' I screamed at him and walked out of the room.

Where is he going to live if he and Lucy move in together and/or are married? Where are they all going to live? I cannot take much more of this. Oliver has been sick on the lawn. Estelle, as usual, is not here. She has taken Plonker to meet Hamish. 'Work experience'. Her phrase for it.

## June 3rd. 10 a.m. More blue skies. No wind at all. No clouds. Sparrow re-emerged. Looks cheerful.

*Estelle 'helping Plonker'. Jakob on Internet. Ruieghey at 'Sleeping Bag' Homeless Seminar with Lucy. Alec, Baldwin, Oliver, Aphrodite, etc., in shed. Laura in there with them? Edwin at school. Me in study.*

Still no one mentioning my birthday. On way in to school asked Edwin what Estelle had got me. He said he didn't know. I spoke of my plan to fight back against Karl/Shirley, Ramp, etc. Edwin said, 'Great! You have to take the initiative! That's what Oasis did! Did you know their second album got terrible reviews?' I said I wasn't surprised to hear it. Edwin said, 'The point I am making is they didn't let that get them down!'

Some truth in this. I intend to gatecrash this Awayday Summit on my future. Seize the day, Slippery!

## 11 a.m.

Called Wainwright. Apparently the three of them will be on some boat at Boulter's Lock, near Henley, this very afternoon! I am going to confront them!

## 11.15 a.m.

In preparation for confrontation, went down to shed and shouted at Alec, Baldwin, Aphrodite, etc. They seemed impressed by my performance. Disturbed to see Laura was in there. Offered her a lift home. She accepted.

## 12 noon.

Outside the Proeks, *en route* for Boulter's Lock. Dropped off Laura, who was wearing a low-cut cardigan. She said in the car on the way down that she knew she and Jakob were right together and she was 'going to work and work and work until it came right'. As she went into her house she turned to me and, giving me the thumbs-up sign, said, 'Chessington World of Adventures!' She is a first-rate girl. If I were twenty years younger, etc. If I could only find her determination to make things work and apply it to my own relationship!

There is, of course, the potion – still unused at the back of one of my desk drawers. Unless Bolt walked off with that as well.

## 2 p.m.

Writing this in undergrowth near Thames. Feel like spy on dangerous mission. Very exciting.

I saw the BBC Awayday boat almost at once. It is a luxury barge, staffed by men in white coats – a double-decker with a gigantic deck astern on which, through the grasses, I can dimly see Howard Porda, Shirley and Ramp. They are being served long, cool drinks. Up at the front of the boat is a man in a nautical hat. Perhaps he is part of the BBC's naval division. I am going in close. If something happens and this document is found on me tell Estelle Slippery I love her.

## 5 p.m.

In different undergrowth. An amazing afternoon!

I slithered through the first lot of undergrowth until I got close enough to hear the three of them. They were, by the time I was close to the river bank, on their own. 'Shirley' – wearing a green trouser suit and green slip-ons — was doing the talking. 'All I am saying,' she was saying, 'is that I want Pennebaker dead. I want *General Practice* moved to the ten o'clock slot. Otherwise I am talking to the press. I have nothing to hide. I have gone to the wall for you, Howard —' Porda said, 'Listen! I know you and Ashley can't bear Paul Slippery . . .' Here Ramp rubbed his hands. 'Loathe him,' he said, 'loathe him! And the "character" he plays!'

I have put up with a lot this year. But this, somehow, was the time to register a protest. I got to my feet. Ramp and Shirley swung round in the direction of the noise. I think they were pretty surprised to see me. There were grasses and twigs in my hair and a large blob of Thames Valley soil seemed to be sticking to my face.

'What,' I said, 'do any of you BBC executives know about anything? Have you ever gone into a studio and given the skills of a lifetime to making an unreadable script speakable? Have you ever done anything? Apart from take the credit for a programme about snails that you never made?' Ramp got to his feet. He groped in his pockets and produced, for no apparent reason, a mobile phone. 'I believe in Esmond Pennebaker!' I said. 'I happen to think he is a pretty great character. The only reason you sneer at him is because he is an ordinary Englishman.' Ramp was looking at his mobile as if it were some form of portable oracle. 'What is the difference,' I went on, 'between Esmond Pennebaker and, say, Anna Karenina? Not a lot. One is a Russian woman, the other an English man. One has an affair with a prince called Vronsky, the other with . . .' Karl was twitching — his mouth as wide open as a fish's, '. . . with . . . a secretary whose name I cannot, for the moment, for some reason, recall. One has medical qualifications and the other does not. One goes on, at great length, about her feelings while the other is, at times, painfully reserved. Both, however, know despair!'

I caught sight of Howard Porda. I thought he seemed to be getting the gist of this. I felt, for some reason, that he was listening to me. Ramp was no longer looking at his mobile. He was peering at me as if I were some form of apparition, some saint, descended from heaven to call him to greater things. 'In denying Esmond the right to be himself,' I continued, my voice rising in pitch as I did so, 'in writing him off as "just another character in a soap", we do violence to our common humanity, to the thing that binds us all together and says, "We are men!" Or, in the case of Anna Karenina, women. Esmond Pennebaker, like you, like me, like that bloke who fell on his head out of a window and can't now speak or move but only waggle his ears, has a right to life!' They were, all three of them, now goggling at me, mouths ajar. But I knew I had them. As with my 1974, Taunton-based Macbeth, I had forced them to listen. I dropped my voice very slightly, allowed its bass tones (once described by a man in the *Guardian* as 'rich and strange') to come through the upper registers and said, 'It may not be much of a life. *General Practice*'s Ashbourne Hill may not be Moscow or St Petersburg or even Los Angeles or Naples – although it has a great deal in common with all these places – but it speaks to the world. It is nowhere and everywhere. It is the deep south and the far north. It is a kind of world suburb and Esmond Pennebaker is its hero. And he speaks to everyone – all over the world!'

There was a long silence. Then Howard said, 'What are you doing here?' By way of answer I turned to Karl. 'If you try to blackmail these two into having me killed,' I said, 'I will tell the newspapers that that is what you have done! That is a warning!' And then, partly because two or three flunkeys were coming up to the side of the boat and partly because I thought this was probably going to be as good an exit line as I was going to get, I dropped once more to my knees and slithered off into the undergrowth.

## 11.30 p.m.

A large removal van has drawn up outside Wickett's house. And – only now do I notice – there is a similar FOR SALE sign outside Porker's. Why did I not notice it? And why did I not notice that the wording on Wickett's sign has changed – so that now both boards read SOLD? Is it because, as Estelle told her lover, I 'have my head up my arse most of the time'? The Porkers and the Wicketts are moving out anyway.

I suppose Rueighry and Jakob and Edwin will move out soon. It'll be me and Estelle. I'd better have sorted out our relationship by the time we face each other alone across the kitchen table.

What, I wonder, will be Karl's next move? Why does Ashley Ramp hate me so much? And what, precisely, is the nature of the tie that binds me and Howard Porda? It feels, for some reason, stronger to me than self-interest.

June 7th. 10.30 a.m. Showery but bright. Sparrow in garden. He has his head under his armpit. No sign of his mate.

*No sign of mine either. Estelle, Jakob, Ruaieghrery, Edwin, Lucy, Laura, Lulu, Snozzer, Alec, Oliver, Baldwin, Aphrodite, etc., all 'gone to Portsmouth in the van with Hamish'. Me here.*

In seventeen days I will be fifty. I will also have been married for twenty-five years. I still cannot remember when I last had sex.

I have looked back through this diary and note that at the beginning of the year I seemed pretty confident about the fact that I must have shagged in the not-too-distant past. I think, on sober reflection, that this is mere routine masculine bravado, an assumption that a man of nearly fifty with three children must have done something along those lines at some point in order to get where he has got. I have a car. I have a house. I have a wife. I have a garden. I have a wife. Surely I must have shagged her! But there is no hard evidence that I have done it to Estelle either this year or at any time before that. I have no hard evidence, come to think of it, that Rueighry, Jakob or Edwin are my sons.

Is this why I have problems spelling Reihyreiry's name? Is this why Jakob has black hair?

I do have a clear image of myself doing some pretty raunchy things. And, as far as I can make out, Estelle is often heavily involved. But these may well be fantasy. Quite a number of them involve such daring feats – sex in the back garden, for example, which I notice from a recent survey only 1 per cent of the population indulge in – that I assume they must be fantasy on my part.

Maybe she has put some kind of chip in my brain. Maybe I am a Stepford husband – a sort of mechanical device for paying the mortgage, looking after the kids and cleaning the house.

I suppose I could consult a psychiatrist. It could be that I have not got Prynne's disease. It could be that it is some sick fantasy dreamed up by the charlatans who compile medical dictionaries. Will look up Prynne's disease in the *New 'Be Well' Family Man Guide to Health*, a volume I bought last week to add to the fifteen other health manuals on my shelves.

I think I bought it to counteract *A Complete Dictionary of Symptoms of Illness*, a dark and forbidding work many of whose entries are terse, unforgiving one-liners, such as 'SARCOMA – usually fatal' and 'CARDIAC ARREST – see under DEATH'. I had to go to bed for a rest after reading the entry on testicular cancer.

## 11.30 a.m.

This is really worrying. The entry in the *'Be Well' Family Man Guide to Health* reads as follows –

### PRYNNE'S DISEASE

Prynne's disease is an extremely rare condition, mysterious in origin, in which the patient is unable to remember when he (it has, to date, never been recorded in women) last had sexual intercourse. Patients with Prynne's disease often become irritable, tense and, occasionally, hysterical, complaining to friends, family or their medical advisers about 'when they last had it'.

Low self-esteem is thought to be a contributory factor in the disease, but Beuler and Shawcross (1987) suggest that it may be due in part to a calcium deficiency. Others (Mathias and Grundeberg, 1989) take the view that it is hormonal in origin, citing the levels of melaporzomyne found in the blood of patients at the Missouri State Asylum in tests carried out in the spring of 1990.

Treatment is usually a course of hot baths, counselling and 'thought visualization' of sexual acts. If you know someone whom you suspect of having Prynne's disease, try to get them to a doctor as soon as possible. Whether or not they have recently had sex – and the disease causes such severe and unpleasant alterations in personality that it is highly probable that they have not – it is vital to reassure them that they have not been deprived of it. Although there are no complications of the disease – Hubbinger's account of a patient who went on to experience a major schizophrenic episode is almost certainly an untypical result – Prynne's sufferers can be become violent if untreated.

See also IMPOTENCE.

I have looked up the disease in three other medical manuals, all of which say different things. Cures seem to range from hydrotherapy to a drug that makes your hair fall out, but almost all involve an intense level of counselling.

One thing they are all agreed on is that Prynne's disease sufferers are nearly always reluctant to go for treatment, since, in the words of one entry 'they do not wish to believe that they have contracted the complaint'. It seems to attack men between the ages of forty-five and sixty (presumably by the time they are sixty they have given up trying to remember whether they ever had a shag) and is particularly common 'in suburban areas of south-east England, especially near woodland and heath'. Three more reasons why this seems to be a plague tailor-made for yours truly.

When do I start to get violent?

## 12 noon.

Several calls on the machine. The first from my mother. It goes –

MOTHER: Is that you, Paul? Are you there? Are you there at all, Paul? (*Long pause. Sounds of chomping.*) I'm in bed. Eating breakfast. (*Long pause.*) Bananas. (*Peculiar laugh.*) I've got this boil. They're coming to look at it this afternoon but that's not what I rang about. (*Long pause. Banging in background.*) What did I ring about? (*Even longer pause. More banging.*) You know that man that used to do Norman's car for him? In the arches by Raynes Park . . . I think that it was there. He was Israeli I think. And he used to do Norman's car. You went to something with him and Norman I think. (*Long pause.*) He may not have been Israeli. He may have been Jewish. He was married to the woman we bought the rabbit off. (*Immensely long pause.*) Anyway he's dead.

The second call is from the thirtysomething. It runs as follows –

THIRTYSOMETHING: Paul, are you there? Not there? No? (*Pause.*) I wondered whether you had heard about Steve? He's had a sort of heart attack! (*Pause. Sounds of cigarette inhalation.*) He's in Charing Cross Hospital and I thought you would want to know. It happened when we were . . . you know . . . well . . . (*More cigarette inhalation.*) We were making love and Steve sort of . . . keeled over. It was ghastly. In a curious way I feel responsible. They think he may die. I've been there but when he sees me he just sort of groans and says . . . 'No . . . no . . . no . . .' So maybe he thinks I'm someone else. Call me and come and see Stevie because he needs lots and lots and lots and lots of love.

And less and less and less and less of the old sexual intercourse. This woman is a nightmare. Is she about to shag all my friends to death? Thank God I managed to resist her. Otherwise I might now be in Intensive Care.

The third call from Howard Porda. It is, as befits a senior executive, short and to the point.

PORDA: You were great the other day, Paul. Don't worry about Shirley. I'll take care of her. Ramp is more of a problem. The reason Ashley Ramp hates you is because of my mother. Paul, you should know that Stella Badyass is actually my mother. It'll all be all right. Just remember Spence's Irregularity!

What does this mean?

## 3 p.m.

No word from any of my family. They continue to ignore me. I have no idea why they are in Portsmouth. Perhaps they are all sailing away somewhere, leaving me on my own. As Ruaighry described me last night as 'a sad old git', I suspect this may be the case. He is not worthy of Laura. She made *oeufs en gelée* the other day. Which was delicious. I had three.

The Porkers and Wickett have gone without saying goodbye. I feel somewhat hurt by this. We were not close but I have been watching them pretty intently for the last fifteen years. I know more about what time they go to bed, where they go for entertainment, what they do at the weekends, etc., than I do about my closest friends. I could answer an A-level paper on the gardening habits of each one of them.

Oh well. Nothing is for ever. Good Old Steve may not be around come tomorrow. Off to see him now.

## 4.45 p.m.

Writing this in hospital Reception.

I have seldom seen a man connected to so many tubes. Steve was pretty cheerful though, considering, and said the bloke in the next bed was even worse. 'He is not,' said the former Economics Correspondent, cheerfully, 'expected to last the night!' They had moved my friend out of Intensive Care and the thirtysomething was sitting by his bed pressing her hand into his when I arrived.

I thought he looked tired so I said I would have to go. He didn't make too many objections. But as I was leaving I noticed he was trying to say something. It was hard to make out the words but it sounded like 'She ain't a brother!' Puzzled, I lowered my ear to his lips and discovered he was saying, as he rolled his eyes towards the retreating thirtysomething, 'She's into rubber!'

I wasn't sure how I was to take this. I thought at the time that Steve was trying to impress me but have now decided it was a cry for help.

I hear the car. Estelle. And the others presumably.


## 10.45 p.m.

Dinner is over. I cooked a dish called Wabberkins pie from a book called *In the Heart of England*. It was generally agreed to be one of the most disgusting things anyone had ever eaten. I seem to have a flair for what goes down well with north African Jews but little talent for the cuisine of my native land.

The meal was not helped by the presence of Plonker, who is becoming completely insufferable. Egged on by Estelle, who plied him with wine, he gave us his views on art, politics and Cranborne School, Wimbledon. 'The Channel Tunnel,' he said, in booming, confident tones, 'is not safe. They should close it! It is leaking.' He gave us his father's views on Tony Blair, Richard Branson and the forthcoming drought. Then he sang. Estelle gazed at him rapturously, occasionally turning to the rest of us and murmuring, 'Isn't he wonderful?'

Laura's new technique with Jakob is simply to sit near him and never allow her eyes to leave his face. I suppose it might work. I think if I were Jakob I would find it disconcerting. Although the boy has nerves of steel.

June 8th. 11 a.m. Summer really arrived. Leaves on tree in garden the size of soup plates. Blue sky, small fluffy clouds. Sparrow lurking in road for some reason.

*Ruairghuy and Lucy at Sleeping Bag. Jakob also at Sleeping Bag. Edwin doing GCSE French. Oliver, Baldwin, Alec, Aphrodite, Laura, etc., in shed. Me in back garden writing this. Estelle in Cologne.*

Or maybe she is buying cologne. Contact between us is now so limited I have almost given up asking where she is going when she leaves the building. I never found out what they were all doing in Portsmouth. Laura's unemployed state is not good for her. She spends far too much time in the shed with Oliver, Baldwin, etc. Think Aphrodite may have lesbian designs on her. I suggested she came with me to the Beeb, but she did not seem keen. She is wearing a low-cut woolly jumper. Jakob even worse with Lucy. Is now offering to 'buy' Sleeping Bag. Ruaigheiughry said, 'It is a charity. You cannot buy a charity.' Jakob said, 'You can buy anything these days.' There is, I fear, some truth in this.

## 11.30 a.m.

Plans for themed evening in Greek restaurant continue without my being informed. Message on machine from Estelle who is (I think) in Germany. She seems to have asked Howard Porda, Stella Badyass, Shirley (who she insists on calling Shirley) and Ashley Ramp. Imagine that lot with the Proeks and the Rachnowskis! She said, 'I think it might do your career some good.' Off now to kick ass at Beeb.

## 12.30 p.m.

Writing this in the canteen. It is German Week and I am eating Knackwurst and potato salad. I am drinking Löwenbrau. The man on the puddings counter is wearing lederhosen and a green trilby. I do not recognize anyone apart from Wainwright, who is sitting in the far corner. I think he may be crying. Laura has come in with me!

## 12.45 p.m.

He wasn't crying. It was onions. It is the thirtieth anniversary of his being given a staff contract. He has, however, told me what Spence's Irregularity is. Apparently Spence is a management guru who came up with a law which states that 'in a period of restructuring those initiating the restructuring will always be restructured themselves before the effects of the restructuring become apparent'. I think this may mean yet more people are to be fired. Let us hope they are the right people, i.e. my enemies. Off now to read-through with Laura! Wainwright peering rather offensively at her jumper. She loves it here!

## 1.55 p.m.

Two lots of scripts. One from Christine. Her nervous breakdown, alcoholism, etc., beginning to show, which is good as I can rewrite her totally. For example, just now I managed to change the line, 'Ooh my back is awful since that terrible accident' to 'I feel so positive and young these days! It's amazing!' Nobody seemed to notice. Christine seems to have taken against my wife and only given her one line, which is – 'Golly!' – a hard thing to bring off when you come to it cold. Karl, or rather, Shirley, is at the hairdresser's. Leo and Witchett have come in and we are going to have creative session!

## 3 p.m.

Their new scripts are rather exciting. For the first time I have become genuinely curious about whether I live or die. Up to now my involvement has been of the 'surely it isn't my turn!' nature but now I find myself turning the page, not simply to see how close Esmond is to the funeral parlour, but to share his adventures with him. Will he live, I find myself asking, only to stop short when I realize that the person I am talking about is me and that if he doesn't I will probably never, ever work again.

Pamela, my radio wife, has hired two hit men called Wallace and Randall. They are Glaswegian drug addicts with a nice line in grim patter and their dialogue is written out in nearly incomprehensible seeming Scots. Sample –

WALLACE: Tae tek a wee shuiter tae his heed?

RANDALL: Fik orff, Wallae. I cannae dae nae shuiters. Havenae ye
heert? Duisnae Pennebaker carry a wee shuiter hisself?

WALLACE: Puss orff, Randall! Yon's a wee maedico!

Etc. I am assured by Witchett and Leo that, with the right actors, all
this will be perfectly comprehensible. At the end of the episode I am
reading now, I am trapped in a garage with Wallace and Randall, who
are dunking my 'heed' in a bath of water and telling me about all the
awful things they are going to do to me. It looks pretty desperate but,
after some discussion, I got them to agree that in the next episode I will
stab one of them in the leg with a syringe and, after an exciting chase
across the rooftops, become temporarily free of them.

The whole thing makes me feel twenty years younger. The fact that I
am finding it increasingly difficult to climb up the stairs without collapsing,
makes lines like 'Dinnae jump, Pennebaker! It's twaenty fuit doon!'
followed by *Jump FX. Pennebaker breathes heavily* even more thrilling
to enact.

Laura v. impressed by my perf., decisiveness with Leo and Witchett,
etc. I sometimes think she is wasted on Jakob. As, of course, does he!

## 5 p.m.

Writing this in the new studio area in basement. Once upon a time a
mysterious warren of heavy doors, blind corridors and carpeted hush.
Now resembling the reception area of a not very successful advertising
agency – pot plants, blinds, low tables with pointless magazines, etc. I
suppose institutions like the BBC are chiefly remarkable for their continuity. Which is why I feel so depressed at the attempts to modernize it
without reference to the best of its past. There is, now, none of the
amateurishness I always loved about the place. Still – things must change,
Slippery!

Just seen Shirley and complimented her on hairdo, which went down
well. She did not speak of my death, which was encouraging. Did my
riverside speech work? Or are the new changes hinted at by Porda working
against her?

I did say, 'Looking forward to the themed Greek evening! What are

315

you going to wear?' This was tremendously popular. There was definitely something different about her. She was, I felt, much more of a woman. Perhaps she has had it chopped off. This could account for her more tolerant attitude to her employees.

I caught Laura sobbing in a corner on her own and put my arm around her. She said, 'It's so unfair, Paul! I love him so much!' I said, 'He'll come round, love! He's a very silly boy if he can't see what a great girl you are, and I'll bang his head on the wall till he does, OK?' She stopped crying and smiled then. She is such a sweet kid. I feel very protective towards her. I said, as we got up to go into the studio, 'Who is this horrible middle-aged perve who's been lusting after you, Laura, while we're at it? I'll bang his head against the wall too!' She smiled and said, 'It was just a joke, Mr Slippery. It was nothing really!' Then she lifted her face and pecked me, lightly, on the cheek. Not unpleasurable!

Love is such confusion. Why does it lead us down so many dark and twisted roads, when all the time the wide, brightly lit highway to romantic happiness lies so close to our wandering feet?


## 5.15 p.m.

Just read through last sentence. I think I definitely have potential as a novelist. Off home now to see how much more furniture is missing, whether Baldwin has strangled a neighbour, whether Estelle has made a grab for Plonker, etc.


## 6 p.m.

Listened to an early evening repeat of the show. Rather moved by it.

Ashbourne Hill, where *General Practice* is set, has not changed much in twenty-five years. It started out as a small market town 'somewhere in England'. I think when we did the first programmes, we thought of it as being in the West Country. There was an elderly rustic character who said 'Eee!' and 'Aaar!' and was always coming in with lumbago. I think we even had the odd farmer coming with gout.

Nobody actually said that Ashbourne Hill was capable of moving, sliding along country roads, creeping up motorways when no one was looking and then finding itself thirty miles north or south or east or west.

But that is what it has done over the years. In the early seventies – when Elspeth the Trotskyite Nurse appeared – the tone of the dialogue began to suggest the inner city. Although which city was never made clear. Some said it was Birmingham. There was an element of the nasal twang of the Midlands in the voices of the patients. Some were sure it was London. Where else would there be quite so many West Indian people?

In the mid and late eighties there was no doubt in anyone's mind that Ashbourne Hill was somewhere in the south. There were plenty of regional accents but these were mainly to be found among the staff. The locals all used received pronunciation. Many of them sounded positively aristocratic. Our receptionist – Camilla – was known as 'Yah!' because that was all she ever said.

And then suddenly everyone seemed to be talking with Cockney accents. Even, for a while, me. Our practice accountant, Gub, who arrived in 1989, sounded like an extra in a Dickens musical – 'Iss orl abaht ver bottom line, Ezzie, innit?' Pilfrey still says 'innit' occasionally, a locution that dates entirely from this period.

And nowadays? Oh, nowadays it is everywhere and nowhere. It has stopped moving because, one feels, the town realizes that if it pitched up anywhere else, anywhere else would be much the same as where it is now. Wherever that may be. Ashbourne Hill is, like England, now no longer really English. There are moments when it reminds me strongly of Düsseldorf and moments when I think it has a vaguely Chinese quality. Its shopping malls could well be in southern California, but when the wind blows through it, in early March, you could easily think you were in Manitoba. It is part of the giant suburb that the world is slowly becoming, and, perhaps because of that, I can no longer distinguish between it and the real suburb in which I dwell.

Which is perhaps why my affection for it is indistinguishable from the affection I feel for the things around me, now, as I write this. For Mafeking Road, with its dumpy red roofs, warm in the spring sunshine, for Wickett's forsythia and Porker's ceanothus, for the cars, waiting quietly for their owners to return and the children's voices in the far distance as another day draws to a close.

## 8 p.m.

Writing this in the kitchen where I am making *foules mesdames*, a Lebanese dish, and frying up about half a kilo of chicken livers. Good evening so far. Have been decisive.

When I got in, Jakob and Mr Scarrotto were in the middle of a business meeting in the front room. There were about eight fridges piled up on the pavement outside and a large swarthy man in a rusty van watching them suspiciously, but, as far as I could see, making no attempt to move them. I walked in decisively, and before Scarrotto could pinch my cheek, tousle my hair or kiss me, I shook him firmly by the hand. 'Good to see you, Scarrotto!' I said, 'I hope those fridges aren't going to stay there all night!'

Then I turned on my heel and strode decisively from the room.

## 8.45 p.m.

Estelle called from Cologne. She was rather businesslike with me. She didn't seem at all phased by the Porda/Badyass news. After a brief chat she asked to be put on to Jakob. Much giggling and secretive whispering. I eavesdropped behind front-room door. Everyone in this house in conspiracy against me. I still determine to be strong! I also heard him say, 'Hamish is so cool! Paul does not suspect a thing!'

Perhaps Hamish, now, will fulfil the role of father in his life. Although what that role is, I must say I am no longer quite sure. It is certainly no longer a simple question of making him boiled eggs and beans (Jakob's staple diet for the first nine years of his life).

## 12 midnight.

I miss Porker and Wickett. They knew how I felt. They were middle-aged, and, in some ways, in even worse shape than me. Am going through latest Christine script and cutting all references to illness and despair. It is now three pages long.

A really sad and touching message on the machine from Laura to Jakob. I offered to play it to him but he said, 'I know what it'll be, I'm afraid.' He is such a curious mixture of hard and soft! Intensely practical. Perhaps that is the key to him. Everyone apart from Edwin is asleep. Edwin is upstairs playing the chord of G minor, very, very quietly. I think I heard him sing the word 'Lulu'.

## 12.30 a.m.

In study with Edwin. It was, in fact, an A major seventh. I managed to broach the Lulu issue by saying, lightly and casually, as if there was nothing significant or untoward or troubling about my remark, 'I once experimented with . . . er . . . love potion! Can you believe it?' Edwin seemed alarmed by this. There was a sudden look of almost childlike terror in his eyes.

'I had a friend at school,' he said, 'a very foolish boy of about my age. Very immature and foolish. He was called . . . Hornbeam. And he sent away for this . . . love potion!' 'Why,' I said, 'did he do that?' 'He wanted,' said Edwin, 'to use it on his girlfriend!' 'My God,' I said, 'and did he give it to her?' 'He did,' said Edwin, 'he gave her quite a lot of it!' 'Did it work?' I asked eagerly. 'Were they . . . you know . . .' 'Were they what?' said Edwin, rather stiffly. 'Were they shagging?' I said. 'I have no idea,' said Edwin, 'Hornbeam and I never discussed questions of that sort!'

He seemed, for a moment, unwilling to go on but after a while continued with his story.

'In fact,' he said, 'it created more problems than it solved. You see, after he had given her the potion he never knew whether she liked him for himself or whether she was just responding to the potion!' 'I see what you mean!' I said. 'He began to wish he had never even heard of this potion,' said Edwin. 'He began to wish he had never sent away for it to . . . Wolverhampton or some such place I think it was . . . I don't really remember . . . He sort of . . . questioned his own relationship, you know? He asked himself whether it was love or whether it was just potion. And he could not answer the question. He was in the middle of exams at the time and it gave him a great deal of concern!'

He fell silent. I said, 'Talking of exams – how are yours going? How was the Chinese?' Edwin gave me a strange look. 'I don't do Chinese!' he said. 'I thought you didn't,' I said; 'I was surprised when you said you were doing the exam!' 'Did I do Chinese?' said Edwin, sounding alarmed. 'I thought you said you did!' I said. He shook his head glumly. 'It's possible,' he said, with a shudder. 'I have taken so many bleeding G C S E s I could well have done Chinese. I could have done Welsh for all I know.'

We fell silent – both looking at the now empty houses of our opposite neighbours.

'What is love, you know?' said Edwin eventually. 'What does real love mean? How do you find it? You know? Hornbeam . . . was . . . like . . . tormented by these questions!' I nodded slowly. 'I am really sorry to hear that,' I said, 'but I don't think Hornbeam was wrong to give her the potion. I think it was entirely natural. Normal. I mean, in certain circumstances I can imagine myself doing something like that!' Edwin's eyes widened. 'Can you?' he said. 'Easily!' I said. 'You have,' I went on, reflecting as I passed on these words of wisdom how easy it is to be philosophical about another's problems, 'to trust your feelings!'

'Anyway,' went on Edwin, staring at the floor, 'he wrote away to this place in Wolverhampton . . . or . . . Birmingham or wherever it was . . . and he got an antidote!' 'How do you mean?' I said. 'I mean,' said Edwin, 'he got a sort of liquid that wipes out the effect of the love potion. So that he would know, when he had given it to her, whether this girl really loved him for himself or was just . . . you know . . . responding to treatment, as it were!' 'My God!' I said. 'And did he use it?' 'Actually,' said Edwin slowly and sorrowfully, 'he didn't have the guts. Because he really liked this girl and she seemed to like him. And he was afraid that if he gave her the antidote she might go off him. So he just had to live with this amazing guilt!' 'I bet,' I said, 'if he had given her the antidote, she would have still been keen on him.' 'Do you think?' said Edwin. 'Positive!' I said.

I leaned forward and took him by the arm. I was amazed by how strong and tall he had grown. A young man really. And yet, as my youngest, always the youngest, with a carefree, protected look in his eye behind which is so much sweetness and vulnerability that the world never really sees. Edwin. My son.

June 9th. 11 a.m. More summer FX. Slightly hazy sunshine. Almost no wind. Sparrow still not in evidence. Hope he has not gone for good.

*Estelle on M4. Jakob on Internet. Ruiueiury and Lucy in Wolverhampton. Edwin doing GCSE Art. Me in study. Oliver, Baldwin, Aphrodite, Alec, etc., sweeping the garden.*

I have put the shed contingent on light household chores. It seems to be working. It is probably about what they would get for their drug-related activities.

Much agitation over themed Greek evening. Apparently we all have to dress up. I am going as Diogenes. Edwin is supplying the tub. Rueigehry is going as a slave, Estelle is going as Sappho (her costume is to be tweeds and stout shoes), Jakob is going as Euripides (he says his costume will be 'to sneer slightly') and Edwin as Hermes.

Laura apparently said her Dad always goes as a hoplite and her Mum as a woman of the streets. I can hardly wait. I hope Ashley Ramp doesn't go for Diogenes as well. Not sure how Estelle has set all this up and have not the nerve to call the Proeks or Rachnowskis about it. I said to Lucy I thought it would be a sticky evening and she said, 'With my Mum and Dad and Laura's Mum and Dad there – it'll be a scorcher!' What is going on with their parents? While we're at it – what is going on with the children? Has Laura given up on Jakob? Why is Mr Scarrotto in hospital? There is a rumour he is being treated for gunshot wounds.

Message on the machine from Peter Mailer, which I have only just picked up, after running Edwin into school to continue work on his traffic-cone installation for GCSE Art. It runs as follows –

MAILER: Hi, Paul, it's Peter here, are you well? I hope you're well I know you to be a hard worker and someone who needs to keep well so I hope you are and also of course your family who are a splendid bunch, I think. (*Pause.*) Christine and I are going to get married! (*Slightly more businesslike tone.*) We are getting married, Paul. (*Long pause.*) On . . . On . . . (*Long pause.*) June 24th. (*Long pause.*)

Christine is leaving *General Practice*, Paul! Paul, she has these . . . costumes, Paul. (*Long pause.*)

For God's sake pray for me!

He sounded drunk. I think he is almost certainly a Satanist. But Christine leaving is good for Esmond! And good for me!

## 11.30 a.m.

Estelle arrived back from wherever she went after Cologne – to have, I think, yet another meeting about the animated film *Mr Slippy Sloppy*. She tells me they have now 'done away with his penis altogether'! She announced her intention of sending Plonker on 'some kind of scholarship'. I asked whether it would teach him a few basic table manners, humility, how to sing, etc. Estelle said, 'Plonker has more talent in his little finger than you have in your whole body!' I asked her what she had been doing in Cologne and she said, 'Flogging my arse, what do you think?'

Enraged by this I have been searching Edwin's room for the antidote to the Wolverhampton love potion. I have not yet found it but have found a great many other interesting things. He has a reserve supply of about fifty unused condoms, a short novel entitled *Why My Father Left* and many riveting personal documents, including the following letter from Lulu.

Darling Edwin,

I do understand your feelings but, as I said on Friday, I just don't think I am ready. It's not that I am worried about getting pregnant, in spite of what happened to Wodge, although that turned out to be a scare. It's just that it doesn't feel right yet and I care about you too much to want to mess it up!

I do love you. It will all be OK. When the time's right we will . . . er . . . get down to it! Sitting up in my bed thinking about you and waiting for the morning to come . . .

Lulu

PS. Tell Snozzer that Wodge does fancy him (I think) . . .

322

Felt unbelievably guilty about reading this. But also unbelievably moved by it. How sane, mature and balanced young people are! And how direct! Why can't I talk to Estelle as openly as this girl talks to Edwin? Because, I suppose, I know her so well. We share so much history.

At the bottom of his underpants drawer I found a small green bottle labelled, in Edwin's handwriting, 'ANTIDOTE TO LOVE POTION'. It was the colour of Ribena so I decanted it into another bottle and substituted Ribena. There is an official-looking label on the back which says it is a 'rhease suppressor' and you should not attempt to drive heavy machinery after taking it.

I must get this down Estelle's face as soon as possible. Otherwise there will be no doing anything with Plonker. Apparently he commanded Mr Horthy, the maths master, to drive him down into Wimbledon for a McDonald's the other day and got quite abusive when Horthy refused.

## 2.30 p.m.

Message on the machine from Good Old Steve. As follows –

> STEVE: Hi, Paul, Steve here. (*Pause.*) Still alive I fear. Need to talk to you about . . . about . . . you know . . . the girl I'm . . . you know . . . sort of . . . seeing . . . can't seem to remember her name but I'm . . . well . . . you know . . . (*Pause.*) Look, she's been in a lot, Paul, and giving me . . . you know . . . lots and lots and lots of love . . . but you know I don't really . . . want it . . . and I . . . I mean apparently stress is bad if you've had a major cardiac arrest and . . . (*Pause. Wheezing.*) I just wish she could . . . you know . . . give this . . . er . . . love to someone else you know? . . . lots and lots of it . . . not to me! (*Wheezing. Tone of desperation now apparent.*) . . . Please not to me . . . not lots and lots of love . . . please . . . (*Line goes dead.*)

I must do something about this. If she really is into rubber the thirtysomething would seem the ideal choice for Ashley Ramp. I am not quite sure how to set about this, however. How to persuade the current girlfriend of my best friend that she really needs a forty-five-year-old hunchback? How to persuade him that he needs her, come to that? Ramp hates me so much that were I to offer him a cheque for a thousand pounds he would probably refuse to cash it just to spite me.

Potion perhaps? Ask her to Greek evening?

I think I have had enough of potion. I would probably end up swallowing it myself and falling in love with Ramp.

## 3.30 p.m.

Rueiughry and Lucy back from Wolverhampton. They seemed disappointed in it. Ruieughry said, with some sadness – 'there are not really very many homeless people there'.

## 4.30 p.m.

New script arrived from Leo and Witchett. They really are motoring. I escape over the rooftops and there is a superbly realized knife-fight – something that is quite hard to do on radio. I emerge victorious. Ep. ends with superb scene between me and Pamela. She brings up secretary-shagging incident and says she has never been able to trust me since. I say, 'Trust is a moment-to-moment thing, Pamela. Love is how you feel now, not how you felt then. Trust is as changeable as life itself. You can't tie feelings down.' Any one of these lines, it seems to me, could be the tag line in the promotion for a major new motion picture.

It works on Pamela anyway. She sobs and says she has always loved me and just as we are moving in for the clinch (in spite of, or perhaps because of, Leo and Witchett's love life, the scene crackles with hetero-sexual tension) we hear a ghastly screech from outside. It is Randall and Wallace, who begin to break down the door of my surgery (where this scene takes place) with shotguns. They shout, 'Yae're gaeing tae friuckin' DAE, yae friuckin' maedico!' as they do so. 'Friuckin' is, I am told, a compromise dialect word agreed at the very highest level of the BBC. If this doesn't increase the audience nothing will. I rang Witchett and got him to give me a last line, 'No! *You'll* die, you bone-ignorant Jock!'

Bolt has returned, bringing my CDs with him. He is not a bad lad really. He is sitting out on the lawn with Oliver, Aphrodite, etc. Edwin has told me I must practise getting into my tub. There has been a lot of controversy about what I should wear underneath it. Edwin says I should be naked. Jakob and Rueigheruy say underpants. Estelle is against the tub.

## 6.45 p.m.

A lot of problems with the tub. It is far too small. I have tried to send out for a larger one but it is apparently not possible to get hold of one at such short notice. Edwin says I should go as Socrates and 'just wear a sheet'. I have refused to do this. There are also problems with my lantern. I tried walking round the house with it, holding it aloft and shouting, 'Where may I find an honest man?' I got hot wax all over my hands. I have sent Edwin out to get me an electric lantern. He is not pleased about this.

## 8 p.m.

Estelle finally returned. God knows where she has been! The Slippery family are dressed and ready to go out. I am wearing underpants under an overcoat. I have stowed the tub on the roof-rack. Estelle is wearing tweeds and a billycock hat. She looks rather sexy. Rueaigry is dressed in a blanket. Jakob is wearing a dark suit and sneering lightly. Edwin is wearing slacks, a rather elegant yellow T-shirt and (his contribution to the Greek theme) a pair of leather sandals with small yellow paper wings attached to them. Estelle made these and seems very proud of them. The girls are coming separately. Oliver and Bolt asked if they could come. I told them they couldn't.

## 9 p.m. The Odyssey Restaurant, Cheam.

This is a nightmare.

Mr Proek is looking as depressed as only a fifty-year-old man dressed in cardboard armour can look. There was a shower of rain on our way here and his sword has wilted. I did try to get la Proek on her own on the dance floor and she snapped, 'How can I think of dancing at a time like this?' She and Bert Rachnowski seem to spend a lot of time muttering in corners.

Shirley is being positively amiable towards me! She and Howard seem to be getting on famously – once or twice she has touched him on the cheek. She is wearing a sort of taffeta gown which, as I told her, is really quite stunning.

The restaurant is billed as having a 'Dinner-dance Area'. Our party is in the private dining-room, where our costumes can be screened from the vulgar. We are about to share a couple of square yards of moussaka and are sitting by imitation wrought-iron garden tables underneath a large Doric column that is, I think, made of papier mâché. There are not many other people in the main restaurant. Earlier, a small man with a moustache tried to smash a glass and was shown the door.

I asked Mr Proek how he was and he said he had taken early retirement – 'because of this business with the Rachnowskis'. I asked how retirement was and he said, 'At least there are no rats!' He then said he was very worried about Ruaieughry and Lucy. 'I hear,' he said, 'they intend to get married.' He gave Ruaiergfhy a venomous look as he said this. Ruarighei-ury was capering around in his blanket waving his arms and saying, 'I'm a spider! Catch me!' He did not, I have to say, look ready for marriage.

Laura wearing gauze dress and looking at Jakob miserably. Help is at hand, my girl! I have brought the potion with me!

Something is up with Mrs Proek. She is coming this way holding a bottle of retsina. Perhaps she is going to tell me.


9.30 p.m.

She did. Writing this at empty table in main restaurant.

It seems she is in love with Bert Rachnowski – and has been for years. She has – she told me – 'simply not been able to break it to Norman, although he suspects and everyone else knows'. I can see this. He would probably take a steam hammer to her and to his daughter. Now that his inner violence can no longer be directed towards rats I imagine Norman is not far away from the Special Unit of Barlinnie Prison. Under the influence of two bottles of retsina she poured out her other troubles to me. She has not had an orgasm since 1989. I thought, but did not say, that this was not bad going. She feels trapped by her life. She only stays because of Laura. The divorce would kill Laura. Laura's hopeless love for Jakob. Etc., etc.

She is, like all of us, ludicrous, but also, like all of us, genuinely sad.

And her passion for her daughter is touching. All of us in these little houses! With these families we love so much! All the same and all imagining ourselves so different!

Perhaps it is my tub that is making me feel these things. It has, however, gone down a storm with the punters. I think I may wear it more often. Off now to administer potion to Laura and Jakob.

## 10.30 p.m.

Writing this in Gents. Oh God! Oh God!

I had put nearly all of the rest of the potion on to a plate of Turkish delight – having first selected all the green ones. I offered this to Laura and she took one, as did Jakob. But, just as they were chewing away, Bert Rachnowski (sensationally stoned) came up and started wolfing them down, staring at Jakob as he did so. I tried to talk him out of eating any more but this only had the effect of attracting other members of the party to the potion-laced sweetmeats. Within minutes everyone (apart from Estelle and I) was chomping away and staring into everyone else's eyes.

What have I done? Will Shirley now shag Mrs Proek? Will Bert Rachnowski make improper advances to Jakob? Is Howard Porda about to try it on with his own mother (of whom more later)? With whom will Ashley Ramp, who has just entered this facility and is being observed by me from my cubicle, fall in love?

Judging by the intensity with which he is staring at the mirror – himself.


## June 10th. 9.30 a.m. Very warm but humid. Clouds massing on the other side of what is no longer Porker's roof. Dark blue-grey. Sparrow in hedge but looking apprehensive. Strong atmosphere of sexual tension in Mafeking Road.

*Estelle at Craftgirls. Edwin 'on study leave with Lulu'. Rueioughry and Lucy somewhere on the Embankment. Oliver, Baldwin, Aphrodite, etc., cleaning kitchen floor. Jakob with Laura in Richmond Park!*

Have just called an agent! A nice woman whose name I found in my address book a week or so ago. I left a message saying that I was Paul Slippery who played Dr Pennebaker and maybe we could meet to discuss things. She probably won't bother to reply but it was worth a try.

## 10 a.m.

Her assistant rang. She sounded very keen. She said, 'Marietta is desperate to talk to you!' Will call her back.

## 10.15 a.m.

Rang agent. She said she was very keen to talk to me. We had a little general chat. She was sorry not to have been in touch earlier. She told me she hadn't been feeling too well. I said I was sorry to hear this and then I said, 'Do you see my career changing?' She said, 'No, I think you are marvellous at what you do!' She seemed quite upset to hear I was thinking of trying to get back into the RSC. I said I was pleased to hear this and asked her what she felt she liked about me most. She said she thought I had a wonderful bedside manner. Then she started to talk about her bowels.

It was not until she asked me about the results of the tests, however, that I realized she had confused me with her GP.

## 11 a.m.

This morning I received another cheque for Wesley Jones, who has gone rather quiet of late. Stricken with guilt I went round to Carslake Road, the address to which his last letter had been directed. It was a most strange experience.

The house was a small, cottage-like dwelling, not far away from the Common. Very English. Not at all my idea of Wesley. I rang the bell and the door was answered by a tired-looking woman of about my age. For some reason, I couldn't have said why, she looked vaguely familiar. As soon as I caught sight of her I heard myself blurting out, 'I'm sorry. Do we know each other?' She gave me a strange look. 'I don't think we do!' she said. I apologized and asked her if she had ever had a person called Wesley Jones staying there. 'No,' she said, 'he's a black man!' I said, 'A big black man!' She gave me another odd look. 'I don't care if he's bright green,' she said, 'he hasn't been staying here. Unless he's hiding in the cellar.' 'That,' I said, 'is perfectly possible!' I held out Jim Baeldi's last letter to Wesley and the woman instantly became more friendly.

'I'm sorry I opened the letter!' she said. 'It was the only way I could think of finding out where to send it . . .' 'I'm so sorry to have troubled you,' I said. 'He may not actually exist anyway!' The woman gave me an even odder look. 'I mean to say,' I went on, 'I think there are two Wesley Joneses. One is sort of in my head. He's someone I made up. And the other one is a real person who appeared to my son near Hyde Park and threatened me!' The woman started to close the door. 'I know this sounds odd,' I said, 'but I could swear your face is familiar! Have you ever worked at the BBC?'

The door was now firmly closed. A small voice came from inside. 'My husband will be home soon!' she said. 'Go away or I will call the police!' I apologized for troubling her and moved back to the car.

I was driving back towards Mafeking Road when I nearly ran over Snozzer. He was walking down the middle of the road smoking an enormous cigar and wearing a black trilby hat. I pulled over to the side of the road and asked him if he was all right. He said he wasn't. He smelled strongly of drink. 'What's up?' I said. Snozzer sighed deeply and leaned against the side of the car. 'It's Wodge!' he said. 'I really like her but she likes this bloke from Wimbledon High!' His face clouded. 'He is a real idiot,' he said. 'He is a real nightmare. His name is Hornbeam.' I didn't, for some reason, wish to inquire too closely into Hornbeam, so I simply said, 'What's wrong with him?' 'He's in the year above!' said Snozzer darkly. 'We hate the year above!' He went on to tell me that this Hornbeam character was two-timing Wodge with a girl called Nuttella. This cannot be her real name.

I asked him if he would like a lift anywhere and he said he would like to go to a pub. He said he didn't mind which one. 'I'm on study leave during the exams,' he said, 'but I'm not doing any work. I just walk around the streets in this trilby and smoke cigars and think about Wodge. I really like love her, man!' He got in the car and we drove off.

He told me, as I cruised around the village looking for a suitable pub, that Hotchkiss has abandoned the Nazi uniforms. Apparently the headmaster objected. He is now going for a traditional approach. Edwin, for example, has wings. When I said Edwin had not told me this Snozzer said, 'We're all keeping pretty quiet about it. I'm in a kind of skirt!' He really was in a bad state. I bought him a pint of lager, which seemed to calm him down. He says he hopes to get me a job at the National Theatre.

## 2 p.m.

Jakob and Laura still not back from Richmond Park, where they went at ten this morning – both looking intense. Message on the machine from Wainwright. It says, 'Paul, it's Wainwright. Have you heard about the new lot of restructuring? Apparently Colin Cross may be coming back. There is a rumour he has never been away. I heard he has been locked up in B34576 ever since his leaving party. Did you go to his leaving party, by the way? I can't find anyone who did. I think it may have been a blind. Remember Spence's Second Law of Irregularity!'

Is this why Shirley has been so nice to me? Must find out more and investigate implications for Esmond, etc.

## 2.30 p.m.

In a major panic attack about my forthcoming birthday I got out my three suits from the cupboard and tried on all the trousers. My stomach is now definitely a presence. I would talk to it – as I believe some feminists recommend – but I have absolutely nothing to say to it apart from 'Go away!'

Edwin, still on study leave, wandered into my room and found me prodding my fat. 'What,' he said, 'are you doing?' I said, 'I am prodding my fat!' Edwin said we should both go to the gym. I said, 'What about Lulu?' Edwin said, 'She is upstairs! Upstairs is for girls! The gym is for men!' So that is where we are going. Apparently I may get something called a six-pack. When I said I could always use a beer Edwin laughed satirically.

## 5 p.m.

Hideously embarrassing session at Parvercourt, the local leisure centre. Edwin and I sat at a desk in the middle of the foyer facing a large photo of the 'Employee of the Month' (an obvious serial killer called Hugh) and were initiated by someone called Kevin. We were both told to go and have our photographs taken in a small booth at the side of the foyer. I came out looking like a mutilated Jambon de Bayonne in a rented wig. Edwin looked rather sexy. When we gave them in to Kevin he told us that at Parvercourt HQ they have a huge wall where they stick up the ugliest customer photographs. I asked whether mine would be there and Kevin said he thought it was in with a chance.

We had to write our ages on a small sheet of paper. Underneath this we were asked, 'HAVE YOU ANY MEDICAL PROBLEMS WE SHOULD KNOW ABOUT?' Edwin wrote, 'Women.' I got as far as 'I get a sort of stiffness and pain in the lower back area when I wake in the morning although it usually wears off by lunchtime –' and then ran out of space. Below that was 'PERSONAL GOALS IN TRAIN-ING'. Edwin wrote, 'To heighten awareness of the world around me.' I wrote, 'To lose fat and strengthen upper body.'

Our instructor, who wasn't called Kevin, looked between me and my personal training goal for some time, nodding slowly to himself as he did so. 'Any particular bits of your upper body?' he said, eventually. 'His head!' said Edwin. The instructor who wasn't called Kevin did not laugh. He said, 'I came here to sort out my upper body!' He was the size of a small furniture van and his upper body looked as if a series of cricket balls had been sewn under its skin. I wasn't sure whether he had acquired the bulges here or was hoping to use the machines to get them down to manageable size.

I was then allowed a go on the walking machine. As I walked I held on to a couple of handles and a screen in front of me told me what my heart rate was. The instructor who wasn't Kevin told me to keep it at around 120 beats per minute. I was unable to do this. I could get it to do about 80. If I walked frantically quickly I could get it up to 160 in a matter of seconds but it didn't seem to want to beat 120 times a minute. Like one of those showers that go from boiling to freezing in a matter of seconds my heart did not seem to have grasped the correct response to a Parvercourt machine.

As a result I developed a kind of slurred, stumbling run designed solely to get my heart to perform. By leaping a little way up in the air, landing with a bump and then doing a series of short skips, I managed to get my beats per minute up to 110. I was just moving in for the kill when I fell off the machine and nearly fractured my knee. I had to be helped to a chair.

Am writing this lying on the bed in our room, about £50 worse off and in severe pain.


## 11.30 p.m.

I have to get Estelle to swallow the antidote. She brought Plonker back tonight and he played his song sequence 'The Dreams are Endlessly Burning'. The unedited version lasts three quarters of an hour.

Jakob talks of going to Sicily with a (fully recovered) Mr Scarrotto tomorrow. Apparently they have to see a man who insulted Mr Scarrotto. I asked Jakob if they were going to make him an offer he couldn't refuse and Jakob said, 'Listen! You are my father and I love you. But please do not make any jokes about Mr Scarrotto being in the Mafia. He doesn't like it. I don't like it. The Mafia are bad people. Well, maybe one or two of them are all right, maybe Louis Finzinetti isn't so bad but on the whole they are bad people!'

Ruaireghry told me afterwards that none of this was intended to be taken seriously. I could not, though I tried, get out of Jakob what happened between him and Laura in Richmond Park. All he would say was, 'We shagged a few deer!'

The trouble is – I never know when anything my sons say is intended to be taken seriously. Estelle says they have picked up this habit from me. One of the many punishments of age is watching your own characteristics duplicated in your children. The inability to be serious, of which I was once so proud, is now one of the things I hate most about myself. It's not that I hate it in my children. More that I'm frightened by how comforting and familiar I find it. Oh, and I'm afraid that one day, like me, they'll wake up and ask themselves why they haven't answered any grand questions or been stirred by sweeping emotions.

It's not that I haven't, at times, been at the mercy of emotions I thought quite as grand as anyone else's. It's just that I distrust them. I have always been cautious about the actions they prompted. And now, looked at as I get closer and closer to fifty, so many of them seem to be the result of self-interest or fear. What is love? 'Tis not hereafter.

This all comes back to Estelle, I suppose. Being married for twenty-five years quite clearly indicates that you don't go in for the kind of love that leads to foolishness. A cautious little Englishman in his cautious little house.

And now, too late, as always, I want to be foolish. I want to be the thing I was not, could never be. I don't want to be the thing Estelle probably always saw I was – since women are so much clearer-sighted about us than we are about them. But because I am the way I am, I remain tied to this street, this house, this family, asking the same hopeless questions any other man in my situation asks, as he watches the last quarter of his life start to tick away. What did Laura say to Jakob today? And what was it Laura thought about Jakob on that waterslide? You know, don't you? You shouldn't take a relationship on trust, any relationship. You should subject it to the same ruthless, critical examination that, to young people, is a natural way of seeing. The old are weak from force of habit. I don't want to be old. I won't be old.

I made meatballs tonight. They went down quite well.


June 11th. 10 a.m. Weather still oppressive. Some distant thunder but no sign of rain. Birds cowering in hedge. No sign of sparrow.

*Estelle and Edwin at school. Jakob 'in Sicily'. Ruaighiury and Lucy on Embankment. Oliver, Aphrodite, etc. in shed. Laura downstairs.*

Don't know what Laura said to Jakob the other day but it has clearly scared him. He is staying with his old schoolfriend Bela Hortobagyi, who is a speechwriter for Peter Mandelson. I am about to go downstairs to lie to Laura. Not happy about this.

Estelle not helping to answer existential questions about the nature of our marriage. Having spent the early hours of the morning on the phone to Hamish – a conversation I was not allowed to hear – she has now gone off with Edwin to the school and Hotchkiss's production. Presumably to feast her eyes on the beloved Plonker.

The antidote must be administered tonight. Although I am not altogether sure about it. I put a little on my finger and nibbled at it while looking at my image in the mirror. I did not, I have to say, find myself totally repulsive. In fact I thought I looked pretty good for a man of my age.

## 11.30 a.m.

Phone call from Wainwright. Sound is, apparently, totally reintegrated with Vision. And all is as it was before. The only problem, according to Wainwright, is that they cannot make up their minds what to call it. I suggested 'THAT THING THAT USED TO BE THE BBC'. He told me that there is a rumour that Colin Cross is to be given back his old department and that I will once more be working for the Radio Drama Continuing Narrative Strand (Domestic). Changing all this round and then putting it back as it was must have cost them thousands. In notepaper alone. According to Wainwright this is all part of Spence's Second Law. What is this?

He did, however, say that Ashley Ramp was 'still dangerous' and, at some meeting or other, had talked of getting rid, not only of *General Practice*, but of all radio programmes longer than fifteen minutes, i.e. most of them. 'John Birt,' said Wainwright, 'is going to leave soon and Ramp may well end up with a very important job.'

Greatly saddened by the imminent departure of J. Birt. One of the few people with the intelligence to grasp what we are trying to do on *Practice*. Must fix up Ramp with thirtysomething. How?

## 5 p.m.

Have gone in myself to what Hotchkiss described as the 'stagger-through for *Dream*'. There is certainly quite a lot of staggering going on from the members of the cast and 'staggered' is probably the only word to describe the expression on the faces of the small audience who have gathered to watch it.

Hotchkiss seems to have lost confidence since he was told he could not have Nazi uniforms. The heart has gone out of him. He, like Estelle, only has eyes for Plonker. Plonker has just announced that he wants to dance on in his ass's head and 'hee-haw' at crucial moments of the action.

Hotchkiss and Estelle seem keen on this. Estelle made his head. It is amazingly realistic. The other day Ruaiertghrey wore it during dinner.

Edwin is about the only good thing in it although he does a bit too much winking and leering for my taste. Oberon is played by a large boy called Ffitch-Presley, who is, I am told, a very good Rugby player and Titania is played by Peter Lugg, the Boy Who Thinks He May Be Homosexual (and blatantly is). Hotchkiss had asked Ffitch-Presley to slap Titania on the cheek before his first line. Ffitch-Presley, who hates Lugg, gave the boy a forearm smash that laid him out on the floor.

Lugg was not really off the canvas until he got to the bit about the nine men's morris being filled up with mud. But he came back in style. When Ffitch-Presley gave his line about begging Titania's little changeling boy off her, Lugg, rather gamely, belted the Rugby captain on the nose. By the time we got to 'Fairies away!' Hotchkiss had to jump on to the stage and pull them off each other.

Snozzer was superb. He has modified his wings in order to enable them to flap lightly. This involves a sort of pulley system on his back and he spends nearly all his time on stage running round in circles and pulling on two ropes draped over his shoulders.

Only one bit of the original plans for promenading the show remains. For no apparent reason everyone rushes out of the theatre during the fairies' song in Act Two, Scene Two ('Beetles black approach not near,' etc.), but as the audience were not told to follow them, we all sat staring at an empty stage while, outside in the playground we could hear Snozzer yelling, 'Lulla, lulla, lullaby!' at the top of his voice.


## 9 p.m.

In the Roland Dune Memorial Area for hot Chinese snacks from Hong, who is wearing a fruit-salad shirt and a Panama hat. While Hong capers around — 'Hotchkiss clearly in love with Plonker, no?' — I plan to stick close to Estelle, with the love antidote held firmly in my jacket pocket.

Luckily Hong is serving some kind of fruit cup and it should be fairly easy to pour all the erotic deterrent into one glass, garnish it with a few bits of pineapple and get it into Estelle's hand. Must get her to concentrate on Plonker. If it is anything like the potion, the antidote presumably only works if you are looking at the subject while you knock it back.

335

## 10 p.m.

Writing this in Gents. Oh God!

I poured the antidote into her glass and only then realized Plonker seemed to have disappeared. I grabbed her arm, anxious for her not to actually drink until I could get him in her sights, and Estelle wheeled round on me angrily. 'What is the matter with you?' she said. 'Why are you behaving like some fussy old man? Will you stop trying to point me in the direction in which you want me to go?' I said, lightly and unthreateningly, that perhaps she would like to see Plonker to give him a few notes on his performance.

This seemed to incense her still further. 'Notes?' she said. 'Notes? What do you mean, notes? Plonker doesn't need notes. He is brilliant. He is absolutely superb.' I said I agreed. He was, I said, absolutely superb. The bit where he ate a large bundle of straw was brilliant. The speech about Algeria was little short of a masterpiece. And the five songs were not a moment too long. Some of the things he did with the bellows were side-splittingly funny. But, I said, perhaps, once or twice, some of the things he got up to with them – especially administering the enema to Mustardseed – might give offence. Not, I said, to broad-minded people like us, but, at a school play there were always a few moaning minnies and dismal jimmies. And, of course, the Headmaster. We should not forget the Headmaster. He was, according to the publicity anyway, a deeply religious man.

Estelle turned her tanned, strong-featured face on me. Her large black eyes sparkled with rage as she said, her slight northern accent becoming, as usual, more pronounced with anger. 'You pillock!' she said. 'You utter and complete pillock!' And now allowing her eyes to unlock from mine she sank nearly half a pint of a substance chemically designed to make you loathe whatever you happen to be looking at when you are drinking it. After she had drained the glass she stopped. I had the impression she was seeing me for the first time. And that she did not like what she saw. 'You're a turd really, aren't you?' she went on. 'You're really just an utter and complete turd, aren't you, essentially? A ghastly little sort of . . . nerd . . . when it comes down to it, aren't you?!' I said I thought that that was not really a fair description. Estelle drained the last of the antidote. She stared into my eyes.

336

'What,' she said, 'is so great about you? What is the point of you?'

I did not find it easy to answer this question. After a while, I said, 'I'm a . . . a . . . human being I suppose!' She seemed to have her doubts about this. 'Just about,' she said, 'but what else have you got to give? What else is there about you that makes your presence on this planet at all necessary?' 'Well,' I said slowly, 'I think I try to be . . . you know . . . kind to people . . . and . . . er . . . decent! And I try to give . . . you know . . . pleasure!' 'To whom?' said Estelle crisply. 'Well,' I said, 'for example . . . to the . . . er listeners . . . the . . . er . . . fans of *General Practice*, for example!'

Estelle gave a short, mirthless laugh. Aware that her reactions were not necessarily an indication of how she really felt I did not lose my temper. 'I think,' I said, 'that I am a fairly ordinary bloke. A fairly typical guy. Who is trying to . . . you know . . . live his life and so on . . .' She was still looking at me as if this was the first occasion in twenty-five years when she had really had the chance to stand back and study the person with whom she was living. 'Why though?' she said. 'Why?'

'That,' I said, 'is a hard question. But . . . er . . .'

The conversation rather petered out after that. I don't think she has addressed more than two words to me for the rest of this evening. She has been on the phone to Hamish. I am sitting here looking down into Mafeking Road, trying to come up with an answer to her last question. Why am I living? I have not, as yet, come up with a convincing answer.


June 12th. 11 a.m. Still humid and hot. Still no sign of rain. Clouds now positively Gothic in scale. All birds cowering in hedges, trees, etc.

*Estelle in studio with Hamish. Jakob 'in Baggage Reclaim'. Ruigherhy and Lucy in East Grinstead. Laura still downstairs. Edwin, Oliver, Aphrodite, Alec, Baldwin, Bolt, etc., in Waitrose.*

Have given the shed contingent £100 and told them to do the weekly shopping. Edwin is in charge of them. The last time I went to Waitrose with Edwin he bought nine bottles of Ribena, ten bottles of Hellman's Mayonnaise and twelve packets of frozen chips. I have told him this must not happen again.

Estelle went out early after giving me brief, puzzled look of distaste. If I had to caption it I think I would go for 'ARE YOU STILL HERE?' Am resolved to get potion down her in order to counteract antidote.

Good conversation this morning with Leo and Witchett, the Writer Who Has Too Many Opinions and Keeps Expressing Them. I visited them at their appallingly twee two-up, two-down house in White Hart Lane in Barnes. Pictures of naked men all over the place and a bathroom that led me to suppose that here were yet another couple who were shagging at least three times a day.

At one point, I grab a baseball bat off Randall and Wallace and hurl it after them. I will give the ensuing scene verbatim.

ESMOND: Take that, you Scotch bastards!
> *We hear Esmond grunt as he throws the bat. There is a dreadful scream followed by FX footsteps. Esmond's voice comes in.*
ESMOND: Oh my God!
> *We hear his voice shake with emotion.*
ESMOND: Pamela! My darling! Pamela!

I have ended nearly thirty years of marriage in the only decent way possible. By braining my wife with a baseball bat. Pamela, Witchett tells me, lingers on for a few episodes' but is 'a dribbling wreck', something that Susan Vullermeyer should be able to convey fairly well. At the moment the plan is for her to die peacefully, although Vullermeyer, who is not happy about going, has requested 'a series of seizures'. I told Witchett that Susan could not act a mild attack of asthma, let alone a seizure. Leo showed me the first draft of a scene between us at the hospital, in which I do most of the talking. It is actually very moving.

ESMOND: Oh Pamela, my sweet! Pamela!
PAMELA: I —
ESMOND: Don't talk! Don't even try to talk!
PAMELA: I —
ESMOND: You must save your strength, darling! Oh my God! To think of all those years we shared! To think of our marriage, Pamela!

All those shared joys and sorrows! The night our daughter was born! My God! Do you remember?

I then go on about our daughter at some length, without ever mentioning her name. I discovered this was because neither Leo nor Witchett could remember what it was. Although I was acting in the series when Pamela gave birth I could not remember either. This was curious. We could all remember that she went to a posh school, went into teaching, revitalized the Ship public house when she worked in its catering department, got pregnant by a bloke called Herbert and then went to Australia to work in graphic design. But no one could remember her name – perhaps because Esmond and Pamela have paid her no attention whatsoever since she moved to the other side of the world.

Apparently our series has been around for so long that most of our listeners have forgotten almost everything about us. 'This might enable us,' said Leo, eyes bright, 'to take you in a new direction. Perhaps you always wanted to be an architect!' I quashed this idea.

The other tremendous news is that Witchett seems to have developed an antipathy to Pilfrey. He twice said he thought Pilfrey was 'smug' and once said something that could be interpreted as suggesting that Pilfrey was about to come down with another disease. I hope it is an improvement on apparent Moeran's syndrome. I said I thought if he caught anything it should be quick – and mentioned the possibility of the ebola virus. Apparently all your orifices spout blood and your skin goes purple. There is no going back.

12.20 p.m.

Message on machine from Jakob. He told me to tell Laura he was 'still in Baggage Reclaim at Heathrow'. In fact he and Hortobagyi are in Camden Town, recovering from thirteen pints of Hochschule 'Mulekick' lager. Laura said, 'Is he really in Baggage Reclaim, Paul?' I said, hating myself for this, 'That is where he says he is!'

Second message on machine from the thirtysomething asking me if I would like to come with her to visit Good Old Steve in hospital. This afternoon. Did not really want to but felt I should. If she sees him on her own she will only give him lots and lots of love and, from the sound of things, this may well finish him off. Told her I have to be at Beeb by five, which is a lie but gives me chance to get away in case she tries to offer me lots and lots and lots of love as well.

## 4 p.m.

Writing this on a seat in the Reception of the hospital where Good Old Steve is confined. This woman is impossible. I have to get Steve out of her clutches and get her into someone else's clutches (or someone else into her clutches) as soon as humanly possible. Otherwise Steve may die and I may well end up in her clutches. Which will almost certainly finish me off. Who knows into whose clutches she may fall (or, indeed, who will fall into her clutches) after I am no longer there to stop her clutching people.

She did quite a lot of clutching this afternoon.

'Tell me about yourself! What's happening in your life?' she said, with great intensity. I started, for some reason, to tell her about Jakob and Laura, and, in a roundabout way, about how hard Jakob finds it to say what he is feeling. As do I, I suppose. 'Sometimes, Paul,' she said, giving me an appraising look, 'I have the impression you're a long, long way away from me . . .' 'Do you?' I said, my voice trembling slightly. 'I do,' said the thirtysomething, 'I do! It's like you're . . . on a raft . . . on a lake . . . drifting away . . . or . . . in a balloon sort of . . . rising in the air!' 'I feel,' I said firmly, 'very close to you! Almost uncomfortably so!' She smiled gently and, once again, linked her arm in mine. 'I think,' she said finally, 'that you're like Steve really. You just need lots and lots and lots and lots of love!'

Then, to my relief, we found ourselves at Steve's bed. 'How are you?' said the thirtysomething. 'I'm . . . feeling . . . er . . .' said Steve, 'as if I'm . . . sort of . . .' The thirtysomething thrust her face into his, 'Drifting away?' she asked eagerly. 'Sort of floating up and off . . . as if you were on a kind of . . . barge . . .' At which Steve's eyes closed. I thought for a moment he had actually stiffed. But, as far as I could tell, he seemed to be still breathing. I managed to get her away but she decided she would like to 'accompany me to Broadcasting House', where she has to meet someone called (can this be?) Ithaca. Even as I write these words she emerges, her red hair scraped back off her forehead, her huge eyes intently

340

scanning the crowd for my face. She quite clearly still has lots and lots and lots of love to give and, this afternoon, I am right in line for most of it.

## 6 p.m.

As I was walking into Broadcasting House with the thirtysomething in tow, Ashley Ramp emerged. He glared at me and then his eye caught the thirtysomething's. Definite erotic interest, I felt. This was the obvious moment to effect an introduction, possibly along the lines of 'Hullo – this is a thirtysomething who is into rubber, would you like to shag her?' but, of course, I was unable to remember the woman's name. I opened and closed my mouth like a goldfish and said, 'Ashley! Hi!'

I was also keenly aware that I must try very hard not to give him the impression that I was at all aware that he is a hunchback. It was important to keep things moving, to not let my face settle into the kind of sneer it seems to naturally wear in repose – especially when people with humps are around.

'Great to see you!' I heard myself saying. 'Really great to see you!' Ramp dilated his nostrils in distaste and then stared, with almost open hunger, at the thirtysomething. I don't think I have ever seen anyone more clearly signalling that he needed to be introduced.

I gave his hunch one more polish and, unable to look either him or the the thirtysomething in the face, fled in the direction of the stairs. Am writing this in the Gents on the third floor. Will not emerge until am sure that both of them have left the building.

## 7 p.m.

Stayed in Gents for forty-five minutes. Very peaceful. I may make a habit of this. I sat looking at the floor while people came in, used the facilities and departed. Not all of it was pleasant – there were some pretty farmyard-like noises, including one man who began by making a noise I have only previously heard produced by novice euphonium players – but I have always found the noise of lavatory cisterns curiously calming.

Writing this in Wainwright's office. He pointed me towards a Telefax message which read – 'Colin Cross, who has been working on Special

Projects out of Room B34576, will now head up the newly restructured Radio Drama Continuing Narrative Strand (Domestic), which includes the popular *General Practice*. Colin will be working to the newly reintegrated Sound and Vision, now renamed The Unified BBC, and its In-House Directorate Controllers – Ashley Ramp and Howard Porda. Ashley and Howard are now Joint Acting Heads of the Core Directorate Policy Unit, which will be looking at a wide range of topics as they implement our paper *Radio in a Digital Age*.'

Wainwright says Cross has been locked in B34576 with three hundred samosas ever since his leaving party. I do not believe this. He also says that Ramp is increasingly powerful and may win a straight fight with Porda. 'He is an angry, ambitious, unsatisfied man!' said Wainwright. Must get him rubber fun soonest.

## 8 p.m.

Message on machine from Jakob. He tells me to say he is still in Baggage Reclaim. I tell him no one will believe this. They will know it is a ploy to avoid seeing Laura. Jakob says, 'I guess,' then he adds, 'there was some kind of commitment' in Richmond Park. I say, 'Does this mean you guys are back together?' Jakob says, 'Who can tell oh Slippery one?' I say, 'This is none of my business, Jake –' (something I haven't called him since he was eight), and he says, sounding very sad and tired, 'It is your business. You're my father. Of course it is your business.' What am I going to say to Laura?

June 13th. 10 a.m. Still hot and humid. The storm threatens but does not appear. Shirt sticking to skin. Sparrow hopped out of hedge looking knackered. Then hopped back.

*Estelle at Craftgirls. Ruaighruyr and Lucy in bed. Jakob 'still in Baggage Reclaim'. Edwin upstairs revising. Oliver, Aphrodite, Bolt, Baldwin, etc., packing. Me in study. Laura also in study.*

A message on the machine from my mother. It runs as follows –

MOTHER: Paul – it's me! (*Long pause.*) It's Granny, Paul! Me! (*Even longer pause.*) What do you think of Tony Blair? (*Long pause while she seems to wait for the machine to reply.*) I don't reckon much to him. (*Short pause. Distant noise of hammering.*) He's too touchy-feely for me. I don't like that. (*Pause. More hammering.*) Do you hear that? (*More hammering.*) It's hammering. Do you hear it? (*More hammering. She sniffs morosely. Long pause.*) Do you remember that woman who used to come out for lunch on Sunday? Who wore those trousers and that green floppy hat? She was Beryl's daughter. You remember Beryl. I went through the war with Beryl and then she married that Portuguese man. I didn't like him. (*Pause.*) Anyway her name was Sheila. The daughter, Sheila. Do you remember her coming out to lunch one day with that dog of hers? (*Long pause.*) Maybe you were too young I don't know but you were there when she came. (*Short pause. More hammering.*) Anyway she's dead.

Laura sitting on my sofa. She has been crying rather a lot. She does not believe that Jakob is still in Baggage Reclaim. Once more, just as she left for work, Estelle came over to me and studied my face very carefully, as if seeing it for the first time. Then she reached up and stroked my face. I said, 'Are you all right, love?' And she said, 'Too old. That's all. Too old.'


10.35 a.m.

Am writing this in the car outside Carslake Road. It seems that the house at which I called the other week, in search of Wesley Jones, is none other than the abode of Wodge! I learned this because of a slip by young Edwin this morning – who foolishly asked me to give him and Snozzer a lift 'to Wodge's place in Carslake Road'. It was then I remembered seeing Snozzer near the mysterious woman's house. I have dropped them off without saying anything.

No wonder the woman looked familiar. Mrs Wodge is the spitting image of her daughter. I can only assume that Wodge or Snozzer or Edwin or Lulu, or possibly all four of them, have been deliberately deceiving me into thinking the man Jones had acquired an independent existence. Now I come to think of it – the figure at the opening night at the Royal Court did have a look of Snozzer about him.

All this from a youth to whom I have entrusted my professional career! I am too trusting.

There is, though, I have to admit, a certain style about Snozzer. I cannot find it in my heart to be angry with him, or indeed with any of them. Like all other middle-aged men, I think I deserve everything I get.

## 1 p.m.

Back at the house to see off Oliver and Aphrodite, who are on their way to Tunisia. I think Bolt and the others are going to Romania. I asked Oliver if he expected problems at the airport. He said, 'With whom?' I didn't like to say 'the police', but Oliver, who has great natural charm, supplied the word for me. He said, 'I will have no trouble with them. I'm not using my own passport.' I didn't like to ask whose he was using. Went upstairs, after we had seen them off, to check that mine was still there. It was.

Lucy and Ruaieiurgy 'resting' after hard day with the homeless in East Grinstead. Apparently the East Grinstead homeless are a pretty tough bunch.

## 3.30 p.m.

Laura still very distressed. My Son the Complete Bastard! I rang him on his mobile and said, 'Where are you? More importantly, where shall I say you are?' He said, 'Baggage Reclaim!' I said, 'No one will believe you have been in Baggage Reclaim for two days!' At first he tried to tell me that this was entirely possible. Then he said, 'No! They won't! But hey!' I cannot deal with him when he is being brittle and facetious. I wonder why this is. Laura tells me her Mum wants to have a drink with me. She says, apparently, I am a really nice person 'who listens'. Can this be why I am not getting a shag?

Tried to get out of Laura what happened with Jakob in Richmond Park. She spoke, evasively, I thought, of deer.

## 6 p.m.

Estelle rang and said she was 'leaving the office right now'. This means she is leaving in about three hours. I have suggested we go out for a quiet dinner next week to celebrate our anniversary. I said, in a very quiet and unthreatening manner, that, as nobody seemed very interested in our anniversary or my birthday it was 'best not to make a meal of it'. Estelle said, 'What's the matter with you?' I said, 'There is nothing the matter with me. I am simply suggesting that as nobody seems very interested in –' At this point she cut me off, saying, 'You just said that! You're repeating yourself!' 'People do repeat themselves!' I said. 'Especially as they get older they repeat themselves a lot. And when they have been married for twenty-five years they probably seem to do nothing but repeat themselves. Because they have a more detailed knowledge of everything the other person has said than anyone else in the world. You have probably heard every single word combination of which I am capable. Twice.' There was a silence and Estelle said, 'Yes. I probably have.'

There was quite a long silence after this. Eventually, I said, in a quiet and unthreatening manner, 'Well. Would you like to go out to a restaurant and hear me repeat myself? Or shall I stay in and do it?' Estelle said, 'I don't mind really either way.' 'In that case,' I said, 'I suggest we scrub the whole thing.' Estelle said, 'What thing?' I said, 'All of it. The marriage. You know. All twenty-five years of it. Shall we celebrate it by getting divorced?' There was quite a long silence. Then Estelle said, 'OK. If that's what you want to do.'

I have not called her back. I suppose it is possible that both of us mean it. I have never believed you can say things you do not mean. To say things is to mean them, isn't it?

Living and dying is all about being alone. Other people are like the noises we hear in a city or the reflection of flames on the wall of a cave – a distraction that can seem like the main event.

I have just tramped round the house – Ruairghy, Lucy, Laura and Edwin have all gone to the pub. There seems to be even more furniture missing. Perhaps Estelle was planning to leave me even before I slipped her the antidote. In desperation I rang Gustave. The woman who answered the phone told me he was in hospital. Sudden rush of sympathy for Gustave. Dear old Gustave! Our years together! The day I got the part of Autolycus at the RSC, etc. I asked the woman if he was seriously ill. She said he had piles. Loss of sympathy for Gustave.

June 14th. 11 a.m. Continuing hot and sticky and cloudy. Wimbledon uncomfortably like Florida. Even the birds are sweating. The sparrow staggered out of his hedge, tottered around the front lawn and crawled back in again.

*Estelle having 'serious conversation with Hamish'. Ruairghery and Lucy at Sleeping Bag. Jakob 'in Crouch End with Hortobagyi'. Edwin performing at open-air rock concert. Shed empty. Me here.*

Estelle and I have not referred to our telephone conversation of last night – a common pattern when we have both been saying unspeakable things to each other. Once, however, I suspect we would have tried to acknowledge the row, even to resolve it in some way. Now we both pretend it has simply not happened.

She did, however, agree to go out with me on the 21st. I suppose we can decide whether to get divorced then. Perhaps, like that guy in *The Loneliness of the Long Distance Runner*, we both want to make almost all of the course, right up to the finishing line, and then, just before the end, abandon the pretence that anything is for ever, or that love, nowadays, can still produce its much-vaunted trick of making two people one.

The new episode has just arrived. At the end of it I seem to be climbing up a rope ladder into a moving helicopter. Wallace and Randall are shooting at me from a nearby building.

1 p.m.

Found Baldwin in shed. When I asked him what he was doing there he said he 'didn't fancy Romania'. I told him to clear off and get a job. Howard Porda rang, asking to meet me in Television Centre as he has to go there to talk about strategy. Have agreed to this.

## 3 p.m.

It proved almost impossible to get into TV Centre, as they have redesigned it to make sure that you always come into the building at the farthest point from where you want to go. They have, however, installed a hairdresser's, coffee bar, shops, etc., on the premises – presumably because they know that, once inside, you will probably find it impossible to get out again. I got lost and found myself walking down a corridor lined with pictures of film editors, cameramen, etc., 'at work', looking glamorous, etc. Although I am told they have fired them all.

Writing this in BBC Club. A changed building. Lots of posters telling you how great it all is. There is almost no one over the age of thirty here – apart from one derelict behind the bar with whom I felt deep, instinctive sympathy. I think I am the nearest thing to a celebrity in the place. Just had meeting with Howard Porda, who arrived with Shirley. She was wearing a miniskirt. It does not suit her but I was tactful about this.

Apparently Ramp fancies Howard's Mum, i.e. Stella Badyass. One of the reasons he hates me so much, according to Howard, is that he blames Estelle and me for the fact that he hasn't got together with Stella. I asked him whether his Mum had a rooted prejudice against hunchbacks and Howard said she had not. 'The problem is,' he said, 'that she fancies that friend of yours apparently. Steve whatever his name is.'

If I can get Ramp off with the thirtysomething and Steve off with Stella Badyass I think it will strengthen Howard's hand with Ramp, i.e., make the hunchback less bitter, angry at world, etc. Howard said he is having a lot of problems with Ramp, who is, apparently, trying to worm his way into John Birt's confidence, playing on his well-known sympathy for the underdog, hunchbacks, etc.

Should I write to J. B.? I know I am on the edge of great things. I do not want Ramp to spoil them.


## 5 p.m.

Drink with Stella Badyass at a pub near Craftgirls, a place that, she reminded me as we sat down, I still have not visited even though Estelle has worked there for six months. She looked at me sideways from under her fringe, and, in her familiar, small, doleful voice, asked me if I found

Estelle's success threatening. I said, 'Very.' It's not quite what I think but it seemed to be the right answer.

Fixed up lunch with her and 'friend of mine who wants to meet her'. Can't wait to see her face when Steve walks in. If he can walk by then. Great feeling of virtue, happiness, etc., even though own life is falling apart. Here's to a new quest – to get other people off with each other! As opposed to the familiar, hopeless search for a never-to-be-recalled shag for myself.

Writing this in pub. Stella has just gone.

## 6.30 p.m.

Ruairehriuy was here when I got back. He was surrounded by pieces of paper, slide-rules, graphs, etc. It turned out he was doing a budget for Sleeping Bag. They are in competition with no less than two hundred other charities designed to help London's homeless. I said there were probably a lot of people sleeping rough. Reuireghy informed me that, according to the 1991 census, there were less than four hundred of them – which works out at about one charity for every two people. Bolt and Alec presumably. He said that they had to get their business plan in by the end of the month, and, sounding rather like a BBC manager, waved a spending graph at me.

He has commissioned a black and white photograph of Bolt and Alec lying in a gutter (I think it is in Mafeking Road although it is hard to tell). Bolt is waving a half-empty bottle of Jack Daniel's and Alec appears to be in the middle of vomiting. They are both wearing fragments of carpet which, I think, come from one of the spare rooms upstairs. The caption reads, 'He is twenty. He is an alcoholic. He could be you.' It appears that Sleeping Bag have decided to target young alcoholics on the theory that we feel sympathetic to drunks – as most of us are drunks. I said I thought it looked like an advert intended to get people drinking seriously and Riuaierhgy said that that would not be a problem. Some of their funding comes from a large brewing company.

Jakob has been at an unknown address for a few days and, when asked, says he is 'with Hortobagyi in Crouch End'. I think, however, that he and Laura may have been in telephone communication because she hasn't asked me about him. Today he suddenly made an appearance with Mr

Scarrotto, who seems to have an affinity with Ruaierghry. 'It's good,' he said, tugging reflectively at his earring, 'to see a young person doing good in the community. You should be proud of your sons, Mr Slippery!' I said I was extremely proud of them. 'God forbid,' said Mr Scarrotto, 'that anything should happen to them!' 'God forbid!' I said.

Jakob told me later that he has been having a few 'business disagreements' with Scarrotto and Vanelli. I was rather disturbed about this and told him to be careful. He put his arm round me. 'Listen,' he said, 'you are my father and I love you. You are part of my family. Do not worry about Mr Scarrotto or Mr Vanelli. If they do anything foolish bad things will happen to them. I believe that.' Then he said something quite long and complicated in Italian. His Italian has really improved amazingly. He was never good at languages at school.

We talked about Laura. He says he had to 'hide up in order to think'. He seems at least to be thinking about it seriously. For the first time tonight he had what I would call a friendly conversation with Lucy. Although this seemed to irritate Ruigueghruy enormously. He described Jakob to me, fortunately not in his hearing, as 'a fast worker'. Lucy made anchovy toast.


## 10 p.m.

Estelle back by nine. Guarded with me. Lucy and Laura came round this evening. Anxious to make things go well between Jakob and Laura, I tried to act my age. I ended up making amazingly middle-aged remarks about state of traffic, foolishness of drivers, routes from Cheam to Wimbledon, etc. Edwin openly laughed at this. Ended up staring at table in complete silence and was accused by everyone of being miserable old git. Edwin in bad mood as he and Plinth performed at an open-air rock concert organized by a Christian youth club in Merton Park. There were only two people in the audience.

Just remember – when your dad sits there stone-faced, not contributing to the conversation, it is probably because he is scared of making a fool of himself. At times like this I recall my own father's mealtime silences with a sharp mixture of love, loathing and nostalgia. I am turning into him, I suppose, the way we all do. He was – is this in any way significant? – a vicar who didn't quite make it.

Could I, perhaps, turn into my mother? I need to work on my answerphone technique.

Both girls smelled even nicer than usual. Laura's upper half was astonishingly prominent. I was so keen not to be seen to look at it I turned my face away when handing her the vegetables and got courgettes all down her jersey. Much harsh criticism from Estelle for this.

Estelle and I still guarded with each other. Or rather, avoiding subjects which we both know may cause offence to the other. Towards the end of the meal I could see she was feeling too tired to get up from the table and she leaned over and touched me, very lightly, on the arm, as she asked me to get her something. Something enormously touching and sad about this gesture. The beginnings of shared old age I suspect. Have now got so paranoid about lack of shagging that I am consciously following internal domestic routes that suggest I am not interested in it, i.e. going to bed twenty minutes later than Estelle, running out of the bathroom when she is in it, etc.

## 11.30 p.m.

Jakob, Ruairghry, Laura and Lucy all off to pub. Was hoping they would ask me but they didn't. It now occurs to me that the reason they used to do so was because they were all too broke to buy drinks themselves. A moment of resentment about this, followed by the frighteningly easy acceptance of the fact that, as a father of young adults, your only role is probably to buy drinks.

Jakob and Laura still v. tense with each other. Is Lucy still interested in Jakob?

Edwin has had to do a draft essay on something called 'Media Texts: Food'. He has to take the exam tomorrow. He has come up with a two-page masterpiece on the evils of junk food, which begins, rather brilliantly, in mid-flow, thus – 'Hamburgers are very bad for you and pictures of thin women make it harder for people to accept that if they eat them they will get fat which they will also the lack of fibre can cause fatal diseases such as cancer which will probably kill you in the end!' He gets pretty worked up about the wickedness of Burger King, BSE, etc. Although something in his tone sounded, I thought, suspiciously like political correctness. When I asked him what he really thought of junk food, he said, 'I love it. Can't get enough. Where shall we go?' I told him he should write this in the exam and he looked at me pityingly. 'They will never pass me if I say I like junk food!' he said. 'This is an exam! They want stuff about apples and shit!'


June 15th. 11.30 a.m. Will it never rain? Unbelievably hot and close. There were even rumbles of thunder last night. Clouds low and bruise-violet in colour. No sign of any birds.

*Estelle 'at business meeting in Madrid'. Jakob also in Madrid. (Why?) Rueiugheiury and Lucy and Laura asleep. All, as far as I know, in separate beds. Edwin at school. Me in garden, writing this.*

Nine days to go to the big 5–0.

I rang up Steve, who is now off his tubes. I told him I could fix him up with a middle-aged woman. He did not seem overjoyed about this. He said, 'The principal task is to get rid of the current incumbent!' I said I thought I had found the perfect person for his thirtysomething – a young(ish), sexually voracious hunchback who was into rubber and had a high-profile job at the BBC. Steve said he thought he sounded perfect.

'She was here last night,' he said, his voice sounding agonized, 'telling me I was like . . . drifting away on a barge or sliding off down a pole or . . . falling over a cliff or whatever it was . . . she was right here by the bed, giving me lots and lots and lots of love! I couldn't get rid of her!'

I was frightened for a moment that he might be about to have a relapse. I finally told him that Stella Badyass fancies him. He did not appear to remember who she was but said, 'If she is over forty send her round!' This is good news!


12.30 p.m.

Edwin called, asking for lift later. He told me that he and Lulu are heading for a crisis in their relationship. I said, 'Join the club!' He gave a brief, incredulous laugh at this. Call on machine from Norman Proek asking to meet me for drink. Hope he is not going to assault me.

## 12.45 p.m.

Another message from Mrs Proek. I have arranged to meet her in the Dog and Fox fifteen minutes after Norman. Feel a bit like a dentist. What is going on?


## 2.30 p.m.

Writing this in the Dog and Fox.

Laura's father arrived, as I might have expected, precisely on time. He was wearing his best suit and had the respectful, respectable air of one of the Peggotty family. If he had been carrying a hat he would have turned its brim in his hands. I put this sudden access of humility down to retirement. Or maybe I just see him differently now. 'Will you have a pint, Norman?' I said, as if his first name was the most natural thing in the world. 'I don't mind if I do!' he said. 'The traffic was terrible getting here!' 'Was it?' I said.

We were both really into this conversation. It was nice, I felt, being in a pub with another boring middle-aged man, able to talk freely and frankly about the state of the A3 without being interrupted by fashion-conscious teenagers. I was genuinely enjoying myself. 'The thing is,' Norman said after we had taken the first sip of our pints, 'I think it's the frequency of the feeder roads!' 'That could be it!' I said. There was another silence. Then Norman said, 'Still – we both don't want to bore for England on the subject of traffic, do we?' We both laughed a lot at this.

'You know,' said Norman, when we had both drunk deeply again, 'I used to think you were a real little shit!' 'I gathered!' I said. 'And I expect you thought I was a bit of an oaf!' 'I did,' I said, pleasantly, 'I thought you were a complete oaf!' We both shook our heads amiably. 'What did you dislike about me most?' I said. Norman thought. 'I think,' he said, 'I thought you were a bit stuck-up. Vain. Thought you were better than other people.' I nodded seriously. 'Yes,' I said, 'I can give that impression!' We both laughed. 'I thought you were mad! Completely crazy! Violent!' I said. Norman laughed lightly. 'Actually,' he said after a while, 'I think I am.'

I looked, slightly nervously, towards the door of the pub. It was full of kids of about my sons' ages. I looked at Norman, as if for the first time. A big, slightly blotched face – like mine, coarsened with exposure to wind and alcohol – hair greying at the temples. An angry look, too, as if its owner didn't want any of these things to happen to it. He must have been a good-looking man once, I found myself thinking.

He started to play with his beer mat. 'It's funny,' he said, 'how quickly thirty years goes. Bert Rachnowski and I were at school together. Bert married his childhood sweetheart. I married mine.' 'Is that right?' I said, with an uncanny feeling that I knew what he was going to say next. As it transpired, I did. 'And I was always in love with her. Bert's girl. Isn't that funny? I was always in love with Bert's girl.' 'It isn't funny,' I said, 'it happens all the time. The wrong people marry the wrong people. All the time.' He looked up at me sharply. 'Did you marry the wrong person?' he said. I looked him straight in the eye. 'No,' I said, 'I didn't. I'm a very lucky man.' 'Yes,' said Norman, 'I think you are.'

There was another companionable silence. I said, 'Are you still in love with her?' Norman lifted his face to mine. 'As a matter of fact,' he said, 'I am. I think it's why I make such a fuss of Laura. It's why I get so irritable. You've been kind to my girl, Paul. It's all a mess. *Si la jeunesse savait, si la vieillesse pouvait!* ' Something in my expression must have told him I was the kind of snob who didn't expect a rat-catcher to quote French at me, because he looked up sharply. 'I'm not just a Blue Nun and Happy Eater kind of a person!' he said. 'No!' I said.

Norman was speaking again. 'Do you have a . . . disappointment?' I looked at him. 'I'd like to have been a better actor . . .' I said. 'In fact I sometimes wonder whether I should have been an actor at all.' 'Actor . . . rat-catcher . . .' said Norman glumly. 'It's all the same in the end!' I wrinkled my nose slightly, to indicate that I might not entirely agree with this remark. I felt a need to get this conversation back on track. 'Have you ever told . . . er . . . Bert's wife about this?' 'Never!' said Norman. 'I think you should!' I said.

I stared over his right shoulder. He was sitting with his back to a large trellis, decorated with artificial flowers. As I looked past him a face rose up into view. It was Mrs Proek. 'You think I should tell her?' said Norman. The head nodded. 'I think you should!' I said. 'And what about Gwen? Would Gwen be able to take it?' said Norman. The head grinned and nodded. 'I think,' I said, 'she would!'

When he had gone Mrs Proek wriggled into view. She was grinning broadly. 'You're funny!' she said. 'You've got such a peculiar, pompous manner. But really you're like some Dutch uncle, going round, trying to be kind and nice to people!' I said I didn't fancy being a Dutch uncle. She put her hand on mine. 'What's the matter with you?' she said. 'Why do you get this lost look sometimes?' I didn't answer. 'Are you really in love with that wife of yours?' said Mrs Proek, with the sudden brutality women can affect when talking of each other. 'Didn't you hear me tell your husband I was?' I said.

I sounded, I now realize, defensive.


## 5.30 p.m.

Have written a letter to Ashley Ramp. It reads as follows –

Dear Ashley Ramp,
   You do not know my name. My name doesn't matter. What counts are my feelings. I had the pleasure of seeing you in Broadcasting House the other day in the company of Paul Slippery (God knows what I was doing with him!). I just felt I had to write. I've never done this before. But I felt such a strong feeling coming off you as you looked at me and what I was wearing, I felt I had to!
   Are you, perhaps, a kindred spirit? Rubber has always, for me, had a powerful sensuality. I am not ashamed of my feelings in this regard but it is often difficult to find like-minded individuals!
   I must confess, too, that I am also attracted to men in high places. By which I refer, not to their elevation above sea level but to 'powerful' individuals such as those responsible for steering and guiding large corporations, such as the one in which we both find ourselves working. The idea of such a man clad in rubber garments is almost irresistible to me! I feel weak at the prospect. I am not saying, by the way, that I am not excited by the possibility of myself wearing rubber. As far as I am concerned – the more the merrier!

I obviously do not wish to give my name. Do you
remember me?

I was wearing a sleeveless dress, am a
'thirtysomething' with red hair which I wear well back
from my forehead and, from the way you were looking at
me, I think you will remember me!

If you decide to look me up, Paul Slippery knows where
to find me. But please, please, do not mention this
letter. I feel terribly forward writing it! But I would
very much like to go out for a 'quiet evening' and talk
about things we might have in common . . .

Yours
An Impertinent
Thirtysomething!

If this does not do the trick nothing will.

## 7.30 p.m.

Letter in the late post from my Personnel Officer. I apparently have an Annual Assessment with Karl, or Shirley as I must get used to calling her. My Personnel Officer — a girl called Norma, whom I have never met, encloses the following chart which I am supposed to return to her. She will then give it to Shirley.

There is a huge blank sheet of paper headed 'OBJECTIVES'. I have written a single sentence in the middle of it. It reads 'My objective is to stay alive.'

Rueirguiry came back wearing a suit! He says that Sleeping Bag has now a 'strict dress code' and as he is involved in the sponsorship end of the operation he must look 'smart at all times'. He asked me if I knew any members of the royal family. I said I didn't. 'Who do we know who's famous?' he then said. I said I had once seen Nick Hornby in the corridors of the BBC. He seemed excited by this.

We are growing apart I think. It is curious that charity work should have this effect.

355

## 10 p.m.

Estelle has just come back, with Jakob. What have they been up to in Madrid? They refused to say. Sudden rush of paranoia about whether Estelle has only been nice recently because she really is about to pack us in. Jakob tense with Laura, who seems to have been hiding in the house all day. Will they ever sort it out? Will Estelle and I? What about Edwin and Lulu? Why do I sort out other people's love lives and do so little about my own family's romantic affairs? Avoidance behaviour re real issue with Estelle – her affair with Hamish, shadowy nature of sexual intercourse between her and self, etc.?

Mr Scarrotto and Mr Vanelli have been involved in a car accident. They have, according to Jakob, had their legs broken. I got the impression, however, that this may have been done after the accident. Jakob says they were becoming very unreliable and that Benny the Greek was finding them 'difficult to deal with'. I asked whether he was going to see them in hospital and Jakob said they were not in hospital. This seemed, I thought, unusually stoical of them but Jakob said they were 'somewhere where no one could find them'. He said, too, that it was 'probably concrete overcoat time' for Vanelli, who has apparently been having some problems with his accountant, a man called Attila.

When I expressed concern about his associates, Jakob said he was moving out of the electrical business. He asked, for reasons that were not altogether clear, whether I had ever been to Malaga.

## 10.30 p.m.

Edwin back late from yet another dress rehearsal for *Midsummer Night's Dream*. Now that GCSEs are over Hotchkiss has devised a punishing schedule for the cast. We had a good quiet chat about him and Lulu. He says that he has decided to stick with her. I said I might come to the same conclusion about Estelle. Edwin looked at me and gave me his wolfish smile. 'You have to stick with her!' he said. 'You're married!' I said that that wasn't necessarily the case. 'Oh,' said Edwin, without apparent concern, 'divorce?' He looked at me shrewdly. 'I suppose that's a possibility!' he said. 'You do argue a lot!' I asked him, again, what Estelle was getting me for my fiftieth and he said 'some kind of suit I think'.

I sulked for a bit after this, which he seemed to find very amusing. I read him bits of the latest masterpiece from Leo and Witchett, in which I shoot my way out of a tight corner, claiming the lives of three Scottish drug dealers as I do so. The effect of all this is to make Pilfrey and the rest of them back at the practice pretty dull and uninspiring. They spend quite a lot of time discussing me — which I find very pleasing. Pilfrey is beginning to sound querulous. Leo and Witchett have mapped out about three months' worth of storylines, which Shirley has approved. I come back to the practice. Pamela is charged with attempted murder and, as a result of my hair-raising experiences, I am 'a tougher, more streetwise GP'. Leo says he sees me as Sippowitz in *NYPD Blue*. He also said that ratings are up and we had a good review in the *Yorkshire Post*. Edwin thinks I will become a national celebrity.

June 16th. 11.30 a.m. More unbearable heat and humidity. Grey haze above the roofs of Mafeking Road. Put out water for sparrow. Magpie got it.

*Estelle at Craftgirls. Ruigheiury and Lucy at Sleeping Bag. Jakob at Club Le Steel. Edwin retaking GCSE Irish Dancing. Laura on sofa downstairs. Bolt poss. in shed. Me in study.*

Did the Kronshoeg Breathing. It really works! Feel much better. Phone call from Gustave.

Creepy in the extreme. 'Just wondered how you were doing . . .' was his opening line. He went on to tell me that Pilfrey is no longer playing the sea slug from outer space. He was fired! Savage pleasure at this news. He wondered if I might be interested in a woodlouse in an upcoming animation from the people who wanted me to do the worm. It is, apparently, a long part. I said, in a superior tone of voice, that I was 'no longer playing insects'. Gustave then said he had been getting 'quite a lot of inquiries about me' and should he tell them he no longer represented me? I said I had hired another agent for public appearances but that I was prepared to accept work from Flaubert if 'it was of high enough quality'. He asked who the other agent was and I said, 'He's very young, very new, very unconventional. You'd like him.' Gustave sounded jealous and

*357*

impressed. If he doesn't find out he is also a sixteen-year-old schoolboy I should be able to use Snozzer as leverage. Apparently we have had several other good reviews and some hack has come out of the woodwork to announce that I am his favourite radio actor. My voice, it appears, has a weathered, suffering quality that 'sounds as if I have lived through pain'. I told Edwin this and he said, 'You have lived through pain! You live at 52 Mafeking Road. It is all pain at 52 Mafeking Road.' I went out and bought the paper for which this madman writes and cut out his review. It is only five lines long but I think I will have it blown up.

If I can sort out my sex/love life (are they the same thing?) then I will be able to face next week's birthday. Resolved to start feeding potion to Estelle in small quantities. If I can get enough of it in her bloodstream she will be feeling so randy and outgoing that, even if I have to wait in a queue with Plonker, etc., I am bound to cop a bit of it.


12 noon.

Call from Ramp. Gave him contact number for thirtysomething.

Article in paper about Viagra, the new wonder drug that gives you back sexual potency, etc., stimulates me to try to remember when I last had a hard-on. I am unable to do so.

What do I remember about me and Estelle then?

I know, for certain, that we were married in 1972 in a registry office in Wimbledon and that I wore a blue-striped suit. I know also that I wore yellow platform-soled shoes and that Estelle had her hair done in the kind of bob that you now only see on the head of the cabin crew of *Deep Space Nine*. This does not, on the face of it, seem a lot to show for twenty-five years of marriage.

Jakob has opened a restaurant called Club Le Steel (pretentious name I felt) and Estelle is with him as they are going to shoot some of the animated film there. I asked him, straight out, what was happening with Laura and he said 'he would be writing to her in a few days'. I said I thought this made her sound like a job applicant. He said, 'She is baby!' Beginning to have some sympathy for Mr Scarrotto.

## 12.30 p.m.

Ran Laura back to East Cheam, where I am writing this. She was wearing the high-necked apricot T-shirt and carrying a paperback copy of *L'Etranger* – in French! She seems calm about Jakob. As I dropped her off she shrugged and said, 'He has to make his decision. We all do, don't we? You decide to love someone really, don't you?' I thought this amazingly wise – although I may just have been responding to the T-shirt. They are both, I suppose, cooler customers than Ruairghry and Lucy.

Norman asked me in. The Rachnowskis were there.

It appears that they and the Proeks had been 'talking all night' – something neither Estelle nor I have the energy to do. They are all tremendously empowered and rejuvenated and more honest and transformed. Everyone is translated and transformed! Porda! Mailer! Steve! Ramp! Karl! Everyone apart from yours truly! Only I plod on in the same marital furrow as my past disintegrates behind me!

Mr Proek is going to live with Mrs Rachnowski. Mr Rachnowski is going to live with Mrs Proek. They will not even have to change colour schemes or move houses, since it appears that Mrs Rachnowski has always wanted to move into the Proeks' house and Mr Proek has always hated his neat living-room, goldfish, etc. Mrs Rachnowski told me, 'Norman always wanted to live somewhere really messy. He has,' she went on, 'always had his eye on the stuffed gorilla!' Lucy and Laura have been told. Lucy and Laura are delighted. Lucy has always wanted her father to shag her best friend's mother, etc., etc. Everything is for the best in the best of all possible worlds.

Romantic love is often embarrassing and usually misconceived. But in people over fifty it is little short of tragic. We are now all off to the pub!

## 3.30 p.m. On bench on Wimbledon Common. On way home.

At the end of our drinks I somehow found myself alone with Bert Rachnowski. He bowed his shaggy, greying head to the table and shrugged, in an embarrassed fashion. 'Tell me,' he said, 'you and Estelle . . .' 'What about us?' I said. 'What's it like?' he said. 'Why do you want to know?' I said. 'Well,' he said, 'people who've been married a long time get this look about them.' 'What kind of look?' I said. 'Oh, you know,' said Mr

Bert, 'the look that says it'll always be this way!' 'Oh,' I said, 'you mean, smug! He said he didn't mean smug, although I thought that that was exactly what he meant.' I said, 'I can't really tell you what it's like. It's always different.' 'But,' said Bert, 'there's something . . .' 'Oh,' I said, 'our secret!'

I thought about this for a long time. Then I said, 'The secret is that I don't know. If you really want to know, I'm genuinely not sure whether I love my wife or not. I've been asking myself that question every day for the last twenty-five years. But I've always thought that one day I would wake up and know the answer. It might mean that I would have to get up and walk away from her. It might mean that I really did love her. You know? Really really truly for ever and ever, amen, like in the story-books. But I don't know the answer to that. Yet. I suppose I am frightened to find out. Or perhaps leaving it unsolved is why we stay together.' 'If you find the answer,' said Bert, 'let me know, will you?' 'Sure,' I said.

I am sitting here on this bench thinking about love and my search for it. Or rather my search for what it means. You do not abandon the search for love when you get married. I want to say that to Jakob and Ruaiergehrey. I think what I said in the pub is true. I don't think I have got the answer. But I'm close. I'm so close. I'm about to make sense of my life and my marriage. That thought scares me. Because if what I said to Bert is true then when I find the answer – it may all have been for nothing, all this shared life, all these children, even, dare I say it, all this happiness. For happiness isn't love, although it is part of it. Love is something that doesn't change, that is purely itself, beckons us on through the darkness, transforms, translates and yet remains true, unchangeable, like the love of God my Dad used to talk about, and, I hope, believed in, at the end, when he was struggling for breath on that hospital bed.


4.30 p.m.

Just read last paragraph. I will never be a novelist. Or any kind of writer. Can't get my sentences to correspond to my feelings.

## 5 p.m.

Jakob, Ruaierhgy and Edwin looked in on me before they went off to the pub. Jakob said there are some changes in his company. It appears that Benny Cammeroni, Toni Gerrasimo, Louie the Greek, Jackie the Horse, Jimmy the Knife, the Albanian, Jodie Sanzarotti and the Twins, and Vittorio Spinetti and Family are no longer involved. I asked why this was so and Jakob said, 'They are all dead!' I said I was sorry to hear this and Jakob said, 'It was for the best.' I asked how it happened and he said, 'Some of them were drowned.' It has not, apparently, affected Jakob's electrical business. I very tentatively and unthreateningly mentioned the Mafia and Jakob put his arm round me as he always does when this word is mentioned. 'Listen,' he said, 'you're my father and I love you. Just because someone can bore for England on varieties of pasta sauce doesn't mean they are Mafia. Some of them were not even Italian.' I said I thought Sanzarotti was an Italian name. Jakob said, 'That was why he adopted it.'

I did not ask further. But I am glad to see that Mr Vanelli and Mr Scarrotto have also not been round recently. Did not like to ask if they were dead.

Ruaierhgy has got on well at Sleeping Bag. His business plan has been accepted and they are firing twenty people. But not him. It appears his attempts to reach young alcoholics has gone down very well – especially with young alcoholics. They have found hundreds of them, which he seems very pleased about. The son of a front-bench Labour spokesman has confessed that he is a young alcoholic and a huge campaign, costing thousands of pounds, is being launched to find more of them. Edwin volunteered to make a public announcement that he was a young alcoholic through his 'press officer', i.e. Snozzer. He said he wished to confess that he and Snozzer drank five pints of Stella Artois last night. Ruewihriuy told him 'not to make jokes about a serious subject'. Then they all went to the pub.

I tried to probe them, subtly, on whether they have organized a surprise party for me. I said, 'I suppose there's no chance of a surprise party!' and Jakob said, 'No chance!'

Still no decision on Laura.

## 8 p.m.

Rang Stella Badyass to tell her the name and address of Steve's hospital/ward, etc. She sounded, I thought, ready to rock and roll, and said she would go round there tonight. Message from Estelle to say she had important news for me about Mr Slippy Sloppy. I managed to sound positive, full of vigour, not in need of Viagra, etc.

## June 18th. 9.30 a.m. Still no break in weather. No obvious cloud – hazy. But temperatures well up in eighties and, to use Edwin's phrase, 'as sweaty as a baboon's arse'. Sparrow may have had heart attack.

*Estelle and Jakob at Club Le Steel (pretentious name). Ruaiughry and Lucy at Sleeping Bag. Edwin at Irish Dancing Gala in Kilburn. Laura presumably at home still waiting for answer. Guess where I am.*
Answerphone messages. First from the thirtysomething.

THIRTYSOMETHING: Paul, are you there? No? Paul, I have something terribly important to tell you and I feel terribly guilty but it's . . . (*Pause. Massive cigarette inhalation* . . . it's that I have been feeling that Steve is . . . is . . . somehow very hard to reach . . . it's like he is on this glider being towed up into the air and I'm towing him or maybe not even towing him, maybe on the ground watching him being towed or maybe not even on the ground, maybe on a sort of other airliner thousands of feet above him not even aware that he's sort of . . . (*Pause. More smoke inhalation.*) The thing is I have met this amazing man, Paul, and we have so much in common. (*Pause. Coughing, followed by reverent lowering of voice.*) He's called Ashley Ramp, Paul, and I think you know him . . . well he knows you and he thinks you're terribly, terribly talented or at least he does now because I told him. (*Pause. Cackling laughter. More cigarette inhalation.*) I've never felt so close to someone, Paul. I feel that Ashley needs lots and lots and lots of love and I want to give it to him. I think a . . . shared interest is so important and we . . . well we just . . . hit it off . . . and I want you to break it to Steve, Paul, because I know how much you care about him and I want you to give him lots and lots and lots and lots of love from me, will you do that? (*Cigarette inhalation. Click.*)

You bet I will.

Second message from Good Old Steve.

STEVE: Paul, Steve here, hi! . . . Just to say that we have accepted delivery of the middle-aged woman as forwarded by you and we find her in every way ideal for the purposes required . . . actually, mate, seriously . . . this is just what the doctor ordered . . . she is a real winner . . . much hilarious stuff to tell you about her son who apparently nearly turned into a woman . . . I just wanted to say thanks for everything you're a pal she is absolutely the woman for me I can't tell you how happy I feel . . . and . . . this is hard . . . (*Hospital FX trolleys clanking, etc.*) but it isn't going to work out with . . . er . . . you know who . . . and I just wondered if you could be a mate and . . . sort of . . . tell . . . her . . . because I think if I see her and she . . . you know . . . offers me . . . you know . . . lots and lots and lots and lots of love or sort of goes on about me being . . . up a tree or whatever . . . I may have another thrombie, mate . . . take care . . . Steve . . .

Third message from my Mum:

MUM: Paul, it's me are you there? (*Long pause.*) Sometimes you're there even though you don't answer . . . (*Long pause.*) It's me anyway. (*Long pause.*) . . . You're working, I suppose . . . I don't like these Scotch people who are trying to kill you, Paul . . . I find the one called Randall particularly unsavoury. (*Long pause.*) Anyway you're not dead yet. (*Pause. Thumping in background.*) Do you hear the thumping? It's all day, the thumping. Thump thump thump thump. (*Long pause. Cackle. More background thumps.*) Do you remember Auntie Elspeth that lived in Newcastle and wrote children's books? She had a cat that had an awful disease and you stayed with her once when you were small. She was a gym instructor. (*Long pause.*) Anyway she's dead. (*Pause. More thumping.*) What do you think of Harriet Harman? I've no time for her. (*Long pause. More thumping. Phone hung up.*)

Fourth message from Estelle.

ESTELLE: Anybody there? No? OK. I'll go away. It's only Estelle. Working my arse off.

Fifth message from my Personnel Officer. I am due in at the Beeb. To be assessed. Now.

## 12 noon.

Just out of my meeting with Shirley.

It all got off to a good start. I saw Ashley Ramp in the lobby. He was looking like a man who had almost enough rubber fun. He gave me a cheery wave and said, 'Keep it up, Esmond!' 'I will!' I said.

If those in positions of power were getting enough sex the world would be a brighter, happier place!

Shirley, too, is clearly at it on a regular basis. She was wearing a loose kaftan arrangement which gave her the look of an Egyptian high priest and she glided around her office like a Dalek. Karl's manner to his secretary – Gillian – was a mixture of the aggressive and the patronizing ('Do me a letter, there's a love!') but Shirley, as she moved soundlessly between the potted plants, was honeyed, persuasive, humorous. 'Some tea, Paul? Gilly, could we possibly . . .') Seeing her at work made me realize how suited women are to executive power. The sooner we all have our dicks off the better really. Although – come to think of it – Shirley has the best of both worlds. Or has she? I was unable to stop thinking about this as she settled herself comfortably on her black sofa and peered at me encouragingly from under her blond wig. No trace of five o'clock shadow. If traces of the old bad, power-mad Karl were there it was only in a slight twinkle in the eyes as she said, 'Well – how are we?' but seemed to be saying 'Go on! Make a fool of yourself, Slippery! Do!'

'Well,' I said, 'we're fine really!' Shirley nodded. 'Good!' she said. 'I feel,' I said, 'that Esmond is really working now!' Shirley nodded. 'Yes!'

364

she said. 'I am getting,' I went on, 'a huge amount of fan mail!' 'Is that right?' said Shirley. 'Mainly,' I said, hoping she wasn't going to ask to see it, 'from women!' Shirley nodded. 'Good!' she said. 'Like yourself!' I said. 'Yes!' said Shirley. Then added, 'How do you mean?' 'Professional women,' I said, 'like yourself!' 'Ye – es!' said Shirley.

Getting into the old bra and pants had made her non-committal to the point of obscurity, I thought to myself. She was certainly not taking any chances. Emboldened by this, I thought I would give Esmond another little shove. 'The new Pennebaker,' I said, 'is also proving popular among sixteen- to twenty-five-year-olds!' 'Really!' said Shirley, her eyes now positively sparkling. 'Yes!' I said. 'So,' said Shirley, 'it all seems to be going well!' 'It does!' I said.

Shirley was clearly now getting enough sex to behave like a normal executive, i.e. do nothing, express no opinions and wait for your pension. Into this vacuum, I and Esmond boldly strode. 'I think, too,' I said, 'the whole Randall and Wallace sub-plot thing is working out well . . . and I am feeling that, on present form, he may go on for ever and ever!' 'Marvellous!' said Shirley.

There was a pause. I had a vision of myself playing Esmond Pennebaker at the age of sixty-five. I shut this out. Then I said, swiftly, 'I would like more money!' Shirley nodded. 'I think that might be possible!' she said, giving me a coy little grin. 'We like Esmond Pennebaker!' Then she held up my objectives form. 'I see,' she said, 'your objective is to stay alive!' 'That's right!' I said. Shirley gave a silvery laugh. 'Stay alive!' she said. 'Stay alive as long as you can!' With which encouraging words I was shown back out into the corridor.

Met Wainwright in the canteen. He seemed drunk. He moaned on about the old days of the Beeb. I said, 'For God's sake, Wainwright! Things must change! People change and grow! We must restructure our lives and ourselves! We have to grow and change!' Wainwright said, 'So they haven't fired you yet!' I told him he was being cynical. He did say one odd thing as I left. 'You think Ashley Ramp is the one who wanted you dead! It isn't as simple as that! The politics of this place can't just be sorted out by who screws who! Something nasty and wrong and sordid happened at the BBC and you are part of it, Slippery!'

He was amazingly plastered.

Spoke to Edwin on the phone, who is beginning to have doubts about his G CSEs. He tells me he wrote a whole essay about 'that weird red mark on Gorbachev's forehead'. It also appears that there is no such thing as G CSE Irish Dancing. It seems to have been some kind of code word he used when sloping off to the pub. He also told me that Snozzer and Wodge are engaged to be married. I asked if anyone else knew this and he said, 'You are the first person to know. You may be the only person who will ever be told. Snozzer thinks you are O K.' I said I was pleased to be in Snozzer's confidence but wondered whether, eventually, he would have to tell some other people. Like . . . his parents for example. Edwin said they were not going to be told. They would not understand, he said.

## 4 p.m.

Have just recorded another episode of *General Practice*. When I started, back in the early seventies, it took us a day. Elderly men in headphones spent hours adjusting the mikes. Producers went around followed by strings of people with stopwatches. Now we all sit around a table, usually with only a director for company, and aim to record half an hour in only twice that time.

Having escaped death at the hands of Randall and Wallace, I have returned to the surgery. I think I am about to start an affair with the man who delivers our surgical bandages, whose name is Jodie. Pamela is on her last legs. Leo and Witchett have decided to send Pilfrey mad – although he has not been told this. The first symptom of his craziness is an obsession with hygiene – he spent much of today's episode washing his hands. 'I feel a little . . . static!' he said to the director. Little does he know that in two weeks he will be pursuing his wife across the living-room with a large axe. In a month or two he will be strapped to a bed while officials in white coats inject large quantities of lithium into his right buttock.

Leo and Witchett's upmarket, sex, guns 'n' drugs approach is paying big dividends – especially as, now the bigwigs have all got their sex lives in order, they are much happier to let us do what we want. I am on the way to becoming a star. The office has had nearly a hundred letters about me, many of them asking for signed photographs! One woman from Cardiff writes –

Dear Dr Pennebaker,

   I had never listened to *General Practice* until last
week, considering it a dull old 'family soap'. Imagine my
surprise! You are definitely the sexiest thing on radio
and my friend and I really snuggle up to our speakers
when you come on.

   She even puts her portable between her legs so your
voice floats up at her from the pelvic regions as if you
were giving her oral sex.

   Speaking of which – if you are ever in the Cardiff area
– do drop in.

   I am twenty-four years old with a good bust, a nice bum
and legs to die for. I long to have you up against the
wardrobe in our downstairs room with my jeans rolled
down over my behind! I would come in a jiffy, I can tell
you!

   We are based at 34 Tregaron Drive,
Aberdevallynaervon, Cardiff, Wales.
I'm hot for you, baby!

Megan


Pilfrey said this letter was obviously written by a middle-aged man. I
asked him how he knew. Did he, perhaps, write it? He wrinkled his nose
like a prune and said, 'I have an instinct for these things.' He then said
that he was glad he didn't appeal to 'people like that'. He is obviously
raging with jealousy.

I seem to appeal to all ages. A boy of eight asks for my autograph and
a woman of eighty-nine says I have restored her faith in British broadcasting. The publicity department are having a special photo of me done to
give me 'an ageless quality'. I am to be snapped walking through woodland
in a shooting jacket, followed, at a discreet distance, by a red setter. Pilfrey
suggested one with a bag over my head would be good. *General Practice*
now has a marketing manager who has identified our niche audience as
'somewhere between twenty-five and sixty, outdoor-loving, concerned
about physical fitness and sexually active'. Thirty per cent of our listeners
are, apparently, illiterate and 10 per cent of them come either from the

Forest of Dean or Northumberland. I cannot work out whether these are the illiterate ones.

The marketing guy, whose name is Gavin, says that the secret of my appeal is that I have been around for so long that the people who stopped telling their friends about me have now found me again and are hailing me as a unique discovery. Even old, loyal listeners, it appears, have forgotten who I am so often that they now feel that they are hearing me for the first time – which is why I have a wider 'age reach' than almost any other British personality apart from Paul McCartney. 'Listener confusion,' he writes, 'has created a new and unique kind of definition for Pennebaker. Many eight-year-olds told us they thought he was "about eight or nine" while pensioners said they felt he was going through the same difficulties that they faced.'

The same is true of the series in general. The writers, plots, etc., have changed so many times that *General Practice* is no longer perceived as a soap. It has, according to Gavin, something unique in broadcasting – it is thought to be not only an institution but also the latest thing. 'What we are looking at here,' he writes, 'is a programme whose fans are so unsure about the ages and identity of the participants – we are talking here about fictional characters and the actors who play them – that we can do almost anything with them.' Eighty per cent of listeners apparently think that Dr Esmond Pennebaker is a real person and 75 per cent of them are equally convinced that Paul Slippery is 'someone they know who is also a doctor'; 15 per cent think of me 'as a friend, someone they can rely on' and 25 per cent 'think I shouldn't have given up medicine for acting'.

What is blindingly obvious, to me, is that all our listeners are idiots. Gavin does not dispute this. In fact he says it is good news for us, since idiots are the highest-spending consumer group yet targeted.

There are huge plans afoot to market me. The strategy at the moment is to 'separate the face from the voice'. Pilfrey said that that probably meant they were going to use photos of a different actor, adding, under his breath, 'a good-looking one'. I rose above this. Fame, I suspect, is going to make me a much nicer person. Off now to give an interview to the *Observer*.

## 6 p.m.

Pretty good interview with the girl from the *Observer* for the 'My Fridge' column. I had to tell her what was in my fridge. I told her – 'Two bottles of vodka, three bottles of champagne, some caviar and three pairs of boxer shorts.' She said that was pretty good. Apparently they never write what you tell them and, by the time the piece appears, I will probably be reported as having three half-empty tins of baked beans and a bottle of Guinness.

She asked me what kind of fridge it was and I said, 'A big, fuck-off fridge.' She liked this and said she would like to do other pieces with me. She also does the 'My Pet' column for *The Times*. She asked me if I had a pet. I said I had a goldfish called Kevin.

A really nice woman, with a first-class degree in biochemistry from Cambridge. Blond hair, sharp features but amazing tits. I am pretty sure I could have 'pulled' (as we say) but in my new nice-but-famous mode decided I would go back to Estelle.

Perhaps I have been a little competitive with her this year. I certainly have been somewhat left behind. But now I am on my way! She will have to work very hard to hang on to me!

## 8 p.m.

Still waiting for Estelle to come home so I can tell her about my new-found fame. Have made something called (I think) 'kib'n el farhiah' – a Syrian dish in which minced lamb, yoghurt, cinnamon and cardamom seeds are blended and deep-fried with okra and the zest of eight limes. I am going to serve it with persiflage – which it will need as it tastes absolutely vile.

Edwin has started to go into retrospective agonies about his History G C S E. I said, 'Edwin – it's been and gone! It's History, man!' He said that that was what he was worried about. He asked me whether the Cuban Missile Crisis happened before the Berlin Airlift and said he thinks he has made a 'grave boo-boo' on the subject of Fidel Castro. He appears to think that Castro was 'something to do with the music business in the early sixties'.

He went on about the Berlin Wall to a worrying extent. 'Who built it?' he kept saying. 'Why was it there? When they got over it did they walk round it or climb over it? Did it have spikes on it? Did the Russians build it or was it always there?' I tried to explain about Communism and said, 'We better start with Lenin and Marx.' Edwin said, 'We haven't done them!' My attempts to explain Communism only seemed to make things worse. And when I got on to Yeltsin his face grew white with terror. 'Who was he?' he said. 'What was he doing in there?'

## 9 p.m.

Told Estelle about huge sucess of self. She said, 'Does this mean we are going to talk about Paul Slippery even more than we did when he was an abject failure whom everyone was trying to kill?' I said I did not think we talked about me much. In fact, I said, I thought this year had mainly been about her and her work. 'Mr Slippy Sloppy, for example,' I said, 'in the old days would have been the kind of role we would have thought of in relation to me. All that has changed. I do not object to this. We have to change. Don't let's talk about me!' This produced a long silence.

I thought this gave me the chance to tell the really very amusing story of my encounter with the 'My Fridge' lady. Estelle listened to this with some impatience.

Everyone hated the Syrian dish.

Jakob has still not given his answer to Laura – although she has rung three times today. He is clearly up to something with Estelle. He has sold his electrical business. Mr Vanelli and Mr Scarrotto, it appears, are not going to be around and Jakob wishes to start up in business on his own. He has opened three more restaurants. I asked how long Mr Vanelli and Mr Scarrotto were going to be away and Jakob said, 'Nine years.' He has acquired a secretary called Gaby. I asked if he could see his way clear to paying me back for my original deposit for the fridges. Jakob said, 'Listen. You are my father and I love you. What's mine is yours and vice versa. All you have to do if you need money is to ask for it!' He put his arm round me and pulled my ear as he did this. He did not, however, come up with the cash. Did not like to ask him again. I am, I realized, a little frightened of Jakob.

Rueighry appeared late and looking, I thought, rather stressed. Are things well with Lucy? She was not there.

June 19th. 10 a.m. Still hot and humid. Still no sign of rain. Clouds circling Wimbledon in threatening fashion however. No sign of sparrow.

*Estelle and Jakob at Club Le Steel. Ruighiury and Lucy having row upstairs. Edwin and Lulu having row downstairs. Me here.*

In five days I will be halfway to a hundred.

Woke at four in morning with suspected heart attack. Pain in left arm. Very bravely decided not to wake Estelle. Better if she just finds me. I have read somewhere that a high proportion of people are found dead in the lavatory so, anxious to do the right thing, I went there. I did not die but, instead, read book about hedgehogs, which Edwin had left on the floor.

Went back to bed and thought about sex. Imagined self being tied up by woman in Viking costume and then beaten with thong. Getting quite aroused by this when she suddenly whacked me over the head with her shield and ran off laughing. Tried to imagine self having sex with Sharon Stone. Failed.

Tried a fantasy that usually works, in which I go into a brothel staffed almost entirely by black women. It somehow got mixed up with the hedgehog book, which was rather interesting. In the end I went back to the lavatory and read the chapter about anointing – which is a bizarre ritual almost all hedgehogs go in for, involving licking, snuffling and other things I cannot remember when I last did with another human. Better deal being a hedgehog, really. By the time I got back to bed it was light. Estelle was snoring but I did not, as I usually do, whack her on the side of the head with a rolled-up newspaper. My new-found success is making me a much more tolerant person.


11.30 a.m.

Message on machine from Ashley Ramp, of all people, to say how much he is enjoying the show. He sounded like a man who is getting enough sex. In fact I am almost sure I heard a sort of squeaking, rubbery sound from his end of the phone. He did say, at one point, 'I and my partner really are enjoying the new upbeat Pennebaker!' I find 'partner' now one of the most erotic words in the English language – it suggests a sexual union without revealing whether the speaker is shagging a man, a woman or a goat.

Also long, rambling letter from Wainwright, who I think is going mad. He speaks of Spence's Second Law which states, apparently, that 'all organizations are restructured to resemble themselves, only more so' and that 'all change is cosmetic and temporary'. More mutterings about a conspiracy against me.

## 12.45 p.m.

New people moving into Porker's house. They bear an amazing resemblance to Mr and Mrs Porker.

## 5 p.m.

Sudden access of rage over Prynne's disease, absence of Estelle, unfairness of life, etc. Decided to try experiment and give self hand-job under controlled conditions and then see if I could remember it.

Tremendous problems finding place to give self hand-job. Edwin was downstairs playing the chord of E flat seventh. Rueirriuy, back early from Sleeping Bag, was having row with Lucy on phone. Jakob was having row with Ruaigurhy because he wished to get on phone so that he could have row with Laura. In desperation scoured house for pornography. There is none. The best I could find was a copy of *Anna Karenina*: some moderately horny descriptions of blouses, necks, shoulders, etc., but not really enough to get the late fortysomething going.

Looked along shelves for other potentially arousing works. *A Country Doctor's Notebook* by Mikhail Bulgakov? I think not. *Making the Cat Laugh* by Lynne Truss? I got it out of the pile and looked at her jacket photograph. A nice, attractive woman, I thought to myself. I could imagine having a nice, attractive conversation with her. Putting the book hurriedly back into the shelves I looked further along. *The Hobbit* by J. R. R. Tolkien? I do not think so. *The Grapes of Wrath* by John Steinbeck? No sex, as I recall. *The Collected Poems of Peter Reading*? *The Trumpet-Major* by Thomas Hardy? *The Rough Guide to Andalucia*?

In total despair I went into the front room. *John Thomas and Lady Jane* by D. H. Lawrence? The mere thought of the appalling gamekeeper running round in the rain and droning on about his cock had an actively negative effect on the project I had in mind. Once again I went into the lavatory, lowered my trousers and stared, resentfully, at my forty-nine-year-old penis. 'Well . . .' I said, 'what about it?' It lay there, sullenly, like an overfed worm. 'Brassière!' I said to it. 'Lacy panties!' It did not move. From downstairs I could hear Edwin playing a major chord on his guitar.

It is over, Slippery. It is all over. Off now to take Edwin to dress rehearsal of *A Midsummer Night's Dream*, which opens tomorrow. It closes tomorrow as well, which I think will probably be a good thing.

## 9.30 p.m.

Watched some of dress rehearsal. Plonker does a reggae number while in his ass's head. Hotchkiss has still not solved the promenading aspects of the production. His game plan seems to be for the fairies to leap on and 'taking the audience by the hand lead them out into the summer night'. He tried this out on the few parents and masters who were assembled in the Lucien Freshman Hall. I was approached by Snozzer (why is he a fairy again?) who, flapping his wings, said in a deep, bass voice, 'Want me to show you a good time, Mr Slippery?' Then he manhandled me out into the playground. The trouble was they had not decided where to put us. Moth, played by an enormous boy called Jason Patel, started to crowd his group into a small huddle over by the bike sheds, while Cobweb, played by a midget called Puntschli, drove his lot out towards the Rugby pitch. The first, second and third fairies (Tooting, Minton and Hughes) ran off into the evening with one or two adults apiece. Hong, who has now been appointed assistant director, chased after them shouting, 'Come back, silly boy! Play not over yet!'

The tensions between Titania and Oberon have got worse. Peter Lugg, the Boy Who Thinks He May Be Homosexual (and blatantly is), has decided to camp it up outrageously in order to annoy Ffitch-Presley. His opening line to Oberon, 'What jealous Oberon? Fairy skip hence!' was given a new dimension by Lugg's pausing after the word 'fairy', turning to the audience, wiggling his bum and pointing at Ffitch-Presley. On the line 'then I must be thy lady', Lugg threw himself to his knees in front of the school's prize Rugby player and lunged for his groin. Ffitch-Presley gave him a forearm smash, to which Lugg responded with cries of 'More! More!'

Edwin has given Puck an American accent. I think I was the only person to notice this.

## 11 p.m.

Estelle still not back. What are she and Jakob doing? Is he going to do the decent thing by Laura? Why are the Porkers returning? Still no mention of what is going to happen for my fiftieth. Presumably nothing. Feeling very Eeyore-ish about this. More furniture missing. Looking out of window at the house where Wickett used to live. Just realized what an important part of my life he was.

Message on machine from Shirley. *General Practice* continues to be the flavour of the month. It is to be translated into French! There are a few changes – I am to be played by a woman and it is set in a cancer ward in Bordeaux but otherwise it is much the same. Apparently there is a huge article about me in *FIGARO* entitled 'Le Phénomène Pennebaker'. Six more journalists have rung up asking to interview me and Ashley Ramp has announced he is now our greatest fan.

Gustave rang a few minutes later to say that he has had offers from a commercial television company to adapt the series for the screen. They want me! Although, as Gustave pointed out, 'They haven't actually seen you in the flesh yet!' He proposes to use their interest to up my fee from the Beeb. But what does all this mean, essentially? What real pleasure can there be for a man who is unable to remember when he last had sex? Can a few newspaper articles ease the pain of someone who is about to have twenty-five years of marriage made light of on the same day his birthday is conspicuously ignored? What has Estelle in mind to tell me when we go out for dinner the day after tomorrow? Has she been having an affair? Why is there almost no furniture left in the house? Why have I not managed to get any love potion down her face? What does my relationship mean? Am I still in love with Estelle and if I am, what does that mean? If I am not, what am I going to do about it? If I am, what am I going to do about it? When is she going to come home? Am I going to go to bed?

Yes.

June 20th. 9 a.m. Weather still humid. No sign of rain yet. Slightly cooler, I think. Sparrow sighted in hedge. Looked cautious about things.

*Estelle at Craftgirls. Jakob gone to East Cheam 'for summit meeting'. Ruighei-urhy and Lucy at Sleeping Bag. Edwin at school. Me here.*

Four days away from saying farewell to my forties. Still no sign of a surprise party. I suppose, of course, if they were going to give me a surprise party they wouldn't advertise the fact. But I am fairly sure I would be able to spot something.

Did manage, however, to get Estelle to swallow love potion last night. She came in at around eleven thirty and told me she was going to offer me the part of Mr Slippy Sloppy! Wild joy on my part. I said I hoped I would rise to the challenge. Said, also, that she must only give it to me if she thought I was right for the part. 'I want no favours!' I said. 'You're the boss! If someone else is right, if Pilfrey is your man, then go for Pilfrey!' She told me not to be ridiculous. I said, 'Let's have a celebration drink!' She seemed agreeable to this, so I went across to the sink and fished out my bottle of potion.

I had forgotten, of course, that it was bright green. The only green liquids in our house seemed to be a bottle of extra virgin olive oil and a plastic tub of something called Squeeze foam. Although Estelle was in an unusually good mood I could not see her downing either of them without questions being asked. I did, however, manage to track down a half-bottle of Sancerre that, in the bottle anyway, had a greenish tinge to it.

I was past caring. I added a huge slug of potion to two large (tinted) glasses. It was, I thought to myself, more than the total amount I had given to both my older sons. My God – we're fifty! We need a little help here, Jesus! The last third of our life is supposed to be fun, isn't it? Don't let's mess around! I carried it over to her. She squinted down at it. 'It's bright green!' she said. 'Sancerre is green,' I said, 'the French call it *vin vert*!' 'Do they?' she said suspiciously. 'This is the colour of Wimbledon Centre Court!' I said, knocking some back, 'It's young! That is why it is green!' Estelle sniffed it cautiously. 'You're not trying to poison me, are you?' she said. I said, 'I am not trying to poison you. Yet, anyway.

I love you!' She looked at me even more suspiciously. 'Oh yeah?' she said. 'Oh yeah,' I said, 'you are everything to me!' I went on, 'Why else do you think I have stayed with you for twenty-five years?' She raised the glass and looked at it against the light. 'Laziness,' she said, 'and cowardice. And because you think your nose is too long for you to get anyone else.' 'That too, of course!' I said. 'But I do also love you!' 'I suppose,' she said thoughtfully, swirling the Sancerre in her glass, 'that there's a strong element of compromise in any relationship!' 'What about love?' I said. 'What about needing someone so much that there is only one other person in the world? What about being half and then whole and marrying their true minds and looking on tempests and not being moved and all that stuff?' 'What about it?' she said, eyeing me levelly over her glass.

I breathed deeply and raised my glass. 'Well,' I said, 'I love you. And I am not ashamed to say it. And I am not ashamed to drink to it either!' Estelle thought about this for some time. Then she said, 'Love, like any interesting thing, is a little complicated.'

I put my glass down. Was she never going to get any of the potion down her?

For some reason I found myself looking at her forearms. She doesn't like her forearms. I thought they looked fine. Tanned, rather muscular. If there were wrinkles I couldn't, or wouldn't, see them. I liked the view of her arm I was getting from the other side of the room – a sensuous, comforting brown blur.

'What is it, then?' I said, a trace of hysteria reaching my voice. 'What is love?' Estelle yawned. 'I haven't the faintest fucking idea!' she said, and keeping her eyes on my face she downed what was probably the largest dose of love potion ever given to anyone since the fatal day when Sex Products of Wolverhampton was first incorporated. I did the same. There was a long silence. 'That,' she said, 'is not fucking Sancerre!' 'It said Sancerre on the label!' I said in a tremulous voice. 'Who cares,' said Estelle, 'so long as it gets you pissed!' She beckoned to me with her finger. 'Come here, little man!' she said. I came. She grabbed the back of my hair and pulled my mouth down to hers. Her lips were wet. I tasted, briefly, the inside of her mouth, sweet and soft.

'That's enough to be going on with!' she said. Obediently I went back to the sink. My mouth still tasted of hers, but, I realized, as I lifted up the bottle, there was something else in there as well. A hardly recognizable fragrance that suggested a curious blend of flesh, perfume and something like cinnamon. For a moment I couldn't think what it was. Then I understood. It was the potion.

'I think,' I said, 'we should talk about sex.' Estelle drained her glass in one gulp. 'I don't think one should talk about sex,' she said, 'I think one should do it.' 'Good idea!' I said in a bright, slightly Boy Scout voice. She continued to look at me as if she was seeing me for the first time. 'The thing is,' I said, 'I was trying to think the other day when we . . .' 'When we what?' 'When we last made love . . .' I said. Estelle nodded slowly. 'The weird thing,' I went on, gaining in confidence and feeling more intimate with her than I could remember feeling for some time, 'I couldn't . . . er . . . remember. Isn't that extraordinary?' 'Not really,' said Estelle. 'You could have that thing you were looking up in the medical dictionary the other day.' 'What thing?' I said, my voice trembling. 'Prynne's disease,' said Estelle, 'The one where you can't remember when you last had sex!' 'Do you think I've got it?' I said. She shook her head confidently. 'You could,' she said, 'just be unable to remember when you last had sex.'

There was an amiable silence. I found I was looking at her eyes. She has a big, strong, intelligent face. The eyes are the best thing about it – dark, energetic, humorous.

'You would think,' I said after a while, 'that I would be able to remember when I last had sex. I mean sex is important.' 'Not to you, obviously!' said Estelle. 'Ah,' I said, 'so we have had sex recently!' 'Of course we have,' said Estelle. 'When?' I said. 'Just now!' she said. 'That wasn't sex!' I said. 'What was it then?' said Estelle. 'It was a kiss!' I said. Estelle held out her glass. 'Give me some more of that peculiar drink!' she said. 'Whatever it is.'

I took her glass and went back over to the sink. With my back to her I poured the rest of the potion into her glass and mine. By the time we had finished, I said to myself, we would have put away enough to make two elephants shag for a week. We drank both glasses down at almost the same time. 'When,' I said, in a threatening tone of voice, 'did we last have sex?' Estelle smiled dreamily. 'About six months ago, I think,' she said, 'maybe more!'

And went to bed. I was so devastated by this remark that, by the time

I summoned up the courage to debate its full meaning, Estelle was fast asleep and snoring loudly. She was out before I woke up this morning.

The implications of this are very, very serious. I am having to face the one conclusion I have never even dared to contemplate. That I can't remember when I last had sex simply because it was so long ago. I am unable to believe that I just sat back and allowed her to get away with this. I think I must have tried, on more than one occasion, and been told she was tired or had a headache. But I am unable to remember any such row. Perhaps, the thought occurs to me, she has bewitched me in some way, possibly involving the little dough men.

Not had sex for six months! And she mentions it, days away from our twenty-fifth wedding anniversary! As if it is unremarkable! As if everyone wandered around not having sex for six months! I am well behind the national average!

## 11.30 a.m.

Jakob called from East Cheam. He said, 'Look. I'm with Laura. O K. It's cool.' This could mean he has decided to chuck her for good. Or, perhaps, that he has proposed marriage to her. I am going to phone Estelle. It is time to stop worrying about other people's sex lives and pay a little attention to my own. I should have been doing that six months ago – or whenever the rot started.

## 11.45 a.m.

Called Estelle. She was in meeting. Sudden panic about Hamish, Turkish men, etc. Left message saying it was 'urgent'.

## 12 noon.

Estelle returned my call. She seemed in a cheerful mood. I said, 'I just want to know one thing. When we last did it – what was it like?' There was a pause. Then she said, 'It was all right!' 'When,' I said, 'will we be doing it again?' 'I don't know!' she said. 'But we will be doing it . . . at some stage . . .' I said, a note of anxiety creeping into my voice. 'I am sure we will!' she said. I said, 'I'd like to drop by and just see you if that's all right!' She said, 'That's fine!' I said, 'Why haven't I done this before?' She said, 'You never suggested it before!' I said, 'We have a lot to talk about! I am a bit of a wally, really, aren't I?' She said, 'Yes!'

## 1 p.m.

Writing this in the car. I have parked in the car park next to Wimbledon windmill. It is a stifling day – thick light, close and muggy.

Craftgirls UK is a group of large, well-lighted rooms. Estelle's office is at the back. On the wall are charts, most of which seem to relate to the animated film. There were long lists of messages next to her telephone, many of them from the production company they have hired to work on the project. I didn't recognize any of the names. When I went in she was on the phone to someone called Mark. She was being pretty authoritative with him. I sat on a black shiny sofa and waited for her to finish.

When she came off the call she pushed her chair back and grinned at me. 'So,' she said, 'you finally came round!' 'Do you think,' I said, 'I've been a bit . . . threatened by all this . . .' 'Probably,' she said. I said, 'Do you think I've been having a nervous breakdown?' She said, 'You've been a bit peculiar!' 'I'm sorry!' I said. 'That's OK,' said Estelle. There was a pause. 'Have you been having an affair with Hamish?' I said. She seemed to find this very amusing. Immediately I had asked the question out loud to her I knew the answer was 'no'. 'Hamish,' said Estelle, 'is an accountant!'

There was another pause. Then I said, 'It's like we're starting over again. That kiss last night. It's still so clear to me. It's like every sensation is new. Do you think that's why I started forgetting? So I could start feeling again!' 'Feeling who?' said Estelle. We both laughed. 'Look,' Estelle said then, 'maybe we have been a bit . . . separate . . . these six months. Maybe I haven't done much about the relationship. Maybe I was waiting, for once, to see what you'd do if I did nothing. Maybe I just got busy, absorbed in these new things I'm doing . . . I don't know.' I didn't say anything. After a while she said, 'I suppose I sometimes feel you don't know me. You don't know what it's like to be me. You don't even make the effort. All you see is yourself.' 'What is it like to be you?' I said. 'Oh,' she said, 'it's like being driven by something . . . that makes you . . . smoke or bite your nails or love your children too much . . . or drives

379

you to . . . work!' 'Yes,' I said, 'work! Is that all there is for you now?' 'It's a lot of what there is for me,' she said. 'But,' I said, 'there might be . . . other things!' She smiled then. 'There might well be!' she said.

Then I got up and closed the door. 'Do you think,' I said, 'I might have another kiss?' 'I don't see why not!' said Estelle. I went over to her and she tilted her head back. My lips found hers and once again I tasted her sweet, soft mouth. I put my hand inside her blouse. Very gently she prised it away. 'That's enough for now!' she said. 'O K,' I said.

Then she got a few more calls. I sat on the sofa watching her for some time, remembering stuff about her. I remembered the first time I saw her walking in some High Street somewhere, her hair full of flowers. I remembered her the night her father died, and how she didn't cry but sat, like a little girl whose toy has been taken away. I remembered her at some political rally, years ago, angry with some man or other, getting to her feet and waving her fist in the air. I remembered her cooking Peking duck in the first flat we ever bought, hanging it on the kitchen door and spraying it with a hair dryer. I remembered her pregnant with Rueighry in the hot summer of 1976, wearing a loose print dress.

The only thing I couldn't remember was how and why and when and where we've made love over the last quarter of a century. I still can't. But I've stopped caring about it. The only thing I can remember about that is the last kiss, in her office and the kiss before that, last night. But those two kisses! I sit here looking across at the trees and think about them and about the other kisses she owes me and how I will steal them from her and how each one will be sweeter than the last. And how I will remember each one very precisely.

I am going to write a testimonial for Sex Products of Wolverhampton Ltd. It is the least I can do.


## 7 p.m.

Just about to leave for *A Midsummer Night's Dream*. Edwin has decided, at the last minute, to appear in a jockstrap. He is wearing it now. He has been persuaded, finally, to wear a dressing-gown over it on his way into school. Lulu has applied decorations to his upper body. Jakob, Rueiaerhy, Lucy and Laura are coming with us. I am crossing my fingers but the signs are good. Laura and Jakob arrived back from East Cheam arm in arm. They both looked extremely pink. They are sitting in the front room, with troubled expressions, but I do not think this is anything to do with Laura. It is probably because Edwin has just told them the play lasts five hours and they are expected to walk about eight miles during the course of it.

## 9 p.m.

Writing this in the pub across the road from the school. The show is not going well. Three of the fairies have gone missing. Hotchkiss tells me they were seen, 'in their wings' drinking lager in the Fox and Grapes. A boy called Appliquant trod on Titania's train and Peter Lugg struck him, savagely, with his wand. Hong keeps interrupting the proceedings from the back of the stalls ('Louder, silly boy! People no hear a thing you say!') About the only thing that is going down well is Plonker, whose songs have received loud applause. Ffitch-Presley is a disaster. On the line 'I am invisible!' he had asked one of the lighting guys to drop a blanket over his head from the flies. In fact he hurled it out into the audience where it landed on the head of Mr Francine, the gay Spanish teacher. Ffitch-Presley was heard to say 'Wicked!' in a loud voice as Mr Francine struggled to be free.

Reiruejhury and I, hiding out from the production, which is now somewhere at the back of the bicycle sheds, have just had a heart-to-heart.

It was quite brief. There was no hugging or crying, as in the American model. It was a very British affair. I said, 'Look. You seem to really love this girl. And if you wanted to get married and stuff . . . I just wanted to say that . . . that would be great.' He said, 'Thanks. I think I would be marrying the right one. I said, 'I married the right one.' 'Sure,' said Rueighry. 'Although you're very different people, you're like . . . suited.'

Ruaieiughy smiled slightly. 'All that sixties stuff. Which hasn't gone away – the way certain generations don't go away. You lot refuse to grown old. You and Mick Jagger both!' 'It is about all we have in common!' I said. 'But,' said Ruaighry, 'I believe in different things. I'm a . . .' 'A Christian!' I said, trying to keep the panic out of my voice. Ruaieghry grinned wickedly. 'I'm not exactly a Christian,' he said. 'I don't know what I am quite yet. But you have to let me find out for myself.' 'I see that!' I said. 'And,' said Ruaighry, 'this business with my name . . .' 'Right!'

I said in as businesslike fashion as I could manage. 'I mean like it's become a sort of . . . I mean a sort of . . .' 'Family joke!' said Ruairghry with a grin. 'Jakob spelt me Rueigheiurrry on a postcard the other day . . . which was almost amusing but . . . I would like to be known as . . . Rerghy!' said Ruaireuirghy. 'My God!' I said. 'Is that . . . sort of . . . final?' 'It is my final word on the matter!' said Rerghy. 'Right!' I said. 'Fine! I'll break it to your mother!' 'It would be good if you could!' said Rerghy.

Then I said, 'Er . . . how do you pronounce it?' 'You pronounce it RERGHY!' said Rerghy. 'Fine!' I said. Then he put his arm round me. 'I love you a lot!' he said. 'Sure!' I said.

That was all. I don't think I ever said that to my father, although I wanted to say it. I just couldn't find the right words, although they are, as Rerghyy has just shown me, devastatingly simple. So I suppose we aren't doing that badly.

God knows how I am going to sell this one to Estelle.


## 10.30 p.m.

Play still going on. The audience are now talking openly among themselves. Dummer, the gay physical-training teacher, who has been asked to write a review of it for the school magazine, is asleep in the third row. Things on stage have got even worse. Lugg, the Boy Who Thinks He May Be Homosexual and Blatantly Is, is weeping in the middle of the stage. His tears are, I think, unrelated to the action, but it is hard to tell. Apparently he demanded counselling during the second interval and Mr Freiburg, the gay Greek master, had to go in and, to use Freiburg's own words, 'listen to him droning on about his problems'.

I can't remember any more at what stage the fairies started to double as mechanicals but it has not helped the show. Neither is it clear to me how Snozzer managed to persuade Hotchkiss that he could play both Quince and Mustardseed, who, in Hotchkiss's production, are quite often on the stage at the same time.

I told Estelle that Rerghy wished to be known as Rerghy. She said, 'That is an absolutely ridiculous idea. You can't call someone Rerghy. It sounds like a car changing gear. You started the misspelling joke anyway. He has a perfectly good name. He is called —' I said, 'I think he is pretty immovable on this one!' Estelle said, 'I shall not call him Rerghy!' I said,

'He will not answer to any other name!' There was a pause. She said, 'What about Fred?' I said, 'It is too late for Fred. It is too late for a lot of things.' She said, 'You're right there.' And she held my hand, briefly, and very hard. Then she said, 'It was you who insisted on calling him Ruairghy. I said it was a stupid idea at the time.' I said, 'I'm sorry!'

Must break off now as Edwin is about to do the song which runs —

On the ground
Sleep sound:
I'll apply
To your eye,
Gentle lover, remedy.
When thou wak'st,
Thou tak'st
True delight
In the sight
Of thy former lady's eye:
And the country proverb known,
That every man should take his own,
In your waking shall be shown:
Jack shall have Jill;
Nought shall go ill;
The man shall have his mare again
And all shall be well.

The beautiful simplicity of Shakespeare!

### 10.40 p.m.

The hideous complexity of Edwin Slippery! Edwin has just finished the song. It took that amount of time, largely because of an elaborate improvised dance with which he entertained us during the long gaps which occurred while he tried to remember the words. I think if this production carries on the way it has been going we will have guys from CNN reporting from the scene. It bids fair to be a major international disaster on the scale of a 747 running into the side of a hill. I am off to the pub with Jakob.

Just about to leave the pub after rite-of-passage conversation with Jakob. I am his father, after all. I don't know why I think I shouldn't be having conversations like this. I should be having more of them. He said he wanted me to know that he was not in the Mafia. I said I never thought that that was the case. He said he had tried hard enough to make me think that it was. Apparently Mr Scarrotto's real name was Byng. Mr Vanelli was his brother. Nothing is what it seems.

Jakob and I discuss emotions in intellectual terms. He said he 'couldn't imagine what had made him think Lucy was right for him'. I said I couldn't imagine either. 'What made me change my mind?' he said. I didn't like to mention Sex Products of Wolverhampton Ltd. I said, with perfect truthfulness, 'Love is a very peculiar thing. We don't know how it comes or what makes it go.' 'Sure,' said Jakob, 'I don't know why I just couldn't see Laura. And then suddenly, I could. Which was so cool.' 'When did it happen?' I said. 'At that weird Greek evening!' said Jakob. 'It has all seemed so complicated. And then it all seemed so simple!' 'It's like that with your Mum and me!' I said.

Then he said, 'Are you and Mum all right?' 'What makes you ask that?' I said. 'Oh,' he said, 'this past six months . . . sometimes . . .' A middle child. He would notice that. 'We're fine,' I said, 'we really are fine. And if there have been any problems they have been mainly to do with me. It isn't easy facing up to . . .' 'The big five-o,' said Jakob, 'especially when no one is giving you a party or anything!' 'Right!' I said. 'Not that I mind, you understand!' I added. 'Of course not!' said Jakob. 'Tell me,' I said, 'are you . . . you know . . . giving me a . . . surprise party of some kind . . . ?' Jakob put his arm round me. 'Listen, Dad,' he said, 'if we were giving you one I wouldn't tell you. And if we weren't giving you one I wouldn't tell you. If I have a criticism of you it is that you don't always . . . take things as they come . . . You have to do that. Stop worrying! Live!'

I intend to do both.

# June 21st. 1 a.m. Still hot.

*All family at school.*

*A Midsummer Night's Dream* is still in progress. Plonker, after his line about 'eat no onions or garlic' did an extraordinary farting and burping routine which created mild hysteria among the crowd. He then sang for forty-five minutes.

Quite a lot of people have left, including the headmaster.

Edwin – who is wandering freely among the audience, voicing his opinion of the proceedings in a loud voice – has just suggested to me that we 'go off for a cigarette'. Although I disapprove of smoking, anything is preferable to watching the play.

## 2 a.m.

Edwin did not seem to want to talk about our relationship, which was something of a relief. He did, however, talk of Lulu (who, by the way, now seems to be playing one of the mechanicals). He had to be pushed into doing this. 'How are you and Lulu?' I said. Edwin shrugged. 'O K,' he said.

'Do you think you'll . . .' 'We'll what?' said Edwin. 'You know,' I said, 'carry on?' 'What else can you do?' said Edwin.

'Are you . . . you know . . . in love with her?' 'Don't use that word!' said Edwin, wincing. 'Even if you don't care to use it – it's there,' I said. 'There wouldn't be any point in your going out if it wasn't! Because "love" means the same as "care for" or "fancy" or any of these other words we use to pretend that what we feel isn't really that important. It's the condition they aspire to. It's what we all want – even if we don't make it.'

There was a silence. In the distance I could hear Plonker. They seemed to be in the middle of the mechanicals' play. To my surprise, he seemed, also, to be speaking lines written by Shakespeare. To my even greater surprise they seemed to be going down rather well. 'Have you made it, then?' said Edwin. 'You've never made it,' I said, 'there is only the attempt. However long you've been together. It changes all the time, you see. Like you and Lulu. That stuff you're feeling – it never sort of suddenly . . . stops. You don't draw a line under it. It goes on – day after day after day – like this damned diary I've been writing. And each day you feel different. But each day should be an attempt to get back to that thing that reminds you why you're there. Love, yes, I'll call it love. And each day is a promise. And each week is a promise. Each month, each year is a promise. Six months or twenty-five years – it makes no difference at all.'

There was a long silence. 'Sez you!' said Edwin.


## 3 a.m.

Amazing transformation! The mechanicals' play went down so well that they decided to do bits of it again. Those of the audience who remained – including the headmaster, who had returned to the stalls after a short kip in his study – cheered Plonker to the echo. The lovers suddenly decided to speak properly. Lugg and Ffitch-Presley made a superb job of their last scene. The line from Oberon about 'all the couples three/ever true in loving be' really worked. Hotchkiss had decided to bring out the lovers in a weird blue spotlight as he speaks the lines. It seemed, after five hours of hell, one of the most amazing theatrical experiences I have ever encountered.

Perhaps Hotchkiss is a genius. Like Peter Brooke or Wagner or Marcel Proust, he has decided to go on so long and to bore the audience so totally and completely that his conclusion has the sonority associated with the end of colossal pain and strife. 'One felt,' said Duncan Hollydene, the gay maths master, 'that it was really worked for! We had all really suffered to get there and it kind of worked on that level!' 'It was,' as a parent said to me on the way out to the cars, 'so wonderful to realize that it wasn't going on any more. It wasn't like stopping banging your head against a brick wall. It was like the end of a war or a serious illness or a ghastly tropical storm!' At which Hotchkiss leaped on us from behind and said, 'Yes! That was the idea!'

Hong said, 'Hotchkiss brilliant, no? Plonker look very tasty tonight I think!' They departed in Hong's yellow open-topped sports car as decorated with flowers as a Hawaiian wedding.

Everyone seems very happy. In three days I will be fifty.

## 12 noon.

Estelle had already left for the office when I awoke.

I lay for some time looking at the ceiling, remembering that the two of us are due to have dinner together tonight. I found the thought overpoweringly erotic. How far will I get with her? What sort of things did I get up to in the past? Ought I to go out and purchase contraception? Or has the menopause taken care of that? Should I get my hair cut? (Good idea.) Shave? Buy aftershave?

Memory of two kisses still very vivid. I think the second one was slightly better than the first. Spent a long time thinking about it.

Much mail for Esmond Pennebaker, forwarded from the Beeb. The ratings are up again. A letter from Leo and Witchett saying they plan to reprieve Pilfrey. Find I am quite pleased about this. I may hate Pilfrey but he and I go back a long way. I have to have someone to hate, as does Pilfrey. Gustave writes suggesting lunch and saying that the Royal Shakespeare Company are thinking of casting me in a forthcoming production of *Henry Fourth, Parts One and Two*. He seems to think I may be asked to play Falstaff. Surely some mistake?

Edwin asleep. Jakob and Laura asleep. Rerghy is on a night-soup run to a group of young alcoholics in Teddington.


## 1 p.m.

Laura has just brought me in cup of tea!

She was wearing a garment I have never seen before. It was loose-fitting and in blue silk and came just below her knees. I stared very intently at her face as she came into the bedroom, so could not describe it accurately, but I think it has little bobbles on it somewhere. I said, 'How nice to have you stopping over! I do hope you'll stay as long as you want!' I think this struck the right note.

Message on the machine from my mother. It runs as follows –

MOTHER: Paul, is that you? (*Pause. Door slams.*) They're banging again. I hate it here. (*Long pause.*) Are you there? (*Longer pause.*) You're not, are you? You're probably off being interviewed. You're getting quite famous, aren't you? With this Pinnybanker man. (*Long pause. Banging. She sniffs*.) I preferred you in that play at the Questors Theatre in Ealing. You played that man whose trousers kept falling down. I tell everyone about that. Anyway. (*Long pause. More banging*.) Do you remember that family who lived next door and used to send us those chain letters? He was in the Customs and Excise and in fact I think he may have been a Drugs man. His wife was a very petite, pretty woman called Lottie. They had five children. Two of them played the violin. (*Long pause. Banging*.) They sent us these chain letters telling us where they had been and what they had been doing. They went all over the world in that jeep they had. (*Short pause. Sniff*.) Anyway, they're all dead.

## 3 p.m.

Oliver has been arrested in Tunisia! He has been sentenced to eighty-nine years in an American prison. The National Drugs Agency (or whatever they are called) say he is 'one of the most dangerous people with whom they have ever had to deal'. I must say I always found him charming. He didn't always wipe the kitchen units after he had made his toast but on the whole he was a fairly exemplary character. I suppose, of course, like everyone, he has improved with distance. There is a picture of him on the front page of the *Standard* looking amazingly sinister. Rerghy says it is a passport photograph, which explains its threatening aspect.

I only hope he does not implicate anyone. Especially me.

Talked on the phone to Peter Mailer, who seems to have lost what few marbles he still possessed. He says he is drinking a litre of vodka a day. I said, 'Well done you!' He and Christine are going to get married.

There is now hardly any furniture in the house at all. We all have to sit on the floor for meals. When I go out with Estelle tonight I am going to use the new-found frankness in our relationship to ask her what this means. Feeling very excited about our date – as it is about the first time we have been out alone together since I forgot when we last had sex. Presumably when I could remember when we last had sex, i.e. shortly before the last time we did it which I failed to remember, i.e. some time last year or possibly sooner – assuming I could remember it then – we were always going out for candlelit dinners. We must have been.

People do, don't they? How else did we manage to have three children?

I have been to buy her a bottle of perfume from the village. I think it is supposed to be for men but it smells pretty good and it has a nice box. I have also written out a small card which says, 'For Our Anniversary'. Underneath this I have written, 'When can we do it again?'

## 6 p.m.

Writing this in the car across the road from Craftgirls UK.

I am half an hour early. I have been trying, as I look across at Estelle's offices, to remember other things about the way we were and how we got here. It's curious. Once she had told me – roughly – when we had last made love, I lost all interest in trying to remember. Why is this? I think because I believe her. And now can't imagine why I ever thought Hamish or anyone else would come between us. I suppose that is one of the most fundamental things about loving somebody. You have to trust them. And, of course, your trust must not be misplaced.

I continue to believe, however, that there is one image that will give me the answer to some of the questions I have been asking myself in this diary. Why Estelle? If I had to explain to a third party why we are together, how would I set about doing it? What, in short, is love?

I can see us holding up Rerghy when he was very, very small and making him fly like a small bird over our heads. He seemed to like it. I can see the two of us on a boat over the Channel, with Estelle standing by the rail and staring out to sea with the wind whipping through her black hair. I can remember . . .

The remembering doesn't seem important any more. What matters is how I behave when I get out of the car, go into the office and take her back out to the street. I have started to worry about something that has not really worried me in twenty-five years of marriage. Should I open the door for her? I've booked a table somewhere and I find myself asking myself whether I should have asked her first. This really is like going out on a first date; the palms of my hands are sweaty. I am checking my hair in the mirror. It looks terrible. What are we going to talk about?

Here goes.

Writing this in my study looking out at Wickett's and Porker's houses. To my alarm, a couple that looked, from here anyway, very like the Wicketts were moving around inside their house earlier on today. What exactly is going on?

Dinner at Franco's. Good.

The reasons for the missing furniture have been explained to me. We are moving! On the profits from Craftgirls U K Ltd, Estelle has bought a large new house in Wimbledon village. Jakob has also supplied her with cash from Club Le Steel. (I cannot think why I did not spot that this is an anagram of Club Estelle.) She drove us past it. It seems the size of a small medieval castle. There is a large lawn, a swimming-pool, a games room and separate flats for Rerghy and Jakob, who will move in with Laura and Lucy – not in that order of course. I have got an enormous study, which has a superb view, not only of the neighbours, but also of a stretch of the Common which, Estelle says, is 'fantastic for peering'. She explained, too, that she was hoping to keep it a secret until my birthday. 'I may have seemed a little strange and secretive,' she said, 'but it has taken rather a lot of organization. Hamish was very helpful. He is an accountant!' This is why she wasn't in some of the places she said she was going to be in!

When we got back to the house I put my arms round her and we kissed again. This time, for slightly longer. Once again, I made some exploratory movements in the direction of her bra. She seemed to tolerate this for slightly more than a minute, and then she gently disengaged my hand. 'Is that it?' I said. 'For the moment,' she said, and smiled in the gloom of the front seat. 'The thing is,' she said, 'we want you to remember it, don't we?' 'We do!' I said feelingly. 'The right balance between expectation and memory is one of the keys to a successful relationship,' said Estelle. 'I am in your hands!' I said. 'You are indeed!' she said and, suddenly and swiftly, she grasped my genitals and gave them a hearty companionable squeeze. 'Oh my God!' I said. 'Oh Jesus Christ!' 'Now,' said Estelle, 'we have to do this under controlled conditions. If you remember that tomorrow morning I will do something else to that area of your anatomy!' I gulped. 'A . . . nice thing!' I said. 'Oh yes,' she said thoughtfully, 'a very nice thing!'

I cannot remember feeling this erotic since I went to the lavatory with Anne Padthaway in 1956 and she let me see her blue gym knickers. Even the sound of Estelle's snoring is erotic.

June 22nd. 10 a.m. It finally rained in the night. A wind got up and drove sheets of water against our window. I lay awake listening to it. This morning it is clear and cool and sunny. The leaves in the garden absurdly brilliant. Sparrow hopping around with what I think is female sparrow in tow.

*Everyone at home – including Laura, Lucy and Lulu – not necessarily in that order. Laura wearing tank top. Estelle* gardening!

Two days to go. They are presumably planning some kind of surprise. What is it? Watch this space on the 24th!

11 a.m.

Talked to Porker in street. The Porkers and the Wicketts are moving back in! But Mr Porker is now with Mrs Wickett and Mrs Porker with Mr Wickett. Apparently they have all been shagging each other for years. He seemed surprised I hadn't noticed it. I said, 'You shouldn't have closed the curtains!' He did not laugh at this. I tried, in a light-hearted manner, to discuss the Wolverhampton sex aids issue. He did not laugh at this either. It is good to have him back.

I did get the impression, however, that he and Wickett may be into Satanism. Of a very respectable kind. He did keep talking about 'the old religion' and at one point said, 'Some of us, of course, have taken the left-hand way!' Going to talk to Estelle in garden.

11.15 a.m.

Estelle was bending over a leaf in a very sexual manner.

With very clear and vivid recall of wet kiss (open-mouthed again) and of pleasurable seizure of bollocks by wife, I approached her and squeezed her bum. She did not appear to mind this. This is excellent news. If this is what it has been like for the last twenty-five years I am a very lucky man indeed. Plus I have no idea what is in store for me. Who knows what we will be up to by my fifty-first birthday? Estelle tells me that Craftgirls U K are going to make a bid to develop Esmond Pennebaker commercially. It appears he appeals to a large number of people because, according to her, 'he has a kind of vital blandness'.

Odd letter from Wainwright.

Dear Paul,
I know you are all right and doing well and I am pleased
for you. But I feel I should remind you that the
institution for which you and I have worked for nearly
thirty years has been destroyed.

I know a lot of other things have been destroyed. The
Trades Union movement, almost all mining communities,
etc., etc. Why should public-service broadcasting be
any different? Does it matter that the community of
creative workers – editors, cameramen, etc. – oh, and
producers too – has been wiped out?

I think it does. I think it matters that a society
should preserve highly trained, impartial people who
don't simply do it for the money. This applies to
teaching, medicine, etc., as well. We none of us fought
for it, Paul. We let the Yahoos take over.

Love
Wainwright

PS. The prophecy is about to be fulfilled.

Apart from the postscript there is some sense in this. I feel a little guilty. Will call him.

Talked on the phone with Wainwright. He sounded very, very strange. He kept going on about Colin Cross. Why? I also learned that Ashley Ramp has had 'a very mild heart attack'. Still walking around, not in hospital but has been 'told to take it easy'. Very worried about this. Feel in a sense responsible.

## 11.45 a.m.

Message on the phone from thirtysomething. It goes as follows –

> THIRTYSOMETHING: Hullo Paul, are you there? (*Cigarette inhalation. Traffic noise.*)
>     It's the girl whose name you never remember here . . . (*Coughing. More traffic noise.*) It's about Ashley . . . I had to ring you because he . . . you see I had been feeling he was . . . (*Cigarette inhalation. Sound of argument in background.*) Sorry, road rage . . . he was . . . sort of . . . up a tree . . . or in some kind of . . . space capsule . . .

At this point I picked up the phone. I said, 'Hi! Is Ashley OK?' She started on again about him being out of reach, down a pothole, etc. I said, before I even realized I was saying it, 'You can have too much sex, you know!' There was a silence at the end of the phone. I continued. 'Don't have sex with him,' I said, 'until he's better. And even then – don't do it more than once a day. He's not a young man. OK? I'd like him to live.'

Then I put the phone down. Never thought I would be working to preserve Ashley Ramp's life. But someone had to say it.


## 1 p.m.

Public excitement over *General Practice* continues. We are up for a Golden Ear Award. Shirley has given an interview for the *Independent* in which she says, 'I have always known that Esmond Pennebaker was a winner. In backing my judgement by pushing him more to the centre of the show and reinventing him for the Millennium I am aware of the tremendous support I have received from Head of Sound and, of course, from Howard Porda, whose recent knighthood confirms his tremendous contribution to broadcasting!'

Nobody told me it was Sir Howard Porda. To think! I could have shagged him! He's a bit young for it. Is this the right title for him, however? It could have gone the other way. He could have been Lady Blake or the Duchess of Porda. If him, why not me? Lord Slippery of Wimbledon? Although I do not feel I have peer potential. Other people in the Beeb are now leaping to take the credit for not bumping me off.

Pilfrey is interviewed in the *Guardian*. He says, 'It's so wonderful working with Paul Slippery. He is a very giving actor and always allows one space. I think in a way he is a genius.' Even in my present, soporifically cheerful mood I cannot quite accept this. Pilfrey is, fundamentally, a disgusting individual. Have just got new script from Leo and Witchett. I seem to have rediscovered my love for Pamela and forgiven her for hiring a contract killer (or rather two of them) to bump me off.

Leo and Witchett are going to America to get married.


## 3.30 p.m.

Suddenly panicked about what happens when Estelle and I finally get round to making love. Since I cannot remember when I last shagged, have I forgotten how to do it? My technique, gathered, as it is, from countless books, plays, films, *The Joy of Sex*, etc., ought to be in good shape. But when we actually get our togs off and confront each other face to face – will I be up to scratch?

Judging from recent experience, of course, Estelle will know what to do. This, I think, is probably usually the case with sex. One follows instructions. But still feel nervous. I tried out a few moves on the cushion of the sofa in my study. Was in the middle of one when Edwin came in and asked why I was humping what was left of the furniture.

She has now left for office. I waved to her from window as she left. Not sure whether she noticed this.


## 4 p.m.

Edwin, Snozzer, Lulu, Wodge, Plonker, Scagg, Bozz and a boy called Garbage are downstairs watching old videos of *Friends*. Edwin has announced that, now he has finished GCSEs, he is going to 'forget all the history, mathematics, biology, etc., that he has ever learned'. I told him that he had not remembered enough to make forgetting it a problem.

## 5 p.m.

Phone call from Beeb. Colin Cross has been murdered! As far as I can make out, Wainwright shot him in the head with a double-barrelled shotgun. 'Of course,' said Pilfrey, who gave me the news, 'Wainwright is insane.' I am not at all sure that this is the case. Off now to have drink with Estelle.

## 7 p.m.

Had drink with Estelle. Was allowed to squeeze her bum in car. Very excited.

At my old school we always used to say that the masters had taken away our rights and given them back to us as privileges. That did not, however, undermine the fierce pleasure of being allowed to walk around in the sixth form with your blazer buttons undone. There is a parallel here in my sex life. Since I have nothing to compare it with I am in a state of wild appreciation at the smallest favour offered. I am reminded of that joke about the man who asks an audience how many times they have sex. Quite a few say three times a week, a few more say once a week, some say only once a month and a miserable handful confess to only doing it once every six months. A little man in the front row, who seems to be grinning cheerfully, says he only has it once a year. The man asks him why he is looking so cheerful. The man says, 'Tonight's the night!'

## 9.30 p.m.

Looked through this diary again. Wondering whether to tear it up. What is extraordinary about it is how little sense I get of what Estelle and I are actually like. This is partly, of course, because when you are as close to someone as I am to her, you simply don't see them. Perhaps that is the key to why I started forgetting our sex life. In order to start it again. I think one of the things I've failed to catch about her is how funny she is. I haven't described the slight droop in her left eye as she delivers some crushing judgement, or the weary inhalation of cigarette smoke when she is told about some new piece of stupidity. And I haven't described the constant laughter and love in her eyes when any of her children are near.

What happens in families, I suppose, is that their members constantly select and refine the myths that represent them. Rerghy was always supposed to be an actor. Jakob was always supposed to be a professor of some kind. Edwin, freed from those kind of restrictions, has the power to be what he chooses – since Estelle and I are too knackered to invent a destiny for him.

And Estelle? I suppose this year she has chosen a destiny for herself. I may not have liked it, but she has. She has disposed of her earlier selves. Neurotic Estelle, Daddy's-not-quite-favourite Estelle (I never said she was the youngest of two sisters, did I?), frightened Estelle, clinging Estelle and all the other Estelles who are now no longer wanted on voyage, have faded like shadows in the sun until there is only gigantic, here and now, in your face, unbelievably present, oh my God it really is Estelle Estelle. There is, it has to be said, something rather magnificent about middle-aged women. Especially when, like my wife, they are six feet one inches and, to use her own words, 'built like a brick shithouse'.

But what of me? I know, like all actors, that my current run of success will not last. That is almost the definition of the actor's trade. But the news about Wainwright has got to me. I have to start standing up for things I believe in. If you can't do that at fifty you will never do it. And if there is one task left to me before the day after tomorrow – when I officially enter middle age – it is to decide whether or not I am to be the hero of my own life. I feel the need to talk about my birth.

Too tired to think about it now. It will have to wait until tomorrow.

June 23rd. 10 a.m. Weather warm and bright. Blue skies and cumulus clouds. Garden packed with birds who all look cheerful. As am I.

*Everyone at home. Me in study writing this.*

Have done new breathing exercises – the Munkkampf System. They are superb! Some complaint from neighbours but I feel even better than ever.

## II a.m.

My birth. As I feel this diary is coming to an end – keep watching this space for the surprise! – I think I should conclude with my beginning.

I was delivered by the local G P – a man who would make Esmond Pennebaker look talented. His name was Harris and I was the first baby he had ever delivered. His opening line to the midwife – who had delivered over three hundred children in the Wimbledon area – was 'Which way out is it likely to come?' He got worse after that. When my mother had what she describes as 'bowel problems' halfway through he yelled, 'Oh my God! This is disgusting!'

The chief difficulty I presented, apparently, was that no one was quite sure what I was up to. First of all I looked as if I was coming out feet first, then I suddenly turned round and made a dive for the uterine canal. Just as they were telling my Mum to push I whipped round and lay, sideways, across the head of her vagina, without moving. For a while they were sure I was dead. After I had blocked the only available exit for about half an hour, I reversed back up towards her belly button and started to do bicycling movements.

By this time Harris was talking of back-up. He went out to look for his partner – we had no telephone in the house – and was unable to find him. When he returned he found the midwife lying with her ear to my mother's stomach. 'I think,' she said, in an awestruck whisper, 'he's buggered off!' They prodded her all over but could see no trace of yours truly. Harris had used his brief expedition to get hold of a medical textbook on birth and he pored over this, while the midwife prostrated herself on the bed and peered up my mother's snatch to see if she could catch a glimpse of me.

Phone going. Will answer it.

## II.45 a.m.

More news of Colin Cross's death. Pilfrey rang to tell me that, in the room where he was supposed to have had his leaving party – before he decided not to leave – i.e., B34576, Cross had amassed a whole pile of clippings and reviews all about me. It appears he was the one really behind the plans to have me killed. His so-called 'leaving' was in fact simply a ploy. He had never actually left the staff of the Beeb, but simply, to use his own words, 'gone underground'. His mission was to find out 'what was happening at the coalface' and in pursuance of this, as Napoleon is reported to have done, he had mingled incognito with employees and listened to what they said about him.

Learning of how much he was hated seems to have finally sent him round the twist. He had been threatening Wainwright – which is why Wainwright bought the shotgun – and was, apparently, talking of killing me in person. There is a strong rumour that Wainwright may get off by pleading self-defence. I think I will not mention the strange postscript of his last letter to anyone.

Back to the subject of my birth. It's important because – if I hadn't been such a tricksy baby, I would not have been born on Midsummer's Day.


## 2 p.m.

Harris found all sorts of fascinating things in the textbook – many of which he read out to my mother. Babies who evaporated in the womb, babies who suddenly became allergic to amniotic fluid and who melted on the way out. Babies who came out covered in hair with no brains. Babies who head-butted their way through the uterus and ended up with their heads sticking out of their Mum's arse. Folktales and true facts became hopelessly intermingled as Harris – apparently oblivious to my mother, who had now started to scream so loudly the neighbours had gathered in the street – read out more and more amusing facts about things that could go wrong with childbirth.

Halfway through this recitation I started up again. I got hold of the umbilical cord and started to thwack it around my head like a lassoo. Then I abseiled round the perimeter of her womb until I was positioned with my feet vertically above her crotch. From this position, she says, I started to do what felt like straddle jumps, landing one foot on each side of her cervix. 'Whatever you were doing,' she always says, 'it was painful!' Halfway through this routine I got the cord tied round my neck and started to strangle myself.

Harris was on his way to the door to try and find an ambulance, or, at least, someone better qualified than he (which would not have been difficult) when I suddenly broke free, spun through three hundred and sixty degrees and started to 'wriggle around inside the womb like an eel'. 'This one,' said the midwife, 'is a very aptly named baby. He is extremely slippery!'

Well I suppose I am. And I suppose I must learn to deal more honestly with people. Stop acting. Unless, of course, I am actually acting. The phone is going. Should I answer it?


## 7 p.m.

Rather drunk. But important to write this down. Now.

It all started out with a message on the machine from my mother.

It went as follows –

MOTHER: Paul . . . Paul, is that you? Are you there? (*Unfamiliar background noise of car engine*). Are you there in your study, Paul, listening to this? (*Car engine noises suddenly stop. Long silence.*)

You often don't pick up my messages, Paul, do you? And you often don't come and see me because I am in Croydon. (*Mad laugh. Silence.*) I hate it in Croydon. All that banging and hammering. Bang hammer hammer bang. (*Sniff. Long silence.*)

Anyway, you're not answering, Paul, are you? You're a bit of mollusc really, aren't you? A bit of a creature in a shell. You shouldn't be a creature in a shell. You should live life to the full even if you're ninety, as I seem to be. (*Pause.*) I blame your birth really. I am, Paul, ninety. (*Silence. Distant traffic sounds.*) You remember that woman, Paul, the one who used to wave the mop around and who hit your father with it? Do you remember? (*Silence. Sniff.*) She was born in north Wales, not that you would remember, and when she was young she was considered attractive. (*Silence. Mad laugh.*)

Some of these women today are disgusting. I read a book by one. I can't see what people see in her. I think it's disgusting. (*Mad laugh.*) Sex sex sex sex that's all they think about. (*Long silence.*) Anyway that woman I was talking about, you don't really remember her, you never really knew her, Paul, not really. You never pick up her answerphone messages although I know you're listening. It's me, Paul. I'm that woman you see. I'm your mother, Paul. I'm not dead yet. I may be ninety but I'm not dead yet. I know you're listening. (*Car door opens. Mad laugh.*) I'm parked outside, Paul. Come to the window! Don't be evasive! Don't be slippery, Paul, even if you are a Slippery! Come and look out. We're not dead yet, Paul. It's not too late. Live life to the max., Paul. Go for it.

It was at this point I picked up the phone. My Mum cackled madly. And said, 'I am! I'm outside! And so are a lot of other people!' 'Mum,' I said , 'I didn't mean to –' My Mum said, 'Happy Birthday, Paul!' I said, 'My birthday is tomorrow, Mum!' And she said, 'Oh no it isn't! It's today! You were born on this day fifty years ago! Go to the window!'

I put the phone down and went over to the window. I looked out. Mafeking Road was packed with people. They were solid from our front wall to the front of what used to be (and now still is) Porker's garden. Porker, indeed, was one of them, standing in the front row and grinning. There were a lot of other people there. Good Old Steve was there and Peter Mailer was there, with Christine, and Leo was there and Witchett and Shirley and Howard and Howard's Mum Stella and Rerghy and Jakob and Edwin and Laura and Lucy and Lulu and the Rachnowskis and the Proeks and a lot of other people. There was Sam Jackson, whom I haven't seen since 1983, and at the back (it couldn't be, surely! Yes it was!) Anne Padthaway, my first girlfriend!

There was Snozzer and Wodge and Bozz and Scagg and Hotchkiss and Hong and a bloke called Manners, who I met on a kibbutz in 1969. There was a girl called Jackie who used to work at the RSC and there was Gustave and Pilfrey (looking amazingly pleased to see me) and there was Alison from *General Practice* and my long-term buddy Dirk and Ashley Ramp, who was holding the thirtysomething's hand and grinning broadly. Helena Twist, Pamela's sister (where was Pamela? Oh there she is!) was there and Wainwright who cannot, surely, be out on bail but has, perhaps, escaped from somewhere. There was the Italian who once tried to put his hand up Estelle's skirt (what was he doing there?) and many, many people that I had always thought were dead or abroad or somewhere else where I would never see them again. Familiar and less familiar faces jostled for my attention. I went from one smile to another (everyone seemed to be smiling) and the faces were as beautiful as flowers in a garden.

There was a banner. It read 'HAPPY BIRTHDAY, PAUL SLIP-

PERY! YOU ARE FIFTY! WELL DONE!' There were even a small group of people over by number 49's – who was peering out of his window – with a placard that read, 'PAUL SLIPPERY FAN CLUB!' For a moment I thought I recognized Colin Cross among them. Then I remembered he was dead.

That was when I saw my Mum. She was parked a little way up the street and she seemed to be on a mobile phone. I went back to my desk. 'Mum,' I said, 'are you responsible for this?' 'Me and Estelle!' she said. That was when I realized. I hadn't seen Estelle in the crowd. Just as I was thinking this she came through the door of my study. 'Happy birthday, Paul!' she said. And kissed me. 'I thought,' I said, unsure of whether I was talking to my mother or my wife, 'that my birthday was tomorrow!' 'It isn't!' said my mother. 'She'll tell you!'

I turned back to Estelle. 'Actually,' said Estelle, 'they always used to tell you you were born at two minutes past midnight, didn't they? On Midsummer's Day. Because you so liked the idea of being born on Midsummer's Day. Everyone in your family always said you were away with the bloody fairies. And you went on about it so much that in the end everyone went along with your obsession. Actually you were born at two minutes before midnight. But they gave in to your idea. Which they shouldn't have done. Because acting isn't being away with the bloody fairies. It's like anything else. It's like what I've been doing this year. It's work, Paul. But work is what made anything of the world. It's all we have. And it's what we have to do now. Work. Get on with it. And stop being so bloody . . . Slippery!' She grinned. 'The bastards!' I said. 'Well,' she said, still grinning, 'your real life starts today, my friend. And maybe now you will have to get on with it and stop messing around. You're on your own after fifty, Paul!'

I could hear singing from out in the street. I said, 'I'm not, love. I have you!' 'Yes!' she said, coming towards me. 'You'll always have me. And tomorrow we'll have a party to celebrate that as well. The day we got married. Or have you forgotten that?' 'Actually,' I said, 'I don't think I have forgotten anything. I can remember everything. All of it.'

And I could. Not just the sex – although, suddenly, I could remember that as well. I could remember the day of our wedding. I could remember the summer sunlight, like today's summer sunlight. And I could remember how her face looked then, as sweet and open and strong as it does today.

I could remember how she looked up at me after we had repeated the words you are supposed to say and how the registrar said I could kiss her and I leaned across and, in front of everybody, I did just that.

I've said I loved her many times across the years. But that was the most public occasion. A marriage, with its ring of spectators, all experts in the field, all with their own reasons for wanting to believe or disbelieve the seriousness of the lead actors, tests, more harshly than anything else I can think of, the validity of that simple, but often misused word: love.

I remember all that, writing in the middle of my birthday party, with the woman I love and my children with the women they love. Not long now and we'll be moving. All of us on the move again, changing places, changing the rules of our lives. But for me one thing never changes and never will change. Love. A very simple thing that almost doesn't need explaining. And that I remember with perfect clarity. Does that mean I at last understand it? Since, in essence, memory is understanding.

I'm not sure. You have to forget love sometimes, in order to remember it, as I've found out this year. You can't live your life on the assumption it's there. Sometimes you have to deny it or ignore it or wish it away, if only to see whether it is strong enough to come back without your bidding it. Love has to be stronger than you are. But you have to be strong enough to see that.

And that moment I leaned over to kiss her in the register office, all those years ago, I knew. I knew the way I think my sons know now. I knew there was only one woman for me, and that however bad life got, or however low I or she were, we would, somehow, always find our way back to it. And even if we didn't, somehow, it would find us. Its meaning was so simple it was all contained in that single word. It wasn't any one thing she or I did or any one quality she had – although she had plenty of those – it was just stamped through every inch of that four-letter word we said to each other over and over and over again in the 1960s – love love love. All you need is love. Love love love. I know people who had it and who somehow lost it along the way. I know people who tried to make it mean something it could never mean, something to do with politics or drugs or great crowds of people waving banners in the breeze. But for me it always meant one very simple thing. It always meant my wife. And the meaning will not change even when there is no longer any me or her or any of our children so bright and brilliant, now, in the sunshine of this June evening.

'Shall we go and join the others?' said Estelle. 'Yes,' I said, 'yes. Let's do that.'